The Laughter of Fools

The Laughter of Fools

CHARLOTTE CORY

faber and faber

LONDON · BOSTON

First published in 1993
by Faber and Faber Limited
3 Queen Square London WC1N 3AU

Typeset by Parker Typesetting Service, Leicester
Printed in England by Clays Ltd, St Ives plc

© Charlotte Cory, 1993

Charlotte Cory is hereby identified as author of this work
in accordance with Section 77 of the Copyright,
Designs and Patents Act 1988.

A CIP record for this book is
available from the British Library

ISBN 0–571–16851–5

For Bob, with love.
And also in memory of my dog,
Grendel, 1978–92.

PART I

The Light That Falls

I still have the chair Rosa sat in. All the other chairs were cleared out a long time back – I do not like furniture cluttering up the rooms, making it difficult to move through them freely. When I have nothing better to do, which is quite a lot of the time, I often come down here and sit in Rosa's chair. I even cross my legs, though they are far from shapely, and I sit quite still and try not to slump. I do not close my eyes. I scarcely breathe.

I see the room as Rosa saw it. Then I picture my young self obstructing her clear line of vision and I look over the top of what would have been my head and keep my eyes fixed on the light that falls inside the deep bay window. The shadows in the late afternoon will be almost the same as when she sat here though a number of the tall trees outside became diseased some years ago and had to be cut down. I have never let these walls be repainted so the dusty ochre is only dustier while all the other walls, in the rest of this large house, have been rendered a dazzling off-white. You can wander from room to room like Goosie Goosie Gander and never know where you are, or where you have been.

But here, in the half light retained in this room, I wonder again what Rosa was up to. Her own life was so glamorous, and varied, I cannot believe she enjoyed her dingy visits to this dull dark house. Nor can she have been fond of me, not when you consider the terrible way she abandoned me, finally. And Rosa *must have known* what an intolerable position she placed my poor mother in all those years, turning up without warning whenever it suited her, getting me over-excited. I don't think Rosa really meant any harm. She was just careless and disruptive the way beautiful women can be and in the end *she* was the one who got killed. We lived on here, quietly enough, without her.

I dare say Rosa pitied my mother and me our quiet, confined lives, dependent as we were on the goodwill and charity of others. My subdued existence must have seemed wretched compared to the wonderfully happy childhood she had enjoyed, cared for by two doting parents who loved each other. Maybe this was why – with some notion, even, of making up for my loss – Rosa told me so much about it. And why I was so keen to listen.

'Jeannie is going to write it all down one day,' Rosa said once, smiling at me in amusement. 'It'll be a bestseller like *Anna Karenina*, or *Tess of the d'Urbervilles*: The Life of Rosa Pegglar!'

My mother pursed her lips. But I laughed out loud at the very idea. Me – *write it down* when I wasn't even bottom of the class at school because the teachers left my name off the lists. It would not have looked good for them, having a pupil who only got 'o'; it was easier always to pretend I was not there. Which suited me. I would watch the other children at their lessons, frowning with concentration, sharpening their pencils and scratching away on the carefully ruled lines of their exercise books. Every so often they glanced up at the clock and I too liked the way the hands went round, one very fast, one not so fast and one that moved tardily through the days as if weighted down, like me.

'Vacant, that child,' the teachers would say, being kind.

The other children did not want me in their teams or sitting next to them at their desks and they said so, loudly. I stood on the sidelines while games were being played and I sat at the spare table at the back of the class ready the moment my friend, the hour hand, touched three to rush home to my mother waiting in the kitchen with a glass of warm milk and biscuits straight from the oven. But what I rushed home for was *not* my mother's baking. I lived those days for the slight chance Rosa might pay us one of her visits. And continue her story.

'There you are, Jeannie dear!' my mother would greet me, trying to hug me, settling me down. Usually the pair of us passed the long boring evenings alone together. My mother did not talk to me the way Rosa talked, making the past and her part in it come colourfully alive. My mother only spoke in uncertain half tones and she rarely ever finished her sentences. She was not good company and, for all her quiet kindness, she was not the company I craved.

Sometimes the old woman who owned the house, who employed my mother, might come downstairs and the three of us would converse politely, although no one had anything much to say. She always descended when Rosa visited, and the house bubbled up overflowing with words and laughter. While my mother kindled the fire, we would gather excitedly round our beautiful visitor, admiring her lovely clothes and pressing her to stay. What warmth and happiness in this drab room those evenings! Of course, I didn't know then that our lives would not go on the same for ever. Nor do I remember quite how it all started. How Rosa must have looked at me and for some reason said, 'Now I will tell you, Jeannie!' And begun what she never finished, and what I have never forgotten.

I cannot light the fire now. I always sat too close to the flames so that my cheeks burned red and when my mother tried to draw me away, I refused to move. Like a loyal dog, I risked being trodden on. I crouched where I could smell Rosa's perfume and know at once if she moved her elegant feet. Central heating, with sensible radiators and neat pipes, was put into the house a few years back, just before they felled the dead elms. The logs were taken away since I could not burn them. The fireplace had been sealed up because of the draught gusting and whistling down the chimney whenever it was stormy outside, making the curtains billow wildly, wrapping themselves around Rosa's chair. Strangling her.

Suffocating me. I am the only one now who knows Rosa's story.

For a long time, of course, I resisted. I tried to tell myself she was only teasing. It was not my responsibility. If Rosa wanted her story written she should have done it herself. Besides, I am not a writer of books. When I looked in the Public Library once, I saw that *Anna Karenina* and *Tess of the d'Urbervilles* had come off production lines. As if Tolstoy and Thomas Hardy had batteries of tidy hens laying eggs a dozen at a time in neat boxes. This is my one story, and it is not even mine except that I have made it mine. Nor am I writing it for the money. I shall tell the publishers so when I send it to them. The last thing I need is any more money – I am, as my doctor tells me, putting it modestly, well provided for.

By the old lady. I was never the least fond of her while she was alive – it cannot have been easy having a young child running about the house and I was such a great gawky thing, always getting in the way. I feel indebted to her now of course, but then, when I observed how indulgent she was of the beautiful Rosa, I resented the way she ordered my mother about although that was what my mother was employed for and why we were allowed to live in this large house, all found. I too learnt to order my mother about. I did so shamelessly. There *was* shame, you see: I had no father. 'As many children are born out of wedlock as are locked into it these days,' the nice doctor told me, 'you must not blame your mother.' But back then, when I was young, things were different.

I knew I should have been grateful for all that was given me, but like most children, in or out of wedlock, the more I had, the more I wanted. How I wanted Rosa sitting here in this chair with us, always! Sooner or later every child will ask about the past. 'I want to know,' I used to whine. And though there was much I could not understand – like how someone as downtrodden and dowdy as my mother had been taken on in this large house and treated so generously – it was Rosa alone who interested me. Her story I wanted to hear. 'You must ask Rosa . . .' my mother always said. She was so humble. It was not her place, she implied, to gossip – even to me.

'Rosa will tell you!' the rich old lady shut me up sharply. I had been impertinent. She did not like my questions. It was as if Rosa was the only one empowered to speak.

And speak she did. Yet, for all that I managed to make Rosa talk about the past and recount things that happened before I was born, I do not think she herself believed in a time before *she* was born. Most people don't. 'Ancient history!' she'd laugh when I mentioned her father but sometimes if I insisted, her voice might soften and her eyes mist dreamily. 'Ah, Pegglar, dear dear Daddy!' And here in this dusty ochre room, she shared him with me, Pegglar who had no head for business. Pegglar, whose passion was for his poultry.

'Poultry!' I would yell like a traveller in a foreign country coming upon some familiar word at last. Pegglar's famous hens might have entered the room, which in a way they had, I was so excited.

'Shush, Jeannie,' said my mother, glancing anxiously at the old lady. 'It's rude to interrupt.'

Rosa did not mind. She smiled at my enthusiasm.

'What was he like?' I demanded childishly. I knew full well, of course, what Pegglar was like but I wanted Rosa to tell me *again*. How Pegglar the Poultryman wore earth-brown trousers that smelled of grass. How the light of far-off stars was reflected in his eyes as he watched over you from a distance, watching you thoughtfully from his great height. But he'd stoop down whenever there was anything you wanted to say. Which often there wasn't. But Pegglar would listen to your childish nonsense as if what you were telling him was of the greatest importance to the world.

No one has ever listened to me like that.

My mother occasionally protested. 'Forgive me, Rosa,' she'd murmur gently, and the old lady and Rosa would turn to her in some surprise. Hadn't this same stupid woman told me, only just now, that it was rude to interrupt? They were both too polite to remind her directly that she was only present because she was paid. But as I got older, I found myself pointing this out more and more. Not that I think my mother was truly in danger of forgetting. Blushing deeply, she stammered, 'I think the child far too interested . . .'

It unnerved my poor mother, you see, my infatuation with

Rosa. At the time, I naturally assumed she was jealous because no one could ever be infatuated with her. She was so plain and put upon; even her lover had left her. My father had, as they say, other fish to fry! Now I can see my mother was only frightened that I would get hurt, as she had been hurt, and she probably also felt I would have done better to have been attentive, instead, at school.

Rosa did not find my interest the least surprising. Or alarming. She smiled her beautiful quizzical smile. 'So, our little Jeannie is *far too interested*!'

She patted my head conspiratorially. In spite of my mother or perhaps *to* spite my mother, Rosa always did continue her narration. But never enough or fast enough for me. 'Be patient!' Rosa would laugh as I urged her on. 'We will get there in the end!'

Children never forget promises made to them, especially those that are later broken. I sit here now thinking what *did* happen in the end, and I am unable to forget all I never had that was cruelly taken away. Like a father who'd have loved me and given me his name. Our Father, they would say at school, Who Art in Heaven, Hallowed be Thy Name . . . My father, I would think rebelliously, Who could be Anywhere on Earth, but here . . .

Here with me now.

Rosa's own father interested me greatly. After she died, I have liked to think Pegglar the Poultryman in some ways more mine than hers, left behind for me along with this old worn chair. I uncross my legs. There is nothing about *my* perfume or *my* shapeless ankles to keep a faithful dog mournfully at heel long after *I* have gone.

It is dark now beyond the window so you would not know the old trees that used to whisper to me comfortingly through the nights when I could not sleep are no longer out there. Nor that Pegglar is not somewhere in all that interminable darkness, stooping down like a breeze barely tickling my cheek, attending to all my nonsense. Dear, dear Daddy!

'Don't sit there on your own in the dark, Jeannie,' I can hear

8

my mother saying. 'And you really ought to pull the curtains!' There was always some task to be done, she herself never sat down for a moment. Neither the old lady nor I would let her.

I'm not just sitting here, I think, but forbear to say. I am not on my own and I am *not* entirely in the dark!

Flying in the Face

Pegglar lived for much of his life with two elder sisters, Edith and Gracie, breeding exotic fowls which strutted and shrieked in the elaborate coops that straddled every corner of the Pegglar family garden. To encourage her brother out of the house and from under her busy feet, Edith had once said: 'How about poultry?' Pegglar only made a face just as he'd done when she suggested bicycling or the collecting of postage stamps, but this time Edith had persisted: 'There are some colourful species,' she urged. 'And a big garden ought to be utilized . . .'

If his sister had it in mind to procure fresh eggs cheaply, she was soon disappointed. Whenever one of the exuberant birds *did* lay an egg, and surprisingly ordinary-looking eggs they were too, Pegglar would flutter and cluck while his exotic hens stood about, coolly preening magnificent feathers and eyeing the man rather disdainfully. But what did Pegglar care? Such high hopes had Pegglar for that magical possibility, tantalizingly concealed within each brittle shell . . .

After years of painstaking pairing and ingenious mismatching, Pegglar had succeeded in creating two entirely novel varieties of fowl. Every spring then, when other men's minds might turn to thoughts of love, Pegglar would journey up to London to exhibit his remarkable species at the Annual Exotic Poultry Show. Never with any success. Though widely commented on in the poultry literature of the period, no *Pegglar's Pride* or *Pegglar's Fancy* ever won a bronze medal, let alone of course the prestigious silver cup. Pegglar was always obliged to stand bravely by while other, more fortunate poultrymen like Bluie Chapman, or Percy Thirsty Higgins, scooped all the prizes.

Edith was not the least surprised. All too clearly she recalled those first half dozen or so bedraggled birds, cowering in the bottom of a soiled cardboard box that had arrived by carrier one cold damp morning long ago. EXOTICS – BEST BREEDING STOCK stamped boldly on the side. Five shillings! Edith had prodded the drooping broilers. The only thing exotic about these particular specimens was the price! Poor Gracie refused to go near them, but Pegglar had paid the five shillings and ordered some more varieties. He then began compiling elaborate stock-breeding books in which the genesis of each of his chickens was fully, pictorially chronicled. In this pursuit he had enlisted the assistance of a friendly local photographer, Mr Philbert Farnol.

Edith could not like Farnol. In the evenings, sometimes, when the two men were outside discussing the hens, she would stand at the kitchen window and consider how these new unnatural birds would never have existed but for her own foolish suggestion. And the readiness with which her brother thrust them together, two by two, in the family garden. These were artificial, unsanctioned creatures Noah had not saved against a rainy day. Pegglar was flying in the face. *She* had encouraged him.

Gracie hovered moth-like and untroubled at the window beside Edith. Philbert Farnol liked to wave to the women inside the house, and occasionally Gracie Pegglar might flap her hands, waving rather vaguely back. 'One of a kind,' Farnol said then.

'What's that?' Pegglar glanced down.

Philbert Farnol grinned. He looked up to Pegglar – yet, as he himself was quick to admit, he was a man who must look up to the whole world. Farnol's short physique gave him a natural advantage in photographing hens, which was as well since other business was scarce. People towered menacingly over him. Though they combed their hair and smiled against some prettily painted backdrop of their own choosing, Farnol's portraits were horrific, giant-like distortions. All the more recognizable for all that. No one felt happy with themselves, or ever came back. Children fared worse. As the grotesque little man clambered and clattered about, they roared with laughter too close to the

11

lens so that even the fondest parent could never again dote on this mocking monster gnashing oversized, close-up teeth. Remarkably, Pegglar's birds looked *better* in Farnol's pictures than they did in real life! And how it pleased the little photographer to touch up their extraordinary combs, crests and plumes with his brightly coloured inks. Enhancing Pegglar's bizarre species in his own special way.

Philbert Farnol's great treat every year was to accompany Pegglar to the Annual Exotic Poultry Show in London. Farnol would pin the second exhibitor's badge Pegglar was permitted to his lapel weeks beforehand and parade round town, even in heavy spring rain, for as many people to see as possible. On the eve of departure the photographer would shut up shop early and hasten to help Pegglar with the final preparations.

Edith did not like having the godless creatures, or Philbert Farnol, in the house but as this happened just once each year, she bit her lip, longed for the long evening to be over and took Gracie safely away upstairs.

Farnol proved indefatigable. Only when all the birds were washed and dried, and packed into their green canvas travelling boxes, did he take his leave, promising to return before cock crow for an early start. Once underway next morning, Farnol scuttled untiringly up and down platforms at the stations either end, instructing guards and whistling up porters, but as soon as Pegglar's party was installed at the Show, he would be content to sit hours at a time, smoothing exotic feathers and reassuring the nervous creatures as they waited for Pegglar to lead them out on to the floor to be judged.

Philbert Farnol was no fair-weather friend. When it came time to leave the bright lights of London again each year, Farnol entered equally eagerly into the annual disappointments. Slumped in the corner of a railway carriage for the weary homeward journey, Pegglar could take comfort from Farnol's indignant animadversions. The little man would rise to this feet and inform fellow passengers that Bluie Chapman had put a wafer of something nasty in the other birds' seedcorn. Percy Thirsty Higgins's cup-winning faverolles resembled nothing so much as puffed-up partridges, while those pompous personages who had made speeches at the Prizegiving only wanted to associate themselves with success and get their pictures in the paper. As a professional photographer, Farnol told the packed carriage, he knew about such things.

Some passengers busied themselves behind newspapers but a few became decidedly interested, even asking to see inside the green canvas boxes! When a buxom lady who sat with her legs forced apart by an enormous shopping basket, powdering a large fleshy mole on her upper lip, remarked: 'Well, fancy!' the exasperated dwarf turned on her swiftly. 'Pardon me, Madam, but *you* weren't there! The bantam I am referring to was *definitely* a *Pride*!'

The railway carriage braced itself for the impact but the large lady only wriggled and smirked. 'Well, fancy!' she said again, dabbing at her mole and winking merrily at Pegglar.

Pegglar sneezed as pungent face powder wafted over him. He shifted his feet. The train stopped. People got out, others got in. The woman edged closer till Pegglar could smell cachou of violets on her lips and feel a plump elbow digging deep into his ribs.

'As I was saying . . .' Farnol continued.

Bluie Chapman had lifted a dapper bowler hat to Pegglar. Letting his mean mocking eyes rest on the iridescent plumes of Pegglar's best hen, which fluttered and flapped and had to be shooed in disgrace from the Champions' Podium, the poultryman had bowed a slight sneering bow to the valiant vanquished. Each year, bucked up no doubt by Farnol's boundless enthusiasm, Pegglar resolved to return the following spring with a new, improved *Fancy* or *Pride* that would wipe the smug smile off Bluie Chapman's ferret face.

Each year also, Edith Pegglar lay awake until she heard the click of the garden gate, at last, and the weary travellers whispering 'Good night'. As Farnol's stout little footsteps retreated into the distance she would hear Pegglar moving stealthily round the garden returning his birds to their coops. Once when everything had seemed too quiet at that point, Edith had risen and peered out into the moonlit garden. At first it seemed empty and she thought Pegglar must already have come indoors, but then she saw her brother standing motionless in the middle of the lawn. He was looking up at her, gazing beyond her out of reach into the darkness of the skies. Later she'd heard him shuffling up the stairs to bed. Next day poor Edith was as tired and irritable as if she too had journeyed with Pegglar and his poultry to the Show. She snapped at Pegglar, and slapped at Gracie.

No wonder if Pegglar's sisters were anxious! They knew the world a hazardous place. Their father, a Captain Pegglar, had long ago placed his various interests in the hands of an agent and gone off to India, and died there. Soon after that tragic death in distant Simla, their mother had died also, nearer to home, struck down in a traffic accident in the High Street. She had been walking to church, on her way to her daughter's wedding.

It happened that Edith Pegglar, eighteen and unbeautiful, had accepted a garnet ring from the town apothecary. The ring had been taken in exchange for poisons and sat painfully tight on the young girl's finger. The man had also bestowed a shilling book, *Lessons in Economy for the Young Housewife*, on his betrothed. In her concern not to trip over her bridal train and to keep a hold on Gracie's hand, Edith had only looked up when shrieking started: three paces ahead, the nine-year-old Pegglar stood bereft on the pavement, their mother lay crushed and bloody in the road. Run over by a runaway horse.

Poor Edith had hurried her brother and sister home and, leaving them huddled together picking at the icing on the now redundant wedding cake, she'd fled upstairs to change. She tore the pretty veil and daisy chain from her hair but, as she began frantically unhooking her dress, Edith caught sight of herself in the mirror. The stitched white muslin gown had never suited her! Why had her fond mother, who'd entered this room less than an hour before and seen her reflected here in this same glass, not said so? Instead, Mrs Pegglar had averted her eyes and begun hinting about the night to come, referring to the errant Captain Pegglar in terms of the very blood and bruising she herself then sustained, not half an hour since, in the High Street. It was as if Mrs Pegglar had personally assumed the fearful injuries that should have been her daughter's that night, for the wedding was postponed in favour of the bride's mother's funeral.

This gave both bride and groom time to think. While the apothecary thought better of taking on responsibility for Miss Pegglar's brother and doll-like sister, Gracie, the sight of all that blood and bruising caused Edith to reconsider also. Besides, she knew a thing or two now about household economy; even had she loved or grown to love him, her fiancé had asked far too many questions about the interests Captain Pegglar left behind when escaping to Simla to disguise his own real motives in the match. Edith had come back downstairs in day-to-day clothes, to find Gracie and Pegglar sitting astride the beautiful wedding cake upturned in the middle of the floor, their mouths chock-full with half-chewed icing, wailing inconsolably for their mother. Edith had mopped the pair down. Pegglars did not need anyone else, she'd said, handing out plates and glasses. The lemonade was too good to waste. Politely Edith Pegglar returned the book on economy, and wrenched the pretty garnet ring from her finger.

When the apothecary suddenly married the new teacher at the school some twenty years later, Edith Pegglar eyed the fresh young bride with her wavy curls and curvy hips, wearing the light garnet ring she herself had worn. 'I have been replaced!' she thought.

The elderly apothecary was not the only one attracted by the lithesome schoolteacher. Pegglar too had watched the girl ushering her class from the schoolhouse to the playing-field, a dainty hen marshalling her chicks. He had almost summoned up courage to address the young woman when she escorted a pupil with a grazed knee into the Apothecary's. While she was comforting the tearful child, the tradesman had lent across his counter to view her full pretty bosom, and squeeze her delicate hand.

No one warned the apothecary's young bride about the dwarf photographer who emerged from his studios in the quiet dusty road behind the High Street, pressing his card and congratulations on her. She took pity on the fellow's deformity so that even if the wedding party had been happy, the large hard jaws glowering down into Farnol's camera did not document it as such. A common or garden pullet, Farnol thought the new schoolteacher. Utterly unworthy of Pegglar.

Edith had her own worries. With each passing year the returns the three of them received on their father's assets grew smaller and harder to live on. Edith even suggested Pegglar should buy less expensive seedcorn for his birds. Pegglar only laughed. Eventually she decided to confront the agent – the son now of the man appointed by her father – but this young man merely leant back in his father's chair and laughed heartily also. He asked after Pegglar's famous hens. Pegglar's sister was not to be distracted so the young man airily waved sheets of tabulated figures across the table; continual costs were bound to be incurred in cases such as this. Edith looked at the upside-down figures and asked what expenses there could possibly be? The young agent shrugged. Shilling books on economy were all very well in their place, he implied. By spending money so freely to prop up the dwindling assets, he had in the long run been saving her, and her brother and sister, money. 'It is all perfectly legal,' he said, smiling. 'I am doing my best.'

'Your best to rob us!' Edith Pegglar snorted.

'Now, Madam . . .' The smooth young man rose to show Captain Pegglar's daughter to the door. The only grounds for restructuring their father's concerns, he said in a low voice, slicking back his hair and removing a thread of cotton from his cuff as she passed, would be if one or other of the three, Edith, Gracie or Pegglar, were to marry. He added that on the whole he would prefer to deal with Pegglar the Poultryman, direct.

Edith went miserably home. On the way she encountered three of her ex-fiancé's grown sons out delivering prescriptions for their father. When Pegglar came in from feeding his hens she could barely bring herself to speak to him. She had tolerated his noisy birds carrying on in the family garden for all to see and she saw no reason why her brother, like an eager young apothecary, or the agent's son, should not apply his mind to *their* father's concerns. She attempted to describe her encounter that afternoon. 'He is a swindler,' she concluded. 'He would prefer to have do with you . . .'

Gracie grimaced, but Pegglar loftily shook his head and stroked his whiskery moustaches: he had no head for business! His only passion was for his poultry. And, he reminded Edith with a straight face, the only thing exotic about those first hens he'd purchased had been their price! Without her diligent studies in household economy, the big garden outside might still be unutilized. There'd be another Exotic Poultry Show in London next spring, and another the year after that. He had high hopes his new improved *Fancys* and *Prides* . . .

Edith Pegglar shivered and drew her shawl about her. We are doomed, she thought. One year, not next year nor the year after necessarily, but as assuredly as the unsanctified fowls strutting and shrieking obliviously in the garden. We have been cast out . . .

Then it happened that, shortly before an Annual Exotic Poultry Show, Philbert Farnol swallowed fixative in the darkness of his darkroom and took to his bed. Pegglar was reluctant to go to London on his own but sick, rasping, Farnol pointed out that if *Pegglar's Fancy* and *Pegglar's Pride* were not exhibited that year, it could only signal weakness, or even defeat, to Bluie Chapman and Percy Thirsty Higgins. Pegglar pictured the mean ferret smile, and was persuaded. Farnol huddled beneath coarse blankets in the chilly room over his studios and gleefully envisaged mayhem on the London Underground. The birds would play Pegglar up.

'I shall worry,' Edith said when Pegglar expressed his stubborn intention of attending the Show after all. He had made the journey many times, he reminded his sisters chirpily. 'Every spring . . .'

'But never on your own!' Edith cried.

17

'I shall have my best *Fancy*, and *Pride*.'

There was more to this, Edith thought, recalling the lone figure standing in the obscurity of the garden. She sighed. Pegglar sighed. Gracie clapped her hands. Edith asked then after Farnol.

'The apothecary has prescribed.' It was the same reliable, unpleasant-tasting stuff Pegglar gave his birds when they swallowed things they oughtn't. 'Very nasty stuff, fixative,' he added, as if apologizing for the limited effectiveness of the medicine. He would not want Edith to think he was criticizing in any way. He would not want her to suspect him after all this time of jealousy over the dainty hen who, in any case, had grown rather matronly. The ample bosom too solidly ample. 'Very nasty. It would take more than . . .'

Edith stared at her brother. 'I hope you enjoy yourself!' she said.

Pegglar smiled. He intended to. Promising to bring his sisters back some souvenir, he journeyed to London with considerably less commotion than usual and, when the wire arrived, informing the sisters of Pegglar's impending nuptials, Edith felt her worst unformed fears confirmed. 'I only hope the woman, whoever she is, knows what she's doing!' was all she said.

Perhaps the stern Registrar, poised to marry the pair, hoped so too for he paused to ask each party, separately, if they were certain they still wanted to go ahead? When Pegglar and his bride both nodded vigorously he had no choice, under the powers vested in him by law, to do other than strap his spectacles behind his ears, and proceed. The Registrar coughed. His eye then registered an exotic hen clucking furiously in a green canvas box. Surely it was in doubtful taste and of dubious legality, that a live lunch witness the deed its consumption must shortly consummate? 'It's not – ehem – customary,' he remarked, indicating the fowl.

'One of my *Fancys*,' Pegglar beamed proudly. Beside him Miss Mary Fanshawe, Spinster, blushed.

The Registrar blinked. With another wedding already

assembling noisily at the back of the room, he sighed and, with slightly less of a flourish than usual, signed what was to be Rosa's parents' marriage certificate.

Rosa's father's motives need little examination. Pegglar had indeed taken a fancy to Mary and asked himself why a man, with two species of exotic chicken named after him, should not take a wife of his own choosing home from London as a souvenir? I am fifty-six, he reasoned. I have been an orphan for nearly half a century. Surely I may do as I please!

Rosa's mother's motives were less immediately obvious, even to her. Far from being an orphan, Mary Fanshawe was the youngest in a large, clever family. One of her brothers was the artist Max Fanshawe, renowned more for his colourful behaviour than any paint on his canvases. Her sister, Nina, a celebrated poetess who had long ago gone to Russia at the outbreak of Revolution, accompanied by a female lover and an Afghan hound, never to be seen or heard from again. Mary, who could only boast a moderately pretty face and a timid disposition, was rapidly attaining that age when a woman no longer takes it for granted she will one day meet a man who will marry her.

Somewhere in the short tunnel between Oxford Circus and Tottenham Court Road, Pegglar had been distracted by all the noise and dust and one of his best hens had taken advantage, seizing its chance to break loose. Poor Pegglar gave chase round the carriage, eventually catching up with the creature angrily flapping its exotic plumage beside a pair of trim little feet. Mary laughed so much at the unexpectedness of the event, and the enormity of the bird's ungainly comb, that the other travellers soon lost interest in the curious lopsided hen and looked only at Mary. Pegglar looked at Mary also: the girl with an enormous red plume in her hat struck him as a pretty rare breed herself. He returned the *Fancy* rather roughly to its box, snapped on the strap and then removed his hat. Gallantly he apologized to the compartment for the untoward curfuffle and invited the girl to ascend at the next stop to take tea with him.

The Annual Exotic Poultry Show ended. Bluie Chapman banked an astonishing three pounds and twelve shillings in prize money while Percy Thirsty Higgins nearly got himself disqualified for repairing damaged tail feathers with an indetectable glue. All part of the fun, Higgins had tried to bluster. The judges took a dim view while Pegglar sat in the Tottenham Court Road, gazing across the tea table into Miss Fanshawe's clear blue eyes, puffing contentedly on his pipe.

When Mary invited her beau back to Bloomsbury to meet her dazzling family, the Fanshawes' lack of interest in him confirmed hers. How she admired Pegglar's unfashionable clothes and slow country-town ways. His want of clever talk, his unaffected ardour. Eagerly she accepted his proposal of marriage, insisting the wedding take place as privately, and soon, as possible.

Edith looked at the new Mrs Pegglar in her outlandish Bloomsbury clothes and laughed bitterly to herself. At most she had anticipated a tin of hard toffee. 'Pegglar always brings us back some trifle,' she told Mary.

Pegglar meanwhile was already hard at work. He had decided to build a new house for himself and his wife and he negotiated right away for a patch of land the other side of town where clusters of nice new houses were already going up. He commissioned some builders to start work at once; Edith told her brother to be sure to take his noisy birds with him. She and poor Gracie and the rest of the neighbourhood would welcome an undisturbed night's sleep after all these years. Edith tried to ask how much this new enterprise was all going to cost, but Pegglar was a man in love. 'There are more things in heaven and on earth than can be accounted for, even by *your* household economy, Edie!' With all the eagerness he had formerly shown devising new coops in the garden, he tied ribbons to stakes and walked the patch of land with Mary and sometimes with Philbert Farnol, recovered now from that unfortunate dose of fixative.

'A Miss Fanshawe,' Pegglar had written to his friend from London. 'I am sure you will like her.' Only look what Pegglar had got himself into, Farnol thought. And without his being there to take photographs!

Gracie stared at Mary. Mary had no idea what she had done to offend Pegglar's sisters. They have had him at home with them all these years, the young Mrs Pegglar thought. It was a relief to everyone when the new house was sufficiently ready for Pegglar and Mary, and Pegglar's poultry, to transfer themselves to the other side of town. It would be better to live on top of the job, Pegglar said, even if everything was not quite finished. We can choose all the fixtures and fittings ourselves.

Next time the local agent called on Edith with more bad news (he'd had to sell off yet more shares, parcels of land and packets of leases at regrettably low prices), Miss Pegglar told him she was only concerned now to secure what was left of her and Gracie's share.

'We'll work something out!' The young man winked. Since her brother had married there were now clear grounds for a lawful restructuring of the Captain's assets.

The new house was eventually finished. Pegglar had been used to summoning workmen to convert orange boxes and wire netting into elaborate coops so when phenomenally large bills started arriving he stuffed them back in their envelopes and sent them directly to the agent to pay.

The young man spoke grimly to Edith. Edith arrived at her brother's new house and found Mary at home on her own. Politely Mary offered to show her sister-in-law round.

'I can see quite enough from where I'm standing!' Edith folded her arms. Indeed she could! The smooth young agent was right, everything in the house her foolish brother had built was unashamedly of the best, and new. Edith stood on the beaten-copper doorstep and gave her sister-in-law a lesson in economics: *What you haven't got you can't spend. If you fritter away your capital you can't then live on the interest.*

When Pegglar returned and found his elder sister bullying his new young wife on his brand-new doorstep he was furious. 'I won't have you interfering here! You've never let me live my own life.'

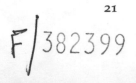

'You had your chickens.'

'You kept me cooped up like a chicken!'

'You never said anything before.'

'I'm saying it now.'

'Fifty years!' Edith gasped. 'I devoted myself to you for fifty years when I too could have married, I too could have journeyed to London, I too . . .' She glanced angrily at Farnol who had followed them unbidden into the house and now stood rubbing his hands, looking up at them excitedly as if they were a side-show put on for his benefit. You are the midget, Edith wanted to say, a freak of nature who should be employed by Barnum! She recalled then the young apothecaries delivering poisons all over the town – artificially contrived variations who might have sprung from her own unutilized loins but for her mother's untimely traffic accident. Wildly Edith blamed Mary's arrival for the ridiculous extravagance of this house. She blamed Philbert Farnol for contriving to be ill and for being present now at this moment of unready reckoning. Most of all, she blamed Pegglar. 'You should never have gone to London on your own!' she shouted at the boy who had jumped up and down in the High Street and frightened a horse which then bolted. 'Your share of our father's money is spent! The agent asked me to mention it. He has paid off your debts. You are destitute!'

Pegglar stared at his sister. 'We'll live,' he muttered defiantly. Edith had never said anything about the horse before.

'That is what I came to tell you, you have nothing to *live* on! What you haven't got you can't spend. You are a beggar, Peg-glar! If I hadn't had lessons and known enough to stop you, you would have beggared us all!'

'I'll go into business,' Pegglar countered calmly.

'You!' Edith scoffed. She would have made a good apoth-ecary's wife, she thought, twisting her ringless fingers. No poison would ever have gone unaccounted for. Edith was glad she had left Gracie winding balls of string back at home. 'You have no head for business, you have told us so often enough! And I'll tell you something else, don't ever come to me asking . . .'

'I won't!' Pegglar cut in. He lit his pipe.

'You fool!' Edith shrieked. How could he afford tobacco? And smoke the stuff calmly in front of her? She strutted about. She had intended offering to tide them over while the expensive new house was sold. She had planned to allow Pegglar and his bride back. She had not meant such things as had been said to have been said at last. She moved towards the door. No one stopped her. Pegglar went over to the sofa and put an arm round his weeping wife. 'My lovely!' he said.

Next morning Mary, née Fanshawe, woke early and puzzled for a moment who the old man snoring heavily on the pillow beside her could be. Then she heard the peculiar cluckings in the garden outside and recollected mayhem on the London Underground. She sat bolt upright and wondered why she had tolerated Edith's hostile gibes, Farnol's stares, Pegglar's nightly fumblings, the over-dullness of life after the over-excitements of London.

The young Mrs Pegglar climbed resolutely out of bed, pulled a gown over her tousled head and reached on top of the wardrobe for her suitcase. While Pegglar snored, his wife struggled with a lock that had jammed. Her family would expect her back; she could write letters for them, see to their laundry and pass round the food at their parties. When eventually the suitcase fell open at her feet, Mary lurched over and was sick into it. She was with child. Rosa, like the *Pride* and the *Fancy*, would bear Pegglar's name. Mary might as well have gone to Revolutionary Russia and been wiped like one of her sister's unwritten poems from the face of this earth; there'd be no going back to Bloomsbury now.

Mary had always been fond of Nina's unruly Afghan hound. What, she wondered as she sat on the cold bedroom floor recovering from that first bout of sickness and listening to Pegglar's snoring and Pegglar's cockerels crowing in the dawn outside, had been the poor animal's fate? 'I want a dog,' she told Pegglar later that day. If Pegglar could keep hens she could certainly have a dog.

'It would chase the chickens,' her husband objected.

'I'll keep him on a lead,' Mary said. Farnol noticed the new determined angle of her chin. He would also be first to notice the swelling up beneath her stomach.

When Edith heard her efforts had resulted in first Mary's acquisition of a large expensive dog, followed by the impending arrival of a young Pegglar, she decided Mary was not as flighty as the ridiculous red plume in her fashionable hat might suggest. A woman who knew how to weep and get what she wanted, Pegglar's bride was made of sterner stuff than *Pegglar's Pride*, Edith informed Gracie unsmilingly.

Not long after Pegglar went into business, his daughter Rosa was born. Mary was amused by what a doting father the old man she had married immediately became. 'My little chick-chicken!' Pegglar crowed, as the baby sucked the tip of his finger.

One catastrophic afternoon the large woolly dog, Alfonzo Bonzo, slipped his lead and got into the coops, barking and worrying at the hens. Exotic feathers flew and the terrified squawking brought Farnol, who was visiting, charging panic-stricken across the lawn. Furiously he flapped his stunted arms. 'Shoo, shoo . . . SHOO!'

The big puppy started a new game then, turning boisterously on the dwarf and pinning him up against a tree. When Pegglar came out to rescue his friend, the dog wagged his tail and darted nimbly away indoors. It was the Annual Exotic Poultry Show next month, Farnol ranted, shaking all over with fury and fear. 'Just look at the state of the birds!'

Pegglar shrugged. They were too unsettled to travel, he agreed, and sent back the two exhibitor's badges. He refused to imagine Bluie Chapman and Percy Thirsty Higgins standing unchallenged that year, or any year after, on the Champions' Podium. How Pegglar pitied those ambitious poultrymen who had nothing better to do! If Pegglar ever gave any thought to his peculiar bantams now, it was chiefly to muse why his peculiar sister had pushed him into breeding exotic poultry when he might just as well have joined a bicycling club, or amassed colourful postage stamps instead. On the rare occasions when a *Fancy* or a *Pride* deigned to lay one of their ordinary-looking eggs these days, Pegglar would boil it briskly, mash the thick yellow yolk and feed it to little Rosa, dandling contentedly on his lap. How the baby gurgled and dribbled! How adorably she grew! How Pegglar loved her . . .

Making Wishes

The sun shone down on the garden in which the infant Rosa played. All summer long, fruit ripened on the little apple tree Pegglar had planted the day she was born, rosy apples which were far too big – Farnol pointed out almost indignantly – for such slender branches. Bees buzzed about the great daisies that grew in the long grass where Alfie, the family dog, gambolled lazily or stretched his wiry body and rolled in the sun. Rosa ignored the dog. She shook the boughs of the tree. She swung in the swing her father had made from two pieces of rope and a plank of old timber. He had rubbed down the wood so the sharp edges would not cut her, nor the splinters hurt her legs. Rosa danced and skipped. Sometimes her friends from the houses close by came into her garden, sometimes she went into theirs, Thelma, Delphine, Norah and Enid, little Winnie who wore round pink spectacles and her bossy, pretty sister, Joan. Others too, there were *others*! Though an only child, Rosa Pegglar never needed to play by herself unless she wanted to. I can only suppose it makes a pleasant change to be alone sometimes when you are not always, of necessity, on your own.

Now and again a hen cackled desultorily from one of the coops along the back fence. When Rosa glanced up, Mary would be somewhere near by. 'Come and have a drink, Rosa dear!' There might be fairy cakes to ice, strawberry jam tarts to eat. Rosa and her little friends would troop into the spotless kitchen. But if Pegglar were present, Rosa told the other girls she was busy.

'Look,' Pegglar said softly, and as he bent down Rosa saw a ladybird perched on his wrist. 'Make a wish!'

Rosa tried, but what could she wish for, little Rosa Pegglar who had everything under the sun? She closed her eyes and frowned hard so her daddy could see she was wishing. When she opened her eyes, the ladybird was pulling back its wings to fly away. 'There!' said Pegglar.

'There!' echoed Rosa, her wish too big, too vague for words but somehow Pegglar understood.

'Let's feed the hens . . .' he said.

This was what Rosa liked best. When Daddy dug inside the large baggy pocket of his jacket and brought out a handful of seedcorn, little Rosa cupped her hands together and held the corn as if it were precious gold glistening in the sun. When they approached the coops, the fowls rushed in a flurry to the gates. A rooster jostled angrily to the front, thrusting his great beak towards the little girl. Rosa looked the rooster in the eye, for they were much the same height. With a jubilant cry, she raised her arms and threw the corn as hard as she could over the back of his bad-tempered head forcing him to turn and scrabble amongst the hens for what he could get. Rosa clapped her hands in satisfaction. 'You are a little Miss!' her father said proudly.

When the corn was all eaten most of the birds wandered off but the rooster stayed close. What kind of a bird are you? he seemed to be saying. 'I don't like him,' Rosa told her daddy.

'Old Guzzler?' Pegglar laughed. This was one of his last remaining *Prides*. Few of the birds left now had been carefully mismatched, or even matched at all. They were kept solely for eggs and eating. Pegglar reached inside the coop and patted Old Guzzler rather regretfully on the head. Vaingloriously the cockerel raised his comb, such as it was.

Once these *Pegglars* had been famous. Rosa knew this from Farnol. There had been coops full of them in every corner of the Pegglar family garden. Not this garden, the large rambling one outside the old aunts' house the other side of town. Rosa knew too that the extravagant combs, crests and plumes had been even more extravagant before she was born and that every spring her father's prize specimens had been exhibited with

Farnol's unfailing help at the Annual Exotic Poultry Show in London. And what happenings there had been . . .

'Something nasty in the seedcorn!' Whenever Farnol came to Sunday lunch, to eat one of the birds he himself had culled – for this was now a job assigned to him, Mary could not countenance such a thing and Pegglar himself was too busy – Philbert Farnol sat opposite Rosa and ate greedily. As self-appointed honoured guest and chicken culler he talked greedily also. He waved his fork in the air, he belched and spat. He spoke with gusto of those epic journeys, year after year, which he and her father, and her father's poultry, had valiantly undertaken in the days before even her mother had known Pegglar. Farnol could recall in precise heroic detail incidents with which neither Pegglar's own memory, nor the present bedraggled state of the birds, quite tallied. 'Bluie Chapman had all the pen men in his pocket!' As Percy Thirsty Higgins's cup-winning faverolles paraded into view beneath the harliquinade lights of London, Rosa's little eyes widened and Farnol brought his fist down hard on the table. A gravy boat keeled over with a splash. 'Plumped-up partridges!' he yelled.

Mary sighed and fetched a cloth. She did not want stains on her carpet. Mrs Pegglar was a houseproud woman. The house she took such pride in had been built before Rosa was born. The building of the house was spoken of many times also. 'They chose *everything* themselves,' Farnol recounted, giggling as if her parents had been naughty children stealing sweets. God expelling Adam and Eve from the Garden of Eden could not, apparently, have been angrier than Pegglar's sisters. 'Only the best, completely modern and new. Your aunts were livid . . .'

'A nesting box – all for *you*, Rosa!' Pegglar told his daughter when she tried to check on what Farnol had told her. 'Your aunts?' Pegglar repeated hesitantly. 'Oh, I dare say you'll meet them one day . . .'

How Mary vacuumed and scrubbed, polished and cooked. The beaten-copper doorstep shone so in the sunlight that it blinded visitors and, in Pegglar's absence, drove away the marauding armies of door-to-door salesmen that frequently threaten a hearth and home. Mary mopped the gravy off the carpet.

The skulduggery at the Poultry Show might have taken place yesterday, Farnol became so indignant at every retelling. Rosa felt she too had seen money change hands sideways and her father's hens, even in their heyday, slighted. Mary and Pegglar did not join in the narration. Unlike Farnol, neither of Rosa's parents had any desire to recapture past triumphs. 'Best forgotten,' Mary once said when Rosa asked her. 'London?' Pegglar queried as if he barely remembered the place. 'Oh yes, we had some great times. You will go there yourself one day.'

'You shouldn't speak with your mouth full,' Rosa told the noisy dwarf. 'It's bad manners.'

Her parents laughed fondly, grateful for the interruption.

After lunch, a ribbon might be tied in Rosa's hair and, while Mary cleared away the dishes, Rosa would go with her father to Farnol's studios to play with toys while her picture was taken. Pegglar was keeping a photograph album as any proud father might, a stockbreeding record he called it. This was such a regular event that Rosa ignored Farnol's antics. She did not laugh too close to the lens but busied herself with the studio toys. She had known them as long as she could remember. 'Are these *mine*?' Rosa once asked.

'Of course they are,' Pegglar chuckled.

Rosa combed the old gollywog's thinning hair. Then she wound round the handle on the musical box and sang to the familiar tune. When her photograph had been taken and it was time to leave, Rosa carefully packed all the wooden animals inside the Noah's Ark and tucked it neatly under her arm. A lion poked its head out of a window.

'You can't take that!' Farnol roared. A monkey tumbled to the floor. Rosa had intended to set up the Ark at home in her bedroom. Noah could stand at the top of the plank while the queue of animals wound in their pairs round the legs of her cot and away across the rag rug. 'Think of all the other children!' Farnol protested.

The infant Pegglar lifted her chin. Rosa did not care about any other children. The Ark was hers, her daddy had said so. She turned to Pegglar.

Pegglar glanced at the disputed toy. 'I see no reason . . .'

'Think how disappointed the other children will be when they come here and find it gone!' Farnol cried.

Pegglar nodded. 'Farnol's right,' he said sadly.

'But . . .'

Pegglar patted his daughter on the head. He stooped down. 'Other children haven't got exotic hens in *their* gardens,' he told her softly. 'Or brand-new houses built specially for them. *You* are the lucky one, Rosa!'

The little girl nodded and rendered up the wooden Noah's Ark.

'There's a chicken!' Pegglar untied and retied the ribbon in her hair.

Rosa bit her lip. It was only a battered old thing with half its pieces missing. The tusks on both elephants had been snapped off, and someone had chewed the paint on Mrs Noah's face. Rosa no longer knew why she'd wanted to take it home with her. The other children who came here were hateful careless creatures. Intruders. *She* was the lucky one, Pegglar's daughter. Rosa took her father's hand and, leaving Farnol hard at work in his darkroom, the two set off home.

Though Pegglar often spent long stretches of time away on business, his reappearances were so deliciously unpredictable that you immediately forgave and forgot his absence. 'An astonishing man, your father,' Mary liked to say, for Pegglar, and her marriage to the man, had never ceased to astonish her.

'My father is an astonishing man,' Rosa would repeat solemnly sometimes at school.

'Really? Why's that?'

And though young Rosa had no answer, she knew with all the quiet certainty of her years that what she said was true.

Late one Saturday afternoon Pegglar returned home unexpectedly. He lifted his little daughter off her feet and swung her high in the air. It left him slightly breathless.

'Let's go to the fair!' he said, although it was nearly Rosa's

30

bedtime. The three set out at once, Rosa swinging between Mary and Pegglar who were each holding one of her hands. As the little family neared the fairground site and sounds of music and people enjoying themselves drifted over open ground, Rosa could see coloured lights flashing and a ferris wheel turning behind a wall of tents. There had come a loud 'holloa' in the street. Rosa twisted in alarm to see Farnol bounding along behind.

'I nearly missed you,' he shouted.

Rosa's heart sank but her parents did not stop him joining them and, when they reached the turnstile, Farnol insisted on paying. 'My treat,' he said.

'Good heavens, alive!' Pegglar exclaimed.

'Alive! Of course we're alive!' Rosa looked up at the two old women who had accosted her daddy. The one who spoke was eyeing her brightly the way Old Guzzler did. What kind of a bird are you, with two legs, no wings or feathers, able to run in and out of the house and even talk to Farnol without ending up cooked for Sunday lunch?

'You must be Rosa.' Rosa understood now these were her two angry aunts, furious still over the house that had been built for her. 'And business, Pegglar?'

'Fine, fine,' her father was saying. 'We didn't expect to meet you here, Edie.'

'I don't see why not. I have always enjoyed the fair.'

'Have you? I never knew that.'

'Well, no, I don't suppose you did.' Edith Pegglar pointed at Rosa. 'The child should come and visit us.' This was a command, not a casual suggestion like the keeping of poultry. Pegglar nodded and twiddled his ginger moustaches. Mary said nothing. Farnol reappeared waving whirls of pink candyfloss on sticks. One of these he thrust into Aunt Gracie's hands. Then he tried to steer them all over to the carousel. 'Rides for everyone!' he declared, jangling the coins in his fist. 'I've already paid.'

'You had no . . .' Edith Pegglar began to protest.

In that moment of distraction, Aunt Gracie let herself be helped up on to the great gobbling ostrich. She sat chomping strands of pink candyfloss, unconcerned that her sister was hissing at her urgently to step back down. Rosa climbed into the saddle of a handsome painted horse and when Farnol made a dash for the strutting rooster, Pegglar got there first and the dwarf had to settle for the donkey behind. Grinding music started up, growing louder and faster as the animals began to whirr and chase. Rosa held on tight to the golden spiral pole that raised and lowered her horse and when she looked back down below, she saw her mother talking to a stranger. Edith Pegglar had stalked purposefully away towards the coconut shies.

Round and round the carousel turned. It was as much as Rosa could do to stay in her seat. Farnol leant forward and waving his candyfloss he yelled at Pegglar, 'Why was it never *Farnol's Pride* or *Farnol's Fancy*?'

Pegglar laughed. Rosa laughed. The wind combed through her hair.

'If it wasn't for me you would never have been born,' Farnol shouted at Rosa then. 'If *I* hadn't swallowed fixative, your father would never have gone to London on his own, and fixed himself up with your mother . . .'

Rosa held on tight but when she glanced up at Pegglar he was staring ahead, smiling into the distance.

'Who was that man?' Rosa asked her mother when eventually the music had stopped and everyone was back on the ground. 'The one you were talking to.'

Mary shrugged. 'I haven't any idea,' she said.

Aunt Edith presented Rosa with a coconut. 'I won it,' she told her niece proudly. 'But I don't like coconut any more than hard toffee. It sticks in the teeth.'

After that, Rosa had been sent every so often, washed and preened and dressed in her best clothes, to visit her elderly aunts. 'Edith's quarrel was with us,' the parents reasoned on the way home from the fair. 'The girl is her niece. Farnol can take her . . .'

Mary bought Rosa a pair of patent-leather shoes and Farnol was delighted by the fresh task assigned to him. When Rosa, wearing her smart new shoes, refused to hold the dwarf's leathery hand, Farnol recollected that he had only ever worn the second exhibitor's badge. He bowed his head and hurried importantly to keep up with the little girl. At the Pegglar sisters' gate he'd refuse to go any further but would always be waiting there later when she came running out.

'Our niece!' Edith told Gracie each time, and each time Aunt Gracie cackled with delight.

'She has straw in her head,' Mary had explained and Rosa would sit scanning the side of Gracie Pegglar's head for the line of stitching where the straw had been stuffed in.

'I don't like tea,' Rosa said the first time. Her shiny new shoes pinched her toes. Aunt Edith raised her eyebrows as if she had not heard properly. 'I drink milk at home,' Rosa explained.

'You are not at home, child,' Edith said firmly. 'This has not been Pegglar's home since before you were born. Try some tea . . .'

Rosa took the cup and sipped at it curiously. 'Alfie drinks tea,' she said, conversationally.

'Alfie?'

'Alfonzo Bonzo – our dog.'

'Drinks tea?' Edith Pegglar sniffed in disbelief.

'Mummy makes him a pot for breakfast and another in the evening. She pours it into his bowl and when the tea is cool enough he drinks it.'

'I never heard of such a thing.' Edith tutted. Behind the plate of ancient-looking biscuits Aunt Gracie tutted also.

'He likes tea,' Rosa said.

'I dare say he does!'

'I like milk,' Rosa ventured. Aunt Edith ignored this. A tea-drinking dog, a growing child shod in patent leather demanding milk – what mockery of household economy was this? The girl should be made to earn . . .

'Tell me,' Aunt Edith said, and began to ask questions about Pegglar and Rosa's mother. About Farnol too, though why she wanted to know anything about Philbert Farnol neither Rosa nor indeed Aunt Edith herself could fathom.

'Postcards! A postcard business!' Edith Pegglar shrieked.

Rosa smiled. 'My father is an astonishing man,' she said happily.

'He certainly is that,' Aunt Edith sighed. Aunt Gracie leant towards Rosa proffering the mound of elderly custard creams.

And then quite suddenly one afternoon, Pegglar died.

'Died?'

'Yes, Jeannie. He died.'

What of? I wanted to know. Everyone died of something, the war, German measles, drink . . .

Rosa nodded. 'It is late,' she said, taking a bonbon quickly from her handbag and slipping it into my hand. My mother did not like me having sweets as they ruined my appetite and rotted my teeth but she could hardly say so in front of our guest. Elaborately I unwrapped the cellophane and popped the sweet into my mouth.

'Say *thank you*, Jeannie,' my poor mother said.

I ignored her. 'But Pegglar . . .' His sudden death was a shock.

Rosa stood up to leave. She kissed the old lady affectionately, and then she turned to me. 'I will tell you all about it next time,' Rosa laughed. She did not kiss me because my face was now sticky. 'There is much to tell!'

And So, Farewell

The girls at school not unreasonably and not unkindly asked Chickenlegs what her father had died of. If they were expected to show sympathy, they had a right to know the facts.

Rosa did not want sympathy. She stood in her pleated navy tunic and regulation short socks looking at them blankly. Her father had been an astonishing man and he had astonished them all. 'I honestly don't know,' the eleven-year-old Rosa Pegglar said. 'But I'll find out.'

I must confess that I too found it difficult to commiserate wholeheartedly. Rosa, after all, had had a father for eleven long years; eleven years longer than I ever had. *And* her childhood had been happy; only later did it dawn on her there'd been anything bizarre. That evening, Rosa went into Mary's bedroom and demanded to know what Pegglar had died of.

'I beg your pardon?' Mary was trying a little black hat on the back of her head. She looked in the dressing-table mirror at her disconcerting daughter and smiled sadly. Mary had enjoyed her quiet marriage. Her daughter's question caught her off guard. 'Old age, I suppose,' she said hesitantly. Her husband had always been an old man to her. She stabbed at the veil with a hatpin. 'I love you,' he had said for no reason, shuffling up here to her room that last time and lingering in the doorway where Rosa stood now. 'Never forget that, Mary, whatever happens.'

'Whatever happens!' Mary had laughed. Taken aback all the same. 'Why, Pegglar dear, whatever *can* happen?'

Anything, it seemed. Pegglar had not replied. He stuffed his hands in his pockets and, late already for wherever he was going, he paused as if he wanted to tell her something.

Something his wife would not want to hear. He smiled shyly and then hurried away. There'd always been business to hurry away for. Her husband's death only seemed another form of his absence.

Rosa, though, was deeply upset. The girls at school were convinced she was holding back some interesting truth. Old age? Daddy? Grown-ups were old, wasn't that the point of them? 'But Pegglar . . .'

'He was an *old* man,' Mary said quickly. 'People die of old age. He was old when you were born, even.'

'But he was *younger* than Aunt Edith, and Aunt Gracie.' Rosa watched in the mirror as her mother's face hardened. The aunts showed little sign of dying of old age: Gracie had stayed much the same while Edith Pegglar was now dislodging coconuts. 'What'll we do?' Rosa asked her mother. There was already a FOR SALE sign standing on a pole in the front garden.

Mary sighed. Life had been easy enough while Pegglar was alive. 'Let us get the funeral over with first. Do you like my hat?'

Rosa nodded and wandered away downstairs. Farnol culled old roosters when their crows became croaks and the hens no longer interested them. She sat in the silent kitchen with Alfie. He too was old, for a dog; he slept most of the day now and his legs were stiff. She stroked his mangy fur. Alfie did not know that Pegglar was dead. He probably would not care if he did, he had always been her mother's dog. Besides, Pegglar had rarely been at home. He'd been busy and important. Men were. Fathers went out to work; their families waited for them to return. But now Daddy was never coming back. Rosa wondered what had happened to his pipe.

She remembered standing in the garden, wearing a pink-and-white check frock, teasing a cockerel that had been far more resplendent than Old Guzzler. Suddenly for no reason, some of the birds had started attacking each other, leaping, shrieking, bejewelled toes clawing, feathers flying. Rosa had screamed and a shadow had appeared behind her. 'That's love,' Pegglar said gently.

'Love!' Rosa was frightened. The screaming and clawing had turned into a frantic fearful dance. 'Love?'

'Absurd as it seems.' Pegglar had taken her indoors then and given her a biscuit.

One day, some time – probably even some years – later Mary had come into the kitchen. 'What a racket outside!' she said.

'That's love,' Rosa told her mother without looking up. The hens were at it again and Rosa was trying to concentrate on her difficult sums.

'Nonsense,' her mother had laughed. 'Love, indeed!'

'Daddy said so!'

'The girl's right,' Pegglar remarked sadly. He had been helping with the arithmetic though nothing he attempted added up. Rosa wanted him to help, all the same.

'Well, human love is different, I'm glad to say,' Mary said brightly. She had the lunch to cook. Farnol was expected. There would be some fresh account of something nefarious at a Poultry Show to endure.

Pegglar shook his head. 'Human love is absurd.' He sounded tired, and matter of fact. 'Look what ordinary eggs even exotic poultry lay! Love, alas, disrupts the natural order for people. Human feelings intrude on any orderly pairing and mismatching. You will find out for yourself, one day,' he told his daughter.

The infant Pegglar chewed her pencil. Daddy did not often make speeches.

'Get on with your homework,' Mary had said.

'What was Pegglar's name?' Rosa asked her mother as they walked together to the funeral.

'Name?' Mary did not understand.

'He must have been something, apart from Pegglar.' Rosa wondered why this had never occurred to her before. Her mother told her some names. Names that were repeated at the funeral so that it had not felt like a funeral for *Pegglar* when there they were in the cold church, solemnly burying a Dear Departed *Rodolphe Arthur George*.

Perhaps because of this, Rosa never felt her father had left

37

her, abandoning her the way she later so happily abandoned me. It was only after Pegglar's death she found out how truly astonishing her daddy had been. After Rosa's death, I still don't know . . .

'You're not regular church-goers?' the priest asked.

Mrs Pegglar blushed. 'Nnno,' she stammered. There had been nothing you could call regular. The Registrar in London had disapproved also but strapped spectacles behind his ears and married them nevertheless.

As the brief service started, Edith and Gracie swept into the pew behind. Edith, resplendent in black sequined gloves and a black Spanish comb swept high in her grey hair, eyed her widowed sister-in-law and bedraggled niece (best breeding stock, indeed!), and sang the hymns exultantly. Gracie did not sing. She opened and closed her mouth, and busied herself with the prayerbook. Rosa saw the book was upside down. Aunt Gracie did not know whom they were burying, either.

Outside, standing in the drizzle by the open grave, Edith blew majestically into a black lace-edged handkerchief and said, 'Mary dear, when this is over we must all put our heads together. Pegglar's business cannot possibly be expected to continue without Pegglar. Whatever our past differences, I would not want you, and the child, to starve.'

'No, indeed,' Rosa's mother remarked meekly.

Rosa looked fondly and for the last time at her father's coffin. Well, goodbye Rodolphe Arthur George! she thought as the box was lowered inch by inch on thick straps into the mud. Rosa read the inscription, *Sacred to the Memory* of one *Captain Pegglar* who had died in dubious circumstances in Simla and *Also, his Beloved Wife* who had been run over by a runaway horse while on the way to a wedding which had not then taken place. The little boy who had picked at icing on an upturned wedding cake was upturned himself now. Aunt Edith caught Rosa's eye and looked away. We all have our own tantalizingly concealed version of events, Edith had told her. Had Pegglar known? Had her parents ever guessed what had gone on during those ghastly visits? Why had they sent their daughter there if they knew that she would be forced into betraying them? Why had she not refused to go? Or refused when she got there to open her mouth?

Farnol turned up then, in time to hear Mary telling her sisters-in-law that food had been prepared. Farnol it was who paid off the priest and, electing himself Chief Mourner, tried to take Pegglar's widow by the arm. Rosa skipped ahead. Pegglar's sisters were not to be hurried.

'We will join you later,' Edith said, dropping back as if wanting a private word with Pegglar. Mary could not help glancing uneasily into the grave. But this was folly, she told herself, and leant on Farnol's stunted arm.

Farnol had killed the hens. What few there were left. And Old Guzzler. Tears rolled down his large squashed-up cheeks anointing the wretched creatures as he wrung their scrawny necks. A vision of all the silver cups and bronze medals that, year after year, the birds he was slaughtering had never won swum before Philbert Farnol's watery eyes.

Mary had bravely roasted and stuffed the miserable carcasses. This was a last rite Pegglar would have wanted his widow to perform, she decided. 'Eat up!' Mary told her daughter sharply.

Rosa Pegglar chewed.

When the aunts arrived, Edith declined any of the sorry fare but Gracie took up a drumstick and picked at the tough stringy flesh, soiling her black crocheted gloves and smearing grease all down the front of her mourning bib.

'Pegglar's passion was for his poultry,' Edith Pegglar remarked. She accepted a conciliatory cup of tea and then asked politely after the extravagant dog. Mary said Alfie was upstairs, out of the way. Philbert Farnol, Edith ignored completely. The dead man may have been the brother she had taken care of for fifty years, but this was not her house. Things had always been done differently here. She sipped the tea. 'You must pardon me for asking, Mary, but as Pegglar's sister I am naturally concerned. I suppose there is no money put by for you and the child to live on?'

'You suppose right.' Pegglar's widow sighed. Pegglar's

business had done quite well when Rosa was small but lately Pegglar had been tired. He and Farnol had created, or cashed in on, a craze for crazy postcards. Farnol's disturbing distorted likenesses of well-known dignitaries and fleshy women in varying states of undress had enjoyed a profitable nationwide vogue. People had liked to be shown how ugly the world in the darkness of a darkroom could be made to look. Even as Pegglar banked the profits he had wondered why we all wish to re-create the world in which we live, touching it up with bright paint. At the height of the craze Farnol had worked flat out while Pegglar organized teams of commissioned salesmen selling postcards up and down the country. Pegglar had not died at home. He had died in a neighbouring town where Mary had not known he had gone. Farnol had been sent to arrange for his body to be brought back for burial.

'What was he doing there?' Edith asked her sister-in-law.

'I don't know,' Mary said. 'Business, I shouldn't wonder.' Minding his own business, certainly.

'I understood the postcard trade to have dwindled,' Edith continued. 'A faddish business.'

Mary couldn't think where this was leading. Edith was somehow well informed. Farnol looked at Rosa. Rosa Pegglar looked down at her feet. How relieved she felt when Edith finished her tea and stood up, pulling Gracie with her. 'When you find you can no longer cope, Mary, you and the child and even, er, Alfie, will always find a home with us.'

With Gracie nodding away beside her the offer had sounded too pressing, too triumphant. Outside it was as silent as Pegglar's grave, Edith only had to look at the funeral baked meats. The overloaded Ark no longer lurched in deep waters. Her brother's godless fowls had all been slain. She inclined her cheek for her niece to kiss, and Rosa obediently did so.

Philbert Farnol waited cunningly like a fox until they heard the door closing behind Pegglar's retreating sisters. Rosa held her breath.

'One of a kind!' Farnol grinned from ear to ear. He and Pegglar had done very well for themselves but while Farnol had cleverly invested all his share of the profits, Pegglar had reck-lessly spent his. His passions had latterly proved expensive. Farnol suspected they had got out of hand. 'You mustn't let Miss Edith upset you.'

'She doesn't upset me,' Mary replied.

'What a business!' Farnol shook the round ball of his head. He was a businessman, he told himself gleefully, about to make a nice killing.

'Pegglar had no head for business,' Mary said. It might have been her husband's epitaph, she thought, smiling.

Farnol coughed. He would give Mary Pegglar something to smile about: 'You don't have to go and live with Pegglar's sisters, you know.' He stroked the side of his wide squashed nose.

'Oh, I expect . . .' Mary had definitely *not* expected this.

Farnol said, 'Yes, I expected it too. I have been saving . . .'

'I wish Pegglar had saved,' Mary said rapidly. 'Money now would certainly save the day!' Maybe if *she* had studied a shilling book before she'd married . . .

Farnol nodded. When the dwarf photographer eventually said what he'd been saving up for this moment to say, Rosa kept very still; Mary's mouth dropped open. 'Philbert!' she gasped weakly, doing her best not to laugh. 'Philbert!'

'Twenty thousand pounds!' Farnol repeated with a bitter smirk. Money in the bank to balance the ugliness and deformity he'd been born with. Buy him Pegglar's bride, pride, fancy – call her what you will. Bring her down to his level, her sweet lips clamped to his, using the most indetectable of glues. All these years he had urged Pegglar on, and now . . . Philbert Farnol laughed aloud in anticipation of his prize. He clasped his leath-ery hands eagerly together. 'Twenty thousand pounds, Mary! Interest and dividends accruing every day!'

Mrs Pegglar faltered. The house her husband had built was heavily mortgaged and houses of this type, the house agent had told her, were impossible at the moment to sell. If the price was dropped any lower, the receipts could not cover the debts, let alone the agent's fee. The agent had stood very close. She had felt his warm breath playing on her skin. If she had not moved smartly away the man would have taken her hand between his. Mary looked with horror at the black hairs on Philbert Farnol's stubby fingers.

'Twenty thousand pounds is an awful lot of money,' Rosa Pegglar sang out, her mouth full of unchewable chicken.

Mary came to her senses. 'Go and check poor Alfie is all right, Rosa,' she snapped. 'You know how he hates to be shut in!'

Rosa did not move. She did not care about Alfie. Her mother readjusted the little black hat, skewed now on the back of her head. She spoke firmly to her late husband's friend, 'Mr Farnol, you are very kind, of course. You were always a good friend to Pegglar and it was clever of you to have saved so much money. But you must not think of *me* in this way . . .'

'I love you!' Farnol's voice trembled.

'That is absurd. I am in mourning.'

Farnol darkened spitefully. 'You never really knew Pegglar,' he hissed at Rosa's mother.

'No,' Mary agreed.

'He had his passions,' the infuriated hobgoblin spat. 'You weren't the only exotic hen!'

There was a long silence. Then Mary said softly, 'I'm sorry if you have been hurt, Mr Farnol. After all you have done, all these years . . .'

'I have been waiting,' Philbert Farnol admitted. He was a patient man. One who could wait however long it took for a *Fancy* or a *Pride* to display unwieldy plumes which he would capture on film and hold tight. A stroke of red ink here, a quick dab there . . .

'Waiting? For Pegglar to die?'

'I suppose, amongst other things, yes.' Pegglar's fowls had looked better in Farnol's photographs than they did in real life. He had made himself useful and they had used him. What could a man, who must by his own admission look up to the whole world, expect? After a while Philbert Farnol said, sorrowfully now, 'What will you do?'

'Miss Pegglar has been generous. You heard her – their house is large and Rosa is her niece. They seem fond . . .'

Fond! Rosa nearly choked on her chicken.

'Live there?' Farnol thought Mary's daughter had more sense: twenty thousand pounds *was* an awful lot of money to turn down rashly. 'With Pegglar's sisters?' Farnol had not considered this avenue of escape.

Neither till that moment had Rosa. She had only kissed Aunt Edith's papery cheek, she had only ever answered her questions, because children have no choice. They are born into this world and before they know what they are doing, they have abided by its laws.

'Perhaps,' said Mary, 'I don't know! I have not had time . . . Pegglar's death – such a surprise . . .'

'I am a disappointed man,' Farnol declared. He stood up to leave and leered at Rosa who turned her face quickly away. I was only little, she thought. Outside the house Pegglar had built for her, the FOR SALE sign flapped listlessly in the wind while the coops in the back garden stood unlatched and empty, as if a fox had broken in and rampaged.

'We're not really going to live there, are we?' Rosa asked her mother. Not in the House of Inquisitions, where they sat you down in the cold musty parlour and interrogated you until you didn't know what you were saying. Until you found yourself betraying those you loved most. Pegglar would have understood. And forgiven her, if he had known.

'You'll have to change schools,' Mary answered, not replying directly to her daughter's question.

Rosa would be glad to leave her school and start again afresh somewhere she was not known. Where the girl who walked in through the door could have been *anyone*. 'Who are you?' she dreamed that the new girls asked her, although *she* was really the new girl, and she had replied: 'I could be anyone. Anyone's daughter.' This, Chickenlegs also dreamed, was her first mistake. She was Pegglar's daughter. The burial of a Rodolphe Arthur George did not alter that.

Moving On

Rosa said 'goodbye' to such of Thelma, Delphine, Norah, Enid, Winnie and Joan as were around the day her mother closed the front door for the last time. Rosa hesitated on the beaten-copper doorstep. Another child would sit in the swing Pegglar had made and reach up for the apples that grew large every summer on her fruit tree. Rosa's mother did not linger even for a second. How she had cleaned, polished and vacuumed. Activities that seemed to Mary Pegglar, now, to distinguish most nearly the Living from the Dead. She was not sorry to walk down the gravel path and leave Pegglar's fixtures and fittings behind. 'Things change,' she told her daughter. 'The world moves on and, if we are sensible, we move on with it.'

'How much did your mother get for that horrible house?' Edith Pegglar asked when she heard it had been sold. Rosa had come of her own free will. Farnol had not delivered her up, he had not been seen since the funeral.

'Not much. I don't know who bought it. We are to rent a shop,' Rosa said. 'And live above it.'

'A *shop*?' What could Pegglar's widow know of *shop*keeping, when she had been unable even to keep her own house? 'The High Street is a dangerous place, your grandmother was killed there!'

'Mummy's turning it into an office. And it's not in the High Street.' Nor yet the quiet dusty road where Farnol had his studios. Their new home was in a run-down part of town where no one would remember Pegglar or his hens. 'We are moving on,' Rosa said and described how her mother had purchased a typewriter and *six* boxes of paper. 'That was the

44

amount you have to buy to get the paper cheaper.'

'I do not need lessons in economy, child, least of all from you! I didn't know your mother could type.'

'She can't, but she's learning. She's teaching herself from a book.'

Edith drew a handkerchief across her brow. What an extraordinary way to mourn a husband, but learning household economy from a book had been an odd preparation also for not getting married, though it had not seemed so at the time. 'And Mr Farnol?'

'He has twenty thousand pounds saved in the bank.'

Edith Pegglar froze. She choked. 'It was my dearest wish that Pegglar would come home one day brandishing the prestigious silver cup,' she said.

'Bluie Chapman put something nasty in the seedcorn,' Rosa told her.

'If you believe that you'll believe anything!' Edith turned to Gracie. 'Did you hear, dear? Twenty thousand pounds in the bank!'

Gracie grinned. She handed Rosa a crumbling custard cream.

The 'office' opened. Business was slow and Mary soon had to cut her original cut-price prices. She typed till her fingers ached and her head throbbed, but still she barely made enough money for them to live on.

Rosa listened to the interminable rattle of the typewriter, less faltering now, and was reminded of the non-stop squawking of her father's fowls. From time to time neighbours had complained. Thelma's father had even got up a petition during the war, protesting that the constant noise would guide in German bombers. Although enemy action remained thankfully distant, countless hostile signatures had been sent to Buckingham Palace. When good King George VI in his wisdom failed to act, it seemed to the petitioners that Pegglar's preposterous birds were Raucous then by Royal Appointment. Pegglar's wife was treated with a new almost deferential, if icy, respect. And when the peculiar little Pegglar child came to play with their daughters she was tolerated in their gardens less unwillingly perhaps than she had been before.

The typewriting went on. People argued the price down to barely more than the cost of the paper because Mary needed the work while they could go elsewhere.

'There are *regular* customers,' Rosa reported to her aunts and tried to exaggerate their interest, for most of her mother's customers were rather dull. Men in ill-fitting suits who often hoped for more from Mary than typing done on the cheap. The monotony of those years spent with her mother was broken by a series of unlooked-for visitations. Maybe it was the recollection of this that prompted Rosa to enliven *my* miserable world with *her* visits. I shall never know. The first such visitor was Eunice Proctor.

'I felt I ought!' Mrs Proctor told Rosa angrily. It was raining, her headscarf was soaked, she had already had to pay for a bus ride, and now there would be the fare back. Under these circumstances, you might expect to be invited in, offered tea or information at least. 'To see how your mother is . . .'

'She's fine, thank you,' Rosa said at once. Mary was out trying to keep clients happy by delivering their finished typing. 'She shouldn't be long if you want to wait.'

'I can't stop.' Eunice Proctor wanted, however, to continue the conversation. Mrs Proctor had regarded herself as Rosa's mother's friend and had often stood up for Mary amongst the neighbours, and even encouraged her own daughters, the bespectacled Winnie and bossy pretty Joan to befriend the poor little Pegglar child. 'Do you like your new school, Rosa? And your new friends? Winnie and Joannie often ask about you.'

What did they ask, Rosa wondered.

Eunice Proctor glared at the Poultryman's daughter. She narrowed her eyes. 'There have been a lot of callers at your old house.'

'Callers?'

'People – women mainly – looking for Pegglar.'

Rosa stared at Mrs Proctor. '*Women*, looking for Daddy? Who?'

Mrs Proctor flicked the water from her headscarf. 'He had his

46

passions, I dare say. Most men do. Your mother forgot to leave a forwarding address, even with me. Someone saw the name above this office. *Wasn't she a neighbour of yours, Eunice, that strange quiet Pegglar woman?* I couldn't deny it of course, not the way I used to stand up for your mother, not knowing for sure. I've never been hereabouts and I did not know your mother could type. But then she always was close . . .'

'It's not a secret,' Rosa said quickly. Eunice Proctor was behaving as if she had found something out. 'I expect Mother forgot, in the rush.'

'So I can send inquirers along?'

'Why not?' Rosa boldly met Eunice Proctor's neighbourly stare.

'Mrs Proctor came,' Rosa said when her mother returned.

'What did she want?'

'To say *hallo*, I think.' Mary looked tired so Rosa did not mention all the women looking for Pegglar.

Alfie never liked living over the shop which was now an office. He did not like the interminable tapping of the typewriter and he was used to a garden and hens to bark at so the tiny backyard was not enough. His fur grew thin, his legs and bladder uncertain.

'He was old,' Mary said, as she had said of Pegglar. 'Very old for a dog . . .'

Mary wept for Alfie as she had never wept for Pegglar. She washed his dogstained blanket and slept with it on her bed.

'Alfie died,' Rosa told Edith.

'I'm not surprised,' Edith said bluntly. The dog had been an emblem of her late brother's folly, as indeed was this new ungodly variant, Rosa herself. 'All that tea!'

Rosa's mother had paid the carter's boy to take Alfie's ragged body away. Rosa stood at the window watching. As the cart jolted off with the dog thrown on top of a pile of dirty sacking, she had seen Alfie open an eye and look straight back at her. The dog lay quite stiff and still, but he had fooled them, he'd only been pretending to be dead. Rosa rapped on the window but the boy did not hear her. She rushed to the door just as he cracked his whip and the cart disappeared in the turn at the end of the lane. Alfonzo Bonzo was gone for good. The old dog had waited, it seemed to Rosa then, till he was out of sight. Then he had sprung from the cart with a yelp of joy and had run as he used to run, back to the long grass full of daisies where he could gambol all day, every day, stretching and rolling in the undimmed sun.

Eunice Proctor began sending callers at the sold house across town to Mary's office. Let the world see what was become of Mrs Pegglar, sanctioned even in wartime by no less an authority than the Crown! The women who came when Rosa was at school, Rosa did not see. The ones who came while Rosa was at home upstairs, Rosa saw but did not speak to. One day, however, her mother was out, delivering work again. She had had a cold and got behind. Her customers were not sympathetic and threatened to take their business elsewhere. An office was an office, illness no excuse. A caller rang the bell and waited.

'Have you brought typing?' Rosa asked, inviting the woman inside.

'Typing? This really *is* an office then? I thought that busybody hanging over the garden fence was joking.'

'Mrs Proctor?'

'She did not look the sort to joke. Only I wasn't sure. I'm not sure of anything any more . . .'

The woman pulled out a chair and sat down heavily. 'You see,' she said breathing slowly, 'I heard Pegglar died.'

'He did. I'm Rosa, his daughter.'

The woman trembled violently. She dabbed a handkerchief to her nose and made emphatic sniffing noises. 'It's no good, I can't pretend . . .' The bright red lipstick daubing her mouth had smudged. Her eyes too were red from rubbing. Her voice reduced to a whisper as she made her ghastly confession: 'Pegglar was with me when he died.'

Rosa stared. 'But he was away on business . . .'

'Pegglar had no head for business. Oh dear!' The visitor wept openly now.

Mary, returning, took in the scene with a woman weeping

centre-stage as if fully understanding the plot at once.

'I'm Mary,' the visitor said.

'*You*,' Rosa's mother corrected her, 'are the *other* Mary!'

'That's a coincidence,' Rosa remarked, but the two women ignored her.

'*Another* Mary, I should say,' Rosa's mother went on wearily like an actor tired of a part. 'There have been others, beside yourself.'

'I shouldn't have come,' the other Mary blurted out.

'No,' Rosa's mother agreed calmly. 'Most likely you shouldn't.'

'I hoped you'd understand. The loss I feel. I haven't slept . . .'

'And what do you think I feel?' Mary asked coldly. 'My child is orphaned!'

'So is mine,' the other Mary gulped. 'I thought I . . . I . . . then I find I am not . . . If I was not Pegglar's wife, how can I be his widow? And yet, I am just as bereaved as you. I too the mother of his orphan . . .'

Rosa's mother glanced sharply at Rosa. Only one of the brilliant plaster animals had had no rider and, though a queue pushed forward (reluctant to sit on the donkey but doing so when nowhere else was left), the flamboyant cockerel with the ungainly strut rode merrily round on his own, coming and going unharnessed. 'Pegglar was an astonishing man,' Rosa's mother said at last. 'Even after death he has not ceased to astonish me.'

'Yes,' the other woman agreed. She sniffed. 'There is comfort in that. If one is to be taken in by a man, let him at least be a man worth the sum of his deceptions. No one – no one person – really knew Pegglar, I dare say.'

'He came and went.'

'You are very calm . . .' The visitor blew her nose and then started crying again. 'I couldn't bear it when Philbert Farnol took Pegglar's body away. He died in my house. In my bed . . . I still have his pipe.'

'It can do no good now to speak of these things,' Rosa's

mother said firmly. Then she added with the faintest smile. 'I dare say Mr Farnol could sort you out.'

The woman immediately wiped her eyes. 'I've been in such a state, I've pawned everything there was to pawn; my little girl . . . I have no money . . .'

'Mr Farnol has twenty thousand pounds,' Rosa piped up.

'*Twenty thousand pounds?*' The visitor returned her handkerchief to her handbag and, closing it with a loud snap, she looked at Rosa kindly. 'I can see Pegglar in you, child.' She sighed apologetically. 'We do what we have to in this life!'

After the other Mary had gone, Mrs Pegglar refused to discuss the visit or refer to it again. Rosa even began to wonder if she had imagined the whole thing. It was some time before the next visitation.

Rosa answered a prolonged ring at the door to find a couple laughing together in the street. The man had a handsome angular face and a fluffy young woman on his arm. He marched straight past Rosa into Mary's office, flung off his coat, swivelled on his heel and surveyed the room. Rosa stared: these visitors looked like filmstars. The girl looked bored. They came from another world and were unlikely to have been sent by Eunice Proctor.

'Where is she then?' the man asked.

'My mother?'

'You must be Rosa!'

'I *could* be anyone.'

'No, you couldn't, not with that chin.' The filmstars laughed as Rosa clutched her chin, the chin that meant she was Rosa Pegglar.

'Who are you?' she asked.

To Rosa's amazement the man said: 'I last saw you when you were a baby. Our illustrious mamma wrote stories for modern women on housing estates, about contraception, which Mary obviously hadn't read because there *you* were, an ugly pink prawn-thing in a pram . . .'

His companion looked thrillingly shocked. 'Max – the child!' she gasped. She was walking round the room, idly picking things up and putting them down. She prodded at the keys of Mary's typewriter with one finger as if trying notes on a piano to see if it was in tune. 'A-S-D-F-G,' she read out, and tittered.

'So, I came to have a look – a nice set-up, wife in apron, baby, dog, cakes in the oven, hens in the garden and old man Pegglar, who knew where?'

'Where was he?' asked Rosa.

'How should I know?' the visitor retorted. 'Your mother didn't know either. That much was clear. Anyway, *you* have grown. Quite the young woman – almost . . .'

'Max!' Mary had known they had visitors for she'd seen the handsome motor outside. Max Fanshawe stared at his worn-out sister. 'This is Lily,' he introduced the fluffy girl with a jerk of his elegant thumb. The two women eyed each other over the typewriter.

'Why have you come?' Mary asked warily.

'To see how you are getting on. To have a look at this office of yours – very bourgeois!' Max Fanshawe waved a hand to take in the typewriter, the filing cabinet, the dead smell of sweat, carbon and paper. He was struggling now to remain exuberant.

'You came to look at *me*,' Mary said. 'This is your uncle,' she told Rosa. 'A famous painter.'

'No need to get huffy, Mary dear.'

'I have work to do,' Mary sighed.

'We'll take Rosa out,' Max said. 'You'd like a night on the town with your famous uncle, wouldn't you?'

'Must we?' Lily hissed.

'There's nowhere to take her,' Mary said.

'We'll find somewhere. Did you notice my *Doublie Royale* outside?'

'Your car?' Mary had seen the vehicle and hoped it was someone rich who wanted typing.

'Oh, *please* can I go!' Rosa begged. Mary glanced at her daughter and she turned to the papers on her desk. Rosa faltered. Perhaps she still hoped her mother might forbid the expedition but Max Fanshawe scooped an arm round each of his fair companions. A lily and a rose. He would give the girl her first champagne. Mary watched them depart and then she bent over her typewriter and her brandy bottle.

'What a dump!' Max said as they circuited the streets of closed-up shops for the third time. 'What a travesty of a place! How can anyone *live* here?' The only cinema was showing a film he and Lily had already seen. It hadn't been worth seeing once and, besides, the performance had already started.

'A paltry show,' Rosa joked. No one paid her any attention.

'Not even a poxy milk bar!' Max was getting cross. For lack of other entertainment he put his foot down hard on the accelerator and sped out of town. He drove fast and carelessly.

'What about the child?' Lily half twisted to look at Rosa sitting in the seat behind them.

'We'll take her to London. I can paint a picture of her: *Portrait of a Provincial Niece*, how about that?'

'Oh really, Max!' Lily giggled.

'Do you want to go to London?' Max called back to Rosa. He was pleased with himself again and Rosa caught the wave of his excitement. She did not mind if they were making fun of her. She saw how dull she appeared in their eyes. Of course she wanted to go to London.

'To the Show?' she had to shout to make herself heard.

'What show? There are hundreds of shows,' Lily drawled. Lily had seen most of them already.

'The Annual Exotic Poultry Show, of course!' Rosa would like to see Buckingham Palace, too, where the neighbours had unsuccessfully petitioned the King against her father's silly hens. Lily convulsed into giggles. Max glanced in his driving-mirror at the absurd creature he could not see in the darkness of the seat behind him. As he took his tired eyes off the road, the vehicle skewed violently at a corner and sped over a bumpy verge, crunching head-first into a deep ditch with a loud long thud and the breaking, breaking of glass.

Rosa came to in the silent darkness. A single torchlight beam twirled around the metal dangling above her. Her eyes focused and she shivered in the icy cold. A policeman on his bicycle at the top of the hill had seen the crash. He pedalled down fast and pulled Rosa free.

'I reckon you was lucky,' he said. He too was in a state of shock. It was the first car crash he had ever seen. The whole of the front of the beautiful vehicle had smashed in. The tiny spot of light from his torch picked out Lily and Max staring up at them, two beautiful dead faces, laughing. 'Who were they?' the policeman asked.

'Filmstars,' Rosa said. The stars above reflected in their open sightless eyes.

'And *you*?'

Rosa hesitated. 'I *could* be anyone,' she said.

'But you're not, are you?' The policeman thought the child dazed. His sister lived on the housing estate next door but two to Eunice Proctor. 'You're Rosa Pegglar, the Poultryman's daughter!'

'Am I?' Rosa felt vague. Only a few minutes ago she'd thought she had escaped. 'My father is dead.'

'Ah!'

'Pegglar died of old age.'

The policeman took Rosa by the hand. She did not resist as she'd have done if he'd been Farnol. Her legs felt suddenly weak.

A woman came from London to see Mary. 'There'll be no more paintings; no girlfriends neither . . .' This was a momentous encounter that was to affect Rosa – and me, and my poor mother – greatly. At the time, of course, Rosa could not know this. She stood at Mary's side and examined this latest visitor. 'I was Max's wife,' the woman said. 'My name is Sarah.'

Mary and Rosa glanced at each other.

'It's all right,' Sarah said. 'I know about Lily. Lily was nothing.' She looked at Rosa closely. 'You must be Max's niece, the one who was in the car. Tell me, Rosa, why was he driving so fast that night?'

'Because there wasn't even a poxy milk bar!'

Sarah Fanshawe laughed, the first time she had done so in weeks. There was a quibble over the insurance. Of course there was. Max had stolen the *Doublie Royale*, he should never have been driving it in the first place. It belonged to the man Sarah had been with. A rich man who had not been amused and who blamed Sarah. 'Is that what he said?' she asked brokenly.

Rosa nodded. The visitor burst into tears. Mary poured her brother's widow a glass of brandy. 'I can't go back,' Sarah wept.

'Of course you can,' Mary said softly.

'I have nowhere to go back to.'

'Of course you have!' Mary took the empty glass.

'What about the man who owned the car?' Rosa asked.

'What about him?' Sarah said. She smiled at Rosa through her tears. 'You must come and visit me in London one day. When you are older and I am sorted . . .'

'I will,' Rosa promised solemnly as if she were getting married. 'My father used to go to London. Every spring . . .'

The Other

Rosa was aware of the other girl's presence before she either showed herself or spoke. The girl had come up quickly behind but instead of walking past, had fallen into step. Rosa stopped. The girl stopped. 'Hallo, I'm Dorothy! My mother wondered if you would like a ride home?'

'A ride home?' Rosa repeated stupidly.

'In our motor car.'

Rosa naturally felt she never wanted to go in another car as long as she lived. This 'Dorothy' was a year or two younger than herself, not nearly as skinny and considerably better dressed. What Rosa *also* saw when she looked at Dorothy was some point of comparison less distinct and as she was puzzling over this a motor car did indeed pull up alongside, purring loudly. Dorothy opened the back door and clambered in, beckoning Rosa to follow.

'You look surprised, Rosa Pegglar.' Philbert Farnol(!) leant out of the driver's window.

'I am!'

'We have caught you on the hop. Well, hop in, then!'

Rosa was too astounded to hop anywhere. She gawped. Seated behind the steering wheel you would not have known there was anything particularly odd about Farnol's size. A woman swathed in a large hat and fur-collared coat sat in the passenger seat beside him, staring fixedly ahead so that Rosa could not see her face. Mesmerized by the novelty of the situation, Rosa climbed obediently in after Dorothy, and Farnol immediately reached out and deftly slammed the heavy door shut behind her.

Farnol drove. His driving was slower, more sedate than Uncle Max's had been. There was no talk now of poxy milk bars, or shows. No one spoke. Dorothy gazed at Rosa with eyes that reminded her of someone she knew well.

'Are you a chauffeur?' Rosa eventually asked Farnol, who did not hear her above the feline engine. The woman in purple turned round. Rosa gasped. 'We were married a few years back,' the other Mary said in a loud confidential whisper, smiling the plump proud smile of one restored to worldly favour by marrying twenty thousand well-invested pounds. 'You *will* come to tea?'

Rosa nodded her acceptance. How could she not? The car braked, and parked. Rosa allowed herself to be led up the garden path. A key was put in the lock. 'You bought it then?' Rosa stammered as she stood on the beaten-copper doorstep.

Mr and Mrs Farnol and their daughter Dorothy laughed. Outside in the garden a dog that was not Alfie gambolled on the lawn. Hens cackled desultorily from one of the coops along the back fence. Rosa's old swing swayed in the breeze.

'Tea' took place in the dining room. Rosa looked at the stain where gravy had been mopped from the carpet. Am I awake or am I asleep? she asked herself, for this was surely some nasty dream.

'Oh dear, yes, the carpet does need replacing,' the other Mary fussed happily. 'I'm not the housekeeper your mother was, I dare say!' Purchased cakes were set out ready on machine-cut paper doilies. There were colourful bone-china tea plates and silver-plated cake forks. This was the woman who had come to them once in despair: *I hoped you'd understand the loss I feel*. Farnol too had undergone a remarkable transformation. Before, his every action emphasized his ugliness but now, if you met him first behind the wheel of his car or here eating cake and making conversation, you would never have known he was Philbert Farnol, the midget Pegglar had long ago befriended for his usefulness. 'You're very quiet,' the other Mary said. 'Don't you like the cake?'

Rosa glanced down at her tea plate. 'I'm sorry,' she stuttered.

'You were very talkative before, Rosa Pegglar.'

'Was I?'

'How is your mother?' the other Mary asked. Rosa knew the difference between polite and genuine inquiry. This other Mary did not want to know how many pairs of stockings her mother owned, what she had paid for them, which shade of flesh. She would not want to know about Mr Gresham. Rosa herself wanted to know more about Mr Gresham. She stored up her information about him but she had not told Aunt Edith any of it. One day she would spring Mr Gresham fully fledged on her aunts.

'. . . so you see,' the other Mary was saying. 'In the right hands, pounds, shillings and pence can be made to go a long way.'

'She married me for my money,' Farnol spluttered cheerfully, spitting crumbs.

'As good a reason as any!' the woman laughed. 'It was Rosa who told me.'

Farnol pointed his cake fork. '*You* were responsible then!'

'I suppose so,' Rosa admitted.

'Like your father, you thought one Mary as good as another!'

'Then we have Rosa to thank,' the other Mary intervened. She moved over and stood beside Farnol, her hand affectionately but firmly placed on his re-shapen shoulder.

'I bought the house as a favour to your mother,' Farnol told Rosa. 'No one else wanted it, I got a good bargain . . .'

'You were always a good friend to Pegglar,' the other Mary said. 'Now, why don't you show Rosa your things, Dorothy. Take her to play with Thelma, Delphine, Norah, Enid, Winnie and Joan . . .'

'I don't want to see them!' Rosa blurted out. 'Do you know Mrs Proctor?'

'Of course I do! She's *my* best friend . . .'

Rosa followed Dorothy up to the little room that had once been her own. It was now painted pink. She sat down on the pink coverlet of the bed. Philbert Farnol and the other Mary were making fun of her parents. It was absurd, but then love

57

was absurd. It confused things for human beings. '*Do* they love each other?'

'*You* were responsible,' Dorothy repeated the charge.

'Yes, but I can't imagine anyone *loving* old Foxy Farnol,' Rosa said. The ugly dwarf had always been there interfering. The two girls looked at each other for a long time then in silence.

'I had another sister,' Dorothy confided. 'I didn't love her, and she died.'

'Our dog, Alfie, died. I didn't think I loved him till he died. He used to drink tea but he didn't like living above the office.'

'*Farnol* used to live above his studio. I used to go there with Pegglar.'

'So did I,' Rosa said quietly.

'*And* my sister who died, to be photographed.'

'What happened to your sister?' Rosa asked.

'She fell in the canal. Pegglar was upset,' Dorothy sounded almost pleased.

'She drowned?'

Dorothy nodded. 'I know where the key is,' Dorothy said to impress the older girl. 'To Farnol's studio. We could take it and have a look. I go near there on Monday evenings for dancing . . .'

'Now, you two little friends! Rosa, perhaps you had better be getting home, I wouldn't want your mother worried.' The other Mary bustled in.

She's uncertain about leaving Dorothy with me, Rosa thought. Her own mother would be far too busy to notice she was late. On the way downstairs she told Dorothy to meet her at the old photographic studios the following week. Monday was the day Mary went to visit Mr Gresham and stayed with him longer and longer each time.

Farnol drove Rosa home. 'Do you like my motor car?' he asked smugly.

'It's not as smart as my Uncle Max's *Doublie Royale*,' Rosa said.

Farnol ignored this. 'You and Dorothy will be friends,' he said.

'Like you were with Pegglar?'

'He was a nasty selfish man. He used to chat up girls on

trains. If it hadn't been for me he would probably have been arrested. It would have killed your aunts . . .'

'You have no right to talk to me in that way. He was my daddy!'

'You ask your mother how Pegglar met her!'

Rosa was not sure whether her mother was more surprised to see Philbert Farnol again, or her daughter arriving home by car. 'We haven't seen *you* for a long time,' she remarked but Farnol had already driven off.

'He looked different,' Mary observed.

'He bought our old house. He married the other Mary. They took me for tea, I had an embroidered napkin and a cake fork!'

'That's nice, dear.'

'Where did you meet Daddy?'

'Why, on a London Underground train!' Mary laughed. 'He suddenly spoke, and invited me out to tea . . .'

Aunt Edith, of course, was immediately interested when Rosa told her how Philbert Farnol had got his hands on the house. 'I always knew he was after something – I often suspected he had designs on Gracie.'

Rosa told her aunts then about the other recharged Mary and the girl, Dorothy, whose sister had drowned. 'She had Pegglar's eyes.' This was Rosa's revenge. Despite all she had ever told her aunts, she had never betrayed Pegglar. 'Dorothy's little sister – who fell in the canal – probably had Daddy's eyes too!'

Edith and Rosa contemplated each other intently.

'Your father looked to the stars,' Aunt Edith said at last. 'Pegglar did not have the temperament for idle, half-hearted pursuits. I knew when he acquired *one* wife, and *one* child, there were bound to be others. Farnol would have encouraged him – Farnol would have whipped up a donkey. I should have warned your mother.'

'She knows – the other Mary came to see us.'

'And didn't she mind, your mother?'

'No. There were others, too. Lots of them. He used to meet women on trains. He nearly got arrested . . .'

59

Dorothy was waiting for Rosa underneath the old decaying sign
P. FARNOL STUDIO PHOTOGRAPHERS. INQUIRE WITHIN. Someone had thrown a stone and the gold-and-black glass had been
fractured like a cobweb into a hundred and more pieces.
Encouraged by their parents, and attracted by the second exhibitor's badge he wore so conspicuously, boys had always thrown
stones at Philbert Farnol, and called the dwarf nasty names.

'I'm meant to be at Dancing,' Dorothy whined.

'Let's get inside. You can dance in there,' Rosa said. The key
turned in the lock with difficulty. It had not been used for some
time.

'Ugh, it's dirty!' Dorothy turned up her nose. 'It smells.' She
and Rosa entered the room where people had waited. Chairs
were still lined up against the walls. This was the room where
customers combed their hair and straightened their collars
wanting to look their best, fearing the worst. A colour-touching
service had been offered. Pictures of hens had been shown as
examples, combs and plumes picked out in red. On the counter
the girls found a few empty boxes they both recognized as
cartons postcards had once been distributed in. Behind the
counter hung a heavy curtain whose faded velvet had once been
royal blue, edged with twists of gold braid and tassels.

'If you'd like to come this way,' Farnol would beckon his
subjects behind the curtain, directing them up on to the stage at
the back. Too late then to run. Backdrops were fixed in place.
Pots of aspidistras, spotlights and lenses adjusted, smiles held.

Under the counter an assortment of postcard samples were
still pinned up, most of them faded now and curled at the
edges. 'There's my mother,' Dorothy pointed at a curled-up
card. 'She was one of their models.' It had been one of the most
profitable cards. Rosa bent down. The other Mary revealed an
intriguing amount of flesh.

'They're not very nice, these pictures, are they?' Dorothy
asked.

'Well,' said Rosa; someone must have liked all this naked
distorted flesh. Farnol's share of the profits alone had been
twenty thousand pounds. On some shelves at the side of the

counter were rows of large volumes tied up with ribbon. Rosa reached one down from the top shelf. The book was full of hens. *Pegglar's Fancy*, she read out. *Pegglar's Pride*. The girls giggled.

'He *fancied* himself, didn't he?' Dorothy said.

'Pegglar?'

'He had everyone on the hop.'

Rosa stared at Dorothy. Dorothy spoke about Pegglar in the way the other Mary and Farnol had taught her. They had not loved Pegglar nor preserved his memory, the scent of grass on his earth-brown trousers, the apples that ripened over-large in the sun. Dorothy continued, high pitched and squawking: 'He had Mr Farnol taking pictures, my mother taking her clothes off. All for his own gain, only *he* spent what *he* took. Who did he think he was with his ridiculous hens, The Lord Almighty? It was left to Philbert Farnol to cull the birds and print the postcards, save his share and sort the mess out afterwards . . .'

'Pegglar was an astonishing man,' Rosa said irritably. She shoved the dusty stockbreeding book back on the top shelf and took out another one from much lower down. The volume contained pictures of herself. All carefully mounted at the corners and described underneath in her father's neat handwriting, just like the hens: Rosa Pegglar, aged 2¾. She turned the pages quickly. Aged 3½. Aged 5 and 2 months. That was when she'd tried to take home the wooden Ark. The painted backdrop was always the same, the carousel at the fair. The pictures grew fewer and further apart as she grew older and there had been less change in her appearance to record.

Dorothy meanwhile had pulled another book from the shelves and was delighted to find it contained pictures of *herself* also, carefully stuck down and similarly described. Dorothy aged 2¾; 2 and 10 months; aged . . . The girls took other volumes out. Other children had been fully, pictorially chronicled like Rosa and Dorothy, like the hens. Rare breeds, all, of his own mismatching. How Pegglar had fluttered and clucked! Dorothy discovered a book recording her sister, who had drowned. Rosa refused to look further. 'How many wives and children did Pegglar have?' she asked flatly.

'Dozens,' said Dorothy, losing interest. The girls did not replace the stockbreeding books but left them carelessly piled open, skewing untidily one on top of the other.

Dorothy drew back the faded velvet curtain. Rosa followed after her, pulling at switches on the wall. A powerful spotlight lit up a circle on the little wooden stage illuminating the dust that danced heavily in the air.

'I liked it here,' said Rosa.

'It's smaller than I remember.'

'I used to like my toys.'

'Oh, the toys!' Dorothy cried. Dorothy and Rosa pulled open the cupboard and there they were, lined up, waiting.

Rosa bit back the resentment she was feeling towards Dorothy and the other shadowy children and she started to turn the handle on the side of the musical box. A familiar tune tinkled. On the stage the carousel backdrop was fixed in place as though Farnol had known Rosa would come. 'Get your dancing things on!' Rosa commanded Dorothy. 'Get up on stage, and dance!'

Dorothy put down the threadbare gollywog she'd been cradling and did as she was told. The delicate cream satin ballet-shoes and matching lace-edged tutu emphasized the plumpness of her blotchy arms and legs, and the roundness of her little protruding tummy.

As Rosa wound the handle on the musical box, the girl posed with her hands in the air, rose unsteadily up on her toes, gave a wobbly skip and then began to twirl gracelessly: a comic little plumpened chicken. Rosa turned the handle remorselessly, Dorothy twirled faster, hopping around the pots of dead aspidistras, knocking them over and sending cameras and lenses flying to the floor. She placed one hand on a chair and pirouetted, her cheeks puffed up like an ungainly partridge gasping in the clouds of dust that rose at each clumsy step. Faster and faster the faverolle spun until at last the handle on the musical box broke. Dorothy overbalanced and toppled into an angry heap, grazing her hands and knees, squawking as she fell.

It was then that Dorothy told Rosa how she would shortly be

going abroad. 'My mother wants to see the world,' she said, catching breath. She remembered her little sister thrashing about like a shrimp, a little pink prawn-thing in the murky canal water down below. She could remember deliberately standing on the bank for a while before running for help.

'I wish *my* mother wanted to see the world,' Rosa said. Mary never ventured far from home. 'I want to go to London.'

'Mummy has booked places on a cruise-liner,' Dorothy went on. 'She has been studying brochures and buying dresses and luggage. Mr Farnol – Daddy, I have to call him . . .'

'He isn't your daddy,' Rosa objected. Why should Pegglar be elbowed aside? Rosa leaned across and gripped the little girl's fat wrist. 'You don't have to be what they want you to be. Say what they want you to say. You *can* be anyone!'

Dorothy shook herself free. The cream satin of her dancing clothes was soiled. She stood up and pulled her outdoor clothes on top. She rubbed her eyes on her sleeve. 'I hate you, Rosa Pegglar!' she yelled, snatching up what was left of the Noah's Ark and dashing it to the floor. 'You don't know anything!' Dorothy scrabbled back through the faded curtain and across the room where the chairs still sat waiting in rows, hopelessly now.

She did not want a sister! She had not then, she did not now. When Dorothy had returned to the canal to point to the spot where the little girl had fallen in there had been something puffy floating upside down on the water. 'Don't look!' they had said, cradling her head with fearful hands as if she had not already seen. As if she were not responsible.

Next time Pegglar came to visit he had wept at the loss of the younger child, at the brittleness of the shells, the impossibility of controlling what you had once so magically created. Perhaps at that moment Pegglar had even been afraid.

Her mother had shouted at Pegglar. Pegglar had not shouted back.

At last we are getting somewhere, the other Mary had thought and only then had she seen he was dead. He had stopped breathing; not lost for words, but for breath itself. His pipe lay on the floor, smoking still like a recently fired gun.

Rosa ran after Dorothy through the deserted studios. She stood in the doorway and watched the little girl disappear at the end of the street, running away into the gathering gloom. Rosa locked the door behind her and put the key in her pocket.

Eastward of Aden

'Why didn't you take the wooden Noah's Ark home with you?' I asked Rosa greedily. *I* would have salvaged the wreckage if *I* had been there.

'I didn't want it any more, Jeannie,' Rosa said, so I asked then what happened to Dorothy. And what became of all the other shadowy children? And those other women sent by Eunice Proctor. Pegglar had had secrets. His daughter had found him out as I would like to find my father out. Rosa sighed. Perhaps in my anxiety to know, I sounded harsh and horrible. Tears glistened on Rosa's beautiful lashes, but she quickly brushed them away. 'We can only ever know so much,' she told me. A little light in the darkness.

Mr and Mrs Farnol and their daughter Dorothy had taken the best suite on board. They headed the printed passenger list. Their luggage was suitably copious, large leather boxes with little compartments lined separately with silk. The other Mary intended they should dine every evening with the Captain. She had read the brochures and knew a fancy-dress competition was always held when the ship crossed the Equator. She had commissioned a seamstress. Farnol was to be got up as Neptune. He had a green scaly suit, a trident and a jagged headdress. She herself would be an attendant mermaid while little Dorothy would dance on deck like a sea nymph.

'You must send a postcard to your friend,' the other Mary said.

'A cruise?' Aunt Edith queried.

'They are to see the world,' Rosa told her aunt, showing her the picture postcard that had arrived that morning.

'They will see a lot of sea while other passengers look down *retrousée* noses at them. Farmyard turkeys who disport themselves like peacocks on twenty thousand pounds can expect no better . . .'

'No,' said Rosa, refusing a stale custard cream from Gracie. 'That is what *you* would see if you went on a cruise-liner, Aunt Edith. *You* would make "polite inquiry", as you call it, and find out everything about everyone else and detect dishonest practitioners everywhere you went. But Dorothy's mother is trusting. She trusted Pegglar and now she acts her part in Farnol's picture: the rich man's wife. She will be happily swindled buying trinkets in every port while Dorothy dances prettily, the sweet stepdaughter. Farnol will disguise his hobgoblin looks because they no longer matter and when they reach the Equator, they will win the fancy-dress competition . . .'

'Oh,' murmured Gracie.

Well, I never! thought Edith. She said, 'You mentioned a surprise for me. If it's Mr Gresham . . .'

'You know about Mr Gresham?' It was Rosa's turn to be startled.

'You were intending to keep him from me?'

'No, I would have told you some time.'

'You are not my sole source of information these days, Rosa.'

Rosa countered her aunt's spitefulness by deliberately, elaborately placing the key to Farnol's studio down on the table between them.

'What is it?' Aunt Edith asked. Rosa pretended not to hear the question. Aunt Edith's fingers twitched. There was dribble running down her chin. Could this be the key at last to the whole mystery?

'You are dying to know?' Pegglar's daughter asked.

'I sincerely hope I am not dying,' Aunt Edith told her niece tartly.

'Oh, no, I only meant . . .' Rosa was shocked. 'This is your surprise! It is the key to Farnol's studios. Dorothy left it in my care. I thought you might like to take a look.'

Aunt Edith's fingers closed greedily on the key. 'I would like nothing more,' she confessed humbly, adding, 'You are a good girl, Rosa.'

Rosa smiled.

When a valuable cruise ship sank eastward of Aden, half a day's sailing south of the Equator, there were no survivors. Hot equatorial waters settled quickly and smoothly over the sinking ship. Someone in a sailing vessel near by reported having seen a sea nymph riding away from the scene on the back of a dolphin. This was agreed to be fanciful but sightings of this sort are not uncommon when ships go down. The waters were deep, no wreckage found. The nymph had been the colour of the sea.

It seemed the Captain had dressed up as usual as Neptune. A rival stocky Neptune had emerged from the First Class quarters brandishing a Bakelite trident and leading a large mermaid by the hand. As the two Neptunes confronted each other on deck, a cheer went up among the passengers who enjoyed a jolly caper. Only rich brash people who had never crossed the Equator before would not have known that the guise of Neptune was strictly the Captain's prerogative.

'It's unlucky,' an able seaman grumbled and, although no one had taken much notice at the time, and the duplicate Neptune's wife had been awarded a mock silver cup, half a day's sailing south the ship had been unceremoniously upturned like a redundant wedding cake. Dorothy had written Rosa a second postcard which Rosa never received as the card had gone down with the ship. 'We are having a nice time,' Dorothy lettered at her mother's dictation in ink that floated off the card and dissolved without trace as seawater flooded into the ship's best cabin, tipping up the little writing desk at which Dorothy had sat down to write.

'It's nice for you to have a nice friend,' the other Mary had said during the writing of the postcard. They were alone together in the cabin. Farnol was showing off his stout little sea legs on deck.

'Like Pegglar and Farnol were friends?' Dorothy asked. Her letters were large and childish and the short message filled all the blank space.

'You must call him *Daddy*, Dorothy dear,' her mother replied edgily. 'He is paying for all this, remember.' I am paying for it too, she thought. She regretted having invited Rosa Pegglar to tea. Seeing Dorothy with that other daughter of Pegglar's had disconcerted her. 'Now get your nice sea nymph costume on, you must do a pretty dance for the other passengers . . .'

This other Mary had been flattered by Pegglar's attentions. Answering an advertisement for photographic models, she'd taken Pegglar for a wealthy businessman. He ran a thriving postcard firm and, recently jilted by a man she had hoped to marry only to find him already married, this other Mary was only too happy to set up home. Once or twice she'd pressed Pegglar on the subject of marriage but he had looked scornful. Marriage, he'd said, was a legal formality true love must e'er o'erleap.

In a short space of time, and despite his many absences on business, she had borne him two daughters. Shouting at Pegglar had never done her any good. 'How can you expect me to live cooped up like this?' she would yell when the precariousness of her situation upset her but Pegglar only smiled sadly, and gave her some extra cash.

It had struck her that Pegglar's interest in his daughters had been almost scientific. 'We are not experiments,' she tried to say. 'To be manipulated like the pictures on your postcards . . .' Later she had seen that this was precisely what they were. She and her daughters. When the younger child had fallen in the canal Pegglar had shaken his head and spoken of the eggs he had lost in his days as a poultryman. The shells had been brittle, the hens often careless. You must expect to lose a few.

The other Mary had been aghast. 'The child did not fall!' she told him then. She had turned on Pegglar. 'You are a wicked evil man! You took advantage of a weak foolish woman!' She confronted him with her suspicions about Dorothy, a girl who had had no proper father.

Poor Pegglar's heart missed a beat. Then it missed another. Mary went on screaming but nobody heard, except perhaps Dorothy sitting in the room she had until recently been obliged to share.

When the ship went down eastward of Aden, half a day's sailing south of the Equator, the director of a small but successful company had gone down also. Confidence in his seemingly rock solid stock plummeted. The share price was wiped out overnight. Aunt Edith's agent called on her. I regret to inform you, Miss Pegglar, he'd begun. He had the good manners to look shamefaced, sorry even, but this could do the elderly sisters no good now. The young man had invested heavily in the successful company. There had been good incentives on offer which he'd been happy to pocket. There was little further to be said.

'We cannot pay the rent,' Edith Pegglar told the landlord's representative when he came. 'In my day it was not done to own houses, one simply rented them for one's stay. It meant one could move on easily, not that my sister and I ever have moved on. Building a house nearly bankrupted my brother.'

'Now look 'ere.' The rent collector sat down. He mopped his brow. 'I 'aven't come for excuses.' He had come for the rent and he knew for certain the old ladies had it stashed away. A wealthy Captain Pegglar with the taste for tiger-hunting had once departed in a hurry for Simla, some two-bit floosie in tow. But that was by the by, and a long time ago. The errant Captain had left assets and property properly settled on the abandoned wife and family. Assets and property legally settled could not be denied, however carelessly mismanaged they may have been meantime. And one heard rumours. It was part of the job to hear rumours. The landlord's representative intimated as much to the old ladies. They had never given him trouble before. He had come only for the rent.

'Times change,' Edith intoned gravely. 'Nothing is fixed, all is flux. Life slips away faster and faster, like sand through the waist of an egg-timer.'

Wandering in the head, the rent collector thought while Edith Pegglar, who had once stood on a beaten-copper doorstep and meted out lessons in economics to a spendthrift sister-in-law, sat staring stiffly at the bald little man with a briefcase on his lap who was only doing his job. 'I have kept myself busy all my life,' she explained. 'But in my day it was not done to earn money. Or spend it. One simply eked out . . .'

'There's an art to money,' the debt collector agreed, accepting a custard cream from Gracie. It was powdery and dry as chalk. If the mind's construction can be found in the face, this other sister so free with her biscuits smiled too easily for the old girls to be in serious trouble. 'I'll be around again next week. You 'ave it ready for me then,' he said.

Gracie smiled and nodded.

It was Edith who now looked vacant and perplexed. She had run out of ideas. I do not suppose I can learn typing like I learned economy, from a book, she mused. The key to Farnol's studio lying on the table where Rosa had left it caught her eye. With Farnol at the bottom of the ocean, could she and her sister not live there rent-free? She had admitted the dwarf often enough to her house, on the eve of the annual bachelors' spring outing. She waited until it got dark and then she packed a small bag for herself and another for Gracie. We will simply disappear, she thought. The earth hath bubbles, as the water has; Rosa will not need a postcard to know where to find us.

Edith Pegglar looked through her brother's stockbreeding books and confessed herself truly astonished. *So many* variants. *Such* pride. *Such* fancy. It was a miracle her brother had never been arrested.

Gracie gurgled and enjoyed the pictures. She pointed at the exotic hens. She pointed, gleeful, at all the pretty children.

'I did not know the extent,' Edith repeated dementedly. Pegglar had not had the temperament for idle half-hearted pursuits. They had looked after their orphaned brother for over fifty years and yet, for all the information she had managed to extract from his compliant daughter, they had never really known him at all. His eyes had been fixed on the stars above their heads. Aunt Edith held her sister tight and wept on her floppy comfortable shoulder. In a flash, like that of the unguarded electricity, Edith saw that *she* had been the one straw headed. For all her knowledge of household economy, Pegglar had died laughing. And at her expense. Rosa had sent her; Rosa had known.

'What were they doing in there anyway?' the policeman

70

whose sister lived next door but two from Eunice Proctor asked. 'The place has been derelict for years.'

They could have been anyone. Two corpses, anonymous as over-roasted chickens; combs, crests, plumage – any distinguishing feature gone. There had been a fault in the wiring, a heavy velvet curtain hung too close to a live flex, a fire once started had quickly spread. Fumes from photographic chemicals, purchased long ago at the Apothecary's, had mercifully overcome the two sisters. They had known nothing. Rosa stood in the street with other bystanders, surveying the smouldering rubble. She watched as weightless ash from burnt paper and dry straw blew about over the glowing embers, light as ragged brown moths whose wing tips had accidently caught the flames.

Mary refused to listen to Rosa's account of all the stock-breeding books that had been burnt. 'Nonsense!' she said to the wilder of Rosa's suggestions. 'He used to keep hens, you know that. I won't hear a word against Pegglar. You were ever a fanciful child!'

'But why didn't *you* have any more children?' Rosa asked. 'Why did *I* never have any brothers and sisters?'

Mary laughed. She had typing to do; Mr Gresham was a patient man but she did not want to try his patience too far. 'I suppose I wasn't good at laying eggs!' Mary remarked with the hint of a gentle, even affectionate, smirk. 'Now I must get on, Rosa dear, Mr Gresham is waiting . . .'

Mr Gresham is Waiting

'My last typist was a woman in her middle years, a Miss Gregg,'
Mr Gresham had told Mary with disarming openness that first
time they met, when she'd thought he was interviewing her for
the post as his typist.

It was an encounter that intrigued Rosa, and one she liked to
reconstruct for me. My own poor mother was immediately suspicious of Mr Gresham. Nothing she heard made her less so. It
was obvious she did not want me to find out about sex, which
was ridiculous considering the other children at school talked
about nothing but, and taunted me mercilessly for not knowing
who my father was and what he had done to my mother to
beget me. I suppose while Rosa was telling me about her own
childhood, my mother accepted this as something people do
with children but when at my pressing Rosa moved on to the
entry of Mr Gresham into her life, my mother became more and
more agitated. She would get up and pace about the room.
Soon, despite all my mother's attempts to distract me, I was as
intrigued by Mr Gresham as ever the adolescent Rosa had been.
Of course I was. He was a literary gentleman. And wasn't I
myself – it pleased me now to rather stubbornly recall – expected
one day to write it all down?

'Do you know Miss Gregg?' Mr Gresham had asked.

'No, I don't think so,' Rosa's mother replied.

'You do not sound sure, Mrs Pegglar. You must *know* whether
or not you know my former typist, Miss Ida Gregg.'

'I have recently been widowed,' Mary Pegglar explained.
Rosa did the voices quite well. She made her mother sound
suitably nervous; Mrs Pegglar needed the job, she was not

sleeping at nights and had started to drink altogether more brandy than was good for her. 'My circle of acquaintances has always been limited. I no longer see my former neighbour, Eunice Proctor, even. I am certain I know no Ida Gregg.'

Mr Gresham nodded approvingly. 'If you *had* known Miss Gregg I should have felt awkward taking you on. No one likes to find themselves replaced, least of all by somebody they know.' He paused, and coughed. 'I may speak frankly?'

Mary thought Mr Gresham was already speaking frankly when you considered it was only a typing job she had come for.

'You have been married . . .' The literary gentleman looked Mary Pegglar steadily in the eye. 'Miss Gregg was twenty-five years old when I met her. Now she is forty. A trying age for an unhappy single woman and, though I may be blamed for much, I do not see that I can be held responsible for the difficult age attained by Miss Gregg on her recent birthday. Do you?'

'Well no, I . . .'

'Fifteen years ago Miss Gregg came to me for work – rather as you now, Mrs Pegglar – she had an invalid mother in those days to care for and there was a man courting her but it suited her to keep this suitor at a distance. A spice merchant or some such. She liked to think her mother could not do without her. I dare say she did not care greatly for the man although she was probably quite gratified by the interest he took. In due course Miss Gregg's mother passed away but by then the purveyor of tamarind and truske had given up all hope of Miss Gregg and consoled himself with another . . .'

'I really don't see . . .'

'Ida Gregg was an adequate typist. I have known better, I have certainly encountered worse. She fussed over details that did not matter and neglected essentials that did. Once a month her work became erratic. But you will not find me a finicky man, Mrs Pegglar. For fifteen years Miss Gregg collected work to be typed every Monday, as I hope you will do, returning it the following Monday by when, of course, the next pages are ready. Miss Gregg made a mistake. Not that I mind the odd mistake, typing error that is. But Miss Gregg made altogether another sort of error . . .'

'Oh!' Mary gasped faintly.

'Two weeks ago, Mrs Pegglar, Miss Gregg sat where *you* are sitting now. *Mr Gresham,* she said suddenly, *time like the tide is running out!* Naturally I asked what she could mean, and it was then that Ida Gregg declared herself. I stared at her, speechless. Over the years I had paid her regularly, I might even have indulged her on the odd occasion when it seemed not inappropriate, yet I had given her no grounds . . .'

'Grounds?' Mary felt as at sea as the Farnols on their cruise-liner, even before it sank. Her head spun.

'The odd glass of ginger wine, maybe. A small box of chocolates at Christmas. Customary formalities. Do *you* have children, Mrs Pegglar?'

'A daughter. Rosa.'

'Ah, good. Miss Gregg, you see . . .' Mr Gresham hesitated. 'Miss Gregg sat where you are sitting and calmly informed me that she had just celebrated her fortieth birthday, only, she said, there had been no celebrations. She accused me of depriving her of the joys of motherhood. For fifteen years she admitted, she had hoped for children . . .'

'Really, Mr Gresham?' Mary coughed painfully.

'*For fifteen years I have been typing for you,* Miss Gregg shrieked at me, *my childbearing days are over. I have nothing to show: my life has been blighted by your horrible typing.* She wept, and I gave her a handkerchief.'

'Oh dear!' said Mary. 'How very . . .'

'Naturally I do not expect to see my monogrammed kerchief again. *My dear Miss Gregg,* I tried to say to the woman who – you will forgive me, Mrs Pegglar, no disparagement on your profession – the woman was ONLY my typist, *You must pull yourself together. I fear you are under some sort of misapprehension.* She stared at me wildly, then she grew calm: *It is you, Mr Gresham, who have misapprehended!* Her voice was cold, hard as the edge of steel; she unclasped her handbag and drew out a knife . . . But I am boring you, Mrs Pegglar?'

'I do not think this Miss Gregg . . .'

'Ida Gregg.'

'This mad woman who keeps dangerous weapons in her handbag, is any concern of mine!' Mary said. 'I have merely bought a typewriter and six boxes of typewriting paper. I know nothing of the former occupant of this chair, I need know nothing.'

'You are a businesswoman, Mrs Pegglar. Time is money and we are wasting time.'

'Pegglar, my late husband, had no head for business. My sister-in-law once tried to give me lessons in economics on our doorstep. Now there is no money left, with a growing child to feed, I have to buy my eggs from the Co-op . . .'

'Poor Miss Gregg could have done with lessons and good-ness knows what else from your sister-in-law.'

'But she worked for you *for fifteen years*, Mr Gresham!' Rosa's mother protested. 'That is a long time out of any woman's life.'

'Miss Gregg deluded herself. She deluded me – there had been no hint till that moment of her violent nature.'

'Oh dear!' Mary remarked, regretting more the uncalled-for disclosures than the self-deludings of a violent, childless Ida Gregg.

'*I am in love with you!*'

'I beg your pardon?'

'That was what Miss Gregg said. And how can I go on employing a woman who had spoken to me as Miss Gregg has spoken?'

'This is why a vacancy has arisen?' Mary asked. It was the vacancy, and only the vacancy, of which she wished very much to speak.

'Ah, yes, the vacancy!' Mr Gresham sighed dramatically. 'I live alone, or so Miss Gregg thought. But a writer never lives alone, a writer's existence is crowded out; sometimes it seems there's no room to breathe the air is so taken up with figments of one's professional imagination pressing and heaving for attention. Miss Gregg harboured hopes and now all her boats have been swept out to sea and are sunk beneath turbulent waves. Emotional storms detract from my work, Mrs Pegglar. A typist must remain calm and, without embellishment or fuss, type out strictly that which is there.'

There was a pause. Then Mary said, simply, 'I am not in love with you, Mr Gresham; I only want to do your typing. I have no knife hidden in my handbag. My terms are reasonable.'

'I am a writer, Mrs Pegglar,' Mr Gresham continued, the sound of his own voice making a pleasant change, presumably, from the scratch of his pen across the empty page. 'All my days are spent writing. You will come here on Monday evenings to fetch what I have written and you will return it to me the following Monday competently typed . . .'

'Who is Mr Gresham?' Rosa had asked.

'A writer,' Mary said.

'What does he write?'

'What I am typing. Now really, Rosa . . .'

'Now really, Rosa,' my mother tried to say laughingly. 'How can you know all that took place between your mother and one other? How can you fill the child's head?'

'Jeannie isn't really a *child* any longer.' Rosa regarded my earnest face thoughtfully. I was hoping it occurred to her that I ought indeed to be told a thing or two. About my father, but it seemed Mary Pegglar turned out to be a born typist even if she had learnt her typing recently, from a book. Born typists unmindfully transcribe on to the typewriter without any regard to the content. They live from word to word though a 'word' to a born typist is a fixed number of letters (any letters) and spaces. Mary's sole interest in what the fixed numbers added up to was the *amount* she could then charge her client. Too desperate earning a living to read what was before her, she merely counted letters and spaces and charged Mr Gresham accordingly. It was left to Rosa to *read* the content:

It has now been six weeks since Ida Gregg opened her heart to me, Ida Gregg of the over-white thighs and the over-large breasts. A man could get lost in all that flesh, if he had a mind to. What will happen when Ida Gregg returns here and begs my forgiveness? Will another already be installed in her chair? Her mother was the one to blame, of course: A spice merchant! My daughter married to a trader in tarmarind and truske, mother of the shopkeepers such a union would undoubtedly bring about! Let her rather live at home and nurse me into my grave, pining all the while for her stony-hearted Mr Gresham, the literary gentleman she worships to sordid distraction . . .

'You're to leave that alone!' Mary told Rosa angrily. My mother too had left the room. Neither my mother nor Mary Pegglar had any more interest, I noticed, in Mr Gresham's outpourings than either of them had had in Pegglar's activities.

No wonder Rosa was surprised when one day Mary said, almost conversationally, 'Mr Gresham asked me to marry him.' Rosa did not expect her mother to surprise her. 'I turned him down of course.'

Mary began staying out later and later with Mr Gresham on Monday evenings.

Miss Gregg was a loose, desperate woman; ever tearful. Sometimes she would arrive, let herself silently into my house and make her way up to my bedroom where she would undress her large body, wash under her armpits, brush her hair and then wait for me to find her like a vast beached whale blubbering in my bed. To say that on a number of occasions she threw herself upon me, engulfing me with slippery passion, would not be to exaggerate. She opened herself and beckoned me Jonah-like inside, this vast wallowing unhappy creature, so disgusted and debased by her own untrammelled longings . . .

What Mr Gresham wrote each week, Mary duly collected and brought home to be typed. And what Mary typed, her daughter blithely read. How Rosa now craved a sighting of the wallowing whale-like Ida Gregg!

One Monday, at long last, Mary was too ill to visit Mr Gresham. 'Rosa, be a love. Apologize to him. Be polite – we cannot do without what he pays.' Rosa followed her mother's directions and eventually found Mr Gresham's large house. She rang the bell and, when no one answered, she pushed at the front door. It was open but she did not like to go inside as the presumptious Miss Gregg had done, tearfully roaming upstairs to the bedroom and undressing herself in voluptuous expectation. Instead, Rosa called out. 'I say, hallo!'

'Come in!' a man answered from somewhere inside. The hallway was lined with bookshelves so that there was only a narrow dark corridor to squeeze through. 'Mrs Pegglar?' the voice called again as Rosa groped her way in the dark towards a voice that was becoming impatient now. 'Well, hurry up! You're already late.'

Rosa entered a cold rather austere room and looked about her. Countless mirrors of all shapes and sizes covered the walls, reflecting what little light there was back off each other. As Rosa smiled ruefully at herself in one of the great gilded mirrors, she noticed with a start that a man was sitting in the tall armchair that had its back to her. He had been calmly watching her reflection all the while. 'I've come instead of my mother, Mr Gresham,' Rosa Pegglar explained. 'She's unwell. I brought the typing and I have come to collect . . .'

'Ah, ha! The daughter! Well, Rosa, let's take a look at you.'

Rosa felt like pointing out that he had already been looking at her. Mr Gresham turned to a tray beside him and poured ginger wine into a glass which he then held out to Rosa. The stem of the glass was sticky.

'I only came . . .' Rosa wanted to get away as soon as possible but she remembered her mother's injunction. We need the money, Rosa. She perched timidly in the chair at the other side of the fireplace.

'How old are you?' Mr Gresham asked.

'Sixteen,' Rosa said. And well versed in inquisitions, she thought, sipping the fiery syrup. I could be a match for you, if I chose!

'Mmmm.' Mr Gresham looked at Rosa who looked at him. He was a thin man with a gaunt hungry face. 'What has your mother told you about me?' Gresham asked.

'You are a writer,' Rosa replied at once. 'You once asked my mother to marry you.'

'But she refused.'

'Yes,' Rosa hesitated.

'She refused because she was not interested. She has never been interested, your mother.'

'I know,' Rosa said. 'She does not take an interest in life generally.'

'And an interest in life generally – as you call it – is the true purpose of life itself!' Mr Gresham sighed, a sigh that whistled harshly through the meagre husk of his body.

'That is what my Aunt Edith thought also,' Rosa said. 'And Miss Gregg?'

Mr Gresham's pale face coloured slightly. 'Miss Gregg,' he repeated sadly, and fell silent.

'Miss Gregg wanted a baby before it was too late and she got angry . . .' Rosa began as if prompting him.

'Miss Gregg thought the true purpose of life was replicating life . . .'

'She should have met my father. Pegglar would have approved. He liked to record the process in stockbreeding books.'

Gresham and Rosa contemplated one another. Rosa felt giddy on ginger wine. 'Why did your mother send you?' the literary gentleman asked drily. Our stories do not overlap. 'The typing could have waited until next week.'

'We need the money.'

'She said that?'

'Yes.'

'I see.' Mr Gresham coughed. 'There never was such an infuriatingly incurious woman – it must have driven your father, the late Mr Pegglar, to distraction . . .'

'I think it drove him away. He had all these other women – perhaps he was only trying to make her curious but she took no notice. Do you write as you do about Miss Gregg to rouse my mother's non-existent jealousy?' Rosa asked. 'Is it a game to you, my mother needing to earn money, and refusing to be interested in your horrid Miss Gregg?'

'No game, I assure you, dear Miss Pegglar! When your mother comes here on Monday nights I pay her to dress up for me. She dresses as the late Mrs Gresham, my dear wife who passed on. There is a cupboard full of the late Mrs Gresham's clothes upstairs. Each week Mary goes up there and selects something to put on. When she is ready she comes down into this room to sit where you are sitting now. She does not speak. She looks so entirely like my poor wife that to speak would spoil the illusion. I, however, speak. I look at her in my mirrors and I talk to Mrs Gresham's reflection about my love for Miss Gregg. I confess all . . .'

Rosa gaped.

Mr Gresham nodded, and continued: 'When Mrs Gresham died, I could not bear the emptiness of the house. I had spent her lifetime at my desk in the study pursuing my literary ambitions. I wrote one or two books that did not sell well enough for the publishers to be interested further. Meantime I regarded myself as a thwarted Thackeray or Dickens and struggled valiantly on, writing one unsaleable manuscript after another. It was like a disease that had got to grips. I hardly took any notice of my poor wife. The more desperate my thwarted ambition the longer grew my manuscripts and the less attention I paid my wife. Then, quite by chance, I conceived a passion for a certain Ida Gregg, a common young woman who had come to the town one summer to stay with her uncle, the High Street baker. Her clothes smelt deliciously of fresh bread and there was flour in her coarse golden hair, for the uncle was a robust man who saw no harm in a bit of rough and tumble with his bosomy willing niece. I had called at the bakery on my morning walk and, as I waited to be served, I glanced through the window at the back of the shop and saw the baker at the great table in the bakehouse, kneading and slapping his niece's floury white breasts together as if they were two vast slabs of pliable dough. My knees weakened. It came my turn at the counter and, nudged into action by the queue of impatient housewives behind me, I continued gazing out of the back window, ordering lardy cakes, bloomers, madeleines . . . Finally I had no choice but to pay up, and stagger home. I took to calling each day at the bakery for pastries and glimpses of the baker making bread. My wife fattened up that summer . . .'

Gresham paused. Rosa stared at him.

'The tragedy of it was that *I never once* spoke to Ida Gregg. Before I got the chance she had been sent packing by the baker's wife. People made the inevitable crude jokes about her hasty departure. It was said she had a bun in the oven and, from what I had seen, this would not have been too surprising. My own wife was also aggrieved. She thought she had married a writer. After only two books I was flailing under the weight of authorship like the baker's niece under the hefty baker. Ida Gregg altered everything. She became my muse, the impossible object of all unplaced desire. I set to work with alacrity . . .'

'Miss Gregg never typed for you, Mr Gresham!' Rosa interjected sharply. She had found him out. 'She was not a typist. You *lied* to my mother!' Rosa swallowed the last of her ginger wine. 'And, if you never got close enough to speak to Ida Gregg how did you *know* she smelt of fresh bread, or that there was flour in her coarse golden hair? How did you *know* she was common – if you never spoke to her she might have been highly educated, well versed in both Thackeray and Dickens . . .'

Mr Gresham ignored the outburst. When Rosa stopped ranting he proceeded calmly, 'One afternoon, while I was out walking, Mrs Gresham came into my study to test her suspicions. A writer bares his very soul, and when he has nothing left to bare, he must invent. What Mrs Gresham found was only in truth the beginning of a work of invention. My poor jealous wife mistook. She read of my passion for Ida Gregg and before I returned from my walk, she had killed herself, a sharp knife . . .'

'Why are you telling me?' Rosa asked. 'I am only your typist's daughter. I could be anyone.'

'I am telling you because you are interested.'

'You don't know that!'

'Your interest is written all over your face.'

Rosa fell silent. This, at least, was true. A manuscript made flesh, easy to read as Aunt Edith dribbling over Farnol's key or Aunt Gracie and the chicken drumsticks, the old fingers closing greedily, greasily in.

'Since then I have tried, for my late wife's sake, to finish my masterpiece. Masterpieces take time. This masterpiece of mine is taking so long, I misdoubt myself. It cannot go on, I think. And yet, in my dear wife's name it must. If I am ever to complete the work inspired by Miss Gregg, Mrs Gresham's life will not have been wasted, she will not have died in vain.'

'And my mother?'

'My typist. My literary assistant. She comes each week to assist. Every literary masterpiece has its own unique requirements requiring its own unique assistance. Your mother assists by dressing up in my late wife's clothes and sitting for an hour or two where you are sitting now as if she were Mrs Gresham. She sits and looks at me reproachfully and she says nothing. Then I recall my passion for Miss Gregg and feel again what it was that compelled me to begin in the first place the book that inadvertently killed my wife.'

'I see!' said Rosa. 'So my mother spends Monday evenings wearing a dead woman's clothes and sitting in a dead woman's chair, looking at a dead woman's adulterous husband with as near as she can to the dead woman's eyes! Why did you ask my mother to marry you?'

'Because I should like to undress her.'

'Would you like to undress me?' Rosa asked.

'You,' said Mr Gresham to Pegglar's daughter, 'are an insolent meatless chicken.'

'If you do not marry Mr Gresham,' Rosa announced to her mother when she arrived home, 'then I will!'

Mary stared at Rosa. She felt iller than ever. 'Mr Gresham is a literary gentleman,' she reminded her daughter. 'You cannot trust a word he says. He dramatizes himself; he tells lies . . .'

'Like Pegglar did.'

'You know I will not hear a word against Pegglar.'

'Mr Gresham is interested in life.'

'You are wrong,' Mary said. 'Mr Gresham's sole interest is in stories about himself. You would soon tire of him.'

'You will not stand in my way?'

'When have I ever done that?'

'You never wanted me to be a sweet little girl, you never painted my bedroom pink or sent me to dancing classes in a cream silk tutu,' Rosa said.

'I should think not!' Mary laughed. 'I wanted *you* to be *yourself.*'

I *could* be anyone then, Rosa mused. And I, who could be anyone, *could* become Mrs Gresham!

'Is it true?' I asked Rosa, afraid Rosa was having me on. That she had begun making things up to make fun of me. 'Is Mr Gresham true?'

'True?' Rosa laughed. The old lady who owned the house also laughed, hoarse and croakingly. She picked up the poker and began prodding the fire. Rosa tousled my hair but I shook myself free.

'*Is* it true?' I demanded.

'What is truth, Jeannie?'

'What indeed!' asked my mother, prosaic as always, muttering under her breath so that only I could hear. She seized the poker from the old lady – there was nothing wrong with the fire – and then, ashamed of her flash of temper, she offered to make a pot of tea.

My mother increasingly left the room when Rosa talked, behaving like the hired servant she in fact was, disrupting us and distracting herself with countless menial tasks that could have waited. How often I wished she was nothing to do with me. My poor mother! It seems to me now that in my ignorance, and my youth, I wished it on myself that I should be living here in this large house, sitting in Rosa's chair, without her.

'I'm not sure what your story has to do with *me*,' I said to Rosa. I did not see that I could really be expected to write it all down. 'Why are you telling me?'

'I thought you were interested.'

'I am . . . But . . .' How could I reveal my suspicions? Luckily my mother was out of the room. 'You *promised* to tell me what

83

you know about my father,' I whispered urgently. If Rosa was the only one who could tell me about him, then she should get on and do so. I was growing out of Once Upon a Time and I'd have thought that was obvious. One of the boys at school had followed me home. Dared on by some of the others, I felt sure, but he had dared to all the same. His name was Gerald Fish. He told me if we did it while I was bleeding nothing would happen. He'd pushed me hard against a brick wall and clutched jeeringly at my clothes but I ducked and managed to get away, the wet from his big slobbery lips still on mine. When I got home I locked myself in the bathroom and washed and washed at my mouth but . . . 'You promised!'

'I haven't forgotten,' Rosa said sharply. She didn't like me or anyone else pinning her down. The old lady had dozed off. We could hear my mother clattering in the kitchen. 'It'll take . . . but I *am* getting there, Jeannie, believe me!'

I wanted to cry. I wanted to believe her. I wanted Gerald Fish and all the others who'd dared him on to vaporize into thin air, and never ever come near me again.

It was myself I vaporized.

There was a time when I thought if I sat here long enough in Rosa's chair, gazing into the shadows Rosa had seen, light might fall on me as it fell on Rosa and I would get inside her beautiful head, and understand at last what Rosa was up to on her many visits to this dull dark house. Let her story become my story, I thought. A dangerous business, I have discovered, shoving one's clumsy ankles into a dead woman's shoes, thinking oneself inside a dead woman's head.

PART II

—I dream horrific dreams . . .

—That is why we are here.

—I look in the mirror, and see . . .

—Go on.

—A chicken. A preposterous lopsided creature staring back at me. Then I wonder if *I* am the chicken in the mirror expecting to see me. Only it is not me. There is a child. A young woman now, sitting alone. Looking into the darkness. There is no fire in the room and this is my fault. I had the trees cut down and she is cold. Abandoned. I cannot comfort her. I tell her stories and I sing her nursery rhymes, but whither she wanders and whether she falls downstairs I neither know nor care. I look at her as if she were myself in disguised distorted form . . .

—She is the product of your unconscious.

—She is my dream. I fear for her, and yet I can do nothing. She is kept in ignorance. Perhaps I only imagine her while she imagines me. I no longer know which is which. It no longer matters . . .

—One can only use the patterns of the past to construct a picture of the future in the present. Not determine what will be, or alter it in any way.

Don't I sound authoritative? And concerned! I must. It is what these mixed-up women pay for. And why they queue half way down Harley Street to lie on my fashionable couch and fantasize. Against the clock. I am paid principally to not look bored.

My name is Gerald Fish. Dr Fish. She loves me of course, this soulful muddled creature. They all do. At night she imagines my fingers stroking the intimate crevices of her slight body. No wonder she dreams of chickens – fouls of the air, *fish* of the sea. Pure Freud. Poor creature. Next thing, she'll accuse me of being the father of this infant . . .

—It's a story, she says.

You bet it is, I think. You ought to write it down, I tell her, glancing openly at my watch. She shakes her head. At first I thought this patient rather plain. The sort of woman who'd not say boo to a goose if it shoved its beak up her skirts and chewed at her knickers. Yet there is a lightness about her, an elfin sweetness that makes me want to crush her. With the truth. I might touch her where it bleeds. Whatever burden she carries, the weight is intolerable. Write it down! I say. Often helps!

—Nothing helps. Nothing can.

—*I* can! I remind her. She does not reply. I am 'nothing' indeed. She has more than enough men already in her glamorous, varied life. Get someone else to write it then! The girl perhaps. It'll be a bestseller like *Anna Karenina* or *Tess of the d'Urbervilles* . . .

The woman looks at me sharply. Her face no longer pretty. She suspects me of flippancy, or worse.

—Dr Fish . . .

—Gerald, please!

—If you lay a finger on that child!

—I have done nothing.

She is silent. Then she speaks: I too have done nothing. I want to love her but I look at her and see a slow ugly creature. The sort of child who sits on the sidelines while games are being played or on her own at the spare desk at the back of the class. I talk to her and tell her things she cannot possibly understand, or want to know. She is so interested, so eager to please. I hate the woman who has charge of her . . .

—Her mother?

—If you like. I drive a wedge. I want to destroy the cosy home. I cannot bear to think of them all sitting round the fire in the evenings when I am not there. I want to cut the trees down outside and stop up the fireplace. I am slow and steady in my narration. When eventually I get to the part about her father . . . Then let her think what she likes about that woman! But I will not be hurried.

—Why should you be?

—I am getting there. Children never forget promises made to them, especially those that are later broken. Last night I dreamed that I would come here, Dr Fish, and tell you this. I would talk to you as if I were the child who sees a chicken. As if she and I had swapped places. By walking through that mirror we had each become travellers in the other's country.

—Such, um, *identification* is not uncommon.

—The child demanded to know if he were true! She suspected me of making fun of her. But she is not really a child any more. She is probably infatuated by Mr Gresham as ever I was. Girls are like that . . .

—Tell me, I say. It is the invitation she needs. No holding her now. I set my stopwatch. She watches the hands going round as she talks, and I listen attentively to the steady ticking.

Mr Gresham of course could not believe his luck: Rosa Pegglar, aged sixteen, tall and thin, standing on his doorstep, a green canvas box at her feet, wearing a coat that had lost all its buttons. 'I have come to marry you,' she said, picking up her box and advancing nimbly into the house.

'I suppose . . .' Gresham shut the door, enclosing them both in the book-filled hallway. Might their stories be made to overlap, after all? 'You could always *pretend* to be Mrs Gresham. A writer's wife.'

'I can be whoever I please,' Rosa said flirtingly. 'My mother could still do your typing, she still needs the money.'

'The widow Pegglar may not – er,' Mr Gresham coughed, typing the last thing on his mind, 'she may not like this particular turn of events.' In the darkness Rosa sensed him moving close, helping her out of her bedraggled coat, smoothing her feathers. I doubt somehow if he pushed her hard against the bookshelves and made a grab at her clothes, thrusting his tongue deep inside her mouth.

—Is that what you would have liked?

—Perhaps. The poor child could hardly talk to her mother about the nasty boys at school but I could see she wanted to tell me. I was frightened for her. This malleable blossoming girl was just the kind of specimen a literary gentleman could use. 'Come upstairs,' Mr Gresham said, taking Rosa's hand firmly and leading the way.

First & Foremost

'I am, first and foremost, a writer!' Mr Gresham declared, resolutely buttoning up his trousers and preparing to get back to work. How easy and tempting to abandon those long lonely hours at his desk and partake indefinitely of the joys of young Rosa's flesh! There is nothing a man so fears as that interruption which must one day come, of which Rosa's sudden appearance now seemed a precursor. Poor Mr Gresham put his clothes back on only to confront the stark truth of his own mortality: one day there would be no more books!

Rosa meanwhile was thinking: well, that was that, Gerald Fish! So much for all the talk at school! There were specks of blood on the sheets. Rosa frowned but Mr Gresham laughed out loud. At his age he might never have reasonably expected to partake again of untried female flesh, however meatless. What it was after all to be a distinguished literary gentleman! He smiled at Rosa Pegglar lying naked like a little plucked pullet on the bloodstained sheets.

'Do I have the run of the place?' Rosa asked. Is the pretend Mrs Gresham to be free-range?

'As you please,' Mr Gresham chuckled. 'Get my housekeeper to rustle you up some lunch if you feel peckish.'

Two flights down, in the basement kitchen, Rosa found a sour-faced woman ineffectually scrubbing a greasy frying pan. 'I am Rosa,' Rosa said. 'I am to have the run of the place.'

'You had better not go running into Mr Gresham's study then! Literary gentlemen do not like to be disturbed.'

Rosa sauntered across the kitchen to a door that stood open and wandered out into a large overgrown garden. How Alfie, once the rival for her mother's affections, would have enjoyed it here. In the end there had been nowhere to bury him. A Russian *émigré* had gone to the house in Bloomsbury to inform the Fanshawes of the poetess Nina's end: her dog barking in the hide-out had alerted soldiers searching for suspect foreigners. The hound had been summarily shot, Nina and her female lover marched away, the poems in her pocket taken as evidence. No one was at home in Bloomsbury but by chance the *émigré* encountered Max's widow, Sarah, at the gate. Are you a relative? the Russian had asked, hope gleaming like gold in his eyes.

'I was married to Nina's brother, the painter,' a subdued Sarah explained. 'He died, looking for a poxy milk bar. His niece, Rosa Pegglar, has promised to visit me one day.'

'I want work,' the man said. He had no interest in the fate of these flimsy people who would only ever get what was coming to them.

'My new husband has contacts,' Sarah said uneasily, scribbling a telephone number down to get rid of the man.

'Poor Nina,' Mary remarked when she read Sarah's letter. 'And that poor, poor dog!'

'You're Edith Pegglar's niece!' the woman in the kitchen said when Rosa returned from the overgrown garden.

Rosa nodded. 'Were you Aunt Edith's other source of information, then?'

'She took to calling with that sister of hers, after your mother began typing for Mr Gresham. She'd sit in my kitchen asking questions . . .'

'Are you the housekeeper?'

'Housekeepers get *paid*,' the woman said grimly. 'Mr Gresham has never paid me but by the time I've earned so much he couldn't afford to pay, then he'll *have* to marry me to settle the debt.'

'Are you Miss Gregg?'

'Ida!'

'Eggless!'

'There's eggs in the fridge. First fridge in town, that once was.'

'I'd like an omelette.' Rosa sat down at the table. Ida Gregg slammed the greasy pan down on the stove. She cracked eggs into a bowl and stabbed repeatedly at the yellow yolks with a sharpened knife. There were traces of blood in the viscous sacs where possible chickens had come to nothing.

'You are a violent woman,' Rosa remarked.

'I could be,' Miss Gregg sniffed enigmatically. 'If I was pushed.'

'Did you know my Aunt Edith used to take tea with Miss Gregg in the kitchen?' Rosa asked. Mr Gresham did not answer. He was concentrating. Rosa shifted herself beneath him.

'Lie still, won't you!' Mr Gresham's voice was muffled by his exertions. Rosa now thought it rather monotonous pretending to be Mrs Gresham. When the literary gentleman had finished, he sat up and asked if he had given her pleasure.

'Pleasure?' Rosa repeated, puzzled.

'If there's anything I can do to – well, you know . . .'

'To give me pleasure?'

Gresham nodded. Rosa's nipples were sore to burning and her legs felt as if they had been hacked apart. Gresham, crouching now on his naked haunches, leant hungrily forward. He thought the girl delightfully reticent. 'Whisper it, my lovely,' he urged, stroking her skinny thigh. 'Miss Gregg may be listening at the door!'

Rosa looked over at the door. 'Tell me,' she said, 'what you *think* of while you . . .' She gestured across the rumpled bed.

'Absolutely nothing, that is the pleasure. It is not a time for thinking.'

'I could be anyone then! Anyone female.'

Gresham agreed. 'Though another little hen might have more meat on her! Your dear mother comes this evening with the typing.'

There was not much meat on Mary either. Mrs Pegglar was not required to sit looking reproachful about the baker's buxom niece tonight. Instead she perched uncomfortably beside her daughter on a sofa and wondered, as any parent might, whether and where especially she had gone wrong.

'There is an old-fashioned fridge in the kitchen downstairs,' Rosa remarked conversationally. 'The first fridge in town.'

'That's nice, dear.'

Mr Gresham poured mother and daughter each a glass of sticky ginger wine which they sat dutifully sipping, looking at Mr Gresham looking at them in the great gilded mirror.

Ida Gregg came and stood squarely in the doorway. 'You owes me!' she said sullenly.

'We'll settle up later,' Mr Gresham replied, without moving. The housekeeper glowered at the three of them in turn, and then at their reflections in the mirrors before departing. Mary glanced at Rosa who shrugged.

'If he doesn't pay up soon, he'll have to marry her,' Rosa whispered.

'To do *nothing*?' Mary was stupefied. 'That's ridiculous! Mothers naturally meddle in their daughters' affairs!' Mary accepted payment nevertheless, understanding that she was to stay away from the house the way Alfonzo Bonzo, in defiance of instinct, had been taught to keep away from Pegglar's poultry.

Mr Gresham came to Rosa that night and took the sleepy girl from her bed. He led her past the stairs up to his study where she was forbidden to set foot, past his own bedroom where he had taken her frequently that week, up another flight of stairs and into a room where Ida Gregg lay, her eyes glittering in the darkness as she listened for sounds that betokened betrayal. Mr Gresham pushed the sleepy Rosa into the bed beside Miss Gregg and then pulled back the sheets to climb on top of them both.

I could be anyone, Rosa thought as they pummelled her, inside and out, Ida Gregg in eggless revenge, Mr Gresham excited by the excitement rising in Miss Gregg.

'That'll teach you,' Miss Gregg cried, holding Rosa in place for

Mr Gresham but at the same time fighting her rival off. 'You are an insolent chicken,' she yelled as Rosa Pegglar wriggled free.

Rosa crept away downstairs.

'No need for tears.' Mr Gresham clad in a red woollen dressing gown entered her room and put an arm round Rosa who was too miserable to resist. 'Love is absurd,' the Old Guzzler explained. 'My poor wife's passions are only roused when she is jealous.'

'What's that?' Ida Gregg fluttered into the room.

'Your passions, my dear,' said Mr Gresham.

'*You* are Mrs Gresham?' Rosa asked.

'She could be if she wanted, but Ida would not lower herself by marrying a purveyor of tamarind and truske.'

'*You* are a spice merchant?'

'My mother was against the match from the start.' Ida Gregg tucked Rosa firmly back into her bed and plumped up the pillows. 'And now poor Mamma has passed on I must respect her wishes. Just as I promised your dear aunt to keep an eye on you.'

'Do you call this keeping an eye on me?' Rosa wailed. 'Telling me lies . . .'

'No one asked you to come here, interfering in our story,' Mr Gresham pointed out.

'We live as we like,' Miss Gregg said lightly. 'Go to sleep now, Rosa. Things always seem better in the morning.'

In the morning Ida said, 'You can cook for us. I have been trying to make out in the kitchen but I was not brought up for menial work.'

'You are not a housekeeper? Or a typist, then?'

'Goodness no! I was a librarian, until I met Mr Gresham.'

'The story changes all the time,' Rosa remarked.

'Your aunt said you liked an escapade.'

'All my life I have wanted to escape, I don't know what from, or where to.'

'You can escape from us: to write your own story you will have to get out of ours. And you may not find that so easy! Meanwhile, you can be the "tweeny" – put on that apron!'

94

When the doorbell rang, one quiet afternoon, Rosa primped her hair and skipped upstairs. 'Yes?' she said rudely as any tweeny might.

'We heard . . .' Eunice Proctor began. She'd had to find for bus fares again while behind her stood a red-faced policeman who had come on his bike.

'I am employed here,' Rosa announced proudly. 'As a tweeny.'

'Mary's story was vague!'

'The story *is* vague; most of it yet to be written,' Rosa said.

The policeman winked. He was used to being dragged out on his bicycle by Eunice Proctor on wild-goose chases. And here was a wild goose if ever he saw one! 'You look very smart in that uniform,' he told Rosa approvingly. What flesh there was on the girl was nicely distributed. He had pulled Rosa free from the wrecked *Doublie Royale* and though he'd seen other head-on collisions since, with blood and petrol gushing all over the road, nothing ever quite matches your very first crash. He recalled the small face peering through broken glass in the moonlight, and here she was entrapped again, in a pretty apron. A young woman you could not rescue.

Rosa did not like the policeman's leer. She closed the door smartly and flounced back down to the kitchen where Miss Gregg and Mr Gresham were waiting for her. 'Did you invite them here?'

'Eunice Proctor has never needed any invitation. She is not that sort of woman.' Ida Gregg and Mr Gresham were looking at her hard. Two sets of identical eyes. 'The policeman has gone,' she assured them.

Mr Gresham returned to his forbidden study.

'Are you brother and sister?' Rosa asked.

'If only it were that simple!' Ida Gregg sighed. 'Poor Mr Gresham, his head is filled . . .'

'My Aunt Gracie's head was filled with straw. I saw the seam. It did not complicate matters though.'

'Mr Gresham's head is filled with ideas . . .'

'You mean he is shifty.'

'The story, as you yourself remarked, is different all the time.'

'*Is* Mr Gresham really a writer?'

'Long ago he wrote two novels and bought this nice big house as a place of literary pilgrimage, like the Brontë parsonage or Thomas Hardy's cottage. Tickets could be issued, postcards sold at the door, his works re-enacted in people's heads . . .'

'He didn't half fancy himself!' Rosa commented, rather as Dorothy might have done.

'Alas, there were to be no more novels, no postcards, only the endless re-enactments.'

'The two he did write?' Rosa asked. 'What were they about?'

'*First & Foremost*, the story of a novelist torn between love for two typists, a greying spinster, and a widow with a young daughter. *Tamarind & Truske*, a more complex work on the same theme. Writing two at once, the books got muddled up and were published with the wrong titles. Not that it mattered; nobody noticed. After that everything started shifting. Most people have a few facts to cling to while their plaster horse bucks and turns. Here, we alter the facts . . .'

'You only alter what you *choose* to call fact.' Pegglar had set about altering the species. Pegglar's daughter felt impatient with this more idle, half-hearted tinkering.

'Oh Rosa!' Ida Gregg cried out. 'We have gone through so many versions. You are the first person who was interested . . .'

One day, Rosa thought, I who could be anyone, who is for the present between things, will escape completely. To London and Aunt Sarah, the Annual Exotic Poultry Show, Buckingham Palace. Anywhere and everywhere. Meanwhile . . .

'Meanwhile,' Ida Gregg was saying. 'Arthur turned up.'

'Arthur?'

Arthur Gregg. Whose father, Colonel Gregg, knew the Pegglars' father. They had gone tiger-hunting in Simla together. Before his death, the aged Captain Pegglar had confided in the aged Colonel Gregg. If he ever returned to England would he please, for the sake of a fellow tiger-hunter, look up the abandoned Pegglars. He named the town. A poxy place without a milk bar. There had been property and assets, doubtless

96

mismanaged. Marriageable daughters, most likely unmarried. A young son, Rodolphe Arthur George, whom he had scarcely seen, and trickiest of all, the discarded wife sitting about looking reproachful.

Colonel Gregg promised the dying Captain to do what he could. The girl who had run away with Captain Pegglar had long since succumbed to the Indian heat. Pretending to be Mrs Pegglar in India had sounded romantic back home, but week after week spent fanning herself, fending off fleas and gossip, while the man she'd lost her home and Reputation for hunted tiger in the hills with his beastly friends was not the least romantic. Neither was the fever when it came, furious and raging like an abandoned wife. Colonel Gregg never did return but, years later, his son Arthur had called on Edith Pegglar.

Miss Pegglar arched her eyebrows. 'My poor mother *died*, Mr Gregg. Careered into by a runaway horse on the way to a wedding which never then took place. You cannot expect me to take an interest in my father's tiger-hunting, or in the offspring of his irresponsible friends.'

Arthur Gregg had been disappointed. On his deathbed Colonel Gregg, with nothing else to dispose of, had mentioned the deceased Captain's property and assets. Arthur had naturally expected more than a few sharp words delivered on a doorstep. He returned to the railway station only to find the last train back to London had already departed. A resourceful man, brought up on a remote plantation who had ridden to school on the back of an elephant, Arthur Gregg set off fearlessly in search of a night's cheap lodgings. When one book closes, another opens, he told himself. The first inn he'd tried had no beds but the inn-keeper directed him to another hostelry. Mr Gregg's sober attempt to follow the directions landed him at last in a tree-lined street. It was cold, with a thick mist gathering.

'Arthur! Arthur!' A woman called anxiously somewhere close by.

'Er, hallo!' Mr Gregg called back. Peering into the swirling darkness Arthur Gregg encountered the astonished face of a woman standing at her gate.

'I'm looking for Arthur,' she said, no little disappointed. She'd thought for one glorious moment that her beloved spaniel had spoken. And had not Mary often yearned for Alfie to talk to her but made do, during Pegglar's many absences, with the wordless gurglings of an infant Rosa?

'Arthur Gregg.' Mr Gregg removed his hat. 'I missed my train.'

'I've lost my dog.'

The unsuccessful search for the canine Arthur culminated in Mr Gregg marrying Ida and taking up residence with her, and her brother, in the tree-lined street. At first the three lived happily. Everything in England was so strange to Arthur Gregg that he did not notice the especial strangeness of his new bride and her brother. Large, loose limbed and dependably grey, there had been an elasticity about his bride he found comforting. Just as the elephants back home always accepted him as he was, Ida and her brother never remarked on his half-Indian darkness, a darkness he'd discovered made life difficult away from the remote plantation. In his hunting days, the gallant Colonel Gregg had chased and caught more than the odd fierce tiger.

When Arthur Gregg found his wife in bed with her brother he merely assumed things were done this way in England.

'We live as we like,' Ida said.

And why not? Arthur Gregg thought, embarking that very afternoon on an active flirtation with a young schoolmistress who had caught his eye.

When Ida Gregg found her handsome dark-skinned husband in bed with the flighty schoolmistress, she trumpeted and stampeded about so that within days, for her own safety, the common or garden pullet had become engaged to an elderly apothecary. The whole town was taken by surprise. You expected reliability when you bought your poisons, not hasty weddings to pert pretty schoolteachers.

Neither brother nor sister spoke to Arthur Gregg after that and when Ida discovered her husband in bed again, alone this time and stone cold dead, his flesh had already started to rot.

Some wondered whether Ida had poisoned him, others openly intimated that they would not blame the poor woman if she had!

With wifely vigour, Ida Gregg ransacked her dead husband's room. She found Edith Pegglar's name and address, scribbled by Arthur Gregg's father, the Colonel, in his dying hour. Furiously the demented Ida wrapped her husband's stinking remains in a coarse hessian sack and ordered her brother to dig a hole, the statutory five foot deep, in the garden. They planted a thorn bush over the spot. With money she found in Arthur Gregg's drawers, the distraught widow purchased a new-fangled fridge.

On entering the kitchen, Edith Pegglar had scrutinized the fridge. An item of domestic utility that superseded anything her shilling book had taught. 'Are you related to one Arthur Gregg?'

Ida was taken aback. Involuntarily her eyes sought the thorn bush through the window. Edith recounted how many years before a certain Arthur Gregg had come from Simla to check on the abandoned family of his father's tiger-hunting friend. 'I was so amazed I shut the door in his face.'

'You never saw him again?'

'No. He came all that way and I refused to talk to him!' Edith sat herself and her sister down at the kitchen table and sighingly accepted tea for them both that had not yet been offered. She spoke then of her sister-in-law who had recently learnt typing from a book. 'I hear Mrs Pegglar intends to replace my poor late brother with yours; the moment the carousel started up I saw her talking to another man!'

'Mary *types* for my brother. That's all. Now, really, Miss Pegglar . . .'

Gracie giggled and helped herself to spoonfuls of expensive sugar she was not allowed at home.

'Visitors?' Mr Gresham had heard voices.

'Your typist's sister-in-law, Edith Pegglar.' Ida did not introduce Gracie.

'I came to see if Ida Gregg were related to a Mr Arthur Gregg, a man I encountered on my doorstep many years back,' Miss Pegglar explained.

'He's under that thorn bush,' Mr Gresham pointed through the window at the grave. 'Now, if you'll excuse me, I must get back to my work . . .'

Gracie Pegglar slurped loudly. Her sister and Ida Gregg let their mouths fall open and a vision of Arthur Gregg, who had ridden to school on the back of an elephant, rose up between them.

I treated him like a spaniel, Ida thought sadly. She'd had the man put down, and buried in the back garden, like a pet that had become inconvenient. She had replaced one Arthur with another, and if Mary Pegglar were to marry her brother, she herself would replace this Edith as Mary's sister-in-law.

'I have a niece, a curious little thing called Rosa,' Edith Pegglar told the woman who had driven a wanton schoolteacher into accepting the garnet ring that had once been hers. 'Captain Pegglar, Rosa's grandfather of course, and Colonel Gregg hunted tigers and goodness knows what else in Simla together.'

'I will keep an eye on your niece,' Ida Gregg promised, for it seemed, in the circumstances, the least she could do.

—What a patient man you are, Dr Fish!
—That is what I am paid for.
—Of course it is, Dr Fish.

You see, Dr Fish, Ida never was a Miss Gregg! She was *Mrs* Gregg. When Rosa taxed her with this she immediately changed her story. If she had been Arthur Gregg's *sister*, and not his wife, then she would be *Miss* Gregg. If Colonel Gregg returned himself, leaving his dark-skinned son in India in sole charge of the elephants and the plantation, returning for medical treatment, a last look at home, or to obtain new boots from his outfitters in Mayfair, it is likely he would honour his pledge and visit the abandoned Pegglars. Colonel Gregg might have taken lodgings while he courted Miss Pegglar and if Edith's brother objected to a match, not wanting his father's assets reorganized in event of a marriage . . .

'Pegglar had no head for business,' Rosa protested. 'He was far too busy with his own passions.'

'Then maybe Colonel Gregg inquired into Miss Pegglar's properties and assets and discovered they were not on the scale he had been led to expect. When Captain Pegglar had propped up his tiger gun and sat with a glass of neat gin, the size of his interests back home would have undergone considerable magnification. By the time the Colonel realized this, Miss Edith had succumbed to the old tiger-hunter's charms and by the time a little Gregg had been born to her, the gallant Colonel was back in India. Your poor aunt had no choice but to have me fostered discreetly.'

'Aunt Edith never had any children,' Rosa declared. 'Only Pegglar and Aunt Gracie – she liked to think they never grew up. And the apothecary's sons who would have been hers, but for a chance accident in the High Street. No, Miss Gregg, you are *not* my aunt's daughter – no amount of invention can make you that.'

'As you say! But while Colonel Gregg was looking up Captain Pegglar's family he lodged with a respectable widow, a Mrs Gresham, who had been left with a large house and a small son. The colonel, disappointed by the preposterous way Edith Pegglar blamed him for depriving her of a garnet ring, was grateful for the attentions the widow Gresham lavished on him. In the evenings he'd sit his landlady's son on his lap and charm the little boy asleep with tales of India. Mrs Gresham, her sights set now on the Colonel's vast plantations, encouraged his tedious story telling but alas, her generosity of mind, and body, was not sufficient to prevent Colonel Gregg returning to India, promising to write.

'When a letter eventually did come, it was from Arthur Gregg regretting to inform Mrs Gresham of Colonel Gregg's demise. His father had taken an heroic and foolish last stand against a man-eating tiger that had been marauding for months in the hills. He had gone on ahead impatiently, and by the time the rest of the party caught up, only half a chewed boot, its label still attached from a shop in Mayfair, was left at the scene.

'In time, the failing plantation failed and Arthur Gregg made his way to England. Having heard of his father's hospitable landlady, he visited us. Imagine his surprise at being confronted by a fully grown half sister when he only thought to meet his father's mistress. My poor mother of course was dead. Worn out by life . . .' Ida Gregg sighed.

'So *Arthur Gregg* was your half brother on your father's side, and *Mr Gresham* a half brother on your mother's!'

Ida sighed again. 'At forty I am too old now.'

'For children?'

'I did have a child. It died. It is buried out in the garden under the thorn bush, wrapped in hessian . . .'

'Beside Arthur Gregg?'

'He isn't buried *there*.'

'What happened to him?'

'I'd have thought you might have guessed that by now! Arthur Gregg and Mr Gresham are one and the same.'

'Oh really!' Rosa felt impatient. 'It isn't healthy not to keep proper stockbreeding books. What you need is fresh blood.'

'That's why we need you, Rosa.'

'I don't count; I am Edith Pegglar's niece. We overlap. It was *my* grandfather who went tiger-hunting with Colonel Gregg. If you were Aunt Edith's child, which you aren't, you would be my cousin. Why can't I go in Mr Gresham's study upstairs? Is he some sort of Bluebeard? Will I discover the bodies of all his previous pretend wives, muddled up and shifting between manuscripts, like the unfortunate Arthur Gregg?'

'Don't be fatuous, Rosa!' Ida Gregg continued then as if nothing had been said: 'I was a librarian when I met Mr Gresham. An ordinary happy girl. One day Mr Gresham came into the library. Nothing was ever ordinary, or happy, again. A man steps casually into a woman's life and before she can side-step him the whole course of her life has shifted. A different backdrop not of her own choosing, fitted immovably in place. The library where I worked was quiet, books and lives were orderly. But Mr Gresham . . .'

'Oh dear!' said Rosa, taking off her apron. 'You were a librarian, maybe. He is a literary gentleman, perhaps. I no longer want to pretend. I want to be me. I am going.' Rosa threw the apron at Ida Gregg and ran upstairs to her room to fetch her green canvas box. She took her coat, still without buttons, off the hook behind the door. As she passed along the corridor she paused at the base of the small flight of stairs which led up to Mr Gresham's study, paused long enough to have no choice. She could not leave until she had entered the forbidden territory, if only to say 'goodbye'. She did not knock on the door. I am prepared for anything, she thought, quite mistakenly.

'It's a machine!'

'You are not supposed to come in here. You will interrupt the flow.'

'You must have known I would come.'

Gresham sighed. How old and tired he felt, small and shrunken beside the vast workings. 'Ah, well,' he said.

'It doesn't look like anything I've seen before.'

Mr Gresham laughed. 'This is my lifetime's invention.'

'I thought you were a literary gentleman.'

'When I was young, a man came to the house and told me fantastical stories about faraway places. I thought they were true or that he was making them up but it turned out he had stolen them from a Rudyard Kipling.'

'That was Colonel Gregg,' Rosa said. 'My grandfather's tiger-hunting friend.'

'So, *you* are responsible! I always knew you were up to something. It was Colonel Gregg who taught me the author is irrelevant; a *process* merely by which a story's variations can be discovered. I invented a machine to process the variations more efficiently. Then I decided to get someone to read the results without realizing they were reading the products of a machine. Which is why I employed your mother. To my astonishment she

103

typed whatever I gave her without comment. And then of course you turned up. A variation I could not have bargained for, Rosa, but one with which my machine has had no difficulty coping . . .'

'I never suspected you were so systematic . . .'

Mr Gresham laughed. 'I was terrified when busybody Proctor arrived with a policeman. In a court of law I would go to pieces trying to stick to a story after all the permutations this machine has contrived.'

'I always wanted to be someone else, somewhere else,' Rosa confessed. 'But no one in particular . . .'

'Well,' said Mr Gresham. 'With the aid of my machine you could be. I could feed *you* in at one end and start you off all over again . . .'

'Please don't! I am not a character in one of your unwritten novels, Mr Gresham. I am me. Anyone I please. My story is my own!' Rosa sniffed. 'There's a dreadful smell of burnt caramel.'

'The machine runs on sugar.' Mr Gresham picked up a Tate & Lyle paper bag and tipped granulated sugar into a funnel. Rosa watched as he wearily cranked a device.

'Is it all worth it?' Rosa asked. 'Couldn't you let the machine wind down? Let the species revert, and die out?'

'When you are first and foremost a writer the writing takes over, Rosa,' Mr Gresham said solemnly. 'The books take over, life is over . . .'

Rosa considered the excitement that had somehow galloped past, a runaway horse with nostrils flaring. Elusive possibilities should probably remain elusive. 'I think you are mad,' she said. 'There is a world out there . . .' Rosa pointed through the window. It was spring. Across the country hopeful bachelors were preparing themselves for their annual excursion. Mr Gresham poured more sugar into the funnel. His eyes travelled lovingly over the machinery's workings and Rosa saw that to Mr Gresham the machine was far bigger than the box where sugar hissed and fizzled over the small flame below. A literary gentleman who could concoct endless stories might equally well imagine a vast machinery outside his head.

'How clever you are, Mr Gresham!' she said and gave the man an affectionate farewell kiss on the thin hair on the back of his old, world-weary head. She retrieved her green canvas box from where she had left it by the door.

'I think Mr Gresham would like an omelette,' Rosa told Miss Gregg in the kitchen.

'You really are leaving us then?'

'If I hurry I can catch the last train to London that Arthur Gregg missed that evening. Goodbye, dear Miss Gregg!'

'Take a sandwich and a couple of books to read on the train . . .'

'Thanks.' Rosa took the books and sandwich, and made a dash for the door.

Tamarind & Truske

'Gone? Gone where?' The visitor was beside herself.

Eunice Proctor eagerly handed over the forwarding address she kept ready these days. 'I have known the family ever since the houses were built and the Pegglars moved in. I watched little Rosa grow up. I always kept a friendly eye even though I did not like the hens they kept. Nasty noisy creatures, not your usual domestic varieties at all. The Pegglars were not usual domestic people. What it has cost me in bus fares!'

The visitor was not listening. She looked around distractedly and looked very distressed.

'There have been a lot of women asking for Pegglar,' Eunice Proctor continued. 'He was away from home a lot, too. And now . . .'

'Now?'

'He is dead. His wife roasted the noisy hens for funeral baked meats.'

'Funeral? Wife? Hens? A *child*, did you say?'

'Rosa. A funny little thing. Not that I was invited to partake . . .'

Ida Gregg pocketed the forwarding address: a typing agency. We need a typist, she thought malevolently as she walked away. I should have known! she told herself also, thinking again of Pegglar and the child he had been so keen for her to carry in her womb. Pegglar who had arrived at the house she shared with her brother, Arthur, stepping into their lives out of the swirling mists.

'Did you apply for a post as a postcard salesman?' Pegglar had asked.

'I think there has been some mistake.' Arthur was immediately suspicious but Pegglar produced a scrap of paper with their address on. He'd come without his notes and was unable to check the origin of the mistake. His assistant Philbert Farnol would be to blame, he said. He was a publisher of postcards and had samples to show them. He was on the look-out for tiptop salesmen. Business was booming.

'People *buy* these?' Her brother was astounded. Pegglar was not a kind of man the Greggs had encountered before. An easy-going, fast-talking, indefinable man. He was also much older than he looked at first sight and the postcards were frankly . . .

'Our father went to India,' Ida Gregg said chattily. It was dead quiet all day in the library where she worked, and she and her brother did not often get visitors.

'Sometimes I think everyone's fathers fled to India,' Pegglar said. 'Mine died in Simla, and my mother soon afterwards. In her distress, she stepped out in front of traffic in the High Street, still holding my hand. I was too young at the time to understand, my sisters never recovered . . .'

The story always touched women's hearts.

'How terrible!' Ida Gregg shuddered, and invited the orphaned Pegglar in for a cup of tea.

'I have often wondered if my sister's bridegroom paid a lad to run down the street and frighten that horse . . .'

'Surely not!'

'You haven't met my sister – I think the poor fellow had second thoughts!'

Arthur Gregg buried himself in his study and refused to see what was happening between *his* sister and the salesman who had wheedled his way into their house and into her soft silly heart. How could he, a scholarly schoolmaster, tell Ida what he knew of men without disclosing, at the same time, something untoward about himself? At the school where he taught, Arthur Gregg found it increasingly difficult to concentrate. In class, two sneaky boys, Mellis and Hobday, took advantage. One afternoon their larking about went too far and Mr Gregg told the pair to stay behind.

Mellis and Hobday quaked. It was their third offence that term and they anticipated a beating. Hobday's father was a governor of the school which gave him the confidence to defy Mr Gregg and go home. Mellis, whose father was dead, thought it best to stick about and, if it came to it, talk grim Gregg-face round.

Arthur Gregg fretted. Ida had always seemed so level headed. Now, of course, he found himself wondering what had truly gone on in the library, and in his sister's head, all these years. That morning, he'd been woken at first light by strange cluckings as if some bantam had got into the house. He traced the sounds to his sister's bedroom. Fearful what the squeals might mean, yet afraid for Ida's safety, he had entered her room to find her heaving under Pegglar, squawking with pleasure.

'Arthur! Your face!' she had said sitting up, her nightdress wantonly ruffed around her neck, Pegglar on the pillow beside her, blinking like a scraggy old rooster in the dawn light.

She had betrayed him! Arthur Gregg entered the classroom at the end of the day and found Mellis waiting. Hobday, the boy informed the schoolmaster, had better things to do and had gone home.

'It was only a prank, Sir, honest, Sir! I didn't mean any harm!' Mellis protested. And then he laughed: the laugh of a man with the wrong address on a scrap of paper, and lurid postcards in his pocket, who nakedly helps himself to all that is precious and not his. 'Only a prank, Sir!'

Gregg seized the tender Mellis and commenced to thrash the boy to within an inch of his young life.

The police had been called. The policeman told Eunice Proctor who lived two doors away from his sister about the maniac schoolmaster who had been dismissed. The boy's only offence, that he had laughed.

'I will not have you in my house!' Gregg had roared at Pegglar.

Pegglar blinked. He recalled the mean ferret smile of Bluie Chapman lauding it up on the Champions' Podium. He did so dislike unpleasantness, and besides there were plenty of other houses where he was welcome.

Ida wept. Later when Pegglar called at the library she took him behind the reference stacks and whispered how her brother had lost his post. 'Arthur is not himself at the moment, you must not take any notice.'

'I could arrange a job,' Pegglar had kindly offered. 'As a salesman.'

'In a few weeks' time,' Ida said, for by then Arthur's spare time, and empty pocket, would weigh. She sent Pegglar off then, arranging for him to call again in a few weeks' time, bringing boxes of cards for her brother to sell.

Once, Ida Gregg had nearly married. A tradesman who'd been jilted by someone else had taken to coming regularly to the library in his lunch-hour. He showed no interest in books but lured Ida Gregg behind the reference stacks to press a garnet ring on her. Since Ida could not envisage putting up with her brother's fussy ways and having to move on every time he disgraced himself, she had slipped the ring on her finger to see how it looked. A fiancée! Ida had permitted the man to put his hand briefly inside her liberty bodice and pinch her breasts. At the end of the lunch-hour she'd reluctantly returned the tradesman his ring and promised to consider his proposal and give him her answer soon. He never came back for her answer, and some time afterwards she found out he had met, married and given his garnet ring to someone else. For years she avoided buying her poisons from his shop.

Poison!

Ida Gregg, a common poisoner? Too drastic and theatrical surely for a librarian in flat comfortable shoes whose only drama- tic moment had taken place one lunch-hour behind the Refer- ence. Yet the thought of living with her stuffy brother for ever . . . *Living?* It was death! Simple draughts simply administered in

Arthur Gregg's tea, and Pegglar would no longer be banned from the house.

Not surprisingly, the disgraced Arthur Gregg had not been sleeping well. 'He hasn't been sleeping,' Miss Gregg told the doctor who came on a number of occasions at her bidding to the house. On each visit her brother had looked distinctly worse.

It happened that the doctor's son had been in the same class as Mellis and Hobday and, although the boy said his classmates had teased the master beyond measure, the physician had no sympathy for men like Gregg. They went against nature. There was no room for their kind in stockbreeding books. 'It isn't medicine he needs,' the doctor said, refusing to prescribe. 'Give him lots of strong tea!'

'Cardiac arrest,' the doctor was later to enter on the death certificate. Then Ida Gregg waited, and waited, but still Pegglar did not come.

'In the *back garden!*' The funeral director totted up his likely losses. You could hardly charge much for a funeral in someone's own back garden, but if Ida Gregg's request was a trifle irregular, so too had been the Deceased. As a favour to the unhappy woman he sent a couple of his men to dig her a discreet hole five foot deep. Unpleasant publicity had already forced poor Ida to resign from the library and in the absence of her brother, and Pegglar, she had been forced also to advertise for lodgers.

When Colonel Gresham's son turned up from India in answer to an advert he chanced upon in the paper, Ida Gregg showed him upstairs. 'I lived here until recently with my brother, a schoolmaster. He died,' she explained. 'And what do you do, Mr Gresham? What is your line of business?'

'Spices. We owned a tea plantation in India but it was failing for as long as I can remember. I was glad to sell up and get out. Spices are altogether a better bet.'

Ida Gregg let the rooms which had been her brother's to Mr Gresham. When she was certain she was pregnant, she had tracked Pegglar to a neat house on a neat estate. The likely explanation for such a domestic dwelling combined with the man's unexplained disappearance dawned on her as she neared the front door. But there was the baby to think of. No one answered her knock. A neighbour leant over the fence.

'A lot of women have been asking for Pegglar.' Eunice Proctor looked Ida Gregg up and down. Alas, the self-deceiving! 'There was one only last week with a daughter called Dorothy. I can't imagine what his widow – Mrs Pegglar – must think. Such a terrible shock after living with a man all these years, if you can call it living with him, he was hardly here. Not like Mr Proctor on whom, you can be sure, I keep a tight rein . . .'

Ida Gregg returned home to the house she had shared with her dead brother. Mr Gresham took his distraught landlady in his arms and pressed her to his suit that smelled richly of tamarind and truske. 'Whisper it, my lovely!' he had said, and she told him about Pegglar with his passions and postcards, and then she told him about the child she was bearing. She did not describe her hand in the untimely unnecessary death of Arthur Gregg. 'His wife, Mary Pegglar, runs a typing agency. There is a daughter, Rosa,' she said. 'Rosa Pegglar.'

'Forget these Pegglars,' Mr Gresham had urged but Ida Gregg could not forget the way she had been duped. Later when the baby was born dead she had lain for weeks tossing and turning feverishly.

'Shall I bury it in the garden?' her lodger had asked but Ida Gregg did not hear him and, having lived in India where flesh rots fast, Mr Gresham dug a hole the statutory five foot deep and discovered another body wrapped in coarse hessian. Little by little, Ida Gregg regained her senses and though she had lost Pegglar's child she had not lost her passion for revenge. Mr Gresham humoured her. 'I will pretend to be a writer,' he said. 'I will pretend to need a typist and we will get Mrs Pegglar here so that you can see her.'

'Pegglar deceived me, it's his daughter I want.' In the kitchen, Ida Gregg sharpened knives. Viciously she stabbed at egg yolks. Once in *her* clutches, the child would have difficulty escaping.

Rosa closed the pages. 'Are we there yet?' she asked the other occupants of the railway carriage who had been watching the young lady with her pretty head deep in a book.

'Another five minutes,' one man said eagerly.

'Depends where you mean by *there*,' another remarked playfully.

'I'm going to the Annual Exotic Poultry Show,' Rosa told them just as the train plunged into a long tunnel which so magnified the noise outside that no one could hear her. Or at least one person did for Rosa distinctly heard a voice in the darkness exclaim: 'Well, fancy!'

'Gerald Fish! You little sneak!' This was no fantasy now. No amount of imagining could imagine Gerald Fish away.

'If we do it while you are bleeding nothing can happen.'

'Nothing is bleeding well going to happen!' I ducked, and ran. The wet from his big fishy lips on mine. The boys who had dared him cheered him on. I got to our gate and inside, panting.

My mother said, 'Is something wrong, Jeannie?'

Of course something was wrong! My mother could be so stupid. I locked myself in the bathroom and refused to say.

Next time Rosa came my mother had words with her but I couldn't hear what was said. Rosa laughed, and when my mother left the room she asked me if I'd been upset. I did not want Rosa upset, so I told her I often had nasty dreams.

'And I dream of Jeannie with the light brown hair!' she said teasingly.

'Do you?' I asked. 'Do you dream about me?'

'Of course not, you silly little goose! Why would I dream about you? I used to dream about Mr Gresham. I had quite a thing about him, because he was a literary gentleman, I suppose. But then he married my mother. No one likes to see their own father replaced. Dear, dead Daddy!'

'I wouldn't know,' I said sullenly, refusing to ask anything about Pegglar. I thought, if we *did* do it while I was bleeding, Gerald Fish could not father a child on me but he could tell the others that I knew what my father had done to my mother, even if I did not yet know who my father was. 'Couldn't you . . .' I began to ask Rosa but the old woman who owned the house came downstairs just then, shouting to my mother to fetch something. Rosa began talking about her Mr Gresham again and, not for the first time, I had lost my chance.

When Mr Gresham heard the tragedy that befell his typist's sisters-in-law, whom Mary had occasionally mentioned on Monday evenings as she and Mr Gresham sipped ginger wine, the literary gentleman expressed polite condolences. 'A fire! In a photographic studio!'

'They were very old.' Rosa's mother felt old herself these days. Life, Mary thought in her maudlin way, had taught her that Death was inevitable. Business was certainly slack. When Mr Gresham proposed, Mary was surprised. She scarcely felt worthy of a distinguished literary gentleman. 'How kind you are, Mr Gresham,' she said, and meant it. Rosa too was surprised. She did not expect her mother to surprise her.

Mr Gresham warned Mary of his sister's likely reaction. 'Ida will not be keen, but she won't be difficult. Her own marriage to one Arthur Gregg was miserable and shortlived. Miserable most particularly in that it was not *more* shortlived. Mr Gregg taught at a boys' school until they sacked him . . .' Another woman might have asked prying questions but not Mary Pegglar. Mr Gresham was grateful for her lack of curiosity.

Rosa met Mr Gresham at her aunts' funeral, a burial of baked meats since Pegglar's sisters had been, in effect, cremated already. Rosa's mother thanked Mr Gresham for coming. 'Your poor aunts!' he said to Rosa, looking her up and down.

'I have read your work,' Rosa told the literary gentleman. 'You'll have to settle on one version eventually.'

'Indeed!' Mr Gresham was taken aback. He wondered what made him, author of two published, albeit out-of-print, novels answerable to the daughter of some long-dead chicken fancier.

'You ought to be grateful Mr Gresham wrote so many – we badly needed the money,' Mary laughed. She took Mr

Gresham's arm. 'She is an only child,' Mrs Pegglar apologized.

'I am not a child any more,' Rosa said. 'And I was not *Pegglar's* only child, as you know full well!'

'She has her fancies,' Mary cut in quickly. How delighted Aunt Edith would have been to hear them squabbling like this at her funeral.

At first, Rosa entertained high hopes of Mr Gresham and his sister. She expected something interesting buried in the garden but life with the Greshams soon proved dull. When Rosa left school she tried to discuss her prospects. 'I could do anything,' she said. 'I wish to see the world!'

'Hush, dear, Mr Gresham is working,' her mother would murmur, sipping brandy and smiling. Ida Gregg snuffled disapprovingly and could not smile. Both women found endless little jobs to keep Rosa busy. 'What it is to be young,' Ida Gregg would sometimes sigh, and poke Rosa in the arm rather viciously. She endeavoured to train Rosa to be useful about the house.

'I shall perish like Alfie,' Rosa thought, staring mournfully into the overgrown garden where a large thorn bush made the basement kitchen dark. The house was so old-fashioned it still had a cumbersome gas-powered fridge, one of the first ever built by the look of it.

'I wish to see the world,' Rosa said, once too often. She was scouring a dirty pan that would not come clean.

'Then *we'll have to see* what can be done,' Mr Gresham promised.

'Her Aunt Edith warned me about her,' Ida Gregg often said, for Aunt Edith and Ida Gregg had somehow mysteriously been acquainted.

'I will buy you a train ticket to London, you can scour the streets of the Capital instead.' Her literary stepfather laughed at his pun. 'I will give you an allowance of five bob a week to tide you over while you look for employment.'

Rosa could have hugged Mr Gresham, but she held back, never having overcome her physical distaste. He was thin and his skin was scaly. His clothes hung off him, his fingernails were long and yellow. She wondered how her mother could bear to have the man near her. He smelt of dust.

'Put that pan on the stove,' Ida Gregg told Rosa sharply. 'The heat will melt the grease and make it easier to clean.' The expense of the train fare grieved her sorely.

'It is more than you have ever done for me,' she reproached her brother in cold jest. Brother and sister maintained a cheerless cordiality, brittle as egg-shells. Mary Pegglar, now Mary Gresham and rescued from an eternity of typing, did not especially notice the strange atmosphere in the house, or the strangeness of her new husband and his sister. When Mary found them in bed together, their sustained hostility out of bed seemed more, and yet less, explicable.

'We live as we like,' Ida said lightly.

And why not? thought Mary, registering only that the rooms in the house were chilly, and the pent-up Rosa become irksome as any large dog thwarted for exercise. Mary began then to drink unmeasured quantities of brandy and insisted, although it was not yet winter, on lighting large fires which she would sit beside, shivering.

'London?' Mary was immediately grateful for Mr Gresham's generosity. 'I will write to Max's widow. I'm sure Sarah, and her new husband, will assist you. You must do your utmost, Rosa, not to need the five bob a week from Mr Gresham longer than you can help.'

Rosa was not certain Sarah and her new husband would welcome the girl who had been in the back of the *Doublie Royale* as it sped into a ditch, but she said nothing. The evening before her departure, Rosa packed a green canvas box such as her father had used to take his hens to London and then she went to say 'goodbye'. Outside the sitting-room door she paused and looked in at the three drowsy occupants reflected in a large gilded mirror. None of them knew she was there. Her mother sat slumped, a half-empty beaker clutched in one hand, her lips skewed sideways, a dribble of dark liquid running down her chin. Mr Gresham stared unseeingly into the fire as if at an invisible machine he had invented long ago, whose workings he was now at a loss to understand. Ida Gregg perched between them thinking poisonously about all she had lost, that she'd never had.

First thing in the morning, before anyone else was awake, Rosa took the train to London. When it arrived Pegglar's daughter alighted eagerly and hurried up the platform, swinging her green canvas box by its strap and disappearing quickly into the crowds.

'Well, Jeannie!' said Rosa, smiling at me. 'We are getting there at last!'

I grinned for I knew that within days of coming to London, Rosa had encountered my mother, my father, the old lady even. Everyone I know and many I only know about. She walked blithely into their lives to devastating effect. That first week Pegglar's daughter spent in London was a week that would change the world. And now, I will tell *you* about it as she told me. Walking back through that mirror, finding her again a character in my narration, finding myself too in the voice of the narrator. Take it steady. Gerald Fish I could handle. I was so excited I told Rosa about him. She wasn't a bit upset. In fact, she laughed. 'You hit him round the chops, Jeannie! You tell him if he doesn't leave you alone, he'll have me to deal with! You tell him.'

'I will,' I said with a new quiet confidence.

'You could always invite the boy back here,' my mother, never an advocate of violence, ventured. 'He could come to tea, dear. I will bake a cake.'

'A boyfriend!' the old lady cackled.

'And why not?' I asked. Wasn't I of an age? What was so odd about me that I mightn't be like the other girls at school? I couldn't imagine what Gerald Fish would make of my home, though. I would not want him to meet my poor mother and hear the old lady ordering her about, but I would have liked him to meet the glamorous Rosa and see how fond she was of me. Perhaps that was why I had sent her to meet him face to face.

—Time's up!

—Already? She looks at her watch and swings her elegant legs slowly off the couch. She shivers and shakes herself as if getting ready to go back, to her varied glamorous life and the busy traffic in Harley Street, outside. For a moment, she looks lost: Is she me, or am I her?

—How should I know? I don't have to sound authoritative, or concerned now, not at the end of the hour. I leer in her face. Does it matter?

—I'm not sure. I no longer even know how it all started. Or why I have come here, and told *you*! In a curious way, it's as though she sent me. I can't think why . . .

—You needed someone to talk to?

—But I have others who listen attentively to every word I say.

—The girl?

—My father, too. Pegglar . . .

These women and their fathers! Poor confused creatures. How quickly when they leave here, though, they dismiss me from their minds. To detain her, I say: When I was at school there was a funny little girl, a preposterous lopsided thing. I used to follow her home. As a joke. I think of her now and hope she is happy. We made her very unhappy at school.

—She should have hit you in the teeth. I'd have done it myself . . .

—She invited me to tea, to meet her mother. But I never went.

—We all have regrets. But there's not much most of us can do about the past. Except sit there with a stopwatch, and not look bored – eh, Gerald Fish? Goodbye, Gerald Fish.

She looked right through me, so that I felt small. Like nothing. Wiped out, vaporized. Goodbye. Goodbye. Goodbye. Then she was gone.

PART III

Five Flights Up

'I'm happy to do anything,' Rosa said.

Mr McCabe was glad to hear it. People happy to do anything were rare indeed. He smiled. McCabe rarely smiled so Sarah smiled tentatively also. 'You'll want to make restitution, of course!'

Rosa frowned. She had been lulled by the welcome into almost forgetting. 'If they are not *at home*, it will mean you are not welcome,' her mother had told her. But Mr and Mrs McCabe *had been* at home. 'This is a pleasant surprise,' McCabe even said, inviting Rosa to sit in an upright chair. 'We don't often have visitors.' Now he leant eagerly forward. 'It hadn't slipped your mind, Miss Pegglar?'

'No,' Rosa mumbled.

'I should hope not!' McCabe puffed on his pipe, still smiling, only Rosa was no longer sure it was a smile, exactly, that split the old man's lips. Sarah was shifting from foot to foot but McCabe could not tell her to sit down and keep still as Rosa was occupying the only other chair. McCabe turned to the intruder, his old eyes bright and vengeful. 'I never had a vehicle I liked as much as that *Doublie Royale*. It wasn't insured for your high jinks, young lady. In the end, *I* got nothing. And I am not accustomed to getting nothing, as you shall see!'

Rosa raised a hand to her throat.

'What have you in mind?' Sarah asked. McCabe appeared not to hear. Considering the skinny scowling niece half Fanshawe, Rosa struck Mr McCabe as surprisingly, almost suspiciously *unremarkable*! The restitutions Miss Pegglar must make could be useful, and it was in just such indeterminate indebtedness

McCabe most liked to trade. Besides, there was that other unfinished business. McCabe took his pipe from his mouth: 'You need somewhere to live in London, a perch, so to speak?'

'Er, yes,' Rosa hesitantly agreed that she did.

'Perhaps I can help.' McCabe sounded grudging. He got up slowly and coughed his way over to a desk. He opened and shut drawers and ledgers.

Rosa and Sarah eyed each other tensely behind the man's back. When McCabe returned he uncurled a clenched fist and held out a key. 'The occupant of this room ran off last week, unable to come up with the rent. I trust *you* will be able to pay rent regularly, Miss Pegglar?'

'I have five bob a week,' Rosa told him.

McCabe gave a bright bitter laugh. 'The young drive a hard bargain!'

'It's all I have.' Rosa produced her purse.

McCabe felt waspish: the girl was undoubtedly taking advantage. Phipps would call him a fool and Phipps would be right. 'It's run-down,' he argued, as if with Phipps. 'I'm emptying the place.' He handed across the key.

Rosa emptied her purse of its five shining shilling pieces. McCabe waved away her thanks. He felt outmanoeuvred and sorry for himself. Rosa read the address on a tag attached to the key: Paddington Mansions, Room 23. A house with twenty-three rooms, at least! Quite how allowing her to live in a run-down mansion cheap was *emptying the place*, Rosa could not fathom. McCabe said a Mr Phipps would be round each week to collect the rent. If there was anything urgent she was to ask Jacob Phipps: by which Rosa understood that she was not to come here again, on any pretext. Sarah had enough to do. The Fanshawes had never done anything for her.

Sarah folded her arms and said nothing.

'Now you watch yourself!' McCabe said.

'I will!' Rosa stood up to go but as she stepped forward McCabe turned away. It was not goodbye, there were no thanks. At first everything had gone according to plan. Max Fanshawe came sauntering along, saw the *Doublie Royale*, spotted the keys and, wanting to impress the fluffy Lily, aware that his wife was carrying on with McCabe – to whom they owed more rent than they could pay – poor Max had been unable, as McCabe anticipated, to resist taking the vehicle.

'We'll visit my sister,' Max Fanshawe decided on the spur of that fatal moment, pulling Lily into the passenger seat, igniting the engine and swinging the magnificent *Doublie* out into the road as if he had often sat behind a wheel. As if it were not dangerous to tangle with McCabe.

The fluffy Lily giggled. 'Your sister?' she shouted, above the roar of the engine. Surely they were not driving all the way to Russia? She knew only of that exotic Fanshawe sister, the poetess who, accompanied by a female lover and an Afghan hound, had gone to support Revolution, and disappeared.

'Rosa's mother,' Max shouted back. Perhaps he could talk to Mary. A shortage of rent, McCabe's designs on his wife and his paintings were ordinary problems dear dull Mary might know how to deal with. What was McCabe, with all his hidden and not-so-hidden interests, up to? He put his foot down hard on the big brass accelerator. Vrumph!

McCabe heard the engine start but did not ring the police; there'd be other authorities to deal with the fellow. McCabe intended *nothing more* at the time than to hold an offence of temporary theft over the artist. McCabe knew nothing about art except that it could be made to fetch fancy prices. He had it in mind to collect the whole collection, while the pictures could be had cheap and were still stashed under the very bed he and Sarah lay on occasionally in the afternoons. He'd tried to suggest her husband's canvases in payment for the rent outstanding, but Sarah said Max did not want to part with his work. He had his pride, his work was out of fashion, not that it had ever been in fashion. He did not want his works collected simply because he had known people who knew Picasso.

McCabe could not have anticipated the crash; the dead Lily turned out to be somebody's daughter. To cover up a scandal and keep the story out of the papers while incidentally acquiring the pictures, it had seemed expedient to quickly marry the widowed Sarah and hope the niece in the back seat kept quiet. He may have lost the beautiful motor but the market in Max Fanshawes was now indisputably finite. A market he could control. Let the smoke die down, McCabe had thought. Cash in later.

And now, just as he intended reaping what he had sown, the girl had shown up. Seeking them out and asking favours. *I could do anything*, Rosa had boasted. And looking at the girl, so unremarkable nobody would ever pick her out at an identity parade, McCabe believed her. 'You watch yourself!' he said.

Sarah heard the warning. She escorted Rosa to the door. The girl's coat had no buttons, her funny green canvas box seemed the extent of her luggage. Sarah tried to recall Mary Pegglar, as feckless a mother apparently as the flamboyant Max had been a husband.

On the doorstep Rosa turned back. 'You have both been very kind. I came here straight from the train, you see. I'm going to be happy in London, I can tell!'

Happy? Kind? Neither Sarah nor Rosa had recognized each other from their earlier brief encounter. Any prettiness Sarah had once used to help pay the rent had long since vanished; she knew what it was to make restitution to McCabe. Rosa too had changed. Taller than Sarah now, she was no longer a child. Sarah thought she ought to *say* something. About Phipps, for one thing. About the cheap rent. London. Looking for work. But how, in a hurry at the door, could she say all she probably ought. 'There'll be a lot of temptations . . .'

'Oh, I do hope so!' Rosa fairly skipped in excitement. Hadn't her father and Philbert Farnol felt airborne also on their way to the Annual Exotic Poultry Show each spring? Rosa, whose purse was now empty, needed to find employment quickly if she were not to starve.

Sarah frowned and tried again. 'Rosa,' she said sternly. 'There are a lot of people out there waiting to exploit . . .'

'What do you mean?' Rosa faltered a little.

Sarah continued, but with less conviction: 'You should probably try and settle down. Find a partner. Marry, maybe.' Rosa stared at the woman who, married to McCabe, stood on a doorstep frantically whispering, who had also been married to Max and had known all along about Lily. 'I'd have thought your mother would have told you.'

Rosa did not say that her mother's own marriage to Mr Gresham had come as a surprise. Impatiently she waved the key.

Sarah looked at the tag. 'McCabe owns lots of shared houses.'

'Really?'

'Hush now. Perhaps we will meet again some time?' Sarah squeezed Rosa's hand and shut the door quickly behind the girl. She had said too much already. Rosa heard countless locks and bolts slide to as if she were a fox and the McCabes were frightened of her.

'What kept you?' McCabe spluttered when his wife returned. 'What does she want?'

'I don't think even *she* knows what she wants,' Sarah said quietly.

'She didn't mention the paintings . . .'

'I'm sure she doesn't *know*. She probably wouldn't be interested if she did.'

McCabe snorted. Look how the girl had bargained him down! 'A bit of a coincidence turning up, right now.'

'She's young. She just wants a good time while it lasts.'

'Well, *she* won't last long, coming here threatening me!' McCabe sighed. Not for the first time he wished he had never heard the name Fanshawe. The absurdity of our lives and schemes, a cruel joke that is played, and played out on us! Once it had seemed simple, only needing a tame art gallery, a showy catalogue mentioning celebrated people the artist had known by which he might himself become known and then, of course, a few highly publicized, highly priced sales . . . The second-rate works of the Dear Departed Max Fanshawe could become highly prized stock. Wouldn't that be restitution enough? McCabe wondered when the girl would make clear her demands and what sort of deal he would be forced to agree to in the end. He must consult Losching.

Rosa fortunately did not know about Losching. Within the hour, five flights up in a large red-brick mansion, her key miraculously fitted a lock. The stairs had been countless, smelling of damp, dustbins and ancient polish, the electric lights dim and intermittent, the paint peeling. The brightness was a wonderful surprise. Room 23 was still lit by the last of the day's sunshine, long since lost in the streets below.

Rosa tossed down her green canvas box and stretched out her arms to the disappearing sun: five bob a week, an iron bedstead, a shared bathroom on the stairs, a little gas-ring in one corner, this was the start of everything. She rejoiced in her great good luck.

Into the Early Morning

McCabe lost no time. He told Phipps and instructed him accordingly. He also told Losching, or Plotschkin, as he had been.

Old and bald, beady as any bullet still, Losching immediately denounced Rosa as a police spy. An informer, maybe. 'Too much of a coincidence, my friend,' he declared, pouring himself more of his friend's whisky. The old excitement flooded his veins. 'Go along with her story a while. If necessary, have her pegged.'

'You think so?'

Losching chewed his tobacco. 'What reason did she give for turning up now?'

'She said she'd escaped, but not what from.'

'Pschah!' Losching spat viciously. 'Too well I know the signs, my friend!'

McCabe usually relished Losching's alarmist deductions, and drastic solutions. Tonight he wondered irritably what a man like Losching could know of a girl like Rosa. Perhaps he had been wrong to consult Losching.

'It is good you consult me,' Losching said. Both men fell silent. While McCabe recalled the loss of his *Doublie* opposite him Losching thought again about Rosa's aunt, Nina. He had burnt the bloodstained poems long ago, but still found sleeping easy, remarkably difficult. He felt unreasonably punished by Miss Nina Fanshawe. He remembered the amused cold face of her disdainful lover, the earnestness of their convictions, the tinkle of their tinny English laughter. When Plotschkin issued orders that all foreigners, and their pets, be rounded up and shot on the spot if subversive material be found about their persons, he'd known she'd have poems in her pocket that could be turned into evidence in the translation.

The last time he'd seen Nina Fanshawe she was lying on a makeshift stretcher, a neat dark hole in the side of her beautiful high-minded head. He'd shown his compassion then, having her companion thrown into the lime pit with her. What happened to the large woolly dog he wasn't sure but dimly recollected a few meals of unusually edible steak. When later his men were in danger of defecting, Plotschkin had fled to England. He'd shunned other Russians in London, adapted his name and cunningly looked to Nina's family for help. 'I loved her,' he'd have said if anyone asked. Were not bullets putting creatures out of their misery, a form of love? Losching had not encountered any Fanshawes directly but for some reason Sarah McCabe had put him in touch with her new husband. McCabe helped Losching settle, bound tight his loyalties and this, even though McCabe was not Nina's family. Here apparently, arriving from nowhere after all this time, was this Rosa, Nina Fanshawe's blood niece. He did not, could not, like it. He suspected Sarah. The less devious women appeared, the more duplicitous their machinations.

'This Rosa is not *family*?' Losching wanted to establish the clear distance between his friend and the girl. Such ties as there were, were tied loosely.

'Not strictly speaking.'

'She has no call on you then.'

McCabe nodded. Losching expressed a desire to see Rosa. Neither he nor this girl were family to McCabe. Both had fled something ill defined. And Nina – there was a bond here. Losching said so. McCabe altogether misunderstood. 'She is very young,' he remarked, one weary old man to another. The sort of girl whose insistence on being taken to a poxy milk bar had done damage enough already. McCabe referred to this relentless velocity, the fearful gathering of speed. 'Ludicrous as it sounds, she is very ordinary.'

Losching licked his lips and raised his glass. 'Life is ruthless,' he sighed.

'She's only young; she wants a good time,' McCabe spoke cheerlessly.

'Who says?'

'Sarah says,' McCabe mumbled. It was like a child's game.

'What does Sarah know!' Losching laughed. McCabe's wife had never liked his usefulness to her second husband. Any suspicions she had, though, the woman sensibly kept to herself. She would survive them all.

'This Rosa,' Losching began again. '*You* want to watch out. She is capable of anything.'

'She will be watched. I have spoken to Phipps.'

'Phipps!' Are we now to be dependent on men like Jacob Phipps to protect us? We are too old for tribunals or even poxy milk bars. The old men sighed; they ordered another bottle. It seemed to them then a man could ask nothing more than that he might live to hear the cock crow and see the start of another day. They drank. They drank to Rosa. Hours later Losching raised his glass again, barely lifting it off the table. 'To Rosa!' he said in Russian this time, adding something slurred and in any case untranslatable.

Distant Music

Rosa had slept three nights now on the iron bed five flights up. Three nights after three days spent roaming alone, returning footsore to the silent building. McCabe, busy emptying the place, apparently wanted her there like a caretaker to keep an eye on the premises. Bombsites dotted all over London made the fates of even the most solid buildings demonstrably uncertain.

'It's not the same London your father and I knew,' Mary had warned. 'You won't find Percy Thirsty Higgins sticking feathers on with putrid glue, or Bluie Chapman lauding it up on the Champions' Podium! That was all long before you were born, Rosa. Nothing remains . . .'

Mary had grown quickly hysterical. Mr Gresham and Ida Gregg had difficulty calming her down. When Mary recovered at last she said she was sorry. London, the place and the past, were irretrievable. 'I have no regrets,' she sobbed in between gulps of brandy. 'None at all!'

Mr Gresham and Ida Gregg looked at Rosa. Who knew what Mary's life had been before she married Pegglar? Her girlhood was something Mary had never discussed. Yet her mother had been right; the war that had hardly touched their tucked-away lives and had been over now a decade, had bled into bloodlessness Pegglar's London. Gone were the harliquinade and all the quiet hidden places Mary had known, sites of those many tender assignations she had put behind her for ever when she married Pegglar.

The war had only affected Pegglar's sisters like an afterthought. Late one afternoon, Aunt Gracie had been standing by the kitchen window, staring into the gloom of the garden just as years before the sisters had often stood watching Pegglar at his coops. As Aunt Gracie leant against the glass, she saw something making towards her, limping and skewing across the lawn: its face distorted, the features picked out with red ink. The apparition caught sight of Aunt Gracie and paused. A splintered hand reached for its pistol but jerked away, having found no grip. Having found . . . nothing! The man – for it was a man – glanced down and saw then that his belt, holster and indeed most of his hip, even his manhood, had been blown away. Blood hung modestly like a fig-leaf in the cavernous wound gaping wide above legs that were now stilts upon which his hollowed-out carcass teetered. He was alive but he was dead. He came towards her.

Aunt Gracie, who merely thought the vision had waved to her, giggled and opened the door. She beckoned the creature, a species Noah would never have invited on his Ark, into the Pegglar kitchen. She helped her visitor to a chair and bent over him, cradling the terrible gashed head and kissing his frozen cheeks with her large warm lips.

When Aunt Edith entered the room and found her sister plying a wounded German airman with biscuits, she shrieked and fell heavily to the floor. Was not this just such a horror as she had spent her whole life guarding poor Gracie against? By the time Aunt Edith came to, blood had seeped through her best tablecloth and was dripping steadily on to the kitchen floor, right beside her face. Aunt Edith scrambled unsteadily to her feet and stared. A half-bitten custard cream dangled from ghastly mis-shapen lips, mingling indistinguishably with mangled smashed-in teeth. Wildly Aunt Edith blamed Philbert Farnol. Only the malevolent dwarf could have contrived a likeness such as this.

From maps Aunt Edith found in the airman's pocket, printed on parachute silk and bloodied, she deduced Gracie's friend had been bombing London. 'There won't be any Annual Exotic Poultry Shows yet awhile!' she'd told Pegglar's daughter gleefully. Aunt Edith was as triumphant as ever Bluie Chapman or Percy Thirsty Higgins had been.

War indeed *had* been waged on Pegglar's London. Muddy bombsites darkened every corner, roads were pockmarked and pavements cracked. Countless hungry, hardened faces avoided each other's eyes as they readjusted to fresh disappointments and disgruntlements after the years of upheaval and hope. You could not imagine anyone releasing a fancy chicken on the Underground these days, wanting to attract the attention of the pretty lady with a bright red plume in her hat sitting opposite. London was heaving with countless lone stragglers like Rosa herself. There were fortunes to be made in this grey restless city and men in neatly tailored raincoats on every street corner looking to make them. The authorities feared a breakdown in law and order. Rosa scarcely dared admit to herself how disappointed she now felt. As for the *temptations* of which Sarah had spoken, or *finding someone to marry her*, poor Rosa had scarcely spoken to a soul!

Rosa was surprised to hear a burst of distant music. It had been playing some time but only now did she open her door to listen. Although the sound was far-off, it came unmistakably from somewhere directly below. She set off in pursuit of the noise and as she moved into and through the building the music grew louder, its tones more distinct: a piano only just in tune was accompanying a rasping violin very much out of tune.

Four flights down, along a corridor and two back up, down another passage and down another different flight of stairs, a ground-floor door stood open. Rosa looked in. A thin woman sat at a shabby black upright piano with yellowed ivory keys. A small boy stood beside her holding an over-large violin uncomfortably to his chin, grinding an equally unwieldy bow dismally across its strings. He saw Rosa but continued his cacophony.

The woman at the piano also noticed Rosa. She turned briefly and smiled brightly, but she too played on, playing as though she dared not stop. Rosa advanced into the room and sat down. They might have been expecting her. A glint in the woman's eyes matched the glint of a ring on her fingers as they hopped up and down on the keys. Apart from shrieking 'And again, Simeon!' every time the boy neared the end of the piece like

Aunt Gracie thrusting custard creams into any lull threatening the conversation, the pianist practically ignored the child and the dreadful sound he made.

'Simeon' eyed Rosa warily. At last the pianist stopped with a resounding thud, banged down the lid of the piano, sprang from her stool and ran from the room. Rosa stared after her. The metronome on top of the piano went on ticking.

'Who is she?' Rosa asked.

The boy took the violin away from his chin and rubbed his jaw. 'Miss Gough,' he said glumly. 'And who are *you*?'

Rosa laughed. 'I could be anyone!' she said.

The boy accepted this. He knelt solemnly on the floor and stowed the instrument in a black wooden case that had been lying at Rosa's feet. Then he looked up. 'Will you carry it home for me?' he pleaded, still on his knees before her.

'I shouldn't think so,' Rosa laughed.

'*She* carried it for me last week,' he said beseechingly. 'Mother . . .'

Miss Gough returned. The violin teacher overheard that one word *mother*. She coloured and handed Rosa an envelope. On it was written, in a large and girlish hand: SIR ARNOLD FARAGHER. 'I'm sorry to trouble you with it,' Miss Gough spoke to the wall. 'The bill for his last ten lessons – *dear* Simeon is coming along *so* well.' She gulped. 'I'm so honoured, so glad *you* came to listen . . .'

'It was quite a job finding . . .'

'Well – goodbye, Simeon!' The simpering Miss Gough, her fingers twisting at the beads round her neck, brought her desperately fixed smile close in to Simeon's face. 'I'll see you next week, dear.'

The boy backed away. Snatching up his violin, he grabbed Rosa's hand and steered her from the room, out of the house and off down the street. In the rush Rosa turned to look back and saw Miss Gough standing at a window watching them closely.

Helen Gough blushed. In her confusion she dropped the net curtain and stepped blindly back into the room. She jabbed a finger into the metronome and then sat down heavily on the piano stool, and began to weep.

'Something extraordinary happened,' Helen Gough was sufficiently recovered to tell Miss Finch. The two friends were sitting beside the wireless in her rooms, sharing a meal of cold meats and scrubbed potatoes and listening to the Home Service. Audrey Finch tipped salad cream on the side of her plate. 'Oh?' she asked.

'Dear Simeon's mother actually came for him *herself* today. He was so pleased. I have never met her before. A charming woman . . .'

'How nice!' Miss Finch said wonderingly. Audrey Finch knew of course of her friend's concern over the boy Simeon and the way he was fetched from his lesson by a different woman each week. Many were the times she had sat in this shabby room and listened as Helen Gough criticized the carelessness of a mother who had other things to do than attend her son's violin lessons.

'I had just got the boy to perform that jolly Sarabande . . .' Miss Gough sliced pink pork luncheon meat. She cared rather more about her young pupils than they or their parents ever supposed.

'I hope she thanked you for all you have done,' Audrey Finch remarked sternly, her mouth full of lettuce. Her friend was too good to people, too inclined to be taken advantage of, she said chummily.

Miss Gough nodded. Audrey Finch looked like a rabbit, only rabbits probably didn't smear salad cream all over their food just because a bottle of it sat on the table, gratis. Helen Gough knew she was not the sort of person anybody ever thought of thanking. She offered her friend more of the rather strong raspberry cup out of the pressed-glass jug. This jug had been a present from another pupil, a little girl called Bryony Bingham who had sadly died during the war. Killed when a flash of lightning caught the steel spike of her umbrella. The gift of the jug had surely been a 'thank you'.

Miss Gough had been a little over-fond of Bryony also. How she had liked the girl to talk to her between the minuets and rondos she had learnt to play so prettily. Perhaps there had been altogether too much talking, for when Bryony had gone and Helen Gough was alone again in her dismal rooms, how miserable she had felt if Bryony had spoken happily of the Bingham family home.

When the little girl went to the seaside in the summer, Miss Gough barely slept, fearing death by drowning or Bryony's being trampled into the sand by a bolting donkey. On Sundays too, while Bryony Bingham and her sisters picnicked or went boating with their favourite uncle, poor Miss Gough passed long afternoons imagining the disasters that could befall a precious child on such outings. It had become harder and harder to let dear little Bryony go at the end of her lesson each week. 'I had a premonition,' Miss Gough would say tremulously now, 'of sudden, untoward death.'

Yet, on that final afternoon when Bryony had arrived wearing a nice woollen coat, death could not have been further from Miss Gough's mind. How she had admired the new coat, and when at the end of the lesson Bryony had said, 'I have a letter for you, Miss Gough,' Helen Gough had held the letter gratefully as she saw the sweet child off. An invitation from Mrs Bingham, a little 'thank you' for all she had done – thank goodness she had purchased that new pad of Pelham Bond note paper on which to write her reply: how kind! How unexpected! Of course I will be delighted to come!

How unexpected, yes; but oh how *un*kind! 'You have been warned!' Mrs Sheringham Bingham wrote, though *nothing* had warned Helen Gough.

A photograph of Bryony Bingham still stood on the mantelpiece. It was something Simeon looked at during lessons. The picture had been taken by a tall adult standing over the girl so that her head and the ribbon in her hair were ridiculously big. The picture had once been crumpled but then straightened out and put in the frame.

Simeon knew the little girl had been called 'Bryony Bingham' because Miss Gough had told him. He also knew that she was dead, that she had been a good pupil and fond of Miss Gough.

Simeon knew, too, how the good little girl had talked to Miss Gough and all the while little Bryony Bingham was talking, Miss Gough had harboured terrifying presentiments of death.

Simeon did not like Bryony watching him each week from the mantelpiece, hearing the mess he made of tunes she had once played in this same room, so prettily. It was something to puzzle over while he played. How could Bryony Bingham, with that stupid ribbon tied in her hair, ever have *liked* horrid hateful Miss Gough? Why had she talked to her, what had she said? And if the girl had been such a good violinist, why had she needed lessons from Miss Gough, who anyone could see was hopeless?

Simeon himself never talked to Miss Gough and, rightly or wrongly, Helen Gough had no premonitions concerning this child. Nor did she possess a crumpled photograph of him that she could straighten out and display on the mantelpiece as a warning to other pupils. Instead she was able to spend Simeon's lessons pretending that the boy was *her* son. As she banged away on the piano and Simeon slurred his Sarabandes, Helen Gough imagined the child prodigy on an international rostrum. When the handsome conductor took his hand and asked him beneath the tumultuous applause who had taught him to play so beautifully, Simeon would point into the darkness with his bow; people would turn in their seats to look at her. The conductor would beg to be introduced. 'How I long to meet such a dear good talented lady!' he would sigh. 'Bring her to my rooms afterwards!'

Miss Gough had not ventured far beyond this point. Lately she had decided that she would not mind if the conductor looked a little like Mr Carnelly upstairs. She pictured Simeon leading her eagerly up the two flights to Carnelly's rooms, rather as he had led Rosa away this afternoon. Miss Gough had managed to pull herself together before her friend Miss Finch arrived by deciding that the man had only inquired after his *teacher*. It was not essential that the dear good talented lady should also be his *mother*. Helen Gough blushed as she recalled Rosa turning round. 'He is mine,' Rosa had seemed to be saying as she hurried her son away. 'You are only a paid violin teacher.' *Of course* Simeon's mother had not thanked her! Miss Gough was not the sort of person anybody thought of thanking.

Audrey Finch sipped the raspberry cup and noticed that it was a touch strong, noticed also how Miss Gough's lipstick had smudged and an unusually higher colour glowed in her unrouged, unpowdered cheeks. Did this explain the slowing down in the trickle of pupils? It was impossible to think that there could be less call for violin lessons now than there had been before the war. 'So what was Simeon's mother wearing, dear?' Audrey Finch asked, mentioning some nice hats she had seen in the window at Swan & Edgar's during her lunch-hour.

'Hats?' Helen Gough gulped. Naturally Simeon's mother's outfit had not engaged her attention. 'I'm not sure,' she said tightly, struggling to recall something about Rosa's appearance. 'I did not notice any hat.'

Audrey Finch smiled. 'Not the sort of woman whose clothes one notices, I dare say,' she said kindly. She suspected her friend had darted about all over the place making a fool of herself like she did whenever Mr Carnelly was prevailed upon to come down to tea. She asked then after Mr Carnelly, a man of the theatre who lived on the second floor whose every movement keenly interested both women.

'He has been out all day,' Helen Gough reported.

Miss Finch hid her disappointment. It was not the same sitting here knowing her beloved was not upstairs. But there was always the excitement that he might return at any minute, and they could ask him in. 'He'll be busy with his new show,' she said.

'Yes,' sighed Miss Gough. 'At least we have *that* to look forward to . . .' She would be able to purchase a ticket when Sir Arnold Faragher paid up.

As they walked along Simeon asked Rosa what she had thought of his playing.

'I don't know why you waste your time,' Rosa told him. 'And hers, though I must say she seemed to be enjoying herself, poor

135

woman. And your parents' money, presumably she expects them to pay this bill.' Rosa waved the envelope Miss Gough had given her.

'My uncle, Sir Arnold Faragher, pays for my music lessons,' Simeon said sadly. 'Mother thinks I will grow up to be a great musician like my father. He's dead. This is his violin, you see, I inherited it. It's terribly valuable!'

Rosa patted Simeon's tousled head. 'Give it here,' she said, for the violin was far too heavy for the little boy.

'Are we going to stop?' Simeon asked. 'I usually have a glass of milk and a cake at Lyons . . .' Rosa could think of nothing *she* would like more just then than a glass of milk and a cake. 'Mummy says I can. You can have some too.'

Rosa wondered how she had got herself into this. 'The trouble is I haven't brought my purse. I came out in a hurry.'

The boy jangled his pocket. 'I've got plenty of money,' he said and led the way into the Lyons Corner House. Rosa felt faint with hunger. Simeon selected a table and hailed a tweeny. He ordered a glass of milk and an *elephant's foot*.

'And you, Madam?' The tweeny turned expressionlessly to Rosa.

'She'd like the same,' Simeon said. The tweeny nodded and left them.

'How do you know what I'd like?' Rosa asked.

Simeon grinned. He could see she was hungry. She could see one of his front teeth was missing. 'I love it here,' he confided. Rosa smiled shyly at him. How lonely she had been. 'I hate Miss Gough,' Simeon added.

'Do you?'

'Her eyes are yellow, she smells of mothballs. She's odd. She hardly says anything the whole time, but not saying anything is odder than anything she says. What's *your* name?'

'Rosa.'

'I haven't seen *you* before. I don't think I have, but all of you change all the time. Is it because none of you like me?'

'Why would I like, or dislike, you?' Rosa asked. He might have been a pretty child, she noticed – blond, and neatly dressed – yet he had sorry sunken eyes underneath that unruly mop of hair.

'I love it here,' Simeon said.

The *elephant's feet* arrived, large choux buns with thick essence of coffee icing and fluffed-up cream oozing out of the middle. Rosa and Simeon gobbled in contented silence. They licked their fingers and they licked their plates. Rosa thought of the baker making bread with his niece. Supposing her foot had shot out and struck some *elephant's feet*, sending up a shower of coffee icing and cream as a whole tray of confection cascaded to the floor. The crash would have brought people running into the bakehouse, catching the old baker at work. And serve him right, though the niece had been the one sent packing.

'I could eat another,' Simeon said.

'Why don't you?' asked Rosa, still hungry herself although not so faint any more that she could hear music playing in the distance. 'Have you got enough money?'

Simeon emptied his pocket on to the table. There were two ten-bob notes and some florins and half crowns. 'You're very rich, Simeon,' Rosa said admiringly.

The boy surveyed his new companion calmly. She had a small white face and warm friendly eyes. She was different from the usual ratty women his mother sent. She had told him the truth about his playing. He ordered sandwiches. He would rather have had another iced *elephant's foot*, but he could see Rosa was hungry and sandwiches were better for real hunger.

'How many rounds?' the tweeny asked.

'Two each,' Simeon said. 'And more milk.'

'Why do you play the violin if you hate it so much?' Rosa asked. 'Surely a boy who can command a tweeny need not be forced to play the violin?'

'They are not "tweenys". They are "nippies". Besides, it is a long story,' Simeon said.

'Tell me.'

'The violin was my father's. He died in the war before I was born. The plane he was travelling in had no maps, they got lost in the fog and crashed into the sea. He was on his way to give a concert to the troops. Unfortunately for me he had *two* violins. This was his best, the one left behind. My uncle says I should play it for my mother's sake.' The boy put his hand to his face and pinched his nose. 'For your mother's sake,' he imitated the uncle. 'So I am sent to Miss Gough's once a week. To play easy-peasy Sarabandes on a priceless violin.'

Rosa glanced at the offending instrument. To retain her interest Simeon remarked, 'He isn't really my uncle, you know.'

'No?'

'He is a rich man called Sir Arnold Faragher who suggested violin lessons as a way of getting my mother to himself for a whole hour each week. He keeps me out of the house even longer by giving me money for tea on the way home. He calls me *a good chap*. He made a lot of money during the war.'

The sandwiches arrived just then. Rosa and Simeon sat munching companionably and not speaking until they were both too full to eat any more. What a waste, Rosa thought, knowing she would be hungry again later. Simeon wrapped the remnants in a napkin and told Rosa it would be a good idea to take them home with her. 'Stuff them in your pocket,' he advised. 'The lions'd be cross if we left anything . . .'

Rosa eyed the boy sharply but took the soggy package and slipped it gratefully into her coat pocket. 'Come on, Simeon!' Rosa said at last. 'Time to get you and your precious violin home.' They walked until the boy stopped outside a house. 'Here we are,' he said.

'Well, goodbye then.' Rosa gave him his violin.

'Aren't you coming in?'

'No.'

'Will I see you next week?'

Rosa shrugged.

'Will I see you again?'

'Of course,' she smiled. 'No promises, mind! Thanks for the tea.'

Simeon walked up the garden path, climbed the steps and stood on tip-toe to press the bell while Rosa turned to go home.

In Simla

The word SIMLA in flashing red lights attracted Rosa's attention. She had walked along this same street several times during the last three days but not noticed the sign before. Now she stopped and peered into the darkened doorway. 'Are you coming in, or aren't you?' a voice in the shadows demanded.

'Oh, yes,' said Rosa meekly and hurried quickly through a set of swing doors to find herself at the top of a steep flight of stairs which she descended quickly. When Rosa dithered at the bottom of the stairs, someone directed her to a door marked *Private*. Rosa entered a large wardrobe full of mirrors and lights. Costumes hung on hooks all round the walls; discarded stockings and shoes lay scattered over the floor. Countless girls were getting dressed and undressed in a hurry, chatting hurriedly, stepping over everything, pushing each other out of the way, brushing their hair and painting their faces. The room reeked of cheap scent and fresh sweat. 'Is *this* Simla?' Rosa asked the girl nearest her disbelievingly.

The girl glanced up and was about to speak when a door on the other side of the room opened and a man stepped briskly in. 'Hurry now!' he shouted at Rosa. 'I don't pay you to stand around chatting.'

'You don't pay me,' Rosa spoke up boldly; someone else said something inaudible. The other girls giggled. The man disappeared. The girl Rosa had earlier spoken to grabbed Rosa's arm. 'Yer 'aven't a clue what yer doing, 'ave yer?'

'Er, no . . .'

'Just my luck! *And* you're late! Look, you can't go out like that. Put this on . . .' She handed Rosa a dress.

'But I . . .'

'You don't know what to do? Same old story. It's always *me* what gets landed with 'em! Look, there's no time. I'm Beryl. Just put that dress on, and – ' she dabbed at Rosa's face with brushes she had been using to dab colour on her own. 'Pale as a mask you are. Stick with me till you get the 'ang of it . . .'

Rosa took the flimsy black dress from the helpful Beryl who then scurried round and produced thin stockings and a pair of high-heeled shoes that more or less fitted.

'She's new, Mr Marcoolyn,' Beryl explained when the man who had shouted at Rosa earlier returned. 'But it's all right, she's with me.'

'I can't have first timers on the floor tonight! What are they thinking of, up there?' Mr Marcoolyn looked at Rosa accusingly and then visibly softened. You could make of this girl what you wanted. 'Still, now you're here . . .' He darted away. As if he didn't have enough to do!

'Don't you take no notice, love,' Beryl said loudly. She was a roundish girl with dark careful curls, sharp eyes and bright red lips. Every feature of her face was carefully enhanced, every movement practised, as if to say, what had to be done she would do it.

An expert, Rosa thought, following Beryl out into a very large dark room sumptuously decorated and buzzing with indiscernible activity. Bright lights in odd corners lit nothing and inaudible music wafted, disguising the excitement and steady murmur of voices. With so much to look at but nothing to see, a lot of noise but nothing to listen to, Rosa stood in her unfamiliar garments and stared around her. Simla! 'Who are they?' Rosa asked.

Beryl shrugged. She did not know or care. 'You don't want to hang back too much,' Beryl advised. 'You don't want them to think you stuck up.'

'Stuck up?'

'Easily done! Don't make no enemies, not with the other girls neither. They only get you in the end. Friends are just as dangerous.'

'I'll remember that,' Rosa said.

'Go on, then!' Beryl indicated a man at a table beckoning indifferently to them. She gave Rosa an efficient push.

'What am I meant to do?' Rosa asked.

'Sit. Chat. Tell him you like champagne, you get a shilling for every bottle he orders. How much tosh you get depends on how much he dishes. In more ways than one, but *you* have a living to earn, don't forget! Be polite whatever and remember to say, if needs must, that it is illegal to consort. Get that straight at the start. I'll come over later and you can introduce me to 'is friend.'

Rosa did as Beryl instructed. Just as she was beginning to feel silly sitting with a man who said nothing and his friend who refused to notice her, some music started up. A spotlight swung purposefully into action, striking a raised stage in the centre of the room where a dancer strutted out and commenced to hop around, defying the audience to bother to watch her. A red feather attached up her spine and over her head twirled as she moved. It was a clever dance in which she appeared to take off her clothes and put them back on at the same time. Rosa thought of Dorothy and while everyone else on the floor completely ignored the spectacle on the Podium, she sat entranced. What would Pegglar have said to see his daughter here? A hand grasped Rosa's knee. Rosa looked down. She had forgotten her taciturn companion. 'Oh, I'm terribly sorry,' she said politely. 'I must warn you if I must that it is illegal to consort.'

The man was amused. 'I like them prim and proper,' he said, nudging his friend who took no notice. Rosa's open interest in the dance had stirred him.

'And you have only ordered *one* bottle of champagne,' Rosa said. 'I don't think one shilling is sufficient recompense for my sitting with you all evening, do you? I have a living to earn, remember!'

'You do, do you?' The man was further amused. He took a roll of notes from his pocket and folded a ten-bob note neatly. He leant over and poked the hard piece of paper into the top of Rosa's borrowed dress. 'That's for you,' he murmured, his lips close to her ear.

'Thank you,' Rosa said politely,

The man ordered another bottle of champagne. Beryl came and sat down beside his friend. They started an unenthusiastic conversation Rosa could not hear. She looked at her own companion for the first time and was surprised to find he was very well dressed, and looked rather nice. 'What's *your* name?' Rosa asked, unable to think of anything else to say.

The man did not answer. He no more liked inquisitions than she did, Rosa decided. She smiled at him compassionately.

After a while the man said, 'You can call me Jack.'

'And you can call me Rosa.'

'Your stage name?'

'You could say that,' Rosa agreed.

'I've not been here before,' Jack remarked.

'Neither have I,' Rosa laughed. The man laughed too and she could see Jack thought she was joking. She obviously looked as if she belonged in SIMLA. 'My grandfather came here,' she said, thinking of the two-bit floosie who had wasted away and been buried in a discreet corner of the cemetery during an interval in a polo match. 'And my father too, probably. To console himself for not winning the prestigious silver cup . . .'

Champagne corks popped like tiger-hunting guns after that. When Jack went home rather the worse for wear, the roll of notes in his pocket considerably reduced, Beryl said, 'They are very pleased with you upstairs. Can you come back tomorrow? I have put your name down.'

'You don't know what I'm called.'

'I put *my* name down, and "times two", that way they think I brought you in and *I* get an extra shilling. Now . . .' She handed Rosa a stash of money. 'You'll need to find yourself a dress. You can't go on wearing that thing, it belongs to one of the other girls who hasn't been back. Mind you, if she doesn't come back, there isn't a problem.'

'I'm tired,' Rosa said.

'You'll get used to it.' A clock outside chimed three. 'A long lie-in and you'll be right as rain. Blimey!' The girls had now emerged above ground. It was thundering and the rain was coming down in torrents. Neither had an umbrella. 'Your coat 'asn't even got buttons,' Beryl commented. 'Where '*ave* yer come from?' She knew better than to look for an answer.

'Night, Mr Marcoolyn!' Beryl yelled harshly at the top of her voice.

The man who had organized the floor downstairs was climbing quickly out of the rain into his car and making as if he had not seen or heard them. Then he glanced at Rosa and seemed to change his mind. He let down the window. 'Go on, then!' he said. Beryl ran round the front of the car and climbed in beside Marcoolyn; Rosa got in the back.

Other girls coming up behind them grumbled at being excluded but hurried away into the lamplit rain. Mr Marcoolyn glanced in the driving mirror but it was too dark to see the girl. There was a flash of lightning and a new sheet of rain splashed heavily on to the roof and the bonnet. Rosa shivered and yawned. She spread her damp coat on the seat beside her.

'Where to?' Marcoolyn asked.

'We're taking you 'ome first,' Beryl told Rosa. Rosa mentioned Paddington Mansions. The man nodded.

'One of McCabe's,' Marcoolyn muttered, and then drove through the wet empty streets and furious flashes of lightning in dangerous silence.

The Sleepless

Miss Gough tossed and turned in her truckle bed. Simeon's mother called again, refusing to pay for his violin lessons. 'You have no cause to be jealous of me,' Helen Gough told Rosa calmly. 'I acknowledge I am his teacher, not his mother.'

'But you have taught the boy *nothing*! He is mine!'

Miss Gough woke at three in the morning when a blinding white flash irradiated the night. *Had* Simeon's mother been wearing a hat? A car door slammed and there were footsteps running in the street. By the time Helen Gough got to the window she just missed sight of the tart upstairs returning, teetering on ridiculous heels, running to get out of the rain.

Miss Gough stood awhile then, a grim smile fixed on her face. The Lord prevent us in all our doings, she thought, thinking particularly of the tart upstairs, in Room 23. From behind her on the mantelpiece, Bryony Bingham also watched the lightning flash and the rain pound down. Why had Simeon's mother shown up that afternoon, returning just now to rebuke her in a dream? Had the woman somehow discovered the truth about her son's violin teacher?

The minuets and rondos had already gone on too long that afternoon when the skies suddenly darkened. Miss Gough tried to persuade little Bryony to stay to tea but the girl had shaken her pretty little head and accepting the loan of an umbrella said, 'I have a letter for you, Miss Gough.' Could Bryony Bingham have known the contents of that dreadful letter? Had she perhaps had a hand, even, in its composition? Helen Gough shuddered and forced herself to imagine sweet Bryony saying, 'I hate Miss Gough!'

'Don't be ridiculous, child,' Mrs Bingham would reasonably have countered. 'How can you hate such a dear, good, talented lady?'

But Bryony had insisted and then the letter had been written: *I must ask you not to detain my daughter with inquisitions. I employ you to teach the violin, not to pry into our affairs. Furthermore, Miss Gough, I must warn you . . . I remain, Yours very respectfully, Mrs Sheringham Bingham.*

When Miss Gough heard of Bryony's tragic death, she had torn up the reply she'd been about to post. On the *very next* sheet of blue Pelham Bond note paper, so that if you held the letter to the light you could detect impassioned underscorings, she'd sent condolences, adding how much she looked forward to the child's funeral. *I feel I know you all, and all about you, already* . . . she had written jauntily, fully feeling the strain.

Mrs Sheringham Bingham detected a clear threat in the violin teacher's words. She instructed Bryony's favourite uncle, Herbert, to reply that under no circumstances would Helen Gough be welcome. Blackmail was a criminal offence. If she stayed away from the funeral, and desisted from all further communication, no action need be taken over the culpable loan of a steel-spiked umbrella during a thunderstorm.

Miss Gough thought of Bryony's mother now as a woman who had slammed down the piano lid hard on her fingers, crushing them and bending her ring. Miss Gough should rightfully have been invited to play the piano, accompanying little Bryony as she played, so to speak, her last minuet on this earth. She resolved to get her own back on the Binghams one day. But before Miss Gough could lift even one of her bruised, disfigured fingers, a swift merciless revenge had been savagely exacted.

War came shortly after Bryony's death, and it was during an air raid that Miss Gough had first encountered her friend, Audrey Finch. One warm, rather active night they had found themselves doing fire duty together on a roof. They were just sharing a fearless flask of sugary tea when someone cycling by below shouted out that a certain street had been hit. An explosion lit up the sky just then and Audrey Finch had glimpsed the horror on Miss Gough's face. 'You go and see if there's anything you can do, dear,' she said kindly. 'I'll be all right on my own for a while.'

It was better than Helen Gough could have hoped for. The Binghams' house had suffered a direct hit. The sharp smell of explosive and the sweet tang of death merged with the dust. While everyone was shifting rubble and laying the dead Binghams out on stretchers, Miss Gough clambered over piles of plaster-covered bricks and, in the beam from her firewatcher's torch, she had come upon the Miracle of the pressed-glass jug. Pretending to help search for more bodies, Miss Gough had been delighted to unearth also the photograph of Bryony.

It had not been looting. Miss Gough was sensible of some greater force, some higher Authority, that had been at work on her behalf that night, for these Binghams had been prevented most assuredly in all their doings. Miss Gough took her acquisitions home for safe keeping before returning to Audrey Finch, still dutifully firewatching on the roof.

'The Inspector was here,' Miss Finch said conspiratorially. 'I told him you had popped to the lav.'

Miss Gough thanked the woman who had lied to cover up for her.

'Much harm done?' Audrey asked and saw at once death reflected in the face of Helen Gough. There was dust in her eyes and blood on her hands.

'A lot of harm,' Miss Gough confirmed quietly. 'I knew the family well, too well, perhaps. I taught the little girl, Bryony.' She gulped, and Audrey Finch poured the last of the sweet tea into the lid of the flask.

'No wonder I had premonitions!' Miss Gough was able to say. If it hadn't been the lightning and the umbrella, it would only have been the Blitz. Death had stalked the whole Bingham family while in between rondos and minuets Bryony and her violin teacher gaily chattered.

Miss Finch was soon to learn of the suit Herbert Bingham had eagerly pressed. 'Was Mr Bingham – Herbert – handsome?' she obligingly asked.

'Well,' Miss Gough hesitated, not wanting to claim too much, 'perhaps not, in any accepted sense. But Herbert was such fun. How he liked jolly picnics and boating parties . . .'

'You went on these?'

'Of course! It was on the last of those picnics we came to a firm understanding.'

'You became *engaged*? To be *married*?'

Miss Gough nodded sadly. Alas, within days poor little Bryony had been killed, the wedding postponed in favour of her funeral, war then started and Herbert Bingham was called up. 'Poor Helen!' Audrey Finch said, patting her new friend's hand, asking nothing about the mis-shapen ring. Later she recounted Miss Gough's tragedy to her mother.

'A likely story!' Mrs Finch said at once. 'I don't think you should have lied to the Inspector, dear. Not on firewatching. Not to protect a woman you scarcely know.'

Audrey had been able to return home to her mother *this* evening and describe the cold meats and scrubbed potatoes she had shared beside the wireless, listening to the Home Service and listening to Helen Gough wittering on about that horrid little boy, Simeon, and his flighty mother. Mrs and Miss Finch sat in the kitchen of their maisonette enjoying a late-night milky drink and laughing together over the foolishnesses of Audrey's friend. 'And Mr Carnelly?' Mrs Finch asked, for she had a shrewd idea what prompted her daughter to visit Miss Gough.

'We didn't see him tonight,' Audrey admitted blushingly. She yawned, and then mother and daughter put papers in each other's hair and retired for the night, so at peace with themselves and each other that they slept right through the storm.

Helen Gough was not so lucky. She stood at the window in the darkness, watched by Bryony on the mantelpiece behind her. One of the bodies dug out of the rubble had been *just about alive*. Miss Gough had quickly rolled up her sleeves, fetched water in a glass jug that had miraculously survived the blast and knelt down over the stretcher. The young woman moaned and, even through all the dust and blood, Miss Gough saw at a glance the piteous creature could never have been one of

Bryony's sisters. '*You* are no Bingham!' Miss Gough said accusingly.

'I'm Jessie Smith,' the girl admitted in a weak and painful whisper. 'I was visitin', gawd help me!' She showed Helen Gough a garnet ring on her finger. The ring and the finger had been crushed in the blast. Herbert had taken up with the girl at the army camp near Brighton. When Herbert was killed on a training exercise that got bungled, Mrs Sheringham Bingham had written to his fiancée inviting her to stay in the very house from which Miss Gough herself had been deliberately, cruelly excluded. While poor Jessie had been taken aback by the gentility of Herbert's family, Mrs Bingham had been distressed by her late brother-in-law's choice of girl. And by the growing bulge about Miss Smith's waist. But then the bomb had fallen on the house, and the Binghams themselves had all been sent packing, without paper and string.

Miss Gough knelt over the stretcher and dashed water into Jessie Smith's loose, pretty mouth. The girl gasped and choked and, in the struggle to evade Miss Gough's ministrations, the fullness of her womb had viciously contracted and she'd let out a long, last strangled scream.

'You have been a Saint,' the warden said kindly, telling the exhausted Miss Gough to go home. 'You did all you humanly could.' It was only when she arrived at her rooms she found she was still carrying the pressed glass jug. The ring was an exact fit on her own crushed finger and might just as well have been given to her as to the feckless Jessie. In the stormy darkness now, the blood-red garnet flashed as the lightning flared.

'I am the sole survivor,' Miss Gough thought as she climbed wearily back into her truckle bed. 'I cannot expect to sleep easy.' Perhaps the raspberry cup she had earlier shared with Miss Finch was to blame. Upstairs she fancied she could hear Carnelly tramping around in his room. Couldn't *she*, oh joy of joys, be the cause of *his* sleeplessness? Somewhere far off, a door slammed. If only Simeon's mother *had* thanked her this afternoon, or shown some gratitude when she returned just now in the dream. 'You are only a paid violin teacher, Miss Gough!' Rosa said.

Somebody's Daughter

Marcoolyn prevailed upon Beryl and spent what remained of the stormy night with the girl. Her brother, Bernard, found them together in the morning but shut the door quietly again, saying nothing.

Rosa woke late. She opened the window and breathed the fresh clean air that had moved into London after the storm. So, the enormous house McCabe was emptying was not empty after all! Rosa was just thinking she might go and visit Miss Gough, the violin teacher downstairs, when someone rapped loudly at her door, vigorously rattling the handle. 'I know you're in there. Open up!'

Rosa unlocked the door and a large woman in a long flowing dress marched in. 'I thought I heard someone!' she declared.

'I'm Rosa,' Rosa said.

'I have a horror of rats.'

'Well, yes.' Rats had occasionally snooped round Pegglar's coops in the garden, making off with eggs and seedcorn, killing the baby chicks with a single bite to the neck.

'I wouldn't put it past him you know. McCabe will try anything.'

'I'm Rosa,' Rosa repeated. 'Not a rat.'

The woman looked at the pile of money Rosa had left heaped on the table. 'Charlotte Lefroy,' she introduced herself. 'Madame Lefroy. I live in the rooms next door – only you have to go down and then up at the other end of the corridor, because fortune has fortunately separated us off! But I can hear you through the wall. I heard you return late last night. You're as bad as the last one, of course . . .'

'The last one?'

Mme Lefroy sniffed indignantly. 'Is there a man with you?'

'Is this some sort of inquisition?' Rosa retorted in a new sharp voice, that of a tart upstairs.

Undeterred, Mme Lefroy persisted: 'So, who is paying your rent, young lady?'

'Mr Gresham.'

'Ah! He's married of course?'

'Yes.'

'As I thought!' The woman paced enthusiastically, worn slippers on her feet, a voluminous dress and several scarves swirling around her. 'He won't get me out of here, your Mr McCabe. You tell him when you see him!'

'I don't expect to see him again,' Rosa said. 'He said he would send Mr Phipps.'

'Phipps is a fool,' Mme Lefroy scoffed. 'McCabe's monkey.'

'Until yesterday,' Rosa said, 'I thought the house was empty.'

'Empty!' Charlotte Lefroy drew herself shakily up to her full height like a volcano wondering whether to explode. 'Let me tell you this, er . . .'

'Rosa.'

'Whoever you are, this house will *never* be empty. I am equal to you all! I am certainly equal to McCabe and any undesirables he cares to send.'

'Undesirables?'

'I know his tricks. Charging cheap rent to riff-raff – how much do you pay?'

'Five bob a week.'

'Five bob a week!' Mme Charlotte Lefroy was aghast. 'It is as well poor Granville never lived to see the day! McCabe thinks he's so clever, sluts banging about at three in the morning not to mention . . .'

'Teaching the violin?'

'You want to watch Miss Gough,' Mme Lefroy said darkly. She screwed up her eyes. 'You're very young to be living like this.' She paused as if deciding on something. 'Come and have

a cup of Earl Grey,' she said. 'But you had better put on something warmer than that.'

Rosa looked down at the dress she was wearing. It was the
skimpy black frock Beryl had handed her. 'I haven't got anything else,' she said, for in her tiredness she had left her other
clothes in SIMLA, and her coat on the back seat of Marcoolyn's
car.

Mme Lefroy examined Rosa as an object of possible charity.
For her daughter Valerie's sake, she might do something for the
girl. 'My dear, even you must be *somebody's* daughter! You need
taking in hand.' So saying she lead the way down the stairs,
along the corridor, up some more stairs and into a suite of rooms
which actually occupied most of the top floor. The furnishings
here were on a grand scale but ancient and used, rather like
Charlotte Lefroy herself. There was a curious smell, and a
gaping hole in the ceiling where damp plaster had come away
and a sharp chill blew in. Mme Lefroy clattered into the kitchen
and began to talk.

'My daughter, Valerie, is the last of the Lefroys. I was a
Verpool, by the way, before I married. The two families, the
Verpools and the Lefroys, have been interlinked by marriage,
and otherwise, over many generations. The Lefroys fled France
during the Revolution. Stripped of their lands and titles, they
came to England with only their necks and a piece or two of
Sèvres intact. Some prospered, some did not. Granville – my
husband – was descended from the Lefroys who once owned
whole areas of London, but fortunes are harder to hold on to
than melting butter. By the time I knew him, only this place was
left. By the time Valerie was born, Lefroy had moved us up into
these rooms and started to let out the floors below. Granville,
alas, gambled away the rights to those rents. I came home one
day and found him, here in this kitchen, his brains blown out all
over the floor. Just there!' She pointed to a large dark stain on
the lino where Rosa was standing. Rosa shifted her feet.

'Good breeding shows at such times: the linoleum was easy to
mop. What a shame if one of the ancestral Turkey rugs had been
damaged. There's little enough as it is for Valerie to come and

collect when I die. No Lefroy can ever be said to have brought this linoleum back from the Crimea . . .

'Not that I blame Granville. He thought he had destroyed us all and took the honourable way out. The Brixton and Battersea Lefroys weren't the only ones who had the gall to come then; McCabe showed up at the funeral waving deeds. I took the documents and pretended to read the signatures. *They're legal*, McCabe said. *So's fishing!* I told him, and tore up the papers right under his nose. Valerie screamed her head off. If McCabe thought he was going to turn Granville Lefroy's widow and his orphan out into the street just because of some . . . Men like McCabe are two a penny. I told him so. I was a Verpool, I entered this house on my wedding day and intend to stay in this house till Kingdom come. A state of armed truce, you might say, prevails. And now you know the full story I suggest, my dear, you decide pretty quickly which side *your* bread is buttered on!' She poured dark tea into a cup which she handed to Rosa. Then she poured tea into another and deftly added something from a little bottle she kept in her pocket.

Rosa held the teacup – pre-Revolution Sèvres, brought from France by Lefroys fleeing the red blade of the guillotine – chipped now. She gulped down the heavily scented tea, itself stashed away and stale from pre-war days. 'So where *is* your daughter, Valerie?'

Charlotte Lefroy acted as if she had not heard. 'Come through!' she called, clumsily clattering the porcelain down on the table and sailing back into her living room with its gilded chaises and faded draperies swathing the dirty windows. 'We must find you something to wear.'

Mme Lefroy's extensive wardrobe occupied one side of another enormous room. A cupboard crammed full of sumptuous moth-eaten stuffs. An extravagant plume attracted Rosa's attention. 'Did you ever go to the Annual Exotic Poultry Show?' she asked.

Mme Lefroy stared at Rosa. 'My dear child! Did I ever go? Why, Granville was frequently called on to give out the prizes . . .'

'To Bluie Chapman? To Percy Thirsty Higgins?' Not, alas, to Daddy. Not while the dwarf photographer sat clapping loudly, over-exciting the fowls so that they played up on the Floor and had to be shooed ignominiously back into their green canvas boxes.

Mme Lefroy laughed. 'I wouldn't know about that, the past becomes increasingly vague the more there is of it.' She started to hand items out of the wardrobe, a green crocodile handbag, grubby gloves of finest kid studded with diamanté, paisley shawls. When Rosa had settled on a shapeless dress which was just about wearable, Mme Lefroy lost interest.

'My daughter, Valerie, always wore nice things,' she said wistfully, wandering back into the main room. 'I don't like to see young people without nice costumes. It's like going to a bad play, got up on the cheap – my dear, you must come and help yourself any time you need something.'

'It's very kind of you,' Rosa said.

'Of course, it was different before the war . . .'

'At the Annual Exotic Poultry Show?' Rosa prompted eagerly.

Mme Lefroy made a petulant gesture. 'When the bombing started I hoped they might flatten this place. It would have served McCabe right to lose his deceitful investment. Bombsites are two a penny these days. He'd not get much for it. There's too much rebuilding with too little regard. I never went down to the shelters with the other tenants. Most of them have been intimidated out by McCabe. Even the girl who was in your room last seems to have gone. Not Miss Gough, *she* never hid from the enemy. She was always out there at night, firewatching and looting from the dead. Neither McCabe nor Herr Hitler could intimidate me. I have to stay here now, you see, it's the only place Valerie would know where to find me. I am always here. In case she comes,' Mme Lefroy was weeping. Then she paused and looked at Rosa sharply. 'I could employ a girl like you.'

'To do what?'

'Run errands. Do missions.' Mme Lefroy bent forward. Her breath smelt extraordinary. 'Find Valerie for me. With *your* contacts, *your* expertise . . .'

Rosa stared at Mme Lefroy. 'I wouldn't know where to begin,' she said.

'Nothing could be simpler.' Mme Lefroy turned away and took a barely concealed swig from her flask. She stood it openly on the table. 'You have only to go about, ask questions, talk to people and Valerie will come to you. I will pay you well. You will find the name of Charlotte Lefroy raises eyebrows. You will have no difficulty, a girl like you . . .' She belched.

Marcoolyn nudged Beryl awake. She moved, moaned and then opened her eyes. Her curls were disarranged, the painting on her face smeared. From behind this dishevelled mask, she smiled sleepily at Marcoolyn.

Marcoolyn had been awake some time, a cigarette jabbed between his lips. 'What do you know of that girl who was with you last night?'

Beryl tried to remember. Yes, there had been. Dimly she recalled Rosa appearing from nowhere, unsuitably dressed and for some reason latching on to her at once. Pretending not to know what to do, and then turning out a natural. Beryl had signed down for her; it had been a good cut and there would be more if the girl returned. 'That would be telling,' Beryl said cautiously.

Marcoolyn didn't like it. 'She's come from McCabe; I'm sure of it,' he said. 'There'll be some angle . . .'

'Oh yer?' Beryl laughed but clipped her laugh short.

'Well, where *did* she come from? No one's seen her before. I hold *you* responsible, Beryl, and you know what that means!'

'I'll find out what I can,' Beryl said sullenly.

'You do that.' Marcoolyn stubbed out his cigarette. He got up and started dressing. His was a wiry nimble frame. He knew how to move quickly when threatened. 'You befriend her, Beryl. Find out all you can.'

'You said *you*'d find something for Bernard,' Beryl said. They could hear the large lumbering brother moving about in the kitchen.

'I haven't forgotten.' Marcoolyn prepared to slip away from

the house. He did not want to meet Bernard's open stare. 'And if you know what's best for your precious brother, Beryl, yer won't forget, neither.'

The Caretaker

Helen Gough waylaid Rosa on the stairs. She did not recognize either Simeon's mother of yesterday evening and in last night's dream, or the tart upstairs returning, clattering on high heels at 3 a.m., waking everyone up. 'Who are you?'

'I am the new caretaker,' Rosa announced proudly.

'Sent by McCabe?'

'Yes.'

'Well, you had better take care then!' Miss Gough spluttered. 'There's no shortage of things you can take care of for me. The storm may have washed my windows outside, but *inside* they are disgraceful. I have mentioned the matter to Mr Phipps of course, but,' Miss Gough giggled girlishly, 'Jacob is usually distracted. Fastidious men like Mr Phipps are so easily . . . Then there's that right Jessie Smith upstairs, bold as brass, coming back here at all hours, waking dear Mr Carnelly I dare say, for he was certainly awake. You had better take care of her, before I do!'

'Certainly, Miss Gough,' Rosa said. She decided to go for a walk to get away. Miss Gough watched Rosa go and then fled back into her room to sit on the piano stool and think.

We have an informer in our midst, Miss Gough thought. Whoever the young woman was, she had known her name! Miss Gough knew she must warn Mr Carnelly about this caretaker who came from McCabe and came well disguised.

Mr Phipps arrived just then with his briefcase and Miss Gough tried to explain that lessons had been given that had not as yet been paid for. Phipps sighed. 'I'll have to take a charge . . .' He looked round the shabby room to fix on something to charge against. There was only a tin music stand worth a few pence and the worn-out piano that would cost more to shift than it could possibly fetch. He saw no use for a ticking metronome. 'You have a wireless, Miss Gough?' he asked wearily.

'I could not live without my wireless,' the woman said firmly.

'If you pay your rent promptly you will not have to.'

Miss Gough gave Phipps her coyest smile and slunk cat-like into the kitchen, returning with some coins she had hidden away in a jar. As she handed these over her dry hand brushed his, lingering slightly. Jacob Phipps shuddered at her touch.

Helen Gough did not mention the new caretaker in case Phipps decided he needed a rise in rent to cover the cost of employing someone to keep an eye on them. Perhaps Phipps did not know. The caretaker had possibly been put in the house by McCabe to check up on Phipps also. There was no love lost between Miss Gough and Jacob Phipps, no love at all, despite years of hands touching as coins were handed across. Helen Gough had no reason to warn *him*. Phipps could take care of himself.

Phipps knew the rents here were not worth collecting. It was only one of many jobs, and he liked to get it over with. He knocked on Carnelly's door and was surprised to find the old man at home. Usually the rent was left in an envelope along with a theatre ticket, gratis.

'Oh, it's you!' Carnelly seemed relieved. 'I overslept.' Mr Carnelly had the money ready but was too preoccupied, or tired, to enter into unnecessary conversation.

At the top of the top flight of stairs, Charlotte Lefroy stood waiting. 'I know your tricks,' she said as Phipps ascended, but Phipps had no time today. If McCabe was soft here, what could he do? A compassionate side to him had Mr McCabe, Jacob Phipps reflected. No one could hold McCabe responsible after all this time for what had happened to Granville Lefroy. Or the daughter, Valerie.

Phipps followed Mme Lefroy into the crowded attic rooms she occupied and handed her the envelope he always brought, ready prepared. She in her turn offered him a glass of red biddy which he declined. The old girl's innards would be completely pickled by now. She could not last long which was probably why McCabe let her stay. The stench up here was terrible. 'She'll help to empty the place,' McCabe had said, laughing.

Phipps knocked on the door to Room 23 and when there was no reply he went in and helped himself to five bob out of the money left lying on a table, although nothing was owing now until next week. He would hold it in advance, as it were. Jacob Phipps ticked Rosa off his list and then looked round the room. Hadn't he been told to keep an eye?

He picked up a black dress that lay lizard-like on the floor, a discarded silky skin. He smoothed a coarse fat hand over the slippery fabric as if sizing up prepared flesh at a poultry show. Slaughtered birds, dressed and stuffed. Wedding breakfasts ready for the eating, not squawking in boxes as they waited like brides to be culled and consumed. There were perks to Phipps's job, and why should not this Rosa, as the girl before her, perhaps be one of them? Phipps relinquished the dress, which slithered to the floor and writhed as he kicked at it savagely with his boot. 'Do what you have to,' McCabe had said.

Phipps started towards the next building on his list. As he passed a newsagent's stand selling magazines, a picture of a celebrated couple seated in their comfortable drawing room caught his eye. Inside the publication, which was not the sort of publication Phipps generally looked at, a series of photographs depicted the couple's domestic bliss. Why not *Mr and Mrs Jacob Phipps, At Home*, he thought, imagining his own face in place of the man's and a face that could be Rosa's instead of the woman's. Why not Mr and Mrs Phipps – the Perfect Pair: eight pages of glossy photographs. Little Phippses playing with a train set running round the feet of furniture from Heal's. Why should it not be fashionable to be, or to know, a Phipps?

Generations of Phippses, his unknown father, his father's father, an endless procession of stout bald men passed before his eyes one after the other, a little light in the darkness as each walked alone his allotted time and then sank back again into the vast cold expanse of friendless water. Jacob Phipps wondered briefly how he had become a man with a briefcase, furtively reading magazines on a newsagent's stand.

'You're Phipps!' someone said. A man he had seen before. Phipps drew himself up. 'We haven't had the privilege,' Marcoolyn said.

Phipps returned the magazine abruptly to its rack.

'Something more suitable for Sir, perhaps?' the newsagent muttered close by Phipps's elbow, but before something 'more suitable' could be produced, McCabe's man had picked up his briefcase and, Marcoolyn at his heel, walked on.

A Liar & A Thief

Mrs Faragher said, 'What kept you, Simeon?'

'She did. She asked a lot of questions.'

'Of all the nerve! She's only a violin teacher!'

'Couldn't I give up the violin?'

'Faraghers are not bolters!' Mrs Faragher had forgotten to organize a girl to fetch Simeon this afternoon but he seemed to have found his way home, all the same. Now Constance Faragher had one of her headaches. His elder sister, Marjorie, never gave her headaches. She hurried to her room to lie down while Simeon wandered round the Faragher house picking up Faragher money. He liked to have money in his pocket. Sometimes he helped himself to money that was not, strictly speaking, lying around.

Marjorie Faragher regarded the little brother who had arrived when she was already in her teens as nothing but a pest. Loudly and laughingly she told everybody so, but she did not tell everybody that she had her suspicions and that she was probably not the only one. A wartime baby, born late, born indeed while Daddy was away supervising his clever inventions in his cleverly camouflaged factories.

If Sir Arnold Faragher had *his* suspicions, which he could not fail to, he never gave any indication. He paid for the boy's violin lessons and teas in the Lyons Corner House. Sir Arnold also paid five shillings a week, and often more, to a Miss Dulcie Dee, a convenient undomestic arrangement that suited both parties. It suited Mrs Faragher too, though officially she did not know of the transaction. Dulcie Dee spent her days working in an art gallery owned by a man who, as it happened, insured with McCabe.

At the moment, Dulcie was taken up with an exhibition of some artist who was somehow connected to McCabe. Max Fanshawe alive might have interested Dulcie (most men did) but dead neither he, nor his pictures, were candidates for her attention. Miss Dee was employed at the gallery more for the artistic line of her calves than her interest in paintings. People came to the gallery to look at Dulcie. Occasionally they purchased pictures. Sir Arnold was one such art lover.

If her husband was busy and famous, Constance Faragher was, if anything, busier and more famous. She ran *the* Agency. The place you could rely on to get humdrum tasks about the house respectably, speedily accomplished at relatively little cost to yourself. Mrs Faragher had been distressed to see all the aimless girls who would once have been permanent domestic servants wandering London's streets when, by an unfortunate irony, Mrs Faragher and her friends found it impossible to find staff. Housekeepers, parlourmaids and tweenys had all disappeared, wiped out it seemed with the war. Factories like her husband's paid women high wages so that they refused to live in someone's attic, all found, for thirty years. Mrs Faragher had set about matching downtrodden girls she waylaid with people she encountered socially who had jobs they wanted done. What had started casually as an exercise in common sense, mutual advantage and the taking of modest commissions, rapidly grew into a large scale business. Mrs Faragher's Agency soon acquired premises in Pall Mall, telephones, tiers of wooden filing cabinets and headed note paper.

'I think of it as harnessing the right horse to a particular carriage,' Mrs Faragher enjoyed telling clients. Dulcie Dee had been one such horse. A girl nobody nowadays could describe as *downtrodden*. When Arnold had been knighted for war-work, Mrs Faragher had been irritated to see the man's neglect of her rewarded, but the title (which she refused on the whole to use) meant people who might have balked at taking on someone supplied by an agency could now claim the distinction of having had Lady Faragher's personal assistance. The only thing Mrs Faragher was ever short of was time. She had no time certainly for the boy Simeon. His presence was a constant rebuke. She applied a cold compress to her head.

Next morning Mrs Faragher was up betimes, fully recovered and at the office in Pall Mall. What a remarkable woman Constance Faragher was, everyone said it of course, and Audrey Finch liked to tell her so to her face.

'You have such remarkable energy, Mrs Faragher,' Miss Finch greeted her employer warmly this morning. When *she* had arrived two hours ago, it had been as much as she could do to drag herself up the steep stairs.

Constance Faragher paused. Since these days the day-to-day running was left entirely in the capable hands of Miss Finch, why this unprovoked burst of admiration, this particular morning?

'Miss Gough tells me you collected Simeon *yourself*, from his violin lesson yesterday,' Miss Finch probed.

'Oh?' Yesterday? What did Constance Faragher know of *yesterday*?

'Miss Gough remarked on your charming outfit, Mrs Faragher, the hat especially. "That'll be the one from Swan & Edgar's?" I said, but she was in such a flutter, and quite incapable of any description . . .'

'Audrey, my dear, I don't know what you are talking about! The boy came home on his own.'

'But Miss Gough . . .'

'I have never once met your wretched friend Miss Gough. You know how pointless social intercourse bores me. How everything bores me!' Mrs Faragher smiled meaningfully at Miss Finch. 'I forgot to send anyone this week, if that's what you're driving at. I had such a headache.'

Many were the times Audrey Finch had sat in Miss Gough's room as the silly woman remarked on the carelessness of a mother who employed girls *from an agency* to collect her son from his violin lessons. Miss Finch had never let on her own involvement with the boy's mother, or that same agency. 'Who *did* collect Simeon, then?' Miss Finch gurgled. 'Somebody must have. Miss Gough cannot have *invented* the creature, can she?'

'How should I know?' Mrs Faragher sighed. 'We only persist with the violin lessons to get the boy out of Marjorie's way. It's a priceless violin, of course. I took it in place of a debt, during the war.'

'Yes.' Audrey Finch had heard of it often. 'We have a busy day, Mrs Faragher. I am interviewing girls this afternoon . . .'

'Again?'

'We never have enough for all the jobs.'

'Don't let our standards slip, Miss Finch. We can't let in riff-raff. Now, I really must get on! I too have a busy day before me.'

Miss Finch sighed. As soon as her employer had gone, she opened a drawer to retrieve the framed photograph of her lover and propped it up for all to see in the middle of her desk.

Marjorie Faragher was a contented daughter, quite determinedly empty headed and with nothing much to do. A state of affairs which accorded happily with her temperament. She wrote occasional letters to old schoolfriends and talked a lot on the telephone to no one in particular. She also had three established suitors who were invited to tea once a week, all three together, at the same time on the same afternoon. Jolly occasions indeed: Miss Faragher exerted herself unsparingly while Binkie, her little black Scottie dog, let rip.

The three suitors would arrive at the appointed hour bearing lavish arrays of flowers and huge beribboned boxes of chocolates and while they jostled together on the Faraghers' wide front doorstep, Binkie barked and rushed about furiously. Like a blushing bride, Marjorie would take her time coming to the door but eventually the three would be admitted, divested of their coats and gifts, and ushered into the cold living room to sit in a row while Miss Faragher presided merrily over them, and over the tea things.

Marjorie's chief occupation the rest of the week was scouring magazines for useful beauty tips. She also enjoyed devising jolly little tasks. One time Freddie would be called upon to drink his tea with the whole contents of the sugar bowl more or less dissolved in it. Charlie might gaily be instructed to sit on the floor beside Marjorie's plump, pampered Scottie dog, and imitate Binkie begging for a custard cream. While Freddie choked on the syrupy gunge or Charlie damaged the knees of his best trousers, Marjorie threw back her head and laughed so compellingly that the others felt forced, albeit uneasily, to join in. Every week Marjorie would openly compare the quality and choice of the gifts they had brought and make mocking remarks about their clothes, shoes, cuts made shaving and pimples shining like red beacons on their noses. Nothing was safe from the afternoon's mirth.

This was a game with rules. Rules William Sharp did not understand. He sat through the tea parties stolidly blinking. *He* was not after Sir Arnold's money. It was his mother who always insisted Marjorie Joan Elizabeth Faragher was destined for him. She and Constance had known each other back in the days when neither of them were yet Mrs Faragher or Mrs Sharp. In vain did poor William return home each week and try to impress on his mother the merciless teasing that had taken place. 'Nonsense!' Mrs Sharp laughed off her son's sufferings. 'An heiress like Miss Faragher is bound to have other admirers – I would never have expected otherwise, William.'

Each week, while Marjorie flitted and flirted about the room, William Sharp surreptitiously fed Binkie tit-bits and attempted to think about happier distant things. Now and then Marjorie would turn on him tauntingly: 'What do *you* say, Silly-Billy?' And William would thrust his hands deep into his pockets, and say nothing.

Marjorie Faragher did not deliberately set out to torment William Sharp. She had known Silly-Billy all her life. The tea party had become such a regular event she gave little thought to its jolly proceedings. The main function of the afternoon was to keep her dear mother at bay. Like most mothers, Mrs Faragher occasionally spoke to her daughter about her future happiness. 'You really ought to choose someone and settle down, dear.' Marjorie would then reach for one of the boxes of expensive chocolates and untie the ribbon. 'I do so like a selection box,

Mummy,' she'd say, and Mrs Faragher could only smile as she helped herself to a gigantic strawberry cream. There the matter of Marjorie's future happiness generally rested.

The afternoon when the suitors called was the afternoon on which Simeon had his violin lesson with Miss Gough. This was Sir Arnold's clever idea after the young Simeon had been caught going through the three suitors' coat pockets. 'You young rapscallion!' Freddie Bodman-Bligh had come unexpectedly into the hall and caught the thief red-handed. Back in the living room, William Sharp eased his collar. Hadn't *he* spotted Simeon, Marjorie's unfortunate little brother, only the week before, his hand in Charlie Chadwick's pocket helping himself to funds?

'I wouldn't if I were you,' William Sharp had whispered, giving the boy a few shillings from his own pocket. 'There'd be such a rumpus . . .'

Simeon had smiled shyly, snatched the coins out of William's hand and run away upstairs. Freddie Bodman-Bligh was all in favour of calling out the Constabulary but Silly-Billy pointed out that Simeon was only nine years old. He ought to join them for cake. Even Binkie had been allowed to catch crumbs. This made Marjorie as angry with her suitors as she was with Simeon. William Sharp had never spoken so much before and seemed not to take the situation seriously. Sir Arnold, summoned home to deal with the crisis, pointed out that the problem only arose once a week on the afternoon the three steadfast suitors came. His eye had alighted on the priceless violin his shrewd wife had taken in lieu of a debt during the war. Surely it was not beyond the abilities of his wife's agency to find the boy some violin lessons and send a girl to collect Simeon and take him out for tea. 'Tea?' shrieked Mrs Faragher. 'And the girl I am to send? Is she to be treated to tea, at a Lyons Corner House, also?'

'I don't see why not,' Sir Arnold said. In his experience, girls were quite partial to teas.

Mrs Faragher had spoken to her assistant, who recollected meeting a violin teacher while firewatching during the war.

Miss Finch had called on Miss Gough in her rooms, re-establishing their friendship. Shortly afterwards Simeon had been sent for the first of his lessons.

Perhaps Simeon had eaten too much tea at the Corner House yesterday. He'd slept badly. In his dream, Rosa said, 'You ungrateful little boy! You lied to me. Why did you say Sir Arnold was your uncle, but not your real uncle, and that your father was a famous violinist who died in the war? You won't get round me with rounds of sandwiches, you know! I shall have to write Miss Gough a letter.' Now Rosa's and his mother's faces were confused. 'Miss Gough will take you over the way she took poor Bryony Bingham over, and we all known what happened to Bryony . . .'

'What did happen?' Simeon asked, advancing towards the photograph on Miss Gough's mantelpiece with a bright red crayon, and colouring the ribbon in Bryony's hair. The colour brought Bryony Bingham to life. She started to scream. Simeon woke then in the middle of the stormy night, too afraid to move or make a sound. Too afraid of his dreams to go back to sleep.

In the morning Mrs Faragher bustled off to Pall Mall without looking in on her son so that Marjorie found Simeon still in bed, later in the day. 'Oh really!' she said impatiently. 'If it wasn't for you . . '

Marjorie stopped short at the sight of the boy peering out at her cautiously from beneath hot sticky sheets: it was the face of a little sick monkey. She sat down on his bed with a heavy sigh.

It was all very well the way Freddie, Charlie and old Silly-Billy came each week to sit downstairs like a row of tame tigers in a ring. Not one of them had ever got down on bended knee and begged for her hand. Only once, that afternoon Simeon had been caught stealing, had matters ever felt they might come to a head. Even William Sharp had spoken out then. And Binkie had taken advantage of the furore to climb up on to Silly-Billy's lap. Marjorie herself had never sat on Silly-Billy's lap! The merriment of all the subsequent tea parties, when

Simeon had been conveniently out of the way learning the violin, might have evaporated had it not been so well rehearsed, and its performance not come so easily to them all.

Yesterday afternoon, however, when the doorbell rang and Marjorie peered out from behind the curtains, only Charlie and Freddie jostled on the doorstep. She'd looked forward to ticking Silly-Billy off, but when Binkie had spent the whole afternoon, like some faithful Greyfriars Bobby moping beside the absent feet of William Sharp, Charlie Chadwick had coughed. Freddie Bodman-Bligh smirked. *Their* flowers had never been more splendiferous, *their* chocolates were as beribboned as ever.

At last Freddie spoke, 'I say, Marjorie, I've got something frightfully exciting to tell you!'

'It's Silly-Billy!' Marjorie cried tremulously. 'What's he done now?'

'No,' Charlie intervened. 'Not William.'

Then Freddie had told her there was to be an announcement in *The Times*. He wanted her among the first to know. 'I'm sure you'll both be the best of friends,' he concluded, speaking breezily of his fiancée. 'She really is awfully topping . . .'

'I'm sure she is!' Marjorie bared her shining teeth. She turned to her last remaining suitor. But instead of signalling to Freddie to leave the room, Charlie had seized the sugar bowl and, tipping its whole contents into Marjorie's own cup, he'd thrown himself down on bended knee and without the slightest regard for his trousers, romped round the floor with a reluctant Binkie, snuffling and begging 'dear Miss Faragher' for yet another of her delicious custard creams!

The flawlessly beautiful Marjorie Faragher looked on with a smile as fixed as the afternoon's capers. The tea parties were over. The steadfastness done with. It was all Simeon's fault. The son of a thief who had stolen into her mother's wartime affections had stolen money from the three suitors' pockets, but *she*, her father's daughter, was the one truly robbed. Sir Arnold's money would have to be divided. Marjorie's inheritance was not what it would have been if Simeon had never been born.

She looked down at the red monkey face and pitied her

brother for the degree of her dislike, but she pitied herself more. She remembered a schoolfriend in Switzerland with whom she had kept up an occasional correspondence for no reason.

Simeon wished Marjorie were not sitting quite so close. He wished his friend Rosa were here to protect him, to whisk him away out of danger rather as she had carried home his heavy violin. His sister's silence recalled the brooding silences and long stares of his violin teacher hunched over the yellow keys of her piano. Simeon groaned and rolled over.

'You need a tonic,' Marjorie said briskly. He needed something to fix him. 'I'll see what I can find.'

She hurried away and returned carrying a spoon and a large bottle of something dark red. She had a suitcase to pack. She extracted the cork. The stuff smelt suitably medicinal. Marjorie poured out a purposeful dose and ordered Simeon to sit up and open his mouth. 'Now swallow! I don't know what it does,' she said, wrinkling her carefully powdered nose; the friend in Switzerland was married and a bore but would have to do. She didn't have many friends. 'Drink it down anyway!'

Simeon drank.

Price Tickets

Losching asked McCabe if he had had any trouble yet.

McCabe said no, the exhibition was going ahead as planned. Perhaps he had over-reacted, the girl had no call on her uncle's pictures. She had shown no interest. If anything, she appeared to have forgotten.

'You cannot be too careful,' Losching commented. Had Phipps reported back?

Of course Phipps had not reported back, there had scarcely been time. And if she didn't manage to pay her rent that was no different from many others.

And how was this girl, Nina's niece, going to pay? Where was her money coming from? There'd be mischief in this somewhere. 'She's an agent of destruction,' Losching said. 'Paid by the enemy.'

'She's a young woman let loose in London,' McCabe contradicted his friend, annoyed to find himself defending Rosa.

Rosa meanwhile was astonished to be accosted by a breathless Beryl who, unlike Miss Gough, did recognize her from the night before. Rosa had returned to the Lyons Corner House to eat some breakfast and Beryl had spotted her through the steamy window. 'I was hoping to find you,' she said. 'This is my brother, Bernard.'

Beryl pushed the bear-like Bernard into the seat opposite Rosa and sat down beside him. She started to ask Rosa questions. Rosa felt very tired. She was unaccustomed to so little sleep but it was not just from tiredness that Rosa was yawning. She hurried away as soon as she politely could, not before Beryl had extracted a promise that she would come to SIMLA again that evening. Beryl also asked about the new dress. 'This?' Rosa had to look down to see what she was wearing. 'Oh, I was given it this morning.' Beryl was happy. She could tell Marcoolyn that Rosa had *indeed* been evasive and *would* be coming tonight and that there *was* someone who gave her dresses. Bernard did not notice Rosa's departure. He picked up a teaspoon and, bending it between his great paws, he snapped it in two.

Rosa saw the name MAX FANSHAWE on the poster outside the gallery and stopped. 'You hadn't forgotten? It hadn't slipped your mind?' The little back street was rather a sedate setting to encounter Uncle Max again, Rosa thought. There was even a children's puppet theatre across the road. She remembered Max Fanshawe carelessly tossing down his great cloak and putting his feet up on her mother's typing desk, like a character coming on-stage in a pantomime, leaving the audience to ask what he had come for? They had never found out.

She entered the gallery. At a desk by the window a girl was vigorously buffing her nails and glancing out hopefully every now and then at the few people passing by. 'Do you want a catalogue?' she asked.

The intruder hesitated.

'Three shillings and sixpence,' the girl said, holding one out carefully to avoid damaging her nails.

Rosa glanced at it and then met the girl's stare. 'Is the artist dead?' she asked, despite the unmistakable self-portrait reproduced on the cover. You had only to look at his chin. 'Did Max Fanshawe die in a car crash?'

Miss Dulcie Dee had not read the catalogue herself and knew nothing about Max Fanshawe except that he *was* dead and had left behind a lot of dull pictures that had needed labelling. The man had somehow been connected to McCabe, which probably explained why he was dead. Dulcie flipped through the short chapter entitled 'Autobiographical Notes' and quickly found a reference to a traffic accident. A loss to mankind. A severe blow to the art world. 'Yes, it seems he did.'

'Ah!' Rosa looked round the gallery with new interest. 'He was my uncle,' she said softly. 'I was in the *Doublie Royale* at the time.'

'Were you now?' Dulcie Dee felt instantly sympathetic. Uncles were Dulcie's way of explaining away older men. Like Simeon Faragher had needlessly, Dulcie of necessity often described Sir Arnold as an 'uncle' whose money conveniently paid for things. 'Look, borrow one of these while you're here,' she said to Rosa, 'seeing as you're . . .' she coughed delicately, 'interested.'

'Thank you,' Rosa said and started to look at the paintings.

Philbert Farnol's photographs had distorted and deformed the world he recorded, Max Fanshawe merely reduced what he saw to canvases covered in overbright paint. Underneath each picture was a neatly printed label with a name and number. 'Are these the prices?' Rosa asked the girl, for the numbers on the labels were somewhat large to be sums of money despite the pound signs.

'Everything has its price,' Dulcie laughed. 'You must know that as well as I! We only expect to sell one or two. To establish a market. Then the rest will be worth far more. McCabe will be a rich man.'

Rosa stared. Most were bold brash townscapes. Pegglar's London. And a few portraits including a picture of Lily, recognizable by the fluffiness. 'Not for sale' the tag said underneath, but an early painting of the young Nina had a red star below it. 'What does that mean?' Rosa asked, pointing.

'It shows the picture is sold.' Dulcie made it clear by her tone that she had answered more than enough questions. The young Nina had been sold to Losching. The red star signifying the exorbitant price on the tag, on her head, had been paid. Rosa slowly walked to the back of the room.

'Excuse me, I couldn't help overhearing.' A man lurking in a corner made Rosa jump. 'Was Max Fanshawe really your uncle?'

'Yes. I was with him and Lily in the car when he died.'

'How very interesting. Very interesting indeed,' the man said lugubriously.

'Does he interest you?' Rosa was surprised.

'Max Fanshawe? No, he was someone who knew people but was not himself known. A flamboyant figure, a minor talent. A minor loss; of social, rather than artistic interest, I would say.'

'Ah!'

'Not much of an artist at all in fact,' the man went on. He hesitated and then stepped out from the corner and looked down the length of the tunnel-like room. 'This,' he announced almost defiantly, 'is *my* gallery. Allington's. And I am Victor Allington.'

Rosa was surprised. 'I thought it was *hers*.' She pointed towards Dulcie Dee.

Victor Allington smiled ruefully. 'My assistant *does* more or less run the place – I can do nothing with Miss Dee.'

'If you don't think much of the artist, my uncle, why have you got his pictures hanging here in your art gallery?' Rosa asked.

A shrewd girl, Allington of Allington's thought. 'A good question,' he said. 'The pictures belong to McCabe. He asked me to exhibit them.'

'They belong to Sarah, surely – Mrs McCabe. She was Max's wife, his widow, my aunt . . .'

'You know a good deal,' Allington said, playing for time, deciding to play. 'Would you care for a weekend in the country?' he asked, abruptly. 'I know its short notice . . .'

'A weekend in the country?' Rosa repeated. The Provincial Niece had only just arrived in London!

'I've been invited to a grand country house where artistic guests are always welcome. *You* would be most welcome. Max Fanshawe is all the rage at the moment, the appearance of his niece would cause a . . .'

'Do you think so?'

Allington smiled. 'Why don't you come, it's always good to get out of London at the end of a busy week. You'd meet a lot of interesting people and I'd be most grateful . . .'

'Grateful?'

'For your help in promoting your uncle's exhibition . . .'

'Thank you,' said Rosa. 'I'd love it.' Hadn't Mme Lefroy said, you have only to go out and about . . . who knew but that Valerie Lefroy might be in attendance.

Victor Allington was surprised. He could have been *anyone*, luring the foolish girl away to *anything*! He thought angrily, these pictures are more this Rosa's than old McCabe's. He took advantage of my good nature. He will not be allowed to take advantage of the girl's stupidity. He smiled at Rosa Pegglar and said, 'If you come here on Friday afternoon, we can get a good start. It is a long drive.'

'You have a car?'

'We won't end up in a ditch, if that's what you mean.' He returned to his cubby-hole of an office, leaving Rosa to finish looking at the disappointing pictures. 'They are historical,' she thought. 'I am the one who is alive now.' She handed the catalogue back to Dulcie Dee by the door.

'You keep it,' Dulcie said, fishing her handbag out of a drawer. She had decided on a long, long lunch-hour. 'I'm just going myself, I'll come outside with you, if you like.'

How friendly everyone was! In the quiet street outside, Dulcie took Rosa's arm. 'What did he want?' she asked.

'Who?' Rosa wondered what Max had ever wanted, apart from that poxy milk bar.

'Mr Allington of course!'

'To chat about my uncle.'

'I thought he might be offering you my job.'

Rosa laughed. 'Why would he do that? I've got jobs enough already.'

'He's always trying to replace me. He keeps going to Mrs Faragher's Agency to see if they have anyone better – have *you* been there? Is that where you get all your jobs – is it they who sent you?'

'Mrs *Faragher's* Agency?' Rosa repeated. 'Not Sir Arnold Faragher's wife?' She'd had a bill for Simeon's violin lessons to give the man from Miss Gough.

Dulcie Dee blushed scarlet and flushed with pleasure. Everyone, she supposed, knew about Sir Arnold Faragher and Dulcie Dee! 'Haven't you ever been there? Look, if you do need a job, you want to get on their cards. You want to get down to Pall Mall right away!' Dulcie reckoned that since Rosa was already doing several jobs and had lost her 'uncle', she must be in straitened circumstances. To judge by the girl's clothes she was probably desperate. Urgently, kindly, she pushed Rosa in the direction of Mrs Faragher's offices. 'Don't let them try and send you back here, though,' Dulcie warned, 'I wouldn't take kindly.' Then she clattered away on steel-spiked heels to keep an assignation by a bandstand in the park.

I ought to explain about the bill for Simeon's lessons, Rosa thought. It had been in her pocket with the sandwiches but she had lost the coat and she wouldn't want Simeon getting into trouble.

The Riff-Raff

Miss Finch looked at Rosa, and sighed. It was all very well for the high-minded, high-handed Mrs Faragher to say, 'Don't let our standards slip, Miss Finch, we can't let in riff-raff!' but *she* never confronted the endless stream of bloodless waifs, crowding the waiting room week after week in hope of employment. Audrey Finch eyed this first comer critically. She was not even wearing a coat! You wanted to direct the creature to Swan & Edgar's for a lesson in fashion. Take a look in the window, dear! Learn how to dress. 'We are a *respectable* agency,' Miss Finch told Rosa sternly. 'We require references for all our girls.'

'References?'

'From respectable people who could be referred to.' Miss Finch picked up her pen. It would be quicker to pretend to take down some details and get the girl out of here. 'Name?' she snapped.

'Rosa.'

'We require your *full* name.' Miss Finch jabbed her nib on a card like a hungry bird pecking at crumbs. Rosa opened her mouth to explain that she had only come to apologize for losing a bill for violin lessons, when the telephone rang. Miss Finch frowned.

Then her face lit up. 'Marjorie, my dear! How lovely to hear from you!' A long pause ensued in which Miss Finch listened. 'No, Mrs Faragher isn't here. I don't know when she'll be back. It's Audrey Finch.'

So, Rosa thought. This is *not* Mrs Faragher!

When the voice down the telephone paused again, Miss Finch spoke with forced politeness into the mouthpiece: 'Marjorie, it can't be done. I'm interviewing this afternoon, I have someone with me just now – a girl . . .' Panic dashed across Miss Finch's face. *'What* did you say?' She glanced at Rosa. *'Where,* Marjorie? *Victoria* Station? The *boat* train? Oh, but you can't leave just like that – your poor mother!' It was impossible dealing down a telephone apparatus with a naughty child who had always had her own way. 'Well, I . . .'

Miss Finch removed the phone from her ear and looked at it in astonishment. Then she scowled across at Rosa, annoyed that anyone should have witnessed Marjorie Joan Elizabeth Faragher *slamming the phone down* on Miss Audrey Finch, her mother's paid assistant. 'Where were we?' Miss Finch faltered. Marjorie had told her that since she had a girl with her just then, she could jolly well send the convenient creature straight round to look after Simeon. 'Send her on one of your Special Assignments, Miss Finch!' Marjorie had yelled against the roar at Victoria Station. The boat train was ready to depart, mind the doors! Marjorie Faragher hung up and pressed Button B. Then she hurried back down the platform to her seat in the first-class compartment, pushing through clusters of sorrowful lovers planting parting kisses before the train drew out. No one kissed Miss Faragher. Even Button B had yielded up no refund.

Looking now at Rosa, Miss Finch nearly laughed out loud. The Faraghers might all be murdered in their beds, the priceless violin that had been taken in lieu of a debt, stolen. Law and order, the world as they knew it, would collapse. Anything could happen once you let in riff-raff. The girl didn't even have a coat!

Audrey Finch sat stunned. Then she recollected the urgency and stood up. She adjusted the belt about her neat waist, sat down again, took hold of the telephone receiver but did nothing with it. Miss Finch glanced at her photograph of Mr Carnelly and fancied herself no better than the dithering Helen Gough, the woman with whom at present she must share his love.

It was too urgent to look through the files for somebody better. The scheme had been Marjorie's. If it was a mistake, the mistake would also be Marjorie's. I am only a paid assistant,

Miss Finch told herself gleefully. A woman on whom other women slammed down phones. No one can blame me!

'I need someone to go to a house and look after a boy who is ill,' Miss Finch said, scribbling the Faraghers' address on one of the Agency's pink Special Assignment cards. 'That is your duty,' she handed Rosa the card. 'Get it signed when you leave the house . . .'

'But I only came,' Rosa butted in at last, 'to tell you about the bill.'

Miss Finch waved impatiently. 'When there are enough pink cards in your file we will pay what is owed. You can sort any problems out with Mrs Faragher later.' Miss Finch did not feel up to interviewing anyone else. As if to gain strength, she glanced at the photograph propped beside the telephone for all to see. She fancied that one heady lunch-hour she had walked up the Tottenham Court Road to Heal's and purchased a nice frame. 'How many more of you are there in the waiting room? Take a quick look will you, dear?'

Rosa looked outside. Gaunt girls in cheap cotton dresses filled the seats and stood in a long shuffling queue that stretched out through the door and away down the stairs. They fell silent when they saw Rosa appear holding a pink card. Rosa shut the door again. 'Two dozen,' she told Miss Finch. 'At least.'

Twenty-four, at five minutes each, would take two hours and you could never get rid of anyone in under five minutes. The more hopeless they were, the more insistent. Look at this one; she'd had to be given a Special Assignment just to get rid of her! 'You'd better hurry,' Miss Finch urged. 'A child is ill.' How could the boy be in need of expert nursing as Marjorie had said, when only yesterday he'd played jolly Sarabandes with Miss Gough? I would put nothing past her, Miss Finch thought, recalling the pink pork luncheon meat, thinly sliced.

The Faraghers' front door was off the latch. Upstairs, Rosa found Simeon in bed fast asleep. The rest of the large house was deserted apart from a plump little dog wandering despondently from room to room. A tag on the tartan collar announced the name BINKIE. An unwashed spoon and uncorked medicine bottle sat on the small table beside the boy's bed. A battered teddy bear lay on the floor staring helplessly up at Rosa with its one remaining eye. 'Come on, Binkie.' Rosa ushered the forlorn Scottie dog from the sickroom. 'Let sleeping violinists lie!'

Rosa went down to the kitchen to find something in the well-stocked pantry to cheer Binkie up but she was interrupted by a loud rap. When Rosa opened the Faraghers' wide front door an enormous bouquet of flowers was thrust into her face. A voice from beneath the flowers cried out, 'I'm awfully sorry I didn't come yesterday, Marjorie, I couldn't face another of your tea parties . . .'

'This isn't *Marjorie*.' Rosa peered into the petals.

There was a pause. The flowers quivered. Then they fell to the doorstep in a colourful shuddering heap exposing the owner of the voice: an amiable young man with doleful eyes. He stared at Rosa in astonishment. 'Wh . . . where is she?'

'Marjorie? At Victoria Station, catching the boat train.'

'Who are you?'

'I could be anyone, but I am Rosa. Your Marjorie arranged with the Agency to send me here.'

'She isn't *my* Marjorie . . .'

'If you hurry you might catch her.'

'I *don't want* to catch her – that's just the point . . .' Binkie charged out of the house, his stumpy tail wagging ecstatically at the familiar sounds and smells of William Sharp. Binkie had missed Silly-Billy at the tea party yesterday. He scrabbled wildly now in the expensive blooms strewn on the Faraghers' wide doorstep. William Sharp bent down and patted the tufted fur. He looked up at Rosa. 'Are you taking care of the house and Marjorie's dog, then?'

'Yes,' Rosa replied. 'I am here on a Special Assignment nursing Simeon . . .'

'Simeon! Is he *ill*?' The poor dog whimpered. The suitor felt like whimpering also. Marjorie had made her choice! Even now she was eloping to the Continent – it would be the ultimate prank, the natural culmination of all the unruly tea parties he had been forced to sit through. Already she would have *Mrs Bodman-Bligh* or *Mrs Chadwick* written on her passport; it was too late to apply to the Foreign Office or anyone else to prevent it. William Sharp had let his widowed mother down.

'Simeon is asleep. There's some medicine by his bed but I don't know what's wrong with him,' Rosa said. Silly-Billy did not hear. He was thinking of his mother. And his father, the virtuoso violinist Petersham Sharp who had died during the war. Shortly afterwards, in desperation, Mrs Sharp had borrowed money from Mrs Faragher. Only a loan, Susan Sharp had decided: when William married Marjorie, of course, the debt would be cancelled. Before long Constance Faragher started sending forthright notes about the money that was owed. Mrs Sharp had no choice but to offer Petersham's priceless violin (the one William's father left at home when his plane went down in fog off the unlit coast) in lieu of the debt. Only a temporary arrangement, Mrs Sharp told herself again: when William married Marjorie, the violin would come back. The music would return.

But now, standing on the Faraghers' doorstep, the most lavish bouquet of flowers he had ever brought shredded about his feet by the lapdog Binkie – who had also been discarded, his wholehearted little affections trampled upon like the delicate petals – William Sharp knew for certain that *he would never marry Miss Faragher*. The violin that had been his father's, and all that Petersham Sharp had left, was gone for ever.

Rosa looked at the downcast suitor. 'You could do with a cup of tea,' she said kindly. 'Why don't you come in – I found some custard creams in the pantry.'

William Sharp wiped his eyes on the back of his cuff and, stepping over the tattered flowers, followed Rosa gratefully indoors. Past the hooks where the three steadfast suitors' coats had hung once a week for the last five years. Past the sitting-room door through which they had all three traipsed to pass the afternoon ranged in a row, Silly-Billy in the middle, unwilling and uncooperative. *If only* he had made more effort to join in the high jinks. *If only* he had found the throwing of sugar lumps, making stupid noises or telling daft jokes as hilarious as had Freddie and Charlie. He was about to follow Rosa into the kitchen when something in a corner of the hallway caught Silly-Billy's eye. It was years since he'd seen the black wooden case that contained his father's violin. Poor Simeon had left the instrument propped up like a tiger-hunting gun resting before its next expedition into the hills.

'Mild for the time of year, isn't it?' William Sharp remarked as he sauntered into the kitchen, his hands thrust in his pockets. He whistled loudly in an effort to keep calm.

'I beg your pardon?' Rosa was boiling the kettle and, what with all the whistling, had missed his remark.

'Granted!' quipped Silly-Billy, as Freddie or Charlie might have done. He had been taken for granted too long. He and his mother had been taken for fools. He watched Rosa rather lovingly warming the teapot as Ida Gregg had trained her to do. He went over and put an arm round the girl. 'Marry me, Rosa!' he said.

Rosa laughed and backed away. She thought William Sharp was larking about the way men did with the tweeny of the house.

'I'm serious,' he said, sounding it. 'I've never been more serious in all my life.'

'I don't know you, you don't know me!'

'I know enough!' Silly-Billy cried. He knew that this Rosa was *not* his cruel tormentor, Marjorie Joan Elizabeth Faragher. He knew also that in the dreadful moment when he had finally realized that his father's violin was lost for ever, this girl had been kinder to him than Marjorie, despite all the chocolates and flowers, could ever be. Without further ado or regard for the welfare of his best trousers, William Sharp threw himself down on bended knee and, like the tartan-collared Binkie begging for biscuits, Silly-Billy begged Miss Rosa Pegglar to become his lawful wedded wife.

Rosa smiled graciously and offered the man a custard cream.

William Sharp rose to his feet and, seizing the whole plate of biscuits, he bent down with an exuberant flourish and set them on the floor before Binkie. Binkie blinked.

'He can't believe his luck.' Rosa laughed as the little dog wagged his tail and began to gobble.

William Sharp took Rosa's hand and gently squeezed her fingers. 'I can't believe *my* luck,' he said. 'I might have gone all my life and never met you. I know it sounds absurd but I . . . I love you!'

Rosa smiled at William Sharp. 'Love *is* absurd,' she told him. 'My father always said so.'

'Your father was a wise man, then.' There had been three wise men but three stupid steadfast suitors, Silly-Billy thought.

'My father had two varieties of exotic chicken named after him. He bred them himself.'

'Did he now?' William Sharp took Rosa in his arms and gazed adoringly into the eyes of Pegglar's daughter, gazing at his own reflection. 'Oh, Rosa!' he said passionately. And then he kissed her.

Back at the Agency Miss Finch banged the door shut behind the last of the interviewees and opened all the sash windows to let out the stench of scents that had definitely not been purchased over the polished glass counters at Swan & Edgar's. She sighed heavily. What a sorry batch of bedraggled broilers this afternoon, she thought as she started filing away the sullied cards. Most were marked 'U' for 'unsuitable'.

'I love you!' Carnelly's dark deep eyes spoke to her from across the desk. 'I love you too,' murmured Miss Finch as she worked. There could be little doubt Mr Carnelly too was impossibly unsuitable. He ran a puppet theatre that could barely pay. If it were not for the money she and Miss Gough spent on tickets, sitting regularly in the most expensive seats in the middle of the front row, the theatre would probably have been forced to close a long time back. We are the Playgoers, thought Miss Finch complacently. If *we* were to stay at home *every* evening and listen to the Home Service on Miss Gough's crackly wireless, Mr Carnelly would be ruined.

Someone rattled the handle of the outer door. 'Come back next week!' Miss Finch called out sharply. 'We have finished for today.'

'Why, so you have!' Mrs Faragher bustled into the room laden with shopping. 'You do work hard, Audrey dear, no one can cope as famously as you do!' She threw her bags and boxes on the floor and herself into a chair. Then she passed a wrist dramatically over her forehead. 'What a trying afternoon! The shops were so busy . . .'

Miss Finch smiled solicitously. 'Can I fetch you anything?' she heard herself asking. She produced a bottle of sherry and two glasses from the drawer beside her desk and as she did so imagined slipping the imagined Carnelly out of view. Then she imparted her news as casually as possible. Audrey Finch had poured out the sherry and handed a glass across before her employer appeared to register that something had been said. '*I beg your pardon*, Miss Finch?'

Audrey Finch gulped down the contents of her own glass. 'Marjorie rang. From Victoria Station. On her way to Switzerland. She said she'd write . . .'

Constance Faragher held out her empty glass for a top-up. As Miss Finch obligingly ran round the desk, Mrs Faragher remarked, 'The dear girl's so fond of chocolate! And Swiss chocolate is much the best, of course . . .'

'Of course,' echoed Miss Finch, pouring more sherry.

Then Mrs Faragher said, 'I wonder why she rang *you*, Audrey.'

'Well, she could hardly ring you. You weren't here!' Mrs Faragher had become impossible to get hold of. So rarely was she ever in Pall Mall, it would hardly be surprising if people began to mistake Miss Finch for Constance Faragher herself!

'Yes, but why ring at all?'

'Simeon is ill in bed,' Miss Finch said tersely. 'Marjorie wanted me to send someone on a Special Assignment to nurse the boy as she was going to Switzerland. For the chocolate. I wonder what can be wrong with the child? Too much violin playing with Miss Gough, perhaps.'

And I wonder what can be wrong with you! Mrs Faragher thought. She did not see what business her offspring were of Audrey Finch's. The woman was acting most peculiarly. 'She'll have gone to see a school friend. Marjorie was always a *sensible girl.*'

Miss Finch looked blank. There had been nothing sensible about screaming against the blare of the tannoy at Victoria Station! Mrs Faragher took her paid assistant's silence for stubborn disagreement and continued rather spitefully: 'I wanted her to come and work in the Agency, you know, but Marjorie never showed any interest. I thought she could take over from me . . .' Mrs Faragher gulped on her sherry. Perhaps she had gone too far. She saw Miss Finch blench. 'Not that anyone could match *you*, dear Audrey,' she said hastily. 'Not even Marjorie could cope as *famously* as you do. Whom did you send?'

'Send?'

'To my house.'

Audrey Finch tried hard to remember. She scrabbled through her piles of unfiled cards rather like Binkie clawing at flowers strewn on the doorstep. She found a card with ROSA written on it. Nothing more. *Full* name, she had said, but then the telephone had rung . . . 'I am not well.' Miss Finch felt herself sinking, drowning, lowered into a chair guided by the firm impatient hands of Constance Faragher. Whom *had* she sent?

'Her name was Rosa,' Miss Finch tried to say. She could hear a voice like her own jabbering. 'It was Marjorie's idea, it is her mistake. I am not myself, I am a Playgoer . . .'

'My dear, you have simply been overdoing it!' Mrs Faragher pressed the switch that lit up an orange light outside in Pall Mall to hail a cab and then, despite her own fatigue and her exasperation with Miss Finch, she shut the windows, turned off the lights and, accompanied by sundry Swan & Edgar carrier bags, nobly escorted her ailing assistant home to the maisonette she shared with her mother. It was in completely the wrong direction, but there you are. We cannot all live in Kensington.

Imagine Mrs Ethel Finch's delight, and horror, at seeing her own daughter brought home in a hired cab by no less a person than *the* Constance Faragher, proprietress of *the* Agency in Pall Mall. If Ethel Finch detected the whiff of alcohol on the breath of the two ladies, she said nothing. The short time she had spent with the late Mr Finch had taught her the efficacy of saying nothing, at times. She'd brought his daughter up to tell her everything – now it was clear, she had *not* been told everything. Where did I go wrong? Audrey Finch's mother wondered. The late Mr Finch had a lot to answer for.

'Can't stop!' Mrs Faragher cried. The likes of Ethel Finch could only stand on the scrubbed doorsteps of their maisonettes with their mouths wide open. The legendary lady had come and gone before Mrs Finch thought to thank her daughter's employer or concern herself even with Audrey's condition.

Audrey, meanwhile, waited bravely, propped up on her own two feet, until the taxi and her employer were out of sight. Then she staggered to the bathroom.

It'll be that Mr Carnelly, Mrs Finch thought furiously as she retreated to heat up a tin of soup in the kitchen. All that talk about listening to an inaudible wireless with Miss Gough had been a cover, all those late-night confidences clearly lies. Mrs Finch tried to blame herself. She should have been prepared. Audrey had reached the dangerous age when a girl needs bedding before it is too late. The fellow had doubtless received every encouragement. Aided and abetted, abedded too maybe by her daughter's foolish friend, Miss Gough. The woman who lived below Mr Carnelly, whose skin her daughter had once lied to protect, must have known of romantic intrigue going on over her head.

Ethel Finch stirred the pan. Playgoers, indeed! She pictured her daughter and Helen Gough in the front row of the stalls, sharing selection boxes and vying between their legs for the showman's attentions. The man would be hiding behind his puppets, but a man cannot go on hiding for ever. A bitch on heat, that's what her daughter had been, under her very own nose. No good sniffing now. The two girls should have stuck to watching fires.

'In the kitchen, Audrey!' Ethel Finch called as the soup

began to bubble. 'You and I need a good long talk.'

She was greeted at first by silence and then she heard a long low moan. 'Audrey!' she shrieked furiously as the soup boiled over.

The Girl of My Dreams

When Mrs Faragher arrived home and found William Sharp kissing a tweeny in her kitchen she said, 'I told that stupid Miss Finch not to let in riff-raff and now I find her sending all kinds of unfortunate creatures to my own house!' Audrey Finch was clearly in need of a holiday. Something inexpensive, but suitably extensive, must be arranged forthwith.

'My fiancée,' Mr Sharp introduced Rosa.

'You are *engaged* to this girl?' That a man, who'd had the honour of being one of her daughter's three steadfast suitors, could turn out so fickle! No wonder poor Marjorie had fled abroad! Mrs Faragher recalled this same Billy Sharp at five years old, leaning over the cot in which her beautiful Marjorie lay milkily asleep, a blank expression on his round stupid face. 'Those two are destined for one another,' Mrs Faragher had teased Billy's mother. As though her baby, the first-born Faragher, could ever grow up to countenance anyone as poor, or as fickle, as Susan Sharp's stout little boy! She had not liked Billy Sharp then and she did not like finding William Sharp consorting with tweenys in her own house now. 'How is your mother?' Mrs Faragher asked pointedly.

For all that had happened since, Constance Faragher had never forgotten. Looking at the son she saw the father, dear penniless Petersham, who had jilted her to marry her friend. The pair had lived, she felt sure – had personally made sure – to regret it. Meanwhile *she* had been left to make do and marry Arnold Faragher. And now, here was Petersham Sharp's equally impoverished son jilting her own darling daughter for riff-raff! Dallying with the girl in *her* kitchen. Mrs Faragher laughed out loud at life's tender ironies.

'I only came about the bill,' Rosa tried to say.

'If you think I am going to sign your pink card!' Mrs Faragher retorted angrily. 'If you think I am going to pay for your doings . . .'

'Oh, but I would like to pay you!' William Sharp interrupted at once. 'I would like to buy back my father's violin.' To do so would always be his idle ambition, Billy knew. He thought of the flowers and chocolates that, week after week, he and his mother had purchased at crippling expense to bestow on this woman's horrid daughter.

'You!' Mrs Faragher turned her laughter on the earnest Silly-Billy. 'Have you any idea what your father's violin is worth? It is a genuine Peristighi, last valued at something over a thousand pounds! At current post-war values . . . Where would you, Mr Sharp, get a sum like that? Unless of course your fiancée here is an heiress?' She looked Rosa up and down and thought of her poor abandoned daughter. Marjorie would certainly have a beauty tip or two to give this creature!

'I understood the violin belonged to Simeon's father,' Rosa said. William Sharp and Constance Faragher both paused, mid-breath, and looked at Rosa. 'If the violin is worth over a thousand pounds, it's far too valuable for a little boy to drag through the streets and play easy-peasy Sarabandes on with Miss Gough, just to get him out of the house, out of everybody's way.'

There was silence in the Faragher kitchen. You could have heard blood spilling.

'You don't know what you're talking about!' Constance Faragher gasped quietly. She sat down. Before Petersham Sharp had left on that last tragic flight to the Continent he had embarked, also, on one of those brief affairs common in wartime. With Sir Arnold away, taken up with his war-work, Constance Faragher had felt furious and neglected. There is nothing more enticing to a good-natured easy-going man, such as William's father had been, than a beautiful woman who feels sorry for herself. Poor Mrs Sharp knew, of course. Constance

187

Faragher was an old friend of hers and an old flame of Petersham's from the days before their marriage. Yet, how could a little infidelity with an old flame count when the nation was at war and London on fire? Susan Sharp had been evacuated to the country with young Billy. She had under-estimated Mrs Faragher and over-estimated her husband, perhaps.

When Simeon was born, some months after the violinist's tragic death while Sir Arnold was still away on war-work, the widowed Susan had called on her friend. This time she did not come to offer needless advice on childcare, as she had done when Marjorie was born, but she came to look at Simeon and, as an injured party, to borrow money to tide her over. With William's studies to pay for on her own now, she was desperate. She said so.

Constance Faragher lent her desperate friend a sum of money to get rid of her but Petersham's widow had called again and, far from offering to repay the original loan, had asked for further help. When Mrs Faragher laughed in her friend's face, poor Susan Sharp found herself gesturing towards Simeon's cradle and threatening to write and tell the wealthy Sir Arnold a thing or two.

Mrs Faragher merely laughed again. 'Do you really think a man like Arnold Faragher does not know already?' The weathy wife had then given the impoverished widow a lesson in economics. Interest steadily accruing on a debt adds up. The sooner it was paid off . . . 'I will, however, because you are an old friend, accept Petersham's Peristighi, in lieu,' she concluded.

'The violin is priceless!' Mrs Sharp spluttered.

'And blackmail is criminal.'

The two women glared at one another. What had already been taken away was theft, neither criminal nor without price. If it hadn't been for the other, each thought, their sons would still have fathers, music would still be playing and Petersham Sharp himself might still be alive. The women were united but divided also by the anger, love and everlasting grief they now shared. 'I have no savings,' Mrs Sharp said helplessly.

'You can always take in mending and ironing.'

'That wouldn't repay . . .'

'And there's the violin.' Mrs Faragher reckoned Petersham Sharp's Peristighi was her Simeon's birthright. The boy was bound to grow up musical and give her headaches by playing jolly Sarabandes. He should do so, at least, on a decent violin. 'I will have the Peristighi as a souvenir,' she said cruelly.

The instrument belonged to young *Silly-Billy*, the sentimental Mrs Sharp inwardly protested. But it would only be temporarily lost. If one day her son had to fulfil the destiny marked out for him all those years ago by Mrs Faragher herself, marrying the buck-toothed Marjorie in order to get the Peristighi back, so be it! And if Susan Sharp were forced to slave night and day taking in other people's mending and ironing to earn the money to buy flowers and chocolates for the other woman's spoilt daughter, then that was probably the least a devoted mother might do.

'Where is Simeon?' Mrs Faragher asked now.

'Asleep upstairs,' Rosa answered. 'At least he was . . .'

Constance Faragher, flanked by William Sharp and Rosa, flew from the room, up the wide wooden Faragher staircase and into Simeon's bedroom. The child was lying awkwardly on his back, one hand stretched towards the battered teddy bear out of reach across the floor, the other curled by his cheek, cupping the air.

'He's dead!' Rosa gasped in horror. The boy showed all the signs of the bloodless death Pegglar's chickens had suffered when her mother's excitable dog had worried at them. Unable to fly away, they had lain on their backs choking on their own breath, claws clutching at nothing as they died of fright in the safety of their coops. 'What can have frightened him?' Rosa asked fearfully, but Simeon's mother did not hear.

'You have killed my son!' Mrs Faragher grabbed the uncorked medicine bottle from the bedside table and threw it wildly at Rosa. The dark red liquid flew up the wall, across the counterpane and dripped down over Simeon's toys. The glass bottle bounced on the linoleum floor and then smashed into a thousand pieces. 'Murderer! Special Assignment, indeed! I'll have *you* specially assigned . . .'

Simeon stirred at the sound of his mother shouting. 'I hate

Miss Gough,' he said, his eyes closed, his breathing thick and chesty.

Mrs Faragher let out a howl. Binkie waddled into the room, sniffed suspiciously at the sticky medicine and stuck his black nose distastefully in the air. Simeon opened his eyes and saw Rosa. 'She's my friend,' he said dopily.

'Nonsense!' cried Rosa and started to remonstrate. The violin had belonged to Petersham Sharp, while Sir Arnold was officially his father and not his uncle. 'You lied to me . . .'

'I was cornered, Rosa,' Simeon Faragher confessed gravely. 'In the Corner House. I am a liar, and a thief!'

'You can tell any stories you please,' Mrs Faragher cried with new-found indulgence for this unwanted son. Why should not the lies the boy had told perhaps be true and the truths not contain something of his own mother's lies? 'Lie if you must, Simeon darling, steal if you need to, but don't die! *She* . . .' Mrs Faragher turned on Rosa. 'She is only a tweeny sent by Miss Finch – you must think of your poor mother, who loves you!'

Rosa retrieved the battered teddy from the floor and, rubbing away the spattering of medicine, set it on the boy's pillow to keep its one remaining button eye on the child. Simeon turned over, smiled blindly at Rosa and at his toy bear and then went back to sleep. He would have to stay alive to stay in the story, he could see that.

Mrs Faragher watched the tweeny fetch a wet cloth from the bathroom and mop the medicine from the wall. 'I did not know you and my son were friends,' she said, looking at the sleeping child and wondering what else she did not know.

Downstairs again, Mrs Faragher said to William Sharp, 'Take the violin!'

'No,' said Silly-Billy, 'I will take the tweeny. The violin belongs to Simeon.'

'He doesn't want it,' Rosa said. 'He hates Miss Gough, you heard him.'

'But he's so musical,' sighed Mrs Faragher.

'Simeon isn't musical at all.'

Mrs Faragher nodded. Since Marjorie had gone to Switzer-

land and her suitors had proved so fickle, there'd be no necessity now to get the boy out of the house to stop him stealing
from their pockets. 'I myself will write to Miss Gough cancelling
the lessons,' she said. Hadn't Miss Finch only that morning
hinted at the woman's unsuitability to teach the violin to Simeon
Faragher, or anyone else? 'Meanwhile, Mr Sharp,' Mrs Faragher
turned to Silly-Billy, 'you will oblige me by taking the violin
away with you. Have it as a present, a wedding present, if you
like.'

She did not want the wretched Peristighi in her house a
moment longer. 'You can take the animal too.' She prodded
Binkie with her toe. 'Since you have driven my poor daughter
out of the country between you, the least you can do is take
charge of her wretched pet!'

William Sharp walked Rosa home. Outside Paddington Mansions, watched through unwashed windows by Helen Gough,
Silly-Billy kissed his beloved and eventually, reluctantly, he
drew himself away to go home. 'When will I see you?' he asked.

'I'm busy this weekend,' Rosa told him. 'I have promised to
go to a country house with my uncle, but I will see you next
week.'

Miss Gough thought, I have seen that man somewhere, I have
seen that girl, even the violin he is carrying is curiously familiar.
She felt confused. She banged on the window to shoo away the
fat little dog that was sniffing about the railings, but no one took
any notice. It was as if the noise she made was heard only by
herself.

Susan Sharp looked on in astonishment as Silly-Billy placed
the black wooden violin case down on her sewing table in the
corner of their small kitchen. She eyed the plump dog with a
smart tartan collar who trotted at his feet. Quietly she said, 'So!
You are going to marry Marjorie Joan Elizabeth!'

'No, Ma,' replied her son. 'I am going to marry the girl of my
dreams.'

Binkie wagged his stumpy tail. Mrs Sharp raised her eyebrows. 'Is she anyone I know?'

'She *could* be anyone,' Silly-Billy mused. 'She is the sort of person you think you have always known.' He took the price-less violin from its case and smoothed resin on to the bow. 'Absurd as it may seem,' he observed as he tuned the strings one by one, 'I love her.'

The violin was desperately out of tune; no wonder poor Simeon had not enjoyed playing it. 'What is she called?' Mrs Sharp asked. 'This girl of your dreams?'

'Rosa,' the son said as he raised his father's violin to his chin. Then the stubborn Silly-Billy drew the bow across the strings and began to play tunes remembered distantly, distinctly, from long long ago. Binkie opened one eye. Occasionally he had heard a violin – this same violin – being played by Simeon, but never had it sounded like this.

'Oh, Petersham,' sighed Susan Sharp, for she had not heard such music since before the war, and the bombing of Pegglar's London.

'Oh, Petersham,' sighed Constance Faragher in Kensington at the bedside of the sleeping Simeon. A doctor had been and gone.

'The boy will either get well, or he won't,' he'd opined, pocketing his cheque and prescribing long, anodyne and inex-pensive sleep.

Nothing Too Extravagant, Please

Mr Carnelly had a new show starting at the end of next week and most of the puppets were not made yet. I am getting too old for this business, he thought.

'Come and have tea!' Miss Gough knocked on his door and refused to listen as he tried to tell her how busy he was. 'We all need sustenance, Mr Carnelly, we all need something to keep us going.' She wagged her finger playfully at him. Only there was nothing playful about Miss Gough. It was as if she thought of nothing else, waiting for him to come home, pouncing on him with invitations and warnings. Today she'd said the rent would go up to pay for a new caretaker.

Mr Carnelly stuffed his hands into his old green cardigan pockets. 'I will try and come,' he agreed, too affable for his own good, agreeing only for the sake of some peace. Sometimes it seemed there could be no escaping Miss Gough or her equally awful friend, Miss Finch. Helen Gough beamed. She felt triumphant. Before he shut the door again she managed to say how much she was looking forward to the new show next week, the new show that was not yet ready. Miss Finch had tried to suggest that her attentions might be unwelcome. That Mr Carnelly might have set his sights elsewhere. 'I think only of him,' Miss Gough had retorted. 'The man works too hard, all work and no play never did anyone any good. I will warn him about the caretaker. I will make him take tea . . .'

'Does the theatre not require a Musical Director,' she had once tried to ask, 'someone who could organize all the violins and pianos?'

'I use a gramophone,' Mr Carnelly replied bluntly, sipping his tea and leaving Miss Finch to smile at Miss Gough, who had pushed herself forward and been gently rebuffed.

I am not a woman to be held at bay, Miss Gough had said to herself. You will regret this. And now, in his rooms upstairs, Albert Carnelly nodded sadly. There was no way he could afford the increase in rent Miss Gough had mentioned. At last he went upstairs to talk to his old friend, Charlotte Lefroy. 'It is a difficult decision,' he told her.

'I knew it would come to this,' she said. 'Old McCabe wants us out and one by one we succumb. Soon none of the old ones will be left . . .'

'Mmmm,' Carnelly agreed.

'The riff-raff drive out the respectable ones like yourself, dear Mr Carnelly. Soon there will be no one who can recall my Granville or my daughter, Valerie.'

Carnelly sighed. He had no desire to take tea again with Miss Gough or her eager friend Miss Finch. 'We are the Playgoers,' they would announce in stage whispers, arriving late after the performance had already started, causing a disturbance as they took their seats in the middle of the front row. Whenever he peeped from behind the scenery there they would be, bedecked in turbans and furbelows, dipping noisily into selection boxes and fanning themselves with their programmes. Because he was busy with the puppets, Mr Carnelly sometimes managed not to let the Playgoers bother him but in the interval he would hear their voices raised, Miss Gough criticizing the gramophone music and Miss Finch slavishly praising the show and informing everyone that as devoted Playgoers they, like Queen Victoria before them, were accustomed to taking tea with 'dear Albert'.

Albert Carnelly suspected the audience thought the realistic but highly unreal life-size figures sitting steadfastly side by side in the front seats were part of the show. People came specially to see the Playgoers. He'd know they had arrived from the shrill excited cries of 'Here they are!' Generally the children would laugh at the antics of the pair but as the pitch of their voices rose, the young audience became gradually quiet, shrinking back into their seats. Albert Carnelly knew he had caught his fear of

Miss Gough and Miss Finch from the children.

'The world isn't what it was . . .' Charlotte Lefroy eyed the large dark stain on her linoleum sadly.

'It never is . . .' Carnelly agreed. Takings were down. The little theatre he had run for thirty years, which had miraculously escaped the Blitz, had become shabby and unfrequented. Other establishments provided entertainments these days, puppet shows were not in demand any more; people had apparently grown up. He was tired. The next show would probably be the last. 'You must come,' Carnelly said. 'I offer Phipps tickets, but he never comes.'

'Phipps is a fool. I never go out. Where will you move to?' Charlotte Lefroy asked.

'There's a little room at the back of the theatre I can use for now . . .'

'I wish I could leave,' Mme Lefroy sighed, 'but this is the only place my daughter, Valerie, knows where to find me.'

Carnelly patted the old unsteady hand. She was sobbing. 'It'll be all right,' he said comfortingly. 'Everyone always comes back in the end. Or we go to them.'

'I have a private detective working on the case,' Charlotte Lefroy confided. 'I lent her some disguises from my own wardrobe. If anyone can find my Valerie, she will.'

In SIMLA, Marcoolyn looked at his watch. Beryl too glanced anxiously at the time.

'I'm sorry I'm late,' Rosa said. 'A man has asked me to marry him. I never said *yes*, I never said *no* . . .'

'I was waiting for you,' 'Jack' said as soon as Rosa arrived at his table, affectionately pulling her down beside him and putting a hand round the back of her waist, a hand he intended to lower as the night progressed and the champagne flowed.

At the end of the evening, in the early hours of the morning, Rosa slipped away, her pockets full of money, her head guzzy with drink. 'I shall be out of town with my uncle this weekend,' she told Marcoolyn who was not best pleased. Fridays and Saturdays were his best nights, he expected all the girls to be there.

'I like *reliable* staff.' Marcoolyn blew smoke into Rosa's face but let the girl – whom he now knew from his inquiries to be McCabe's niece by a marriage or two – go. He had spoken to Phipps and sent word to McCabe. He had also sent word to George Braid. Let them fight it out between them. Meanwhile he'd let the niece have a free run. It was nothing to do with him, he insisted, wondering whether he should warn the other girls. 'We have a spy in our midst,' he told Beryl. He had found the buttonless coat in his car. A squashed packet of sandwiches and an indecipherable letter to Sir Arnold Faragher in the pockets.

Beryl perked up at this. She asked if Marcoolyn had found a job for Bernard yet. There must be *something* he could do. 'He's very strong.'

'Don't pester me,' Marcoolyn replied. That afternoon he had confessed several of his lesser doings to an old deaf priest. But it was not a priest Marcoolyn needed. He might need Bernard, but he did not like the way Beryl carried on. And on. As a mark of his displeasure he did not offer Beryl or her friend a lift home that night, favouring one of the other girls with his protection.

Albert Carnelly did not come down. Miss Gough had boiled her kettle but waited in vain. There was the new show next week to look forward to, Miss Gough thought as she waited. I do not *always* have to oblige Miss Finch, I do have *other* friends who could be Playgoers. She pictured herself surrounded by a jolly party, tapping each other on the shoulder, lending programmes, offering round chocolate boxes. Fingers would riffle and dip companionably in the darkness, there would be whispers urging her to 'Help yourself, Helen!' 'Do help yourself!'

Mr Carnelly, Albert, she would tell these other Playgoers, lives in rooms directly above, in a house full of artistic people. Why, if you look in your programme you will find I am named as Musical Director. I teach the violin to infant prodigies. Not that I can teach the little geniuses much . . .

Cries of 'Don't be so modest, Helen!'

Such a special friend, of course, she would say, referring to Mr Carnelly but implying there were other friends as well. One of her pupils would be giving a concert; they were all, of course, welcome to attend. Carnelly and the conductor were actively vying for her hand. The Playgoers would glance at one another, too polite to comment or ask questions but in the interval, just as they were digging wooden spades into twopenny buckets of ice-cream and recalling the hazardous seaside holidays of childhood, a stampeding donkey, the tide running out fast leaving them alone and stranded, Carnelly himself would emerge from the door at the side of the stage. 'Helen, my dear, what a pleasure!' His eyes lighting up and his arms outstretched as he advanced on her in his shabby green cardigan. Her happiness would be complete. No one could be sceptical after that. She thought of the smile she had fleetingly glimpsed on Audrey Finch's lips. It seemed to Miss Gough then that her friend Miss Finch had been getting in the way. Of late, Audrey had always been there, had taken to sharing her meals and pretending to listen to the Home Service while actually listening out for Carnelly.

We are not Playgoers sitting side by side on faded velvet seats in the darkness, but rivals keeping an eye on the fire, Miss Gough thought. The same fire! It was at that moment that she began to pity Audrey. No one had ever set themself up against Helen Gough and survived. Who knew what might happen if Audrey Finch persisted in her foolish infatuation?

Victor Allington, of Allington's the art gallery, asked Dulcie Dee to do him a favour. He was taking Rosa to Lady Hester and Lady Harriet Traquair's country seat for the weekend in an attempt to promote the exhibition and he asked if Miss Dee would lend Max Fanshawe's niece some suitable clothes from her own wardrobe. 'You are about the same size,' he said. The niece had had none of Dulcie's clothes sense and indeed, as far as he could see, made little sense at all.

'You must be joking!' Dulcie Dee exclaimed. 'I'm not having some drunken sod's red wine down the front of one of my dresses, ta very much, even if it is being worn by someone else!' Why wasn't *she* being taken to visit Lady Hester and

Lady Harriet; who was this Rosa, anyway?

'Max Fanshawe's niece,' came the answer.

Dulcie Dee huffed and eventually volunteered to take Rosa to Swan & Edgar's for a lesson in fashion. 'I will kit her out at your expense,' she offered. 'I saw some nice hats in the window.' Hats with extravagant feathers.

'Nothing too extravagant, please,' Mr Allington pleaded, agreeing to the arrangement, hoping it would not cost him too much. Hoping McCabe, as chief beneficiary from any sales of Fanshawe's pictures, could be induced to foot the bill.

The Necessary

'She has been seen in SIMLA.'

'You should cut your losses, my friend.'

'My throat, more like.'

'It might come to that. Collect and have done, the time has come.'

'You think so?'

A pause. 'What does Sarah say?'

'What does Sarah ever say? She prefers not to know . . .'

'A sensible woman, Sarah,' Losching conceded.

McCabe nodded. Hadn't he married her because she had been a sensible woman who would keep her mouth shut? 'And Phipps?'

'Phipps has a soft spot for the girl. His eyes were dewy when he spoke of her . . .'

'He betrayed himself. He will betray us all. Phipps is a fool and fools are dangerous.'

McCabe nodded and puffed on his pipe. 'Give the job to Marcoolyn. He has the necessary. Tell him a thorough job. Or else . . .'

'He has dealings with Braid.'

'Marcoolyn will do it, Braid or no Braid.'

A Little Place in the Country

'It is good to get out of London at the end of week,' Victor Allington ventured. He did not know what to say to the girl but supposed that they could not pass the whole journey in silence. At some point he would have to tell her about the overnight stop he proposed to make *en route*.

'But I like being *in* London!' the Provincial Niece replied.

'It is still quite nice sometimes to escape. Everyone keeps a little place in the country to go to . . .'

'Do they?' Rosa looked down at the new clothes she was wearing. Dulcie Dee had conspired with the shop assistants at Swan & Edgar's to treat Rosa like the new doll at a nursery tea party and run up Allington, of Allington's, an enormous bill. These were not clothes Rosa would have chosen for herself. They made her look like any other fashionable lady about London. Perhaps women with a lot to escape from found dressing up a pleasant way of doing so, Rosa reflected, as Mr Allington drove and the city thinned and daylight faded. I could be anyone, she thought, wearing this dress.

'You will meet art lovers,' Mr Allington was saying, 'they will talk to you about your uncle, they will want to hear your memories . . .'

'But I don't *know* very much. I only met Uncle Max once, I hardly remember . . .'

'I am sure it is not beyond your abilities to elaborate, Rosa! People only listen to what they want to hear. You are the niece of a great artist whose pictures will be worth collecting now he is dead and the market is finite. When they buy a picture at vast expense from Allington's – and we need all the sales we can get to pay for your new outfit – and they hang the picture from a nail on their drawing-room wall, they want to be able to boast how one weekend years ago they met Max Fanshawe's charming niece. The artist being dead, the pictures will be rapidly increasing in value. They will be seen to have invested wisely. Other people will follow suit and Allington's will acquire new customers.'

'I was with him when he died . . .' Rosa said.

'You might mention that. People like to hear of death.' After a while Mr Allington spoke again: 'I hope you don't mind, Rosa, but we are not going directly there. The Ladies Traquair will not be expecting us until the reception lunch tomorrow.'

'Oh?'

'No. First of all I have a visit to make. A poor widow I provide for. A little place in the country. I will have to explain who you are . . .'

'I see.'

They drove on in silence. Mr Allington thought, this is not going very well. I have managed my life badly. I am a man with a unique facility for managing things badly. 'I am not really Allington, of Allington's,' he confessed at last, talking into the darkness as he concentrated on the road.

'I never thought you were!' Rosa said sarcastically. She was fed up with people telling her things they did not have to and then going out of their way to strenuously deny what need not have been said. The boy Simeon she could excuse, he was only a child and feverishly confused. A respectable man like Mr Allington should know better.

'It is a long story,' the respectable Mr Allington sighed.

'It usually is!'

'The real Allington of Allington's was a friend of mine, you see. We were boys at school together. My father died when I was fifteen. He blew his brains out . . .'

'All over the linoleum in the kitchen?'

'I do not know *where*. I was at school at the time. My mother and I were left penniless, I would have had to leave the school as there was no money for the fees and I had my mother to support.'

'The widow you provide for in the country?' Rosa asked, anticipating the story.

'No. That is another widow. I will get to her shortly. Victor, Victor Allington, the real Victor Allington, begged his father to pay for me to stay on at the school. I was his friend, we did everything together. We even looked alike, everyone said. In the school photograph you could not tell us apart, we were rarely apart. His father, Mr Allington Senior, agreed.'

'That was kind,' Rosa said.

'Kind? If only it had been. You see, my poor friend couldn't stand his family's business. He was *the* Allington of Allington's, one of the oldest commercial art galleries in the world. It has been handed down father to son since Hogarth's day. There are plenty of people who have always bought from Allington's, only ever bought from Allington's in fact, noble families whose art collections were assembled for them by one of poor Victor's art dealing ancestors. Fusty reliable men with pince-nez. Men who looked rather as I look now. The nobility found they didn't need to know anything about art when they could rely on an old-established gallery to supply what was worth having. No point wasting valuable fox-hunting time learning up about boring old canvases. The Lady Traquairs' priceless collection was sold to their grandfather by my friend's grandfather. The pedigree is unbroken and impeccable . . .

'It was to be a joke at first. At least, *I thought* it was a joke, it was so absurd. Victor did not want to be stuck in a little office at the back of an art gallery in a back street, however distinguished the back street, however old established the gallery. He had no interest in paintings, in the images our artists create of the world. He wanted to be *out there* seeing the world for himself. As the time to leave school approached poor Victor became deeply melancholic. His father, being a practical businessman, knew that his son could never have become fusty and reliable or wear a pince-nez. I was summoned. I was reminded how much, over the years since my father died, I had cost the Allingtons in school fees and one thing and another. My mother had also been amply helped. Indeed, she and old Allington . . .

'It was decided between them all then that Victor and I should simply swap places. *Her* son for *his*. We looked alike, everyone said so. I was to become Allington, of Allington's. For the time being, they said. When Victor had travelled the world, he would come home and we could swap back. It sounded so reasonable at the time . . .

'At first I was delighted with my good fortune. Much as I missed my friend, I found myself hoping that Victor would never return. I wanted to be Victor Allington, *the* Allington of Allington's for ever. I went to countless weekend parties, I moved among the best families, I developed a taste. In short, I . . .'

'You?'

'It all went wrong.'

'What went wrong? Did the real Allington of Allington's come back and point you out as an imposter?' Rosa asked. 'Did you have to murder him to retain your position. Did all the noble families who'd been conned by you both turn nasty?'

'No.'

'Well then?'

'My friend never came back. His parents died. My mother died. I am still Allington, of Allington's, while he presumably is out there somewhere still being me . . .'

'But who are you?' Rosa asked.

'That is part of the problem. I am not at liberty to disclose. It was part of the original agreement and I am too fusty and reliable now to break my word. Besides, it is so long since I was anything other than Allington that I can, in truth, scarcely remember . . .'

'Perhaps it does not matter much then,' Rosa said. 'Perhaps it doesn't make much difference . . .'

'Not matter? Not make much difference?' The man swerved violently, skidded and stood on the brake. Rosa screamed. 'Oh it matters,' Allington said bitterly. 'It makes all the difference. *That* is just my point. *That* is what I was coming to . . .'

There was, however, no time to explain further. The car had halted outside a run-down cottage without any curtains. At the sound of the car stopping countless grubby children who had obviously been awaiting their arrival came pouring outside and surrounded the vehicle. A dishevelled woman stood in the door, a dirty baby under each arm.

Allington, of Allington's, climbed out of the car and beckoned to Rosa to stay where she was. 'It's not what you think,' Rosa heard him saying as the troupe of children surrounded them, tugging at his coat with cries of 'Uncle' and pulling him inside the cottage so that they all disappeared at last, leaving Rosa outside in the car in the silent starlit darkness.

Eventually Rosa was fetched by the eldest of the children. 'Dinner's ready, Miss Rosa.'

A meal was served at a long scrubbed kitchen table. The biggest pan of stew dished up and the largest loaf of bread divided but as it all had to be apportioned between so many mouths there was scarcely any food on anyone's plate. Rosa sat at one end of the table. Innumerable children eyed her sideways. Their mother remonstrated with them so frequently to behave themselves that she made Rosa feel like some fashionable lady from London who must be treated with awe. Rosa wanted to explain that her gloves and matching handbag were new, so too the clothes they matched. Her hair hurt from all the hat pins. Every time she moved her head she could see the tip of an extravagant feather bobbing somewhere out to her left. This was what it must have felt like to be one of her father's exotic hens! How she pitied *Pegglar's Fancy* and *Pegglar's Pride*, led out on to the Exotic Poultry Show Floor year after year, and eyed sideways. There was no way she could try and explain away her costume. Mr Allington himself had paid for her clothes and, since the same man was obviously paying for everything here, Rosa was obliged to sit at the end of the table playing the gracious lady condescending to do so. She heard herself politely asking each of the children their names, and their ages, and admiring the treasures they shyly brought to show her, a four-leafed clover, half a clay-pipe and a dead beetle.

When one of the grubby children tugged at her sleeve, he

was smartly called off by his mother, who apologized profusely, 'I'm so sorry, Miss,' she kept saying.

'Do call me *Rosa*,' Rosa said, but the woman refused to hear her.

'What is *she* doing here?' a little girl asked.

'I am taking Miss Rosa on a visit,' Allington, of Allington's, said patiently. He was very good with the children, who were clearly fond of this uncle.

'To see us?'

'To see Lady Hester and Lady Harriet Traquair.'

'Is *she* a lady too?'

'She certainly could be,' Allington said pleasantly, smiling at Rosa.

'Lady Rosa?' the child persisted, but then another child piped up.

'Are you a choffer, Uncle?'

'A *what*?'

'He means *chauffeur*,' the mother laughed.

'I am this weekend,' Allington chuckled. They were holding hands under the table. The woman no longer felt threatened by Rosa's presence. She trusted entirely the man whose deceptions and debts shaped her impoverished life. Rosa understood now that Victor Allington – so called – could not marry the woman he loved, and who was the mother of his many children, because to do so he would have to reveal that he was *not* Allington, of Allington's the established art gallery, but a boy at school whose father had died penniless. There had been no priceless violin to pawn, no exotic chickens to cull and eat. His mother had been befriended, his school fees paid but everything in life has its price. If he revealed that he was not the last in a long line of reliable art dealers he would lose his livelihood and the means by which he supported this enormous brood. Meanwhile his family lived discreetly in a little place out in the country looking forward to his weekend visits but more especially, Rosa suspected, looking forward rather hungrily to the food they could buy with the money he would bring. A family this size ate a lot of stew. The children had been raised to regard Victor Allington as their 'uncle' and generous provider. Only the older ones perhaps had yet made the connection between this *uncle's* steady visits and *their* own steady proliferation but in the interests of their bellies they hung their heads, collected four-leafed clovers and dead beetles, and said nothing.

Shall We Dance?

'Go on in! Introduce yourself!' Victor Allington said. 'Tell the butlers I brought you. Talk about your family.'

Rosa mounted the white stone steps that swept effortlessly up to a pair of palatial front doors. How mean and dwarf-like even the Faragher residence seemed by comparison, trying too hard to impress. As Rosa approached, the elegant doors glided noiselessly open, moved by unseen gloved hands. 'I am Max Fanshawe's niece,' Rosa said to the resplendent butler. 'Allington, of Allington's, brought me.'

The butler bowed low and Rosa was ushered up a long flight of carpeted stairs and into an enormous ballroom. At the far end of the polished wooden floor a small orchestra prepared to strike up. Near the entrance two old ladies sat side by side on a sofa.

'Hallo,' Rosa said, taking pity on the old ladies. Although crowds of well-dressed people were milling up and down chatting to each other, no one paid the pair any attention. 'What are you both waiting for?'

'One is always waiting for something in this life,' one of the ladies said in a loud cracked whisper as if conveying some great secret.

'We are the Lady Hester . . .'

'And the Lady Harriet . . .' the sisters interrupted each other.

'The Traquairs?'

'We are sisters . . .'

'We expect you to muddle us up . . .'

'We will correct you when you do!'

'I had a sister once,' Rosa told them. 'A half sister, really. But she drowned. Half a day's sailing east of Aden. She too had a sister and she drowned also, in the canal . . .'

'Hush now, child!'

'All this chatter about drowning is not good for us!'

'We are all drowning . . .'

'In our own separate seas . . .'

'Are you poets?' Rosa asked, for the ladies struck her as rather poetical. 'I had an aunt who was a poet – she was shot in Russia after the Revolution . . .'

'How perfectly dreadful!' The old ladies clutched their pearls. 'We can all expect that sort of thing now the Socialists have taken over . . .'

'I am also Max Fanshawe's niece.'

The two old ladies smiled. 'A charming man, of course,' one of them said.

'Do give him our regards,' the other added and then they both looked away to show that they had exerted themselves sufficiently, Rosa's audience was ended. She must move off now and mingle with the other guests who all this time had been observing her deep in conversation with their illustrious hostesses.

Rosa joined a queue of people helping themselves to food from a vast and opulent dining table. She picked up a plate with a blurred Latin motto stamped on it, some clever and ancient pun on the name Traquair that no one had understood for generations, and hungrily began piling food from huge silver dishes on her plate. If only some of this could be transported to the cottage where she had stayed the night. The obscure Latin motto was obscured by a chicken leg. Rosa started eating and walking up and down the large room weaving in and out of conversations.

'He killed his wife for one, you know,' a woman was saying. 'One will be seventy-seven when he comes out of prison. He really should have thought of that first, don't you think?'

'Well, I . . .' Rosa didn't know what to think.

'Of course one has dinner sent in to the fellow now and then, and there's a committee got up for his release. But murder is murder, and murder will out and one is not at all sure one wants the man roaming the streets. Who knows what atrocity he may commit next?'

'Excuse me,' Rosa interrupted the speaker. 'Is Valerie Lefroy here?' There were a lot of people in the room.

'One hasn't seen her, dear. Do fetch one another glass, would you be so kind?'

Rosa reached out and took a glass of sparkling wine from a tray held by one of the many silent tweenys dotted about the room. She did not expect kickback here.

'Did you motor down this morning?' the woman asked.

'No, last night,' Rosa said.

'Have you known the Traquairs long?'

'No, have you?'

'As long as one can remember but frankly, my dear, one can never tell the Lady Hester and the Lady Harriet apart . . .'

'They enjoy getting muddled up,' Rosa said. 'Then they can correct one.'

'How perfectly clever you are! So that is the secret! One saw you getting on so well.'

'Ah, yes,' Rosa said, filling her mouth quickly with chicken. 'They knew my uncle.'

At that moment St John Ranalphe Trippias, Bart, known as 'Trip' to his many friends, caught sight of Rosa, started disbelievingly, regained his composure and then contrived (although he stood close and could hardly miss her) to look straight past. 'Hallo, Jack!' she said softly but he gave every appearance of not hearing or even recognizing the girl he had consorted with the evening before in the warm darkness of SIMLA. Why, thought Rosa, with a silent giggle, it is *his* money jangling in my pocket!

'Of course, Scotland is out of the question this year,' someone else was now saying. 'After that fool of an Arab prince got in the way of the grouse last summer. One has been advised by the Yard to lie low . . .'

'Rotten luck . . .'

'Foreigners . . .'

'Very funny at the time though. Jolly hilarious . . .'

Across the room an elderly man had raised his monocle and, unlike St John Ranalphe Trippias, Bart, he stared directly at Rosa. He looked as if he had seen a ghost. Every time Rosa glanced up from her plate the old man was still openly staring. Then she sensed him making across the enormous room towards her as if he could scarcely believe what he was seeing and must touch her to know she was real. A tiger-hunter spotting fair game.

As the old man advanced on his quarry, Rosa felt Jack's eyes return towards her also. He himself was now deep in conversation with a couple of pretty girls in flouncy satin who had him neatly pinned beside the puddings. 'Oh, Trip, you are so funny!' one of them shrieked. The whole room paused mid-sentence to glance indulgently at the lively creature. A niece of Lady Harriet's, as it happened. A veritable party-goer.

'I know you,' the old man said close to Rosa's ear. Rosa caught her breath. 'You are a Fanshawe!'

'I am Max Fanshawe's niece,' Rosa said, a little too quickly.

'You are *Mary* Fanshawe's *daughter*,' the man corrected her. Rosa nodded. It had been inevitable probably that one day someone would look at Rosa and recall Mary. It was a cruel trick of nature. All the best families were represented in the room but Mary Fanshawe's daughter was a Pegglar and an imposter. Her clothes had been purchased only yesterday. Mary Fanshawe had not been good enough for the man who loved her to marry. He, and she, should never have let things develop but she had been brought up in Bloomsbury where the parameters of accepted behaviour were fuzzy. Mary had not sufficiently understood that a man of Lord Marcus's standing needed a wife of equivalent breeding solely to produce an heir, he owed it to the ancient and established family from which he was descended. Love was an absurdity that had nothing to do with it. Lord Marcus had wanted to go on seeing Mary, however. The sort of wife he needed would not mind that he saw Mary also, but Mary minded. She minded bitterly. There had been a tearful parting and Mary, her wounded heart still gaping, a goodbye kiss planted only recently on her pretty lips, had found herself riding on the

Underground one warm spring day when a bizarre bantam started clucking at her. Attracted, no doubt, by the bright red feather in her brand new hat. 'You're a match for him, all right!' some had said and Mary, in the mood for absurdity, had been grateful for the ridiculous distraction. She had alighted at the next stop with the hapless Pegglar for the purposes of taking tea. Next thing she knew, she was living in a neat little house in a small provincial town, married and with Rosa on the way.

St John Ranalphe Trippias, Bart, saw Rosa talking to the distinguished old gentleman and as soon as he could he slipped away from his pretty companions in their frilly party-frocks and moved involuntarily towards the curious pair. Lord Marcus had been at school with Trip's father, and had watched the young rogue growing up. He slapped a fatherly hand now on Trip's shoulder. 'You know Rosa, of course,' he said.

'Of course,' replied Jack, nodding in Rosa's direction, hardly daring to meet her eye. Before he could say anything further or elicit some sort of explanation from the girl, Lord Marcus had slipped a hand through Rosa's arm.

'I knew her mother,' he said proudly, an heirless old man in his dotage. 'An English rose!'

Rosa flushed with pleasure.

'Such a talented family,' he went on referring to the Fanshawes, for he had mellowed with the years, had perhaps gone a little Socialist after the war even and could now imagine a world used to this sort of thing. The orchestra struck up and Lord Marcus, who had promised the first dance to Lady Hester, forgot he had done so and led Rosa out on to the floor.

'I can't dance,' she protested.

'A woman must learn how to dance,' Lord Marcus said. 'If only your mother had stepped in time, all would have been well. Given time,' he sighed. 'Just tread up and down, my dear . . .' The old man held Rosa close to him and, enjoying the warmth of the girl who might have been his daughter, thought of Mary Fanshawe who had fled his embrace and married a poultryman. Lord Marcus's own wife had been an invalid for many years, having never recovered from the birth, and death, of their only child. She had taken to her bed and stayed there.

In the comfort of Rosa's young arms Lord Marcus remembered how often he had been tempted to apply the morphine – his wife needed to allay her pain – a little too enthusiastically. He had restrained himself then, he restrained himself now. He did not ask Rosa questions about her mother and felt saddened by the questions he could not ask and the answers he did not want to hear. Eventually he returned Rosa to St John Ranalphe Trippias, Bart, in the belief that the girl was there for the weekend with him. The country, after all, had gone Socialist. 'Look after her,' Lord Marcus said tenderly, his old eyes wet with tears. 'She is very precious . . .'

'Hallo, Jack!' Rosa said again and this time the man who had earlier looked past her did not do so.

'Shall we dance?' he asked, slipping a hand round her waist.

'You'll have to show me how,' Rosa said.

'Who is that frightful creature, Hatty?' Lady Hester nudged her sister. She had been stood up by Lord Marcus for the first dance at her own party in her own house and did not take kindly. The *country* may have gone Socialist but Lady Hester Traquair had no left-wing leanings. She perched very upright.

'Never seen her before in my life.'

'No breeding at all.'

'It's the butlers you know, they let in all kinds of riff-raff for larks.'

'Communists, shoot as soon as look at you . . .'

'Her first name is Rosa,' an attendant informed the sisters.

'What sort of appellative is that?'

'Red – I did tell you.'

The sisters clutched strings of pearls about their necks and sat as straight as poor Nikolayevich before the execution squad. If one knew how to live, one knew also how to die. Not a motto to be idly obscured by some chicken leg.

Toy Money

At the *Gare du Nord*, Marjorie Faragher had been unable to make herself understood so she heaved her suitcase into the nearest café, banged it down and demanded *un café*. The *Simplon Express* did not leave for an hour. What was an English heiress, with a heavy suitcase, expected to do for a whole hour at a railway station in Paris? Marjorie wondered.

The unmistakable dulcet tones that sent quivers through attendant *garçons* had a palpable effect on a fellow traveller who dived behind the day-before-yesterday's *Times* and went, by turns, very hot and very cold all over.

Frederick Bodman-Bligh had fled the country. He had told whoppers at Miss Faragher's tea party: he had no fiancée! What started as yet another prank – he couldn't for the life of him recall what prompted such foolishness – had snowballed rapidly downhill. Now he sat engulfed in his own confusion, unable to read a word of outdated newsprint. There would, of course, be no Announcement next week, or any week, in *The Times*. He had no one to name as his fiancée, he had no one to blame but himself. In the past men had got themselves outposted to far-flung Simla. Freddie Bodman-Bligh felt it expedient to take the first boat train out of Victoria. He had obviously been followed. It hardly seemed possible and yet, here *she* was.

'I'd lie low for a while if I were you, old chap!' Charlie Chadwick had advised, slapping him on the back and saying 'these things happen'. Charlie had been glad 'these things' had not happened to *him* and resolved to resolve matters himself and ask his sweet cousin Felicity to marry him. She was a good sort, even if she did read too many novels.

What agonies poor Felicity had endured these last five years while her darling Charlie courted the beautiful heiress, Miss Marjorie Faragher. How could the poor girl with her talk of Jane Austen and the Brontë sisters hope to compete? In vain had she purchased magazines containing beauty tips and locked herself away for whole afternoons to follow the complicated instructions. To worse than no avail; tricks and treatments that might enhance Marjorie Faragher's bold allure only made Charlie's funny cousin even more of a fright. 'What have you done to yourself?' her family would cry. 'Oh, Fizzy darling, we liked you well enough as you were!'

There had been that memorable tea-dance in someone's heavily furnished drawing room one Christmas while they were still at school. Charlie had got chatting to the aloof Miss Faragher and, for something to say, had pointed out his cousin Felicity. He was just explaining to Marjorie what an intelligent girl she was for a girl, when Fizzy turned round too suddenly and knocked over a vast collection of Fifth-Dynasty Ming. Though it turned out later they were only forgeries purchased at great expense from some less than reputable source, and a costly law suit had ensued and a whole trade in fake artefacts been exposed, poor Fizzy had died a thousand deaths. Marjorie burst out laughing and everyone joined in unsparingly so that Charlie's cousin spent the rest of the afternoon refusing Christmas cake and weeping with shame. Only a kiss from Charlie when he caught her under the mistletoe had sent her home happy.

'Well, if it isn't old Bodders! I simply don't believe it!'

Freddie Bodman-Bligh stood up. He shook hands limply. His assailant was a man with whom he enjoyed a nodding acquaintance at his London club. But a nodding acquaintance in Mayfair evolves instantaneously into full-blown camaraderie in the steamed-up café of a railway station in foreign parts.

'Just passing through!' the man said, his official briefcase implying important government business. He might as well have been shining a torch into a field full of rabbits for a marksman to pick off with his gun. Freddie trembled. Out of the corner of his eye he could see Marjorie Faragher turning her beautiful sights in his direction. She made no further move, just then, but all the time Freddie stood there blathering to the man he hardly knew, the skin on the back of his neck prickled and the little hairs stood on end. Eventually a Non-Stop to Calais was called and the fellow traveller, whose name Freddie could not recall and had probably never known, moved on at last. 'Well, Bodders, *bon voyage* and see you back in Blighty. We must have a drink . . .'

'*Bon voyage* yourself, old man!' Freddie knew himself rumbled. He might never live to enjoy that drink.

'Your fiancée not with you?' Miss Faragher asked stonily.

'I left her in London. Buying her trousseau,' Freddie said quickly, throwing far too many francs at the supercilious *garçon* who arrived just then with Marjorie's *café*. 'Toy money!' he laughed nervously as some coins tinkled weakly on the floor.

Marjorie arched her pointed eyebrows pitilessly. 'And you, Mr Bodman-Bligh, what can *you* be doing *en France*?'

'Oh, er, I've been buying wine,' Freddie stuttered. 'For the wedding!'

'It is to be a boozy affair then, the wedding breakfast?' Marjorie inquired. 'I do hope the future Mrs Bodman-Bligh will not fall down dead – dead drunk, I mean – and have to be carried senseless on the first leg of her honeymoon!' She laughed nastily.

'Certainly not!' Aware the whole café was enjoying a free lesson in the English language at his expense, Freddie came gallantly to the defence of his defenceless and non-existent fiancée. 'The future Mrs Bodman-Bligh knows how to deport herself. And are you catching a train, Miss Faragher?'

'One is usually at a railway station *avec bagage* for precisely that purpose,' Marjorie replied, icy as the Alpine glaciers whither she was bound. 'If you really want to know, which I'm sure you don't, Mr Bodman-Bligh, I am on my way to Switzerland. I was unable to get a porter, despite my purse and *parlez vous*, so perhaps *you* would oblige with my suitcase . . .'

'Delighted, of course.'

'Of course!' Marjorie and Freddie looked at each other. If this was a film, Marjorie thought, Freddie would melt at this point and tell her there had been a dreadful mistake, one of those inexplicable aberrations that happen sometimes. He had been lured into a foolish arrangement by some scheming minx. Violins would strike up and despite all the *garçons* and language students, he would take her masterfully in his big strong arms . . .

Old Bodders, however, seized a bowl of *sucre* and, boisterously tipping its entire contents into her cup, told Marjorie rather roughly to drink up *le café* he had paid for. 'Sweets for the sweet,' he said, marching Marjorie Joan Elizabeth Faragher, and her enormous suitcase, as fast as he could over to where the *Simplon Express* now stood awaiting the signal to depart. As soon as he spotted a cluster of porters smoking and joking together at the head of the platform he handed the maiden and her luggage over to these unknown bit-parts.

'I shall keep my eye on *The Times*,' Marjorie called out before the porters could entirely sweep her away. 'I shall see the Announcement, two or three days late . . .'

Poor Freddie! It was all right for Charlie Chadwick. He had the owlish Felicity to fall back on, even if she did often forget to wear her thick spectacles so that she walked into things, causing untold damage to property wherever she went. In spite of himself, Mr Bodman-Bligh stood for a moment to watch the Faragher heiress being shepherded to her seat through clouds of steam and smoke that billowed cinematographically from under the roaring engine. This *could* have been the moment when the girl of his dreams walked soft focus out of his life for ever, the audience fumbling for their handkerchiefs. Fortunately for *our* hero, this same sight only filled Frederick Bodman-Bligh with immense relief. He was alive, and he was free! He kicked his legs high in the air. He could go anywhere he chose (except to Switzerland just now), he might even go straight back to dear old Blighty! Why, tomorrow evening he could be sitting with his feet up at his club enjoying that drink with the man whose name he did not know. If he dashed he might find the Non-Stop to

Calais miraculously delayed! Turning joyously on his heel and holding his hat on his head, Freddie Bodman-Bligh ran like a rabbit let loose in the dark.

On Monday morning Miss Finch received a letter from Mrs Faragher dispensing forthwith with her services. Audrey Finch had spent the entire weekend in bed refusing to speak to her mother. 'I have nothing to say,' was all she said, burying herself in the bedclothes and sobbing incessantly.

On Friday night, poor Audrey Finch had had a dreadful dream in which she sat in the front row at Carnelly's, waiting for the new show to start. Beside her Miss Gough crinkled chocolate wrappers and prepared to find fault with the music, although quite what Helen Gough knew about music, Audrey Finch had never been able to fathom. Was the woman she had met on firewatching duty *really* a violin teacher? In Miss Finch's dream, though, Miss Gough sat beside her, real enough.

The curtain rose. An apology of a puppet came on stage to explain that due to a series of untoward interruptions, interferences by a fellow lodger of Mr Carnelly's, the new show due to begin tonight was not yet ready. This was a puppet they saw now in every show, for Albert Carnelly was growing old and finding it difficult to construct new puppets. From where they sat in the best seats right at the front, the Playgoers often caught glimpses of Mr Carnelly working his puppets from above. This evening no strings were visible in the darkness. The familiar puppet talked on. She said she was fed up appearing in every show in a new guise, expected to act according to another's unseen whim. She said she would like to be herself for once.

Fair enough! thought Audrey Finch, but the children in the audience began to hiss and mock. This was not what they had come for. The puppet wept. She tried to dance to entertain them, but no one was entertained. Some one jeered. Whistles and shrill catcalls followed. Orange peel thrown at the stage landed, dangling from Miss Finch's ear. Bravely she half rose from her seat and turned to face the mob.

'Give the creature a chance!' Audrey Finch pleaded tearfully, but already the audience were tipping over their seats. Indignant parents marched stormy offspring outside, the bolder ones demanding their money back, hammering on the box office windows so that etched glass cracked, and caved in.

Miss Gough sat solidly in her seat, steely vengeance flashing like lightning in her eyes. At last, when the auditorium was empty but for Miss Finch and Miss Gough, the puppet stopped dancing and flopped down on the stage in an untidy heap. She raised her head to gaze at the Playgoers. They gazed at her.

'Who are you?' Miss Finch asked.

'Rosa,' came the reply.

It was not her full name. Audrey Finch tossed and turned. Any minute she expected the telephone to ring and interrupt her dream but instead she found herself mounting the steep steps of an old charabanc, joining a party heading for the coast. Behind her came Miss Gough wearing her firewatcher's mac and carrying a valise and thermos flask. The two women were being seen off on holiday by their beloved who stood with the puppet Rosa, waving 'goodbye'. The Playgoers chose separate seats so that they could both sit by a window and wave to Carnelly.

'Only *one* will return,' the puppet master predicted, picturing the scene along the windy cliff edge as storm music howled from the gramophone. Two figures left the rest of the party far below and walked together against a backdrop so high above the raging sea that they looked like tiny puppets jostling along the narrow path: battling, in fact, for their lives. One of the two must lose her foothold, slip over the edge of the cliff and hurtle into the raging sea far below; the other would return in triumph on the smoky coach to marry the puppeteer.

'*Which of them* will come back?' Rosa was asking as the engines of the charabanc started up. Try as she might, Miss Finch did not hear the reply. She and Miss Gough waved cheerfully from the windows. Now she lay in her bed, sobbing into the pillows . . .

Where Mrs Ethel Finch had stood boiling soup, she now

furiously boiled soiled handkerchiefs. Her high-handed daughter was treating the maisonette like a luxury hotel and herself like some unpaid tweeny. Being employed in fancy offices in Pall Mall, and then arriving home in a metered taxi escorted by the legendary Mrs Faragher, had turned the girl's head. It was probably as well for them all that the situation had been terminated, forthwith. 'How very generous! How extremely kind,' exclaimed Ethel Finch when she read out the letter her stubborn daughter refused to open and read for herself. *I would like to arrange a holiday for you*, Constance Faragher had written. *And for your friend, Miss Gough, too . . . a mark of my appreciation . . . at my own expense . . . you have both earned . . . much-needed rest . . . an escorted coach trip . . . beside the sea . . .*

Audrey stifled a piteous cry.

'Miss Gough, too! Well I never!' Ethel Finch was impressed. This was more than most employers would do, in the circumstances. Some of the shame was bound to rub off and sea air would certainly benefit a woman in Audrey's condition.

'I'm not in any condition,' Audrey tried to tell her mother.

'You're in no fit condition, that's for sure!' Mrs Finch resolved to take matters into her own capable hands and call on the showman Carnelly. It was her maternal duty not to let him get away with his doings. At the same time she would be able to discuss the holiday with Miss Gough, who must be made to take some of the responsibility also. She had surely been aware of what was going on upstairs.

On Monday morning, Helen Gough also received a letter from Constance Faragher but she had no anxious mother to insist that the envelope be opened and its contents revealed at once. *She* merely noted the Kensington postmark and assumed that her invoice for Simeon's music lessons had been paid. 'You are only a *paid* violin teacher,' she had been told by Rosa in *her* dreadful dream and by not opening the envelope immediately Miss Gough could elaborate a little on its contents. Why, she might purchase a selection box at the box office. 'Do help yourself! I received a little bonus from the grateful parent of one of my pupils, the child prodigy Simeon Faragher . . .'

'Not *Simeon Faragher*?' would be the astonished cry, as friendly fingers dipped in the chocolates.

Life felt good to Helen Gough when she propped the unopened envelope beside the smoothed-out photograph of Bryony Bingham and, playfully setting her metronome to mark quick time, bobbed happily upstairs to call on Mr Carnelly. 'My boat has come in!' she would sail in and tell him. 'I am full of the joys of spring . . .'

'You have driven the man out!' cried Mme Lefroy from the stairs above as soon as the violin teacher appeared on the landing. The wind dropped, Miss Gough was becalmed. The door to Albert Carnelly's room stood open. 'He left on Friday.'

'Where has he gone?' Miss Gough gasped.

'Never you mind! You are a wicked woman . . .' Mme Lefroy belched majestically and, openly swigging from her bottle, heaved her way down to join Miss Gough.

Miss Gough backed away, backing into the room which for years she had longed to enter. Carnelly had been gone all weekend and she had missed him. How fully in this empty room she experienced the absence of the man whose absence she had enjoyed for so long. Joyfully Mme Lefroy witnessed Miss Gough's confusion. Helen Gough averted her nose from the stink of drink and urine. I will not be seen to weep publicly. A woman in love, I am marking quick time. I have suffered worse setbacks than this in my life, and come through . . .

'You need some tea,' Mme Lefroy observed dispassionately. 'Not that I'm offering, mind,' Mme Lefroy said hastily for there was a glint in the woman's eyes that frightened her. The ancestral Sèvres had not been rescued from the guillotine, and conveyed across France concealed in a poultry cart, to be set upon now by the likes of Miss Gough.

'I would not in any case accept,' the violin teacher remarked with dignity. 'I have my own tea, my own sustenances . . .'

'You will need them!' prophesied Charlotte Lefroy. 'In the dark days that are to come, you will be grateful for all you can get.'

'I have always been grateful,' Miss Gough replied. How she feared for dear Mr Carnelly! No one had yet crossed her and lived to tell the tale. She knew he needed warning but little did she know it was already too late. Lightning, so to speak, had struck old Albert Carnelly and all his poor puppets with him. 'I have had a lot in my life to be grateful for.'

While Ethel Finch loudly collected useful items into the red plastic handbag she kept for best, Audrey refused to notice her mother's protracted preparations.

'I'm ready for the orf!' Mrs Finch called out at last, calling it again before finally entering her daughter's room and prodding the snuffling bundle in the bedclothes. 'I'll see myself out,' she sighed huffily when Audrey still did not respond.

Ethel Finch enjoyed her long bus ride. At one point they passed the end of a street where there had been a big fire. If she had not been bound on an important mission she would have liked to alight and take a closer look; fires had been lacking in Mrs Finch's life for too long. She had depended on Audrey for her excitements, and Audrey had been less than forthcoming. I will get out and about more, Mrs Finch decided, clutching her red plastic handbag and envisaging the excursions she would undertake once Audrey had returned from her coach trip and needed to stay cooped up at home with the child.

Victor Allington, of Allington's, stood in the street beside a jubilant Dulcie Dee. She had turned up late for work and found no work to turn up for. The gallery and most of the back street had been burnt to the ground. 'How did it happen?' she was asking the firemen who were themselves nonplussed.

It would be in all the early editions. Mr Allington found himself photographed, flashlights bouncing off his perplexed pince-nez. The very picture of a gallery owner who had suffered thousands of pounds' worth of damage over one weekend. Every painting by the late Max Fanshawe had gone up in flames. The word arson had not been mentioned (except by the incorrigibly indiscreet Miss Dee) for it was not a word the fire brigade and the police brought into action lightly. 'You were insured?' they had asked though, needing a note for their files.

'Of course,' Allington said stiffly.

'Could someone have held a grudge?'

'Of course not.' Allington's was – had been – a reputable gallery, generations old. Most of the fashionable back street had gone up in flames also. It was impossible to say how the conflagration might have started.

'It'll be a chip-pan,' Dulcie declared. 'My granny once set fire to her house with a chip-pan . . .'

Apart from the fact that it had happened at all, there were no suspicious circumstances anyone could see. No one had seen anything. Fires in commercial premises at the weekend were bound to go unnoticed. People liked to get out of London.

Dulcie Dee giggled. 'I'm out of a job,' she said and, not one to hang around, she decided to go straight to Pall Mall and throw herself on the mercy of Miss Finch. She had finished with Sir Arnold Faragher. She did not know why she had ever started with him and had told the man so only yesterday.

Sir Arnold felt old. He was old. War-winning inventions no longer interested him. Young women were tiring and, if he were honest, tiresome. He'd returned home and was surprised to find the dreadful Marjorie gone and Simeon ill in bed, his wife in attendance. He sat and read some stories from Kipling to the funny boy he accepted as his son. He told the feverish Simeon not to call him 'Sir'. 'Call me Dad,' he urged. 'Or Daddy!'

'Call me Mowgli,' Simeon replied. Marjorie had called him a monkey.

'How did you get on, by the way?' Dulcie Dee asked Allington, of Allington's, before she left. 'With the niece, at the Lady Traquairs'?'

Allington shrugged. It was irrelevant now the paintings were destroyed. Max Fanshawe's niece had been a phenomenal success. Allington could have expected plenty of sales this week. Many would be eager to boast a Fanshawe in their drawing room after an Announcement appeared in *The Times*. It had turned out that Rosa and St John Ranalphe Trippias, Bart, were already acquainted. Lady Hester and her party-going nieces had not been amused. 'He'll trip himself up!' they predicted, punning bravely on Trip's name in a way that was neither Latin nor obscure, for veritably they were disappointed women. The handsome baronet had been a good catch. And who was this Rosa, anyway? A mix-matched *Fanshawe*, as it turned out. Now the paintings were burnt and there was nothing to sell . . .

The Braid Brothers called on McCabe. McCabe puffed on his pipe. He could have done with Losching, or Sarah even, but McCabe sat in his chair, facing George Braid alone, wondering how the man had managed to slip into the locked and bolted house.

'We *know*,' Braid said, clicking his fingers.

'You can't possibly,' McCabe mumbled.

Braid laughed like a knife slashing silk. '*Knowing* and *proving* is not the same. And not necessarily necessary.'

McCabe nodded. He knew all right. It was only in a court of law you had to prove anything, and this was no court of law. Allington's had been insured with McCabe (McCabe knowing what he knew had naturally ensured this. And who had tipped McCabe off many years ago? Why, the authentic Victor Allington of course, to keep his puppet on a string indefinitely). McCabe was glad of the steady business and this he had placed over the years with the company the Braids were employed to protect. But the Braid Brothers had failed to protect that company's interests. The incident would do the Braids' own business of protection no good at all. The thousands owing was relatively small fry, it was the *principle* of the thing. The Brothers could not be seen to be weak. 'Insurance is an expensive business,' McCabe tried to say. 'There is always a risk . . .'

'The point with insurance is that *we* take no risk,' Braid said flatly. 'We *eliminate* the risk . . .' When something was insured with McCabe it was meant to get taken care of. There hadn't been much care taken this weekend. The Brothers wanted to know why. What had Jacob Phipps, for instance, been doing?

'Ah, yes, Phipps.' McCabe was silent for a moment. Phipps

was expendable, but McCabe tried a new angle first. 'I understand my niece was in the country promoting the Fanshawes. I would hardly have had her doing that, generating sales for next week, if I had been *planning* this. This fire. The exhibition was genuine enough, it was meant to start a rising market. All we stand to get now are the prices on the tags. Besides, it cost me real money – the girl is no fool. She only agreed to participate when a whole new wardrobe had been purchased . . .'

'Your niece?' Braid asked as if this was the first they had heard about Rosa. A valuable asset, was how the man described her. (Marcoolyn had not mentioned McCabe's change of plan. Going for the insurance money, forgetting the rising market.)

'She's Fanshawe's niece, too,' McCabe said, as if spreading the risk.

'Well connected then,' Braid sneered. He clicked his fingers, and clicked them again. Bit by bit he was piecing the thing together. This same girl was the key to it all. She had been in the *Doublie Royale* driven by an uncle who'd been uninsured. 'So you did crash the car deliberately.'

'No!'

'You think you had us fooled.' They had thought McCabe had got nothing, but McCabe was not a man accustomed to getting nothing. Max Fanshawe's death had given McCabe his finite market that could have risen indefinitely. McCabe felt old and unprotected. His pipe was going out. As he struggled to light it, he eyed his visitor over the match's flickering flame.

George Braid was not a man often encountered face to face. His physical presence was smaller than one expected, or remembered. The man clicked his fingers rather too often and referred to the deadly twin brother who had died beside him in the pram. He still thought of himself as The Brothers, always speaking for both of them, and the business they shared. He had found early on that this instilled fear in the woman, their mother, whose breast milk they had sucked before they drained her dry. If the twin had lived, they would have been formidable; as it was, George Braid did not do badly, an absent brother at his side. The Braids' reputation went before them and was usually enough. George Braid was not a man encountered face to face. You found yourself looking for someone else.

'We don't like it, get that? It stinks. You stink, McCabe! You and us'll have to come to an understanding.' The understanding, Braid let it be understood, should include this piece, the niece, Rosa.

McCabe recalled his beautiful *Doublie Royale* and the restitutions Miss Pegglar was bound to make. McCabe wondered what the girl herself would make of George Braid. Or he of her.

'I want to marry her,' Braid said. He would sort it with his brother later.

'I can see no objection,' McCabe said lamely.

Braid laughed. He leant over, still laughing, and clicked his fingers in McCabe's face.

When Sarah returned home she went into the kitchen to boil the kettle and called to her second husband to ask if he would like a cup of tea. She was singing tunelessly to herself and would not have heard McCabe if he replied. She was accustomed to his ignoring her so she made the tea anyhow. It did not matter to her if he would not drink it.

Sarah took the two cups and went to tell her second husband what she was sure he already knew. She had seen the headlines in the early editions and a photograph of Allington, of Allington's, that most reputable of old-established art galleries, looking properly distraught. As well he might: his livelihood had burnt down during his absence in the country over the weekend and every trace of Max Fanshawe's artistic genius had gone up in flames.

Poor Max – even the catalogues had burnt, the autobiographical notes that omitted all mention of Lily. He had finally been laid to rest, a market so finite as to be extinct.

Because Sarah was singing she had not noticed the deathly quiet. She found McCabe curiously slumped, his pipe lying on the floor beside him had mercifully extinguished itself. The man had had a massive heart attack.

I am free, Sarah thought as she sat down on the rug at his

feet, leaning her head almost affectionately against his legs as if the two of them were picnicking together. She drank from her cup, and then from his. 'Mustn't let it get cold, dear . . .' she said solicitously.

Sons & Lovers

'I am the mother!' Mrs Finch announced.

'Do come in.' Miss Gough led the way. When both women were sitting down facing each other, Ethel Finch said pleasantly, 'A nice place you have here.'

'Yes, it is,' Miss Gough replied, thinking: another parent, another pupil. She eyed the red plastic handbag. Mrs Sheringham Bingham would never have countenanced such an article about *her* person. I will probably have to get used to this sort of thing, Miss Gough thought sadly. Her life had been spent getting used to things she would rather not, living with what was possible, aware of what was missing. Like the handsome young soldier of the 8th Gloucestershires who had kissed her mother 'goodbye' and never come back. He'd sent a letter, written the day before a sniper bruised his heart. The letter had bruised hers. It seemed *en route* between training and the trenches he had met another and married her. A few months later, after Helen was born, her mother sought out the father's young widow and confronted her with the evidence. When the poor woman threw up her arms in horror, Helen's mother had thrust the sleeping bundle into them.

'I had no idea!' Mrs Gough had stared at the baby. It had only been a romance of weeks, a common enough episode in 1916 and one she had thought concluded. As a music teacher, though, she recognized an irrevocable coda tacked on to the end. 'What am I to do?' she asked.

'Your best,' Helen's mother replied, picking up the fruit basket she had used to carry the baby, and disappearing back into the evening gloom.

The woman *had* done her best but in the struggle to make ends meet, teaching music in her home to the reluctant children of gentility, young Mrs Gough had worn herself out. She had given the baby her name, so at least little Helen received that from her father, but she'd been careful the child, and everyone else, knew that what was done for another woman's child was done out of the kindness of a cold good heart. When Mrs Gough died she had bequeathed the seventeen-year-old Helen her metronome, piano and book of pupils. What Miss Gough could not so easily inherit was any musical inclination, but on the whole this had not mattered. She smiled bravely now and made a determined effort to ignore the red plastic handbag and get the conversation swiftly on to the subject of violin lessons. She asked professionally, 'You have a son – daughter?'

'Only the daughter, in fact. I wanted a son, of course.' Ethel Finch had been cruelly deprived. 'It was not to be,' she remarked simply, not wanting to elaborate on the painful truth, for a pair of twins had been born to Mr and Mrs Finch, identical to anyone peering casually into the pram but, in fact, a girl and a boy. The babies had *both* been fragile and yet the wrong one, the boy, had died. Mrs Finch wondered what business he was of Miss Gough's. Perhaps the woman was setting her cap at her friend's non-existent brother. At least there had been none of that sort of thing to contend with! Mothers, she supposed, could have just as much trouble with sons and *their* lovers as with daughters and *theirs*. Audrey till recently had been pretty tractable.

'Ah well, everyone knows that boys are much more difficult,' Miss Gough was saying. Simeon Faragher had never chatted freely the way little Bryony had done. 'Can I offer you a cup of tea? I was just about to make some.'

'How kind!' Mrs Finch said cautiously.

'My day is positively punctuated by cups of tea.' Miss Gough liked to put parents at their ease. 'In novels people never seem to drink tea but I'm afraid I do it all the time.'

Hmph! thought Mrs Finch. This over-friendly talk of novels and tea was clearly an attempt to throw her off her guard. While the violin teacher scurried into the little kitchen next door, Mrs Finch ran a finger over the dust on the piano and then tried to stop the ancient metronome's infuriating ticking but the busy little thing throbbed against her finger, and carried on regardless as soon as she left it alone. Mrs Finch sighed.

'I understand Mr Albert Carnelly lives upstairs,' she called out.

All the rattling in the kitchen ceased abruptly. There was a crash followed by an uncanny silence. Ethel Finch raised her voice again: 'Albert Carnelly is the child's father.'

Miss Gough reappeared suddenly in the doorway, her mouth wide open, her eyes ablaze, the string of beads about her neck dangling wildly. 'The child's father!' she repeated.

Audrey Finch's mother could see Miss Gough was suitably shocked. 'I am glad you are shocked, Miss Gough. You too have been unwittingly . . .'

Helen Gough clutched her beads and lurched across the poorly furnished room where over the years she had given music lessons to little girls and boys whose parents wanted them out of the way. In the kitchen the kettle had started its low gentle whistle.

Mrs Finch was slightly taken aback by the effect her news was having on her daughter's friend. Some shame, of course, was bound to rub off – the girls had watched fires together and both been Playgoers – but Miss Gough sat on the piano stool staring and showing no sign of any ordinary or rapid recovery. Eventually the music teacher managed to gasp, 'You have come here, whoever you are, with your horrid red handbag, to laugh in my face and ridicule me!'

'I came here,' Ethel Finch began. She had come to discuss arrangements for a coach trip. 'I believe Bournemouth is considered equable this time of year.'

'Get out!' yelled Helen Gough. By now the kettle's whistle was loud and shrill. Steam gushed into the room through the entrance from the kitchen. Someone had tampered with the metronome on top of the piano, it ticked louder and faster than ever. 'Get out!' yelled Miss Gough at her friend Audrey Finch's mother. 'If you think for one minute I am going to teach your horrid daughter the violin . . .' She fixed her eyes wildly on Ethel Finch's plastic handbag and she yelled again and again, 'Get out, before I call the police!'

Ethel Finch did not hesitate. She had not understood that Audrey visited Miss Gough out of the kindness of her heart. The poor woman was deranged and although it had been a dangerous foolhardy thing to do, like lying to the Inspector that night in the war, it was undoubtedly a selfless act of charity such as she herself had never knowingly committed. Outside on the steps of Paddington Mansions, the fleeing Mrs Finch ran straight into Rosa. 'Do you live in there?'

'Er, yes,' Rosa admitted. 'I am the caretaker.'

'Tell me where can I find Mr Carnelly.'

'If he isn't at home, he'll probably be at his theatre.' Rosa mentioned the street. She had seen Carnelly's little puppet theatre opposite Allington's Art Gallery. A poster in large bold type had announced a new show, THE LAST SURVIVING PUPPET IN THE WORLD, starting this week. Ethel Finch did not stop to thank the caretaker for her help. She wanted to put a bus ride between herself and the unhinged Miss Gough ranting and raving in her cold rented rooms. I under-estimated Audrey, she thought meekly, renewing her resolve to do all she could for her unborn grandchild.

Rosa meanwhile flew up the five flights of stairs in a dream. She had had a lovely weekend. In Room 23, she closed her eyes and waltzed again in Jack's arms. Or would she ever learn to call him 'Trip'?

She stopped dancing abruptly, and frowned. Whatever will I tell Mr William Sharp? she wondered.

The firemen had found the body by the time the busy figure of Mrs Ethel Finch could be seen trotting purposefully towards them up the narrow back street, waving a red handbag and calling 'Coo-ee!' It had not been a pleasant sight, the charred flesh, the half-burnt face gazing up from among the heap of smouldering fabric faces, for Carnelly had perished among his puppets. It was police business now a body was involved. Police flashguns were already popping, carrying out their grisly recording, as there would have to be an investigation. The destruction of an entire art gallery was one thing, but the loss of human life ... The man had been asleep in a little room back-stage.

'I used to go to Carnelly's as a child,' a fireman remarked. 'Fancy him still going after all this time ...'

'He ain't going nowhere now,' someone else said of the man to whose roasted carcass pieces of melted green cardigan had adhered.

'Did you say Carnelly? Albert Carnelly?'

The men nodded suspiciously. 'What's it to you?'

'I'll tell you what it is to me,' Mrs Finch drew herself up. 'The man has fathered a child on my Audrey!'

The officials standing around examined the woman. Could this be the *motive* that until now had been missing? Members of the public often stepped forward, though, making wild allegations just to get themselves admitted beyond the barriers. Once they had seen all they wanted they generally retracted their statements, without signing them, and disappeared back where they had come from.

'I'm telling you ...' Mrs Finch shook her large bright handbag.

'If you'd like to make a sworn statement?'

Ethel Finch would most certainly like to make a statement. For the baby's sake. 'My daughter is a good woman, whatever you may think. She visits lunatics after work to eat pink pork luncheon meat. Her only crime is she's too soft hearted. Carnelly got my daughter into trouble.'

Crime? Trouble? 'There's trouble all right. We have reason to believe the poor man perished in the fire.'

Ethel Finch glared. 'It'll be deliberate, of course!' The puppet master had chickened out of his responsibilities! His puppets had got out of control, but Audrey was no ordinary puppet to be strung along, her virtue held cheap, her mother's willingness to pay bus fares made calculated use of. 'And,' Ethel Finch

231

added, recalling the demented Helen Gough, 'I dare say my daughter is not the only one who has suffered from the man's attentions, or lack of them!'

Someone whose stomach had churned at the sight of fried human flesh pointed out that it was not a nice way to go whatever trouble you were in. But Mrs Finch held firm. She knew about men. Mr Finch had been a shirker also. He had eluded her by long spells in His Majesty's Prisons. The nearest she herself had ever got to a seaside holiday had been that long trek to Parkhurst the one time she went. A man on the Isle of Wight ferry had told her he was a chaplain at the prison and touched her knee through her thick lisle stockings so that she had been thinking about that gentleman of the cloth all the time she'd had her final talk with Prisoner No. 3416.

'Deny everything, Ethel!' her husband told her, whispering it through the grille, asking after Audrey, pressing her for a photograph of the little girl to put on his cell wall. 'Take care of little Audrey for me.'

He had hanged himself that night in cell 3416. Strung up like a chicken, he too had chickened out. Audrey had always been a daddy's girl. A daddy's girl without her daddy.

Mrs Finch was asked if she'd be prepared to identify the body. Someone would have to do so.

'Oh, that's him all right,' she replied at once without stirring from the spot or being told what she was meant to be looking at. 'No doubt about it – I'd know the man anywhere. Audrey has been dismissed from her post in Pall Mall. She has given herself airs and is to go to Bournemouth for sea air, taking a mad woman along to walk the dangerous cliff paths. Lord above knows what the neighbours will say . . .'

'Never mind the neighbours!' A senior policeman had arrived on the scene and been told of a woman's allegations.

'Pardon me!' Mrs Finch swung round. 'It's all very well you *never minding* the neighbours but I'm the one who lives in a maisonette, whose only daughter goes firewatching with lunatics, telling lies to the Inspector.'

'If you would like to come this way, Mrs er . . .'

'Finch,' Mrs Finch said. 'Ethel May Hilda Finch.'

The detective racked his brains. He'd had dealings with a Finch before.

'No,' said Mrs Finch, keeping tight hold on the red plastic handbag she used for best. 'I deny everything!'

A Walk in the Park

How long Sarah sat on the rug at the feet of the dead McCabe she herself hardly knew. Later she supposed she had been waiting, as if waiting for him to die, but had mistaken the time and, arriving too late, had sat down and waited with the old man all the same. It was only when Rosa entered the room that she knew what she had truly been waiting for.

'How did you get into the house?' Sarah asked Max Fanshawe's niece.

'George Braid brought me,' Rosa said. No doors were barred to the Braid Brothers, Sarah knew that. She also knew that the burnt-out Allington's had been insured through McCabe and the Braids so she nodded wearily and let Rosa help her into a chair.

Rosa had been walking along a street when a car with darkened windows had pulled alongside, close in to the kerb. It had probably been following her for some time. 'Get in,' Marcoolyn had said and in the back, when Rosa had done so, sat George Braid. He clicked his fingers and introduced himself.

'It's like playing gangsters,' Rosa laughed.

'There's been . . .' Braid hesitated.

'An accident?' Rosa asked.

'Not exactly.'

'Where are you taking me?' They were driving fast, jumping lights.

'To your aunt, Sarah. You are to look after her.'

'On a Special Assignment?'

'If you like.'

'But . . .' Rosa found herself looking for the pink card. Braid took hold of Rosa's hand. This was a valuable asset he had no intention of sharing with his brother. 'We do not have to share everything, not now I've got her,' George told his twin firmly. They had occasionally shared a mistress in the past and blamed each other when things had gone wrong but eventually cemented the rift, accusing the woman of deliberately causing trouble between them, uniting again by sending someone to punish her. This time there was to be no trouble, no virulent acid distorting, Farnol-like, a beautiful face. Nothing was going to go wrong.

George Braid squeezed Rosa's hand. There were large gold rings on his fingers like there had been metal tags wrapped around the feet of her father's roosters. Braid did not tell the girl just then that he intended to give her his name and keep her by him as close as the partner who had died beside him in the pram, the stupid woman who had been their mother wheeling them round together for hours before she noticed anything wrong.

Rosa looked at the hard-bitten face and handsome watchful eyes. A deep scar ran down the side of his cheek. Braid was a man who knew what he wanted and, with a click of his large strong fingers, he took it. 'I am to make restitution,' she thought, in no way averse to the prospect.

Rosa picked up the two teacups and carried them into the kitchen. She carefully washed and dried them. If she wondered whether Sarah had put something reliable in Mr McCabe's tea she had more sense than even to think about it. The marital routines of Sarah and the old man McCabe had never interested her.

The mortal remains of McCabe were speedily dealt with while Rosa and Sarah went for a walk in the park. They stopped and watched some children playing with wooden boats on the pond.

'I had a whole Noah's Ark when I was small,' Rosa said. She had been taught that animals went in two by two, the elephant and the kangaroo.

'I looked forward all those years to your visit,' Sarah said. 'And when you came, you were no longer a child and I . . .'

'Yes,' Rosa replied. 'I dreamed of coming but when I got here . . .'

She and Sarah held hands. It was like starting out in London all over again. Only now, there was no McCabe. There was McCabe's money though. And the insurance pay-out. And the three suitors – William Sharp, St John Ranalphe Trippias, Bart, and George Braid – all three quite set on marrying her. I never said *yes* and I never said *no*. I never got a chance to speak, Rosa thought.

'You told me to try and settle down, find a perch, marry maybe,' Rosa reminded Sarah.

'Did I?'

'Well, I have found three perches to choose from,' Rosa told her.

Sarah laughed. Max's niece was delightful! She had always thought so. 'I am a very wealthy widow,' she said. 'You are my niece, you must live with me now and do whatever you like, no questions asked . . .'

I am alive, Rosa thought. She recalled the fixed plaster rooster strutting vainly round and round on the painted carousel. As Pegglar's daughter, she had always been in flight. And I am free!

A Letter from England

High in the Swiss Alps and despite the calming influence of the mountain air, a hitherto happily married couple, Lettice and Grahame, were having a horrible row. Their three small sons looked on agog.

'You should have stopped your friend coming. You should have stopped Miss Binns going!' Grahame raved. The boys stuffed toilet paper into their mouths to stop *themselves* laughing until Crispin started choking and had to be shaken upside down.

The nanny, Miss Binns, had gone to Lucerne. Miss Binns had not had a day's holiday in all the years she'd been with the family so Lettice could hardly object to the short break. Marjorie Faragher's arrival, the morning after Miss Binns's departure, could not have been forestalled either since there had been no warning. Marjorie Faragher had simply stepped off the *Simplon Express* and summoned Grahame to convey her large suitcase up to her room, and run her a nice hot bath. When Lettice had invited her old schoolfriend to visit them, any time she was in Switzerland, there had been no real hope she would come.

'Marjorie is *the* Faragher,' Lettice informed her husband importantly. Her own father was a country parson so she had been easily impressed by Miss Faragher's friendship during schooldays, and grateful to receive news and beauty tips from England in recent years. Marjorie had treated Lettice like her personal maid at school. High in the Alps she did so again. She ordered Grahame about as well but he, unused to fetching and carrying for the heiress, was not amused. 'This isn't a hotel,' he told his wife. 'I'm not some pre-pubescent bell boy in his first job!'

Lettice giggled and said not to be silly. 'You can be so pompous, Grahame.'

'Did she say that?'

'Yes, and it's a wonder I never noticed it before.'

Whatever Grahame did or said, his wife's friend capped or belittled but when he then pretended to be deaf, Marjorie only spoke about him to his face, mocking his deafness. 'How did you marry such a common little man?' she asked his wife in his presence. 'A lavatory attendant – really, Letty!'

'He's an engineer, Marjorie.'

'At the waterworks!' Miss Faragher laughed.

Grahame walked out of the room. 'Grahame isn't one for conversation,' he heard his wife saying.

'You were always so pretty,' Marjorie remarked.

Lettice blushed with pleasure. 'Was I, Marjorie? You never said.'

'But you have rather let yourself go.' The two women locked themselves away and spent the whole afternoon in front of the mirror. When Grahame saw his wife again he thought they had (God forbid!) another visitor, or even a new nanny, Miss Binns presumably having taken a liking to Lucerne. When Letty spoke, he gaped and said he preferred her before the beauty treatment. Lettice wept and smudged her make-up. She accused her husband of having no taste.

Grahame tried to ask *why* Miss Faragher had come. Lettice did not care *why* her friend had come. Wasn't it enough that she had done so? 'Do keep your voice down, Grahame. *She* is not deaf, she might hear us!'

'I don't care if she does. I'm not whispering in my own house, for anyone.'

More tears. 'You are ruining everything,' Lettice told her husband and wondered how she had come to marry a man who mopped out toilets on a large scale.

'I am an expert in hydro-electricity,' Grahame tried to say. Nothing at all to do with sewage. Hadn't she and her ghastly friend been taught *anything* at school; hydro-electricity was a major industry in Switzerland. Caspar, Crispin and Caspian looked on. They watched the visitor and they watched their parents. They wished Miss Binns had not taken it into her head to go on holiday, especially now when she was needed.

'Old Binnsy must have *known* she was coming.'

'She had premonitions.'

'If *I* had known she was coming, I'd have gone away too.'

'We could all go away . . .'

'*She* is the one who should go away.'

One afternoon, during the hour of *Mittagsruhe* when Miss Binns had liked to enjoy forty winks but the three boys rarely let her, Caspar, Crispin and Caspian stood at an open upper window watching Marjorie Faragher sunning herself on the veranda below. 'We could pee down on her,' Caspar suggested.

'And say we thought a fire had started,' Crispin added. Caspian giggled. Marjorie looked up.

'Go away you horrid little boys!' she shouted waving angrily at them. They stood at the window waving back.

'You were always so clever at school, Letty,' Marjorie said that evening. 'I always thought *you* would *do* something splendid with your life!' She gestured towards the piles of clean laundry Lettice was helplessly attempting to sort. Her friend sighed and apologized.

'Dear Miss Binns is usually here,' she said meekly.

'I expected so much more from you, Letty,' Marjorie continued. 'You're not secretly writing novels are you?'

Lettice hung her head. When would she find time or the inspiration to write novels? Even with Miss Binns in charge, the boys, the house, Grahame, Miss Binns herself, all took a great deal of organizing. She felt Marjorie's disappointment keenly. 'And what about you, Marjorie?' Lettice asked.

'Me?' Marjorie eyed her dull little friend folding a small pair of trousers.

'Why have you come?' Lettice had meant to inquire what glorious things Marjorie had done with *her* life but, to her dismay, the real question in her tired head slipped out by accident.

'*Why have I come?* What a perfectly silly question! I came to see

239

you of course.' Marjorie laughed, and Lettice knew there'd be some reason she could not know. She'd once been told about the orange light used to summon taxis in Pall Mall. Anybody really anybody would send out the pantry boy, the mutual friend had said. The Faraghers for all their wealth were only business people. Their money had been made only yesterday. As a country parson's daughter, Letty had not understood. She was one of the few girls at school who had ever been kind to Marjorie without wanting something (usually something expensive) in return.

Every morning Marjorie grabbed Grahame's copy of the day before yesterday's *Times* and scanned the Announcements. She has murdered someone, Grahame concluded, and fled the country. She'd be checking to see if her victim appeared under DEATHS. He'd not put it past her to send some flowers. Before long Interpol would arrive on the doorstep and he would cooperate fully, handing Miss Faragher over at once.

'When is she going?' Caspar asked.

'When is Miss Binns coming back?' Crispin added.

The expert in hydro-electricity had to admit *he did not know*. That night, the three little boys woke screaming in their sleep. They knew their father dammed up vast lakes of water but for the first time in their young lives they understood there were things in heaven and on earth beyond even their father's power to control. They were terrified.

'You be quiet at once, all three of you!' Lettice shrieked at her sons. 'You'll wake my friend . . .'

Grahame moved in to sleep on the floor with the boys. Letty thought the bald patch on the back of Grahame's head, which she had never noticed till Marjorie pointed it out, was growing bigger and balder by the hour. On the morning Binnsy was due back from Lucerne a letter arrived for Miss Faragher from her mother. 'Mrs Faragher runs *the* Agency,' Lettice informed her husband. 'They have their own orange light to summon taxis in Pall Mall!'

Grahame did not know, or want to know, what his wife was talking about and told her so, sparking off yet another fierce row. Marjorie, meanwhile, took the letter out on to the veranda and sat calmly breathing fresh Alpine air, a box of chocolates open beside her. 'Darling,' she read but what she read next, combined with three accurately aimed streams of pee raining down from an open window above, sent Marjorie Faragher straight back indoors to pack. 'No time for explanations!' Miss Faragher cried, ordering her schoolfriend's husband to escort her and her *bagage* to the station.

How could Marjorie Joan Elizabeth Faragher ever have explained to the likes of Lettice and Grahame that Binkie had wandered off, the priceless Peristighi been stolen, riff-raff had entered the house. Simeon had nearly died, poisoned by person or persons unknown. Miss Audrey Finch had been wilfully negligent and had had to be pensioned off, while Silly-Billy Sharp, of all people, had been discovered in the most compromising of circumstances in the Faraghers' own kitchen!

Letty watched her friend go, and she wept. 'I have been a failure all my life,' she said.

'We liked you as you were before,' her three sons told her.

Miss Binns returned from Lucerne in time to spot Grahame seeing a blousy woman on to the north-bound *Express*. Noticing how red about the eyes poor Lettice was and how unruly the three boys had become, old Binnsy could not help rejoicing at the chaos that had reigned in her absence.

PART IV

Epilogue: The Inheritor

I was born in September, 1956. It was an Indian Summer. And a difficult birth. My mother nearly died. At one point they thought it was her, or me. But somehow, for better or worse, we both survived.

'Oh, Jeannie, you were the most wonderful thing that ever happened to me!' Miss Finch gushed once, hugging me close and, young though I was, I remember thinking that if *I* was the best thing that ever happened to the poor woman, I would not much like to be Audrey Finch.

I have always loved this large house. I was meant to stay in the basement, with my mother, but if the old lady went out or I knew she was likely to be asleep, I would climb the stairs and roam from room to room. Sometimes I stood staring out of the windows at the tall trees whispering together. Unlike the teachers and children at school, I knew what they were saying was kind. My mother worked hard so that we could live here in this large house. She had not been young herself when I was born but however downtrodden and tired she felt, seeing to the old lady's needs, cooking and cleaning, looking after me, keeping me out of the old lady's way, my mother was invariably cheerful, and never complained. Nothing Audrey Finch did for me was too much trouble. I was the light of her life in those days. And I knew it.

We lived quietly, though a few visitors came now and then, and there would be a lot of boring talk that went over my head. The old lady was very particular about locking and bolting the doors, keeping the world outside at bay, protecting my mother and me from prurient interest and prying eyes. My poor mother washed and cooked and ironed all day. Her greatest pride was in my appearance. I can still remember the drawers of neatly folded little vests and pants. My bleached white socks and polished red shoes. Sometimes my mother's own mother would come. 'I am your grandmother!' she would shriek, bearing down on me so that I got giddy and screamed.

'I am your grandmother,' Ethel Finch then repeated, but in the tone of someone who has been pushed away. What I remember most about Granny Finch was the bright red plastic handbag which my child's eyes would fix on until everyone looked to see what I was looking at and when they saw what I saw, they laughed. I was the fool who made fools of them all.

Ethel Finch's visits were hurried occasions. She referred to us as if we were Parkhurst, and there had been the expense and discomfort of the Isle of Wight ferry. The only restrictions on visiting hours were imposed, though, not by my mother or the old lady but by scheduled stop-offs in the coach holidays Granny Finch became addicted to in her later years. 'I am seeing the world!' she would say, sending me copious postcards from Clacton, Frinton and Great Yarmouth to prove it. 'I would have taken you to see the puppets,' she had told me with a sorrowful sniff. 'I would not have kept you from your father . . .'

I did not have a father, but this was something rarely mentioned. Once Miss Gough who liked to invite herself to our house took me aside and confided that she and Miss Finch had both been passionately devoted to a Mr Carnelly who wore a shabby green cardigan. 'How we longed to smarten dear Albert up!' she recalled, adding that she still loved him and dared say Audrey Finch did too, not being the kind of woman who would ever let go. They were rivals; more so now than ever since there was only his memory to fight over.

'Your mother stole your father from me,' Miss Gough said on another occasion, sighing not with pity for herself but fearfully for those who had crossed her. When I looked into the veils of her eyes, and saw that my mother and I were doomed, I reached out and grabbed the ugly cheap beads that dangled about Helen Gough's neck. I pulled and tugged, refusing to let go. If the string had not broken, scattering the beads all over the floor, *she* would have been the one strangled.

When I started at school my mother walked me proudly to the gate each morning, disregarding all the cruel comments and cold stares. I was better tended, better turned out than any of the other children but I spent the day anxious not to scuff the shoes my mother had so lovingly purchased and polished, or tear the frock she had made for me with such care. I sat quietly and watched the other children. I was not interested in their rowdy games. I wanted to be back at home with the tall trees whispering, and my mother in the nice warm kitchen. I was the most wonderful thing that ever happened to her and I did not want her left alone. When I took my satchel and went in with the other children Audrey Finch stood apart from all the other mothers. Sometimes I would turn back at the last moment and see her standing on her own, hoping for a last glimpse of me before I was swept away into the noisy smelly school.

I hated those partings, and felt them as keenly as she did. I suppose we had been so much together in my infancy that the legal requirement to deliver me to the school gate hurt us both inordinately. I paid little attention in class. I lived in my own busy world. The other children called me a cry baby. They called me 'Chickenlegs'. I made few friends at school except among other misfits to whose homes I would occasionally be invited. The parents of these strange children lavished hospitality on me in the form of big teas, delighted their offspring had found a little friend to play with at last. I was not, however, someone people took to. The teas merely rendered me bilious. The friendship, such as it was, always ceased abruptly after the visit, and no invitation was ever repeated.

I still have the chair Rosa sat in. Even though I often come down to this dusty ochre room and sit for long hours in this chair, I find it impossible to imagine what went on in Rosa's beautiful head. She cannot have enjoyed her dingy visits to this dull dark house. Maybe she pitied my mother and me our quiet confined lives, dependent as we were on the charity and good-will of others, but if my subdued existence seemed wretched and furtive to her, compared to the wonderful childhood she had enjoyed, she was wrong! Audrey Finch and I were very happy.

Until, that is, my encounter with Marjorie Faragher.

Marjorie had returned from Switzerland in a fury and raided the offices Miss Finch had so wilfully neglected in Pall Mall. She found an unfiled card marked ROSA and an invitation to the forthcoming nuptials of Charles Montague Chadwick with his clumsy cousin, Felicity. The Agency had gone to rack and ruin in her absence, Miss Faragher declared and, shuddering to recall all that shattered fake Ming, she promptly took charge. She took on a Miss Dulcie Dee who claimed to be destitute, working the poor woman to the bone. Her incompetent mother she instantly banished. 'I'm afraid, Mummy dear, you are past it!' Marjorie had said, pressing the switch that lit the famous lamp in Pall Mall and sweeping old Constance Faragher straight out of her own door and into the metered cab that already stood revving its engine. 'New brooms, Mummy dear! Go home!'

The worn-out Mrs Faragher had not been sorry to sink back then and devote her declining years to her husband and son.

'I want proper records kept in future, Miss Dee,' Marjorie Faragher had cried. No more muddles, no monkeying. How dare Sir Arnold pass Simeon off as his son! Miss Faragher blamed the incompetent Miss Gough. The violin teacher should have taught her pupil, as she'd been paid to. Had Simeon mounted the Podium of an International Concert Hall, the priceless Peristighi under one arm, pointing his useless teacher out with the other, everyone would have known that her brother had Petersham Sharp's talent and that Marjorie alone stood to inherit the Faragher millions. By now she would have Mrs Sharp, Mrs Chadwick or Mrs Bodman-Bligh written indelibly on her passport and later there would be little Sharps, Chadwicks or bare-faced Bodman-Blighs running amok round her elegant feet. 'In future, Miss Dee, we must have names written out properly *in full!*'

The Agency had been asked to find a nurse for a child that was due. A discreet arrangement, it was understood.

A substantial reward was also offered for the return of Binkie, a plump Scottie dog wearing a tartan collar. WANTED posters of poor Binkie were posted widely and for three whole days the traffic in central London had been brought to a standstill as hundreds of plump Scottie dogs with newly acquired tartan collars were rushed to Pall Mall by owners hoping to pass the creatures off as the missing pet.

Bluie Chapman, ancient and unshaven, slinking from pub to pub at closing time, cadging the last of the evening's warmth and the dregs of other men's drinks, cowered in a doorway from this remorseless stampede. The toothless ferret saw then a vision of a new heaven and new earth and he cried out to the murderers, whoremongers, liars and idolaters who charged blindly past with their plump Scottie dogs, for Bluie Chapman had seen into the lake which burneth tartan with brimstone and the aged poultryman was afeared. Later, when the excitement died down and traffic flowed freely again, he'd been grateful for the few scattered fag ends that had miraculously escaped trampling underfoot.

After her dismissal from her post in Pall Mall, poor Audrey Finch had languished in bed for a long time. As soon as she felt strong enough, she quit her mother's maisonette for ever and visited the Agency to collect her things – there was a framed photograph in the drawer of her desk she'd been particularly anxious to recover – and to beg her former employer to find her a live-in post. 'I cannot bear having my handkerchiefs boiled!' she had cried in desperation. 'I will be happy to do *anything* where accommodation, if nothing else, is provided in return.'

The debilitated Miss Finch was not altogether surprised to find Marjorie Faragher, who had once slammed down the phone on her in front of witnesses, installed at the stuffy offices, clearly in charge. Nor had Miss Finch been amazed to see Dulcibel Dee sitting at what had been her own desk and looking – even Miss Finch felt – less like Miss Dee and more like Miss Finch. 'I have been replaced,' Audrey Finch observed. Her drawers had been emptied, their contents thrown away.

'We are none of us irreplaceable,' Miss Faragher replied, in a tone more matter of fact than malicious. 'I have replaced my mother and once that too would have been unthinkable.' She mentioned the holiday with Miss Gough that her reckless mother had offered to pay for. 'Naturally, the Agency will stand by its obligations.'

Audrey Finch shook her head. 'I must seem ungrateful.' She swallowed hard. 'But I could not countenance such a companion in a boarding house beside the raging sea. We would be turned out of our rooms after breakfast, and who knows what could happen in the long windswept hours before they let us back in. No, I need work. And somewhere to live.'

Relieved at this unexpected saving of unnecessary expense, Marjorie Faragher told Miss Finch she had just the job for her. A pink card was handed across.

Not long after I started school, I was taken to the Agency on a visit. Perhaps Miss Faragher summoned my mother, for a ribbon was tied in my light brown hair and I wore my best frock. I was lifted up, and perched on a desk for inspection. Dulcie Dee prodded me with a pencil and Miss Marjorie Faragher laughingly filled my mouth with rich chocolate. I did not know then that this was my chance to ask if Binkie ever came back, or to find out whom Mr Frederick Bodman-Bligh had eventually married. What I did learn was momentous. It choked me up, and turned my world upside down. *Miss Audrey Finch was only a woman on a Special Assignment!* I saw her thick file of pink cards with my own eyes. I saw details of the small sums of money that had changed hands. My mother, indeed! It was worse than any skulduggery at an Annual Exotic Poultry Show and, like Philbert Farnol, I was righteously incensed. Whoever she was, Miss Finch was *not* my mother!

'Of course she's not your mother!' Marjorie Faragher laughed. She shoved an enormous cherry cream down my throat and told me to buck up. 'Really, Miss Finch, you were only asked to . . .'

I said nothing at all until we were outside. My indignation and the chocolate made me ill. 'I HATE YOU!' I spluttered as I doubled up, red faced and retching into the prestigious gutters of Pall Mall. Dark sticky vomit dribbled from my lips as I screamed and yelled at Miss Finch. 'You make me sick!'

'You were the most wonderful thing that ever happened to me, Jeannie dearest,' Audrey Finch tried to say as she sobbed, but I pushed her roughly away. I could see Marjorie Faragher and Dulcie Dee standing at a window enjoying the scene. Mine was no ordinary temper tantrum. Passers-by passed quickly by. I was nobody's dearest, I told Miss Finch. Not from now on.

Young though I was, my resolve was absolute. Thereafter I called the woman Miss Finch. She was *not* my mother. She had been sent on a Special Assignment to live with a rich widow as a nursemaid for a child she must henceforward pass off as her own. She should first take herself away somewhere remote until after the baby was born and then return and accept the shame that was bound to rub off. 'You will live quietly with the child and the child's Great Aunt. I understand that the mother will occasionally visit. You will, above all, be discreet. These arrangements are not so uncommon, our files are full . . .'

Audrey Finch had nodded meekly. She did not need Marjorie Faragher to tell her what was hidden in the Agency's files. She gratefully accepted the pink card and, at the height of an Indian Summer, returned unobtrusively from a long lonely sojourn somewhere suitably remote and moved into this large dark house to look after me. I began ordering her mercilessly about. I treated Miss Finch now like the nursemaid she was employed to be. I did my best to hurt her feelings as she, and her horrid pink file cards, had hurt mine.

Of course I did not tell the children at school that not only had I no father, but the woman everyone took to be my mother was paid on a monthly basis, and not very much, to act the part. Although I was furious with Miss Finch for her deception, I have to say that inwardly I rejoiced. I felt specially placed, alone and apart in this world, watched over from a distance. My parents could have been anyone. I would roam from room to room in this large house then, a fairy-tale princess waiting to be rescued. I was an heiress. I had inherited a puppet show complete with audience, life size and laughing. When my puppets leave the stage I can always summon them back. I can even have Bluie Chapman scratting for seedcorn in Pall Mall.

'You are too . . .' Miss Finch said once.

'Yes?'

'Interested. In Rosa's stories. You're more interested in her stories than she . . .' Miss Finch gulped.

'Than she is in me?'

Miss Finch turned briefly away. 'Perhaps.'

I hope you will not feel that I have been misleading you if I say now that Rosa was only a woman who came occasionally to sit and talk about nothing. With a little girl's admiration and schooled by Miss Finch who knew about these things, I was a keen observer of Rosa's varied and glamorous guises for she was as varied and beautiful as the seasons and, like them, her changeability was her charm. But in those days, I was an impressionable child readily enchanted, and really she was not unlike other visitors to the house. She did talk rather a lot about herself, but most people do. My real recollection of her was of someone rather ordinary. She told me about the uncontrollable dog they had had when she was young, the raucous hens they kept during the war, the stepfather she'd never taken to. When her own father had died she hadn't understood at the time, or for a long time after, that his death meant he wasn't coming back. He had married her mother late in life and she dimly sensed there had been other shadowy families her mother had hushed up from her. 'You can only know so much!' she had said cheerily. This was all borne out by the coroner. Rosa, he'd said, had been just another provincial girl who'd come up to London and got pregnant. Fortunately for her, there'd been a relative by marriage, a rich old widow who was happy to bail her out, taking charge of the child and releasing her to continue her life of folly. 'You live your own life, dear!' Sarah McCabe had said to Rosa. Perhaps feeling guilty about her first husband Max, a second-rate artist who'd died in a car crash, she'd wanted to indulge his niece.

Once or twice, Rosa had produced crumpled brown photos. People like talking to children about their own childhood. I hardly looked at them but I remember once my eyes alighting greedily on a wooden Noah's Ark. 'Did you own that?' I asked. I had never had many toys myself.

'No, it was one of the toys kept in the studios for children to be photographed with. Old-fashioned things. I once tried to take that Ark home, but they wouldn't let me. *Think of all the other children!* they said and I did think of the other children, and I hated them for chewing Mrs Noah's face and snapping the tusks off the handsome elephants.'

No photographs of me were taken, and fondly preserved, as I grew up so mercifully no record exists now of what I looked like as a child. I have the impression Rosa wanted it that way. My very existence might have been hearsay except that *here* am I, in defiance of her, sitting in her own chair determinedly telling you this.

I am not sure at what point we dispensed with the fiction. I must have noticed how uneasy Miss Finch always became whenever Rosa talked to me, getting up and banging about the room, attempting to distract herself and disrupt us. Whenever I did ask Miss Finch or the old lady questions, they would always say, 'You must ask Rosa. Rosa will tell you.' No one explained why they deferred to Rosa in this way but when she did visit, which wasn't very often, once or twice a year, probably, I could not bring myself to ask her anything. Increasingly I had my own concerns.

I had got blood on my skirt which made the other children jeer. Gerald Fish had taken to following me home, egged on by the others. School was insuperably boring. I had no idea how the others made friends. Alone and apart in this world, I was not a happy adolescent.

Now of course I find it unbearable to think how the woman who was my mother would come to this house and sit in this chair. I was made to come and perch beside the hot fire, but all the time she talked loudly or sat looking out of the deep bay window, I fidgeted and was bored. At times, I felt outraged by this loud laughing presence that would burst occasionally into our lives, making fun of Audrey Finch and teasing me with questions I could not answer, commenting inanely on my appearance. 'My, how you've grown!' I would stare at Rosa dumbly. I had to live with the old woman and do as the irksome

Miss Finch told me: 'Eat your tea, dear. Wear a hat. It's all for your own good, Jeannie!' But for all the noise Rosa made when she came, she was silent. And if her silence was painful to her then, it is even more painful for me now. I have tried to reconstruct her visits, telling myself how absorbed I had been, how I took in every word she said, the joy and laughter in this dusty ochre room those evenings. I like to think Miss Finch jealous of my infatuation, and how amused Rosa had been by my interest in all she said. How mother and daughter actually conspired together to disconcert poor downtrodden Audrey Finch, who was only there because she was paid. 'I think Jeannie is going to write it all down. It'll be a bestseller like *Anna Karenina* or *Tess of the d'Urbervilles!*'

The merriment, such as it was, came to an abrupt end one afternoon in the High Street. A tragedy that cut short the narration, leaving me held in suspense like some puppet dangling hopelessly on a string: which of the three men had my mother married, William Sharp the internationally acclaimed violinist, George Braid the gangster or St John Ranalphe Trippias, Bart? How had she chosen between them, and what on earth had she told the others? And then: *me*. Where had my father been in September 1956? More to the point, who and where was he now? And that I do not know, I blame Gerald Fish with his squishy lips and slimy schoolboy fingers.

'Why don't you invite him to tea, Jeannie dear?' the stupid Miss Finch said. She did not understand. *Tea* wasn't what Gerald Fish was after when he pursued me home every evening. It had become a blood sport, me lumbering along, dodging the traffic, the others goading him with loud whoops and vaunting slaps on the back.

I did think of inviting Gerald Fish as she suggested. If he saw what a miserable life I lead he might have mercy and leave me alone. He might even protect me from the others. I don't really know what I thought. Perhaps I intended to let him do what he wanted with me, and have done. I was almost past caring.

One cold damp afternoon, I was hurrying home to get away from him as usual when I spotted Rosa, of all people, further down the street. I would have recognized her anywhere, but I had never seen her out like this before. In fact, we hadn't seen her for about a year. I thought she must be on her way to visit us.

She didn't hear me at first. She was all dressed up and very beautiful. I thought she could speak to Gerald Fish and tell him and the others to leave me alone. Tell him that if he didn't, he would have my father to answer to. I thought she might even hit him round the chops as she had wanted me to do. I called out again, and started to run. Behind me, Gerald speeded up too. He liked a good chase.

I shall never forget the moment Rosa saw me. I was waving and calling excitedly, lolloping eagerly towards her, Gerald Fish closing in, at my side now, pushing and shoving. Rosa half turned and in that instant, a look of sheer horror and animal panic filled her face. The next thing I knew there'd been a screeching of tyres and the tinkling of glass smashing. Two cars had collided and a pedestrian lay in the road, covered in her own glistening blood. At first no one moved and then everyone started screaming. I pushed through the crowds to the front and knelt down. I took hold of one of her slender hands. It was still warm. As I started to stroke it, I looked right into Rosa's dead eyes. 'It's me, it's Jeannie,' I said. She didn't respond. 'Jeannie with the light brown hair.' It was like a dream, the worst dream of all. But nothing, not a jot of recognition, flickered in her eyes. All I could see was the blob of my dark reflection; all I could hear was the splash of my tears as they hit her cheek. And a moan welling up from deep inside me that would cry out for ever and ever. 'Don't die! Don't leave me!'

Someone leant over and closed her eyes, they unlocked my hand and pulled me firmly away. Someone else covered my mother up with a blanket. I don't know what happened to Gerald Fish. I never saw him again. I was escorted home, the blood washed away. I never went back to school. My part in the traffic accident was not mentioned. 'I never saw her!' one of the drivers kept saying. It had been a shock. When I looked at her lying there, covered in blood, blood of my blood, lifeless and frail, crumpled like thin paper, she could have been anyone.

All sorts of things were said at that Inquest. Some were true and some ridiculous. The papers were full of the story. They said it was a scandal that, for nearly fifteen years, a woman had got away with being married *simultaneously* to *three* different men. In this day and age. The puppet had played too many parts. What were national stockbreeding records at Somerset House kept for, if not to guard against such abominations? No wonder all the books of births, marriages and deaths had to be shifted somewhere else sometime later. Surely one or other of the husbands ought to have noticed something was up and prevented the woman in all her doings? As for the child secreted away, Rosa had enjoyed a longstanding joke at everyone's expense.

The teachers and children at school were reported saying they had always known there was something odd about me. Loopy, they said. Like mother, like daughter, I used to chase the boys!

Marjorie Faragher, meanwhile, was forced to close the Agency after the offices were raided one night and confidential files removed, by person or persons unknown. Someone, presumably, who feared discovery or intended blackmail after the foolish Miss Finch blurted out under pressure from the press that she had been recruited in Pall Mall back in 1956 to look after me, all found. Such arrangements were not unusual, she had said. The Agency's files were full of them.

Traffic in Pall Mall was brought to another standstill as journalists fought each other for an exclusive story. They battered down the door to the Agency and gave poor Dulcie Dee such a fright, she suffered a nervous breakdown, and had to take indefinite leave at the seaside. A perpetual invalid inhabiting hotel foyers, getting other women's husbands to run harmless errands, fetching her a shawl, buying her a drink. Miss Faragher hurriedly left the country, cursing Audrey Finch, a woman her mother had encouraged to let in riff-raff and who now, by blabbing indiscreetly, had brought disaster cascading down on them all. In the café at the Gare du Nord in Paris, beneath the eyes of *garçons* and fellow travellers, the fleeing Miss Faragher had an interesting encounter that was to change her life. On this occasion, however, *my* interest in Marjorie Joan Elizabeth Faragher ends strictly at

256

Calais. She is as welcome to her new heaven and new earth as poor tartan-collared Binkie. If you think I have abandoned my characters cruelly to their fates, remember I was abandoned also, by those who should most have loved me.

My nurse comes and sits with me.

'Everything has been left in trust for you,' Great Aunt Sarah told me the day before she became unconscious, the week before she died.

'We don't trust you Jeannie!' the nurse said bluntly. By 'we', she meant herself and the doctor who came every so often in a white coat and shook his head in a preoccupied fashion and wrote notes. *I* did not trust *him*. I knew for a fact that his poisons were not always reliable because when Sarah McCabe died, I had swallowed everything left over from her and Miss Finch's last illnesses. To no effect. The medicines that did not cure them, did not kill me. I woke in a hushed white ward where all sound and sense was muffled, as if heavy snow had fallen overnight. I refused to talk to the ineffectual doctor but he went on shaking his learned head and writing pages of notes which I tried to read, upside down.

Then the nurse told me that if I didn't talk to the nice clever doctor, I would have to stay in the hospital which reeked of disinfectant and that this was a pity. She said I could go back to the big house that had been Mr McCabe's. It was mine now. 'We could all go back, if you liked, Jean!'

I did like. I tried to talk to the doctor then. I tried to explain that when Miss Finch died I sobbed and refused my tea. I vowed *never* to wear a hat again. I gave Sarah McCabe so much trouble and wouldn't come up out of the basement and in the end the poor old lady spluttered and choked in her room upstairs and then I wept till I spluttered and choked too, but unlike Sarah McCabe and Audrey Finch, I did not die. I sat about in the large house on my own then, and it was very like death.

I told the doctor about Gerald Fish. Boys behave like that he said. Did you behave like that? I asked. I might have done, he said. You'll probably find he's grown up into a respectable citizen, he might even be a doctor now!

Then I tried to tell the doctor that it was because of Gerald Fish my mother had been killed. Many happy homes are broken up by the arrival of some oafish boyfriend, the doctor said at once. I mentioned Rosa. And Audrey Finch's pink cards. Ours had not really been a happy home.

The doctor knew already. Rosa was a *cause célèbre*. 'Your mother has a lot to answer for.'

'But what is extraordinary,' I tried to say, 'is that if it hadn't been for that traffic accident, Rosa might have gone on getting away with it for ever! Think of all the other women out there who hide away children and get away with being married three . . .'

'Now, Jeannie, you must try and understand her. It would help you. It was difficult for your mother, because of the *shame*. It was different then. Nowadays more children are born out of wedlock, than locked into it . . .'

'Rosa told me stories, they were only ever stories.' She gave me an entry into her world even as she barred me from it. That's what stories do. I tried then to recount: *Pegglar lived for much of his life with two elder sisters, Edith and Gracie, breeding exotic fowls which strutted and shrieked in the elaborate coops that straddled every corner of the Pegglar family garden . . .*

The doctor glanced at his watch and said he was a busy man. If I had stories in my head I would do better to write them down. It would give me something to do. Then when I'd finished I could pack it all up and send it to Faber & Faber. 'In some ways you are the lucky one, Jean,' the doctor told me. '*Your* mother could have been anyone. A lot of people know only too well what their mothers are like – they don't have the freedom or latitude allowed you . . .' He shuffled back through his notes and discovered at some point that I was an heiress. I had inherited, all right, but he was referring, at that point, to the house. 'You must be a good girl, Jean,' he said. 'You must not do anything silly again. You must eat your tea, wear your hat, and not swallow medicines that are not yours.'

I hung my head.

'I will come and visit you,' he promised, sending me home to the great house that was now my own.

They came together, the two of them, he and the nurse and I admitted the pair into my ark. They are very nice, no trouble at all.

I live in my Great Aunt Sarah's room high up in the house. The trees that used to screen me from the outside world became diseased some years ago and had to be cut down. I have a desk I sit and write at. My door is usually locked. By them on the out, by me on the in.

The large house is full. Every room like every chapter. The doctor and the nurse have their work cut out. There is a sign up outside in the front although I have not been out to see what it says. I sometimes wonder what the old man McCabe would think of his large hollow rooms echoing ceaselessly with the laughter of fools. No one paying rent for their stay.

'It is your birthday,' the nurse says. I nod. I am thirty-five. There are questions that need answering thirty-five years on that never will be. These are the imponderables that enliven my plot. I cannot compensate distortions and omissions of my mother's making. No daughter could. I no longer try.

The nurse says I am to have a birthday cake, no candles mind. I am not surprised, there are too many arsonists in the other rooms only too keen to sit drinking sweet tea, watching fires they themselves have stoked.

On one of my birthdays when I was little, Rosa brought me an apple. I put the apple in my pocket and refused to eat it. Maybe it had been brought straight from a priceless silver fruit bowl that had been in the ancient Trippias family for generations. Or from a luxury hotel in America where Rosa had gone on a concert tour with the internationally acclaimed violinist, William Sharp. Or the apple had come from one of the high-security dens inhabited by the clever man, George Braid, and his mob. A man rarely encountered face to face. A man too clever to have gone to prison though others had not been so lucky. Loyal frightened men who took the rap and often took their own lives also, hanging themselves in their cells as Mr Finch and poor bear-like Bernard, Beryl's brother, had done when Marcoolyn smiled and pointed a manicured finger.

'Eat your nice apple, Jean!'

I kept the apple stubbornly in my pocket. I took it with me to school, polishing it when I should have been doing sums. The apple started to go off. I polished it more. Then one day Rosa's apple was completely rotten, its shiny skin may have hidden the secrets of other worlds from me but it could not hide the brown rot within.

'Throw the nasty thing away, Jean!' they said. At first I refused. Then the apple was taken forcibly from my pocket and thrown away for me. 'It was only a rotten old apple,' they said when I would not be consoled.

'You have a visitor, Jean.'

It is Simeon Faragher. 'I've got a birthday present for you,' he says, giving me chocolates he knows I will not eat. Hadn't chocolate once made me as sick as a dog, lost and wandering, in Pall Mall?

We walk in the garden in the cool of the day, he and I. They trust him. He tries to tell me he is my friend. Which may be true. I'm sure like the parents of all the other friends I'd ever had, Sir Arnold and Constance Faragher would never have approved of our friendship if they were still around to disapprove. I try and tell Simeon that it was *my mother* who was his friend. She with whom he had eaten *elephant's feet*. He laughs and offers me his arm. We limp along.

'You must forgive them,' he tries to say. At least I think it is what he is saying.

'She could have been anyone,' the coroner said of the woman on the slab some claimed to have been a Mrs Sharp, others were equally adamant was the missing Lady Trippias and others again swore to be none other than the wife of George Braid! Without photographs, distinctive clothing, distinguishing features or an identity parade, what could the poor coroner do?

There had been no children by any of Rosa's marriages because my birth had been a difficult one. She nearly died. At one point they thought it was her, or me. But somehow, for better or worse, we both survived. No more children, she'd been told, and I cannot suppose that as I grew up she was sorry.

I was such a great gawky things with my big floppy head and large flappy hands. A mild case, the doctor was kind enough to say when I insisted something must be seriously wrong. Very mild. There were others much worse off than myself. I am well provided for and well looked after.

Mild or not, I am no one's idea of a daughter. I know this because after my mother's fatal accident they each wrote to me, William Sharp, St John Ranalphe Trippias, Bart, and George Braid. Perhaps they thought the world had changed sufficiently for the shame of illegitimacy no longer to rub off. Maybe they reasoned that since Rosa had been married three times, that ought to legitimize something. Generously they each wrote that they were prepared to overlook . . .

I was so excited that unlike with Gerald Fish I did as Miss Finch suggested and invited them all to tea, all three at the same time on the same afternoon and there they sat like three anxious tigers in a ring, waiting.

As soon as I walked into the room you could see I was not their idea of a daughter. The three men, who might have been my father, all took one look at Rosa's daughter advancing eagerly towards them with hand extended – dear, dear Daddy – and they backed hastily away. Not one of them wanted to take such a stupid great lump of a girl home. They could not get out of the house fast enough. Not one of them could even bring himself to take me by the hand.

Poor Rosa, they said sorrowfully as they rushed for the door. If only we had known. What a dreadful secret – how the poor woman must have suffered . . .

They were not angry with each other, or with Rosa, any more then. She can be grateful to me for that. The three left the house wiser men. They had not been watching over me from afar. They had none of them known, till Rosa died and there'd been all the fuss in the papers, that I even existed.

Only Audrey Finch ever held me close. 'Don't forget to eat your tea, and do wear a hat, Jeannie dear,' she'd whispered painfully when I sat beside her last year, watching as she shrivelled up beneath my gaze, like an apple steadily rotting away inside. It was then that I knew how much I loved her, but by then of course it was too late. Her breathing became intermittent, then impossible. She died before I could say anything, and I still do not know what I should have said but I wish I had returned the feeble squeeze of my hand. I wish I had bent over her, and kissed her. I wish I had called her 'Mummy', if only that last once. She'd have liked that.

Oh yes! She'd have liked that. Audrey Finch had come in that afternoon with a tray of tea things, expecting a jolly tea party, laughter and pranks. A daddy's girl herself, she thought me incredibly lucky to have found *three* daddies. How surprised she was to find me sitting in the dark, on my own. 'Jeannie!'

'They've gone,' I said unnecessarily, seizing the bowl of sugar lumps and tipping the whole lot all over the floor. I had meant to ask William Sharp what happened to Binkie. I had questions for them all but my mother's three husbands had departed before I could get my big lolling tongue round the words.

'Don't cry, Jeannie dearest,' Miss Finch murmured, stroking my light brown hair. 'We've always managed perfectly well, you and I . . .'

Not for the first time, I pushed her roughly away and watched sullenly as she bent over and picked up the scattered sugar. She too was crying.

'You can't force people to love you,' I told her. She was so plain and put upon even her lover had left her. But I too was discarded. My father had, as they say, found other fish to fry. And by *fish* I do not mean slimy Gerald at school, whom any father should have battered and fried in hot fat. I had been so sure one of the three would have wanted a daughter and taken her home to protect her, if only for my beautiful dead mother's sake. But you can't force people to love you and call you their little chick-chicken.

'I didn't even look like *any* of them!' I wailed.

'No, Jeannie,' Miss Finch said quietly, drying her eyes. 'That's because you look exactly like her. They'll have thought they were seeing a ghost. When they looked at you they probably saw poor Rosa, for the first time. They were frightened men.'

'Hah!' I laughed. It was nonsense. How could a mobster, a baronet and an internationally famous musician have been terrified of me! Rosa was beautiful, while I could have been anyone. A princess waiting to be rescued, not from a dragon breathing fire, but from herself.

At least I still have the chair Rosa sat in. All the other chairs may have gone, a lot else has been lost, but I can sit here quietly and see the room as she saw it and picture my young self obstructing her clear line of vision. I have no real idea what she must have felt or thought. There was a time when I hated her. Now I feel sorry that we had to hide behind fiction.

One morning during the turbulent time following the death of a woman I now know to have been my real mother, I was standing at my window like a conscientious rooster waiting for the sun to rise when a press photographer climbed on to the wall at the end of the garden and pointed his camera up at my window. The dazzling dawn light bounced off his lens straight into my eyes. Perhaps I'd been a bit enthusiastic in my waving, because when the picture was printed in the newspapers, I looked blurred and wonky. This was rather a shame as it was the first time I had ever had my photo taken and I was very excited.

'But it's a lovely picture, Jeannie,' Audrey Finch said at once, holding it up admiringly and smoothing away my disappointment. She cut the photograph out carefully so at least my edges were straight and then she neatly trimmed away the caption she could not like: 'Rosa's daughter'. One afternoon, when the excitement had died down, and we could go about again unremarked, she and I walked all the way up the Tottenham Court Road to Heal's and purchased an expensive wooden frame to hang the picture in on the wall. It hangs there still. The photograph faded away to nothing long ago, but whenever I need strength or comforting sometimes, I look at the lovely frame and think of dear Miss Finch, who could only afford to buy me such an extravagant present because she'd been paid all those years to look after me.

'It is my birthday!' I shout now Simeon has gone, and the nurse and doctor have retired to bed. The same bed. In their ardour, they have forgotten to lock my door so that I wander round the house calling in all the other rooms. 'Come to my party, Mr McCabe! Come along, everyone, come and eat cake!'

When the birthday cake without candles is eaten, I remove the cellophane wrapping from Simeon's chocolates. I don't eat them myself as you know, but there are plenty here who will. A murmur of agreement runs along in the pipes beneath the floorboards as the heating goes off for the night. I hold out the box. 'Help yourself, dear darling Miss Finch . . . Audrey . . . Mummy! Come along everyone – do help yourselves!'

Fingers reach forward and riffle companionably in the darkness. I hear Miss Gough with her mouth full, conjecturing whether the chocolates are not some gift from a grateful pupil. An infant prodigy. The rest of us laugh, enjoying the joke but in the morning the box will be empty and the nurse will accuse me of eating the whole lot myself.

'We had a full house, last night,' I will say. 'Even Bluie Chapman came on the cadge, and Percy Thirsty Higgins brought his pot of indetectable glue; Aunt Edith asked endless questions, while poor Aunt Gracie made free with the custard creams. That's why there aren't any . . .'

'Really, Jeannie!' my nurse will shriek in the uproarious manner the doctor clearly loves. 'You are a one!'

I *am* a one, that is precisely what I am. Pegglar's granddaughter. As novel a variety as any *Pride* or *Fancy*. And so absurdly happy I could fly. When I came downstairs this morning, some men were in the dusty ochre room busily painting over the dusty ochre. They had actually stood on Rosa's chair to reach the ceiling! One of the arms was broken off, and the whole thing was covered in splashes of off-white paint.

'That's Rosa's chair,' I said indignantly and, as I clucked and fluttered about, I remembered the lopsided chicken in the mirror waggling its ridiculous scarlet plume at me. I started laughing and when I found I could not stop, the painters threw down their paint brushes and started laughing too. We have a lot of fun in this large house.